"I want you," Ash said softly

Christie froze. Her knuckles whitened on the handle of the hairbrush she was holding. "B-but you promised... you gave me your word."

"I gave you my word not to do anything you wouldn't like," he said, a dark flame burning in his eyes. "It's useless to argue with a woman who believes she is frigid. Words will never persuade her she's wrong. There is only one way to convince you, my nervous bride."

Self-preservation—the ancient human instinct—leaped to Christie's aid... and she grabbed at her one chance to escape.

The passionate new novel by the author whose romances have sold more than 40 million copies!

Anne Weale was born in Liverpool, England. She is married, with one son, and currently lives with her husband on the Mediterranean coast of Spain. Her first Harlequin novel was *Castle in Corsica*. Since then she has written more than forty romances, which have been translated into eighteen languages and sold in eighty countries. Sales of more than forty million copies have proved Anne Weale's reputation as one of the world's finest authors of romance fiction.

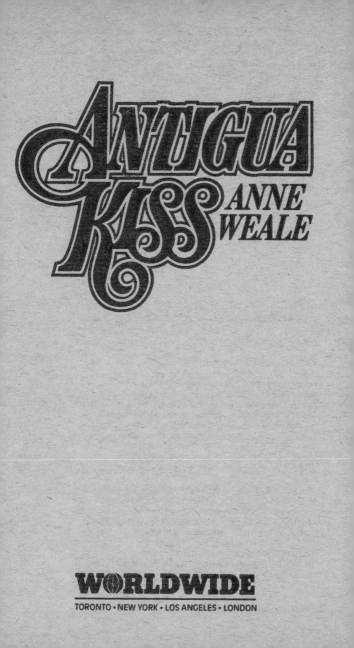

ANTIGUA KISS

ANNE WEALE

WORLDWIDE

TORONTO · NEW YORK · LOS ANGELES · LONDON

Published February 1983

Second printing February 1983

ISBN 0-373-97001-3

Printed in Canada

For Cynthia Borg, Rhonda Fitzgerald, Jackie Lafaurie, Nancy Machata, Mary Lou Riker and Cathy Ungaro, the six charming Americans whom I met while staying in Antigua, and whose entertaining company is part of my happy memory of that lovely island.

ONE

In the middle of the night—or so it seemed—she was woken by a sound which at first she didn't recognise as her door-bell. When she realised what it was, Christie raised her head from the pillow and peered at the faintly illuminated dial of her electric alarm clock.

She had been asleep for two hours, having come to bed early at ten. It was now only just after midnight, but still an extraordinary hour for someone to be ringing her bell in that persistent series of three rings, a pause, then three more rings.

Thinking it must be one of her neighbours in some sort of urgent trouble, she fumbled for the switch of her bedside lamp, threw back the bedclothes and swung her feet to the floor.

Her pyjamas, her snug sheepskin slippers, and her plain, warm cream woollen dressing-gown were those of a woman who rated comfort above glamour. A woman who slept alone.

Yet the sleep-flushed face reflected in the dressing-mirror as she flung on the cosy robe was neither elderly, nor what Americans call "homely".

A few years ago, before the events which had quenched her sparkle, the youthful Christie had been considered a beauty. Now, at twenty-four, she still had the fine, clear skin, the silver-grey eyes and

7

full lips. But time and experience had tempered her personality and made her almost unrecognisable as the glowing, effervescent young creature she had been on her nineteenth birthday.

As she went through the flat switching on lights, it occurred to her that the reason for the insistent ringing might not be an emergency, but the act of hooligans or a drunk. For this reason she left the safety chain in place when she opened the door, and was glad she had. The man outside was a stranger.

'What do you want?' she asked cautiously.

The narrow aperture and the dim lighting in the corridor made it difficult to see him in detail, but he was very tall and broad-shouldered, with a skin as dark as those of the fathers and brothers of her Indian pupils. But as far as she knew the only Indians of his stature were Sikhs, and he was not wearing a turban.

'Mrs Chapman?'

'Yes.'

'I'm Ash Lambard. Your sister's husband was my half-brother. Perhaps you'd like to check my identity.'

He passed something through the gap. It was a passport, open at the first page, with *Mr Ashcroft Lambard* written in the space for the name of the bearer.

This was the moment which Christie had dreaded ever since the discovery, after the motorway accident in which her sister, her sister's husband, and four other people had lost their lives, that her normally feckless brother-in-law had actually made a will.

As Paul's house had been heavily mortgaged, he had driven a company car and had stopped the payments on his life insurance, his estate had consisted of liabilities rather than assets. Christie had not cared about that, except in so far as it affected the welfare of her orphaned nephew.

It was the clause in the will about the child which had upset her. In the event of Jenny's death, Paul had consigned his son not to his sister-in-law but to his half-brother, a man about whom she knew little except that he had been expelled from a famous public school, and sent abroad in disgrace.

Neither she nor Jenny had ever met Ashcroft Lambard. Although invited to her sister's wedding, he had not attended it.

The generous cheque he had sent as a wedding present could have meant that the erstwhile black sheep had done well for himself overseas. Or it could have meant that, like Paul, he loved to play the big spender, and had happened to be in funds at the time the younger man wrote to announce his forthcoming marriage.

She undid the chain and stepped back to let him come in. In the better light of her lobby, she could see that the swarthiness of his skin was a deep tan superimposed on the colouring which went with dark hair and very dark eyes. She seemed to recall hearing that his mother had been a foreigner from one of the countries surrounding the Mediterranean.

Having walked through into the living-room, and dumped a small grip on the carpet, he turned and offered his hand to her.

'I'm sorry to have dragged you out of bed, Mrs Chapman, but I haven't any time to waste. I landed at Heathrow an hour ago, and I have to fly out the day after tomorrow. As you'll be at work most of tomorrow, it seemed a good idea to come here at once rather than waiting until the morning.'

Although, in the last week of term before school broke up for the Christmas holidays, the weather was chilly, his ungloved brown hand was not cold. His fingers closed firmly on hers in a powerful but not crushing clasp.

'How do you do, Mr Lambard,' she said, a little nonplussed by the unexpectedness of his arrival. 'If you'd cabled you were coming, I would have stayed up and had a meal waiting for you.'

'I didn't know until the last moment that I was going to be able to come today. This is a busy time of year for me. I ate on the plane, so I'm not hungry. But I wouldn't mind a drink.'

As he spoke, he took off his light-coloured rain-proof blouson. Christie, who liked good clothes even if she could not afford them, noticed the label—*Aquascutum*.

Once, when her sister had been in London on a shopping spree, Christie had tried on a beige silk Aquascutum shower coat. Jenny had thought it boring; her taste ran to the latest fashions. She hadn't cared if they were of poor quality and inferior finish. She would wear them only until the next fashion came in.

But Christie had loved the feel of the fabric, the understated elegance of the style with its stand-up

collar, fly front, flared line and classic strapped cuffs.
It was the kind of coat which would go anywhere,
winter or summer, and always look right. The price
ticket had made her blench. Two hundred and fifty
pounds! And that had been some time ago. What
would it cost now?

Underneath the blouson Mr Lambard had on a
navy blue seaman's sweater which she recognised as
a guernsey. She had had one herself at one time, but
had given it away because of its associations. Guernsey, although a lovely island, was not a place she
wished to remember.

'I'm afraid I haven't any spirits. Only sherry or
wine,' she told him.

'In that case—' He unzipped his grip and produced a bottle. 'I took the precaution of bringing my
own supply of rum. Will you join me in a tot?'

'Oh, no, thank you—not at this hour. I'll get you a
glass.'

While she went to the sideboard in the dining end
of the room, he moved to the sitting area. As she
brought the glass to him, he asked, 'Is this your only
form of heating?'—indicating the gas fire set into a
rather ugly artificial fireplace.

'Yes, but it gives a good heat. I'll light it.' She bent
to do so, then, straightening, said, 'Would you excuse me while I put on the kettle? Do sit down. I
shan't be more than a few moments.'

As well as filling the kettle, she went quickly back
to her bedroom to brush her fair, shoulder-length
hair and smooth it back from her face with a tor-
toiseshell clasp at the back to keep it neatly in place.

She never wore it loose by day.

'Why are you here, Mr Lambard, if this is your busiest time?' she asked, returning to the living-room to find him looking at her bookshelves with what seemed a very generous tot of rum in his hand.

He took in her tidied hair, the concealing dressing-gown and her slippers. She had the feeling he thought her a dowdy, mousy-looking female.

'As we are, in a fashion, related, why not call me Ash?' he suggested. 'Your name is Christiana, I believe.'

'Yes, but I'm always called Christie.' She moved closer to the fire and perched on the edge of a chair.

'I've come to take charge of the child,' he said, in answer to her question.

'To take charge?' she said warily.

'You've had to hold the fort so far because you were near and I wasn't. But you can't be expected to cope indefinitely. I'm here to take him off your hands.'

She said in a quiet, pleasant tone, 'But I don't want him taken off my hands. I'm very happy to take care of my sister's son. I'm the natural person to do so.'

'Had he been a girl—yes, perhaps you would have had a stronger claim. But it isn't good for a boy to grow up under a woman's aegis with no masculine influence as a counterbalance. You're young, and perhaps may remarry'—she felt he thought it unlikely—'but that's all the more reason for me to take him. I know from bitter experience what can happen to a child whose mother dies, and whose stepmother or foster-mother comes to regard him as a cuckoo in the nest.'

His strongly marked brows had drawn into a forbidding frown, and she saw his jaw muscles clench.

But his tone remained even as he continued, 'I'm not married, and never likely to be, so that circumstance won't arise if he grows up with me.'

'Why are you never likely to marry?'

A faint gleam of cynical amusement lit his sombre dark eyes as he answered her.

'Because, unlike most men who depend on your sex for all their creature comforts, I do not. I find my life runs more smoothly without the continual presence of a woman in it. I don't dislike them. At times I find their company very necessary. But I don't need it all day and every day.'

In the solitary evenings of her widowhood Christie had turned to books for solace. History was what she liked best, but before discovering this preference she had sampled almost every genre, including the works of all the leading champions of Women's Lib from Simone de Beauvoir to Germaine Greer. Their cause had never excited her, and only rarely had she felt a twinge of their indignation at certain entrenched male attitudes.

But now, when Ash Lambard made it clear that his only use for women was as what the liberationists called sex objects, she understood their resentment.

She said stiffly, 'You may not but, while he's little, John does need a woman's daily care. I'm afraid you can't just march in here and remove him from mine.

You see, Jenny left John in *my* custody, Mr Lambard. Paul was killed outright, but my sister lived for three days after the accident. She made me promise to keep John, which I did—very willingly.'

Her voice was not perfectly steady as she spoke of her sister's last hours. The tragedy was too recent to be referred to dispassionately. It had seemed such a cruel irony of fate that Jenny, with so much to live for, had been the one to be taken while she, Christie, a childless widow with no possibility of remarrying, lived on.

'But Paul left the boy in my charge. Not verbally merely, but legally, in his will. It seems unlikely that his wife had no say in the matter. She must have agreed to it.'

'She may have—or she may not. She was very happy-go-lucky and easily influenced. She may have agreed because she felt it was impossible for anything bad to happen to her or Paul. If she'd been a person who worried, she could never have stood driving with him.'

'You thought he drove badly?'

'He'd had several minor accidents, and he often drove above the limit,' she answered, forbearing to add that it was not only the speed limit which her brother-in-law had disregarded.

After a moment, she went on, 'Jenny made no mention of any will in the time I spent at her bedside. But she had to be heavily sedated, and it made her very confused. The only thing which did seem clear in her mind was that I should swear to look after John. I had to promise not once but repeatedly.

Several of the medical staff would be able to vouch for that if you didn't believe me.'

'Certainly I believe you, but a promise made in those circumstances may often be seen to have been injudicious in the light of mature reflection.'

He finished off the rum and put the empty glass aside. Then he went on, 'I'm sure we both have the child's best interests at heart, and I think there can be little question but that I can give him a better life. He won't remain four years old for ever. A growing boy needs more scope for healthy activities than a flat in the suburbs can offer. With me he can swim and sail, and live a fine outdoor life in a year-round good climate.'

'But he may not be the outdoor type, and if he should turn out to be scholarly, surely London has far more to offer than wherever it is that you live?'

'At present I live on a schooner,' he answered. 'My base is Antigua in the Leeward Islands on the eastern side of the Caribbean. It's spelt A-n-t-i-g-u-a, but we don't pronounce it as the Spanish would. We leave out the u and call it Anteegah.'

'I've no doubt it's lovely,' she began, 'but—'

'It's one of the most beautiful islands in the world, and I've been to a great many islands, so I know what I'm talking about. If you lived where I do you wouldn't be pale-faced all winter, and you wouldn't need to be muffled up as you are now. You'd be brown and healthy, and sleep in a thin cotton night-dress.'

'I daresay, but the Caribbean must have its drawbacks, like everywhere else, or why have so many

West Indians come to live here?' she asked dryly.

'That's true. The Caribbean isn't a paradise for everyone. But for such as myself it's very close to it. I've done well over there. I can afford to send the boy to school here, or in America, if he turns out to be unusually clever. You work for your living, I understand? Your husband left no provision for you, as Paul left none for his son. Only debts and a massive mortgage. So for you to bring up the boy would be quite a financial strain.'

It was hard to refute that argument. Her job as a domestic science teacher was not badly paid but, like many others, she was a victim of inflation, high taxes and soaring interest rates. Even with the advantage of being an expert manager, she had little to spare after the payment of her overheads.

'Excuse me: I think the kettle must have boiled by now. Would you like tea or instant coffee?' she asked, as she rose to go to the kitchen.

He shrugged. 'Whichever you prefer.'

Christie made decaffeinated coffee. She took dietetics seriously, and had given up drinking ordinary coffee, except on special occasions, after reading that heavy coffee and cola drinking was linked with fatigue and depression.

'Where are you staying tonight, Mr Lambard?' she asked, as she brought the tray back to the living-room.

He moved forward to take it from her. 'Here, if you have no objection.'

'Here? But I can't put you up. The only bed in my spare room is John's.'

'Your sofa looks long enough for me. Unless you don't wish me to stay here?'

Was it only her imagination or did his dark gaze hold a gleam of challenge?

She found herself saying, 'Not at all, but surely you would be much more comfortable in a hotel?'

'If I sleep here we can continue talking over breakfast. You don't want to stay up too late tonight, I imagine'—with a glance at his watch. 'What happens to the boy during the day while you're working?'

'One of my neighbours looks after him. She used to be a children's nanny, so she likes children and knows how to manage them. You seem to know a good deal about me. Who told you?'

'Paul's solicitor, when I spoke to him on the telephone. He said you were a teacher and had lost your husband. You must have married very young.'

'I was nineteen. My husband was twenty. He didn't know it, but he had a congenital heart defect. He died very suddenly six months after our wedding.'

He looked at her thoughtfully. 'Life has given you a rough deal—losing your husband and now your sister. Are your parents alive?'

Christie shook her head. 'Other people have had rougher deals. I'm healthy. I like my job. And now I have John.' She returned his scrutiny with a resolute look. 'Paul may have named you as John's guardian, but I'm not sure that a father's wishes count for more than a mother's; and even if you were half-brothers, and lived in the same house as boys, Paul didn't know you as a man. Having more money than I have doesn't necessarily make you a fit person to have charge of John.'

He lifted one well-shaped dark eyebrow. 'Are you hinting that you'll contest the will?'

She shook her head. 'It would be a bad thing for John if the two people who are all the family he has now resorted to litigation over him. If I were really convinced that you were the better person to have him, I would give him up—not gladly but with a good grace, for his sake.'

'Perhaps we can arrive at a compromise,' he suggested.

'Perhaps.'

But during the restless night which followed, Christie could see no way in which they could compromise when they lived in different parts of the world. Had he lived in England, it might have been possible to work out a system for sharing John in the way that separated parents did. But when the people concerned lived on opposite sides of the Atlantic . . .

The alarm clock woke her at six. She had always got up at seven but, with John to attend to, she needed the extra hour.

This morning she made the fatal mistake, instead of jumping out of bed immediately, of thinking, *I'll just have five minutes more.* The result was that she fell asleep again.

The next time she woke, someone was shaking her gently, and a deep voice was repeating her name.

'Oh, my goodness! What time is it?' she demanded, realising what she had done and, at first, being much more concerned about being late than by the alien presence of an almost strange man in her bedroom.

'Only twenty past six. You've plenty of time. I heard your alarm clock as I was leaving the bathroom. I guessed you'd had a disturbed night, and thought you might like some tea to get you going.'

Ash indicated the cup and saucer he had placed on her bedside table. He was wearing a short silk dressing gown of navy silk over apple-green cotton pyjamas. He had had a bath the night before, after she had gone back to bed, and this morning he had washed his hair. The angular lines of his jaw, shadowed when they said goodnight, were now no darker than the rest of his face. She could smell, very faintly, his after-shave.

'Thank you . . . but you needn't have bothered.'

Why didn't he go away, instead of standing there, his hands in the pockets of the dressing-gown, looking down at her as if he had never seen a woman in bed before? She suspected he had seen many, but perhaps never one in warm pyjamas. His sort of woman would sleep in clinging satin, filmy chiffon or, more probably, nothing at all but an aura of expensive French scent.

'What time does the boy wake up?' he asked.

'I expect he'll be awake now. He usually reads until I go in to him.'

'Reads? At his age?'

'It's not really reading. He looks at picture books and talks to himself.'

'Will it frighten him if I say hello?'

'I shouldn't think so. He's a very friendly little boy.'

As he moved to the door Christie sat up, her selfconsciousness submerged by a more important consideration.

'Mr Lambard—'

'Ash.'

'Ash,' she amended. 'He . . . John doesn't know his parents are dead. He's too small for the word to have any meaning, and one can't say they've gone to heaven because his parents were not religious, and he hasn't been taught to say prayers. He's been left with me before, during the school holidays, and sometimes with other people when I couldn't have him here. So far he hasn't even asked me when his father and mother are coming back. You may not agree, but Mrs Kelly and I—she's the neighbour I mentioned last night—both feel it's better to say nothing. I wouldn't ever lie to a child,' she added earnestly, 'but with one of John's age, it's not difficult to dodge an issue. So, please, be careful what you say.'

He nodded. 'I won't say anything—for the time being. I was thinking while I was shaving that it's a fortunate circumstance that your job involves long holidays. You can bring him to Antigua and stay with him for a few weeks while he settles down in new surroundings.'

Before she could protest that he was taking far too much for granted, he had left the room and closed the door.

*   *   *

It took Christie a little less than twenty minutes to wash and dress. She had not worn make-up for four years. A box of cosmetics given to her by her sister on Christie's last birthday remained unused in the drawer of her dressing-table.

Jenny had not understood the reason for Christie's refusal to revert to the ways of her girlhood. She had thought it was grief for Mike which accounted for Christie's continued lack of interest in current fashions and social activities. The real reason was something which Christie could never confide to anyone, not even her sister. Least of all to her sister who obviously did not suffer from Christie's secret incapacity.

One of the reasons Paul had not liked his sister-in-law was, she knew, that he had thought her a prude. But it wasn't narrow-minded primness which made her tense and uncomfortable when anyone mentioned sex. The explanation was far more complex.

Had Paul but known it, Christie had not disapproved of the fact that he and her sister had lived together for some time before getting married. She had often regretted her own virginity on her wedding day. If she and Mike had emulated Jenny and Paul, the unhappiness of her short marriage could have been avoided, and she would have had fewer harrowing memories to haunt her all the rest of her life.

When, dressed in a pleated grey skirt, white blouse and grey lambswool cardigan, she left her bedroom, she could smell bacon cooking and hear her nephew's piping voice coming from the kitchen.

Before she reached it she heard Ash ask, 'Where

does your aunt keep the marmalade?'

In answer, the little boy must have pointed to a cupboard because, when she joined them, her unwelcome house guest was opening the cupboard containing her stores of home-made marmalade and jam.

'Those are unopened jars. The one we're using is in here,' she said, opening another door.

Having put the marmalade on the table, she bent to kiss John's rounded cheek. 'Good morning, my lamb.'

He responded with a vigorous hug. He was an affectionate child who liked to sit on her lap to be read to, and who rushed to clasp her round the legs when she fetched him from Mrs Kelly's flat after returning from school. The thought of losing him, of living alone again, filled her with dread. To spend the rest of her life without anyone on whom to lavish her deep reserves of affection seemed unendurable. But the usual outlet for those feelings was something she had had to renounce. To love and be loved by a child was all that was left to her.

'One egg or two?' Ash asked her, as she straightened after being hugged.

He had gone back to the cooker and was breaking eggs into a pan of hot oil. Tomatoes, cut into halves, were sizzling gently in a second pan, and several days' supply of bacon rashers were visible under the eye-level grill.

'One, please.'

She couldn't help being impressed by the deft way he rapped the eggs on the edge of the pan and, using only one hand, swung the shells open. Her brother-in-law and her husband had both been useless in the kitchen, prevented from acquiring even the most rudimentary skills by their doting mothers. She wondered how Ash had acquired his competence, and remembered his remark the night before that he didn't depend on women for all his creature comforts.

'Why do you scrape your hair back like that? It looks nicer loose,' he remarked, with a glance in her direction as the last of five eggs plopped into the fat and began to set.

'In my job neatness and hygiene are more important than looks,' she answered stiffly, knowing that she probably sounded priggish, but resenting so personal a comment on such short acquaintance.

'You aren't at work yet,' was his reply, with another glance which took in her clothes and low-heeled black shoes. But if he was critical of them, he didn't say so but left the cooker to draw a chair out from the table for her.

With a murmur of thanks Christie sat down and unrolled her napkin which matched the red linen cloth. It felt strange to be treated like a guest in her own kitchen.

The importance of a nourishing breakfast had been impressed on her during her training, and evidently Ash also believed in beginning the day with a hearty meal. Having eaten two eggs, five rashers of bacon and two whole tomatoes, he cut himself a second thick slice of Christie's home-made wholemeal bread, and helped himself to the marmalade and some more butter.

But there didn't appear to be an ounce of unnecessary flesh on his muscular frame, suggesting that his intake of food was balanced by a high output of energy.

'You said you'd done well in the Caribbean. At what?' she enquired as she filled John's blue mug with milk before pouring out coffee for Ash and herself.

'I'm a charter skipper. I cater to people, mostly Americans, who want to "get away from it all" but still have good food and modern conveniences. I provide them with a combination of the *Swiss Family Robinson* life with inner-spring mattresses, dry Martinis and all the other comforts of home. It's the way I like to live, too, but I have it all the year round and they only enjoy it for two to four weeks.'

'Does the schooner belong to you?'

He nodded. 'She was left to me.'

'By someone on your mother's side of the family?' As far as she knew none of his paternal relations had ever owned a large schooner.

'No, her previous owner was no relation. She was just an old lady I knew. She had no one to inherit the boat, so she left it to me. I'd been knocking about the Caribbean for a year or two by then, and the cost of buying anything seaworthy was rising a hell of a lot faster than I was earning money, so probably I should still be crewing if I hadn't run into Tugboat Annie, as some people called her.'

Christie knew him to be at least five years older

than her brother-in-law, who had been twenty-seven. 'How old were you when this happened?' she asked.

'Twenty-two. The boat badly needed a refit. It took me some time to get organised for the charter game, but at twenty-four I was in business. I've never looked back. It wasn't the future which was forecast by my father or my schoolmasters,' he added sardonically. 'I'm sure you've been told that I left England under a cloud.'

'I believe so. But that's long ago,' she answered, with a meaning glance at John.

The little boy seemed intent on his breakfast, but he might be taking in more of their conversation than Ash realised. Most of it would be over his head, but with children of his age unguarded remarks by adults could result in embarrassing questions at awkward moments.

In case Ash didn't take the hint, she asked, 'What was your mother's nationality?'

'She was Greek. I don't remember her, only my father's second wife who didn't care for foreigners of any sort, but particularly those of my complexion. It's as well she isn't alive to see England becoming increasingly cosmopolitan.' His dark gaze flicked over Christie's fair hair and pale skin. 'Perhaps you share her views?'

She shook her head. 'I teach at a very mixed school. There are problems when people of different nationalities and races start living together on terms of equality, but I don't believe they're insuperable. I think life would be a great deal duller without the

very mixed cuisine which most people eat nowadays.
I certainly shouldn't like to think I was never going
to eat another pizza, or a curry, or a doner kebab.
Food-wise, there's everything to be said for a multi-
racial community.'

'My stepmother wouldn't have agreed with you.
She disliked even French food,' said Ash. 'But as you
have a more adventurous palate, how would it be if I
took care of the supper tonight and gave you a
Caribbean speciality?'

'It would be very nice—if you think you can get
the ingredients.'

'With the number of West Indians in London—no
problem,' he assured her. 'John can come shopping
with me instead of staying with Mrs Kelly. It will
give us a chance to get to know each other.'

John had finished his breakfast. Christie sent him
to the bathroom to start brushing his teeth.

Alone with his half-uncle, she said, 'Liking small
doses of other people's children is not the same as
having a child on one's hands all the time. Frankly, I
just can't see how you could fit John into your life.
Surely your wealthy passengers wouldn't want a
small boy underfoot? And how could you captain a
schooner *and* nurse him through measles and
mumps, which he's sure to have sooner or later?'

'Your Mrs Kelly has her equivalents in my part of
the world. How could you manage without her?' was
his calm reply.

'At least I can give him my undivided attention for
two days every week, and all through the long school
holidays.'

He looked at her long and intently, and after some moments she found herself unable to meet that oddly piercing scrutiny.

'More coffee?' she asked uneasily.

'Thank you.'

As she refilled his cup and waited for his comment on her last remark, she was suddenly intensely aware of the sinewy brown forearms resting on the edge of the table, and the breadth of his shoulders under the blue cotton shirt. The kitchen was not so warm that she felt uncomfortable in a cardigan. Yet he, newly arrived from a much warmer climate, had his shirt sleeves rolled up to his biceps, and the top two buttons of his shirt open.

Obviously he was superbly fit, with the kind of vitality induced by an energetic outdoor life in an unpolluted atmosphere. Most people looked like that for a few days after a holiday, but not all year round and especially not in the winter. Maybe it would be wrong of her to deprive her nephew of the chance to grow up like his half-uncle: tall and strong, with a dark coffee tan.

Ash said, 'I think we should postpone any further discussion until tonight. What time do you get home?'

She told him, and excused herself to go to the bathroom to supervise John's morning wash and explain the change of routine to him.

By the time John was dressed, Ash had put the kitchen in order, and was washing out a shirt. 'Where shall I hang this to dry?' he asked.

'There's a line which goes over the bath. If you

hang it on that, and leave the wall-heater on for an hour or two, it should be ready for ironing by this evening,' she suggested. 'I'm going to pop upstairs and tell Mrs Kelly that John won't be coming today.'

Her neighbour, also a widow but thirty years Christie's senior, came to the door without delay, for she too was an early riser, but wearing a cherry red housecoat and matching lipstick.

From time to time she had hinted that Christie's appearance would be enhanced by make-up and more colourful clothes. But although she had been devoted to her late husband, Mrs Kelly admitted that she would like to marry again if she met a suitable widower.

Whereas Christie had put marriage behind her and, by dressing like a modern nun, except that she wore no veil, attracted little male interest and re-minded herself—although this was scarcely neces-sary while she still had occasional nightmares which brought the past vividly back to her—that she had no right to encourage such interest.

'Christie! Is anything wrong, my dear?' asked the older woman, finding her on the threshold.

'No, nothing. I'm sorry to interrupt your break-fast, Margaret. Did you enjoy the play last night?'

For a few minutes, as she greeted her friend and listened to her enthusiastic report of a visit to a West End theatre, Christie's clear grey eyes were alight with the friendly warmth which made her well liked by her women colleagues and popular with her pupils.

But, when Margaret enquired where John was,

the smile left her eyes as she answered, 'He's with his uncle, Paul's half-brother. He arrived late last night from abroad and is only here for a short time. John is going to spend the day with him. I thought you would like to know early, in case you felt like spending the day with one of the girls.'

Margaret Kelly had two married daughters living on the far side of London.

'No, I must spend today at the sewing machine, or I shan't have my Christmas presents finished. What's he like—your visitor?'

Christie had always been the kind of person who received confidences rather than gave them. Very often, while standing beside her in a bus queue or at the supermarket check-out, some lonely fellow human being would begin a conversation which would rapidly develop into their life story, or details of ill health and other problems. Perhaps they sensed that she had been through life's storms and would not reject their need for sympathy.

But although Margaret was a kind, understanding woman, Christie felt that she did enough for her by looking after John during school hours. She had not told Margaret about her past unhappiness, or about the worries which had loomed over her since learning the conditions of Paul's will.

'He seems very pleasant,' she said guardedly. 'He's certainly the most capable man I've ever met. He cooked our breakfast, and I left him washing out a shirt. John will be quite safe in his charge, I'm sure of that.'

'He stayed the night with you?'

'Yes.' Christie knew that Margaret's surprise was prompted by her knowledge of the limited sleeping facilities in the lower flat rather than by any moral disapproval. 'He didn't turn up until after twelve, and we talked for some time, and then he suggested dossing down on the sofa. At that time of night it seemed rather inhospitable to push him out to a hotel.'

'Oh, yes, I was forgetting about your sofa. Mine, being a two-seater, is no good as a makeshift bed. Where has he come from?'

'From Antigua in the West Indies.'

'An expensive journey,' was Margaret's comment. 'He must be a good-hearted man to concern himself with John's welfare. What age are his own children?'

'He's a bachelor.'

'Oh?' Again Margaret looked surprised. 'In that case perhaps he'll be able to help you financially.'

'Perhaps. Enjoy your sewing day. You'll be able to get on faster without having John on your hands.'

'Oh, he's never any trouble, bless him. Thank you for letting me know, dear. See you later.'

Descending the stairs to her own floor, Christie was inclined to wish that she had confided in Margaret and could have asked her advice.

She found John contentedly playing with a simple wood and plastic construction set, and his half-uncle still in the kitchen.

'May I use your shoe cleaning brushes?' he asked her.

'Of course.' She fetched them for him from her broom cupboard.

His chestnut brown leather slip-ons did not look in need of a polish, but evidently he was as particular about his appearance as her father, an Army officer, had been. "Never trust a man with dirty shoes" had been one of the adages he had impressed on his teenage daughters.

Looking back, Christie thought she might not have married so young if her father had lived. He had retired from the Army at about the same time that she had started her domestic science training. Her mother had died when Jenny was sixteen and Christie thirteen; and the plan had been that he and his younger daughter would set up home in a cottage on the south coast near the large resort where she was training.

For a year this arrangement had worked well. Then, shortly after her engagement to Mike, her father had become seriously ill. He had died when she was not quite twenty.

With none of the home-making problems besetting most young engaged couples, she and Mike had married forthwith. He, like her, had lost both his parents, and was living in uncomfortable digs which he had been glad to exchange for the comforts of the cottage and Christie's already expert housekeeping.

He had been twenty-one when he died, still in love with his bride and, she felt sure, with no suspicion that her father had been wise in trying to dissuade her from becoming engaged before she had finished her training.

She knew now that she had never really loved

Mike and, if he had lived, she would have grown to
detest him. But if some of the fault lay with him, a
great deal more lay with her for not recognising the
difference between herself and other girls. There had
been plenty of signs, but—

'Do John's outdoor shoes need cleaning?'

Ash's question interrupted her thoughts. With a
slight start she returned from the unhappy past to
the uncertain present.

'They may not be up to your standards,' she
conceded, forcing a smile.

She fetched the little boy's shoes. They were fairly
new but, at the rate he was growing, would soon need
to be replaced. The price of keeping him well shod
and comfortably clothed was one of her many worries about him. With the worst of the winter still to
come, he would probably need a new fleece-lined
anorak before the cold weather was over. She felt a
sudden pang of envy for Ash living in a climate where
thick clothes were never necessary, and the rain
came in short heavy downpours instead of long days
of drizzle.

'You may need an umbrella before the day's
out,' she said, peering up at the sky through the
kitchen window. 'I'd better leave you mine. It isn't
far to my bus stop, and I have a good waterproof
mac.'

'No, no—you take your umbrella. If it starts to
rain while we're out, we'll pick up a taxi.'

'There aren't many about in the suburbs. You
have to ring up for them.'

'Then we'll ring up. Don't worry about it.' There

was a note of raillery in his voice which made her feel
foolishly fussy.

She flushed. 'I'd better be going.'

It seemed a very long day. Christie found it difficult
to concentrate for thinking of Ashcroft Lambard and
his right to take charge of the child who was all the
happiness left to her.

During the mid-morning break, she rang up the
local solicitor how had acted for her when she had
bought the flat. His clerk said he was very busy and
couldn't possibly see her at such short notice. When
Christie said it was a matter of the greatest urgency,
he relented and made an appointment for her. The
consultation made her half an hour late getting
home. When she unlocked the door—having given a
spare key to Ash—instead of entering a flat which
had been empty all day, she was greeted by an
appetising smell of cooking, and the sound of music
from the living-room.

Christie hung her raincoat in the cupboard in the
lobby. It had been a grey day, but dry.

There was nobody in the sitting-room. But a vase
of dark red carnations stood in the centre of the
dining-table, and the room was warm instead of
chilly, suggesting that the gas fire had been alight for
some time.

She crossed the passage which led to the kitchen
and bedrooms. The kitchen door was half open. Ash
was sitting at the kitchen table, wearing her striped
butcher's apron, with John perched on one of his
thighs, poring over a large new picture book.

In the moment before they looked up, she was struck by the contrast between the child's rounded, unformed features and the hard angularity of the man's face. No painter could do justice to that remarkable bone structure. It would take the skill of a sculptor, and some dark burnished metal, to capture the shape of his cheekbones, the lean jaw, the forceful chin.

'Hello! How have you two been getting on?' she asked, with a cheerfulness she was far from feeling.

The man set the child on his feet and rose to his own towering height.

'We've had a good day,' he said, smiling. 'How has your day gone?'

'Oh . . . quite well. Something smells very good. A new book, John?'

'Yes, Uncle Ash bought it for me. He bought a present for you, too.'

'The carnations . . . yes, I saw them. They're lovely. Thank you very much,' she said to Ash.

'No, not the flowers,' he replied. 'In America, flowers or a pot plant are the usual offering to one's hostess. As you won't be here to water a plant, cut flowers seemed more suitable.'

'What do you mean I won't be here?'

'Run and fetch the envelope I left on the table in the other room, will you, John?'

As the child scampered out of the kitchen Ash turned to open the refrigerator. He took from it a dark green glass bottle, the top sealed with dull gold foil.

'I hope you like champagne.'

'I've never had it.'

'Never? Not even at your wedding?'

'It wasn't that sort of wedding.'

He shot a swift, narrowed glance at her, but he said only, 'Any glasses will do if you haven't flutes.'

Christie turned to a cupboard containing lemonade goblets. 'What did you mean—I won't be here?' she repeated.

John came back with a large white envelope. Wide-eyed with interest, he watched his half-uncle ease the cork out of the bottle and fill two glasses with pale golden, bubbling wine. His long, square-tipped fingers had the deftness of much practice.

'You wouldn't like this stuff, my lad,' Ash's free hand ruffled the child's hair.

It was clear that in less than twelve hours he had become an established member of John's small world.

Ash handed one of the glasses to Christie. He raised the other. 'To the future.'

'To the future,' she echoed uncertainly.

He drank, then handed her the envelope, his eyes amused by her hesitance.

Christie set down her glass, and tipped out the contents of the envelope. When, having examined the tickets, she looked up at him, he said, 'I think you'll find Christmas in the sun just as enjoyable as a white Christmas over here—and maybe it won't snow this year.'

Her beautiful teeth—only noticeable when she was laughing—bit into her soft lower lip. How could she rage at a man who had paid a great deal of money for her to cross the Atlantic? Yet what intolerable arrogance to assume she had no other plans; to dictate her actions in this high-handed manner.

TWO

'I THINK this is something we should discuss later this evening,' Christie said, in a carefully controlled voice.

He said, 'As you wish.' But she could see he was confident that his wishes would override hers.

'By the way, I invited your friend Mrs Kelly to join us for supper,' he said casually.

'Margaret? Where did you run into her? At the shops?'

'No, I called on her at her flat.'

'Really? Why?' she asked, thinking—To pump her about me, I suppose.

'I needed to know the name of the school where you teach, so that I could ring up and check the dates when this term ends and the next one begins before booking your flight. Mrs Kelly is a nice woman. You're lucky to have her to help you.'

'I know. Very lucky,' she agreed.

'You don't like this champagne?' he asked, reminding her that she had taken only one small sip of it.

Christie drank a little more. 'It's delicious, but I'm not used to drinking. It may go to my head if I drink it too fast. Is it true that champagne is the only drink which doesn't give people hangovers?'

'I wouldn't know, never having had an excess of it.

I suspect that a split of champagne would do most people more good—and cost the Health Service less—than all the tranquillisers and sleeping pills which Mrs Kelly tells me are prescribed far too freely over here. Do you take them?'

'I did for a while after my husband died. I don't any more. Why do you ask? Do I strike you as being a neurotic?' she asked, somewhat indignantly.

'Not neurotic. A little tense, maybe. But that's understandable in the circumstances, and three or four weeks in Antigua will relax you. It does everyone; even businessmen with ulcers and high blood pressure.'

His cool assumption that she would fall in with his plans had an anything but relaxing effect on her. But she said only, 'What time were you planning to have dinner? I usually bath John about six, and give him his supper at half past. Then he plays in bed till he's sleepy.'

'So Mrs Kelly told me. I suggested she joined us at seven, to eat about eight.'

Ash watched her bath John that night. The bathroom seemed even smaller than it was with the tall, dark man as an audience while she knelt on the bathmat and lathered the child's rosy body as he played with his fleet of plastic boats.

Having bathed him, she left him with Ash while she went to change the white blouse which her nephew had accidentally splashed.

When she rejoined them, wearing a grey flannel shirt-dress, she saw Ash looking critically at it. But it wasn't until she had tucked the child into bed that his half-uncle had the effrontery to remove the clasp which held her hair back.

'It doesn't suit you like that,' he said, when she made a small sound of protest.

'In *your* opinion,' she retorted.

'Your husband wouldn't have wished you to mourn him indefinitely. Even Mrs Kelly, whose husband died fairly recently, wears lipstick and coloured dresses.'

'Please . . . give it back,' she insisted, holding her hair back with one hand and stretching out the other for the clasp.

Ash shook his head. 'It's time someone made you snap out of this state of withdrawal you've sunk into. You're a young and potentially beautiful woman. However much you loved him, however bleak the future seems without him, life still has plenty to offer someone of your age.'

'You don't understand—'

'No, I don't,' he agreed, rather curtly. 'If it had been you who had died, would you have hoped that your husband would never look at another woman . . . never enjoy life . . . never marry again?'

'No . . . no . . . certainly not!'

'Then why commit suttee yourself?'

'I haven't. I—you don't know anything about me.'

'I don't have to know you to see that there's something wrong with a woman who deliberately plays down her assets. You've an excellent figure, good legs, and the kind of streaky blonde hair which some of your sex pay a fortune to achieve by artificial means. But you're trying to pretend you're a flat-chested spinster of forty.'

Christie opened her mouth to deliver a furious riposte, but was forestalled by the doorbell.

'That'll be Mrs Kelly, I imagine.'

Ash went to answer it, leaving her fulminating with annoyance at his high-handedness.

'What a charming man,' said Margaret, in a confidential undertone when she and Christie were alone for a few minutes while he went to the kitchen for another bottle of champagne.

'Do you think so?'

'Don't you?' Mrs Kelly looked surprised.

'I'm not sure. I haven't known him long enough to form any definite opinion.'

'Nor have I, but my first impression—and I think I'm a reasonably good judge—is that he's a very nice person. Kind, sensible, very concerned to do the best thing for John.'

'I'm not sure. It seems most peculiar to me—a bachelor wanting to bring up someone else's child. He and Paul weren't as close as all that,' was Christie's reply, in a low tone.

Before Margaret Kelly could comment, Ash returned to dispense the champagne.

Dubious about him as she was, Christie could not fault him as a host. During the excellent meal he had prepared, and which he served single-handed, insisting the women should relax for a change, she felt more than ever like a guest in her own home.

While they ate a Dominican dish called *Pato con piña*, a stuffed duck garnished with pineapple, which

followed the creamy aubergine soup, a speciality of
Nevis, an island not far from Antigua, Ash kept
Margaret amused with tales of the idiosyncrasies of
some of his charter passengers. He was a good
raconteur. Christie had to join in the other woman's
laughter at some of his most absurd anecdotes. Long
before the meal was over—it ended with a cold rum
soufflé—she had forgotten her vexation at being
made to wear her hair loose.

It was Margaret who reminded her that the evening had not begun amiably. She said, 'I don't remember ever seeing you with your hair as it is
tonight, Christie. It suits you. The other way is too
severe. Don't you agree, Ash?'

They had been on first name terms for some time
by then.

'I do,' he said, looking at Christie with a quizzical
glint in his dark eyes.

Suddenly her mood changed. It occurred to her to
wonder how much several glasses of champagne had
contributed to her feeling of cheerful relaxation. And
how much of his cordiality was a deliberate strategy
to overcome her resistance to his wish to take John
away from her.

'*Why* do you want to bring up John?' she asked
abruptly. 'It doesn't make sense to me, a man in your
circumstances voluntarily encumbering himself with
a young child when there's no necessity. In general,
men aren't interested in babies and children, except
their own—and not always then.'

She saw that this unexpected broadside had surprised him, and was glad she had revived the point at

issue between them instead of allowing him to distract her from it.

'In general, you're right,' he agreed. 'But most men—particularly those who, starting with nothing, have built up a profitable business—hope to have a son, if not to follow in their footsteps, at least to inherit the fruits of their labours. My problem is that I should like a son, period. Now if a woman feels an urge to have a child, she will have very little difficulty in finding a man to sire it for her. She's not obliged to marry him. He may never know that he's performed a service for her. But how many women, do you think, would be willing to bear a child for me? Apart from the fact that gestation takes a great deal more time than procreation, the kind of woman I would choose to be the mother of my son wouldn't consider such an arrangement. Nor do I stand much chance of being able to adopt a boy. So, although I should never have wished it to happen, the tragedy which has left John an orphan doesn't put me to any inconvenience. Rather the reverse.'

Christie glanced at Margaret, thinking she might have been shocked by his outspoken statement. But her expression was unruffled. She asked, 'Have you ever been married, Ash?'

'No.'

'Oh, so it's not an unhappy previous experience which puts you off marriage?'

'Not at all. My relations with women—other than with my father's second wife—have always been extremely enjoyable—to me and, I hope, to them,' he added, rising to his feet. 'I'm going to wash the

dishes. No, sit tight, you two. I can manage. Perhaps
you can convince Christiana that my attitude isn't as
outrageous as she seems to find it, Margaret.'

'I should have thought you would find it even *more*
outrageous than I do,' said Christie, when they were
alone.

'No, not really, dear. My views have broadened a
lot in the past few years. My husband could never
accept that manners and morals change with every
generation. In his day it was all right for a young
man to sow his wild oats, but a nice girl had to
behave herself. It upset Matthew very much when he
realised that neither of our girls were nice any more,
in that sense. But they've settled down now, and
they're just as good wives and mothers as my generation. Looking back, I realise it was largely the fear of
having a baby which kept us in line.'

She paused. 'To return to what Ash said just now,
I think girls always have marriage in view. They're
always searching for the right man. But men aren't.
They want to make love to as many pretty girls as
possible until, suddenly, one girl comes along who's
special, and they lose interest in the others. Ash
hasn't met the right girl yet.'

'If he hasn't by now, will he ever? He's not a boy
any more.'

'Round about thirty. That's no age. A lot of men
settle down earlier because they're not particularly
attractive and feminine companionship isn't too easy
to come by. That can't be a problem in his case. He's
a charmer of a high order.'

'He may be God's gift to women, but it doesn't

make him an ideal guardian for a child,' was Christie's somewhat acid comment. 'Not that I can do much about that,' she added, with a heavy sigh. 'My solicitor's advice is to give in gracefully. He thinks Ash has a better claim than I have.'

Margaret said, 'I hate to agree, knowing what John means to you, but one can't ignore the practical difficulties of someone in your situation—in effect, a single woman—bringing up a small boy.'

Ash came back. 'Did Christie tell you she's going to spend the Christmas holidays in Antigua with me?'

'No, she didn't. Oh, my dear, how exciting! It will do you the world of good, the best part of a month in the sun. You'll need some new dresses . . . sundresses. They won't be easy to find at this time of year. You must let me run up a couple for you. It doesn't take more than an evening, that sort of dress.'

She chattered on, full of enthusiasm, while Christie sat, saying little, unable to feel any excitement at the thought of four weeks in Antigua because, at the end, she would have to come back on her own.

After Margaret had said goodnight and returned to her own flat, Christie asked Ash, 'What time does your flight leave tomorrow?'

'A little after ten, from Heathrow. I need to leave here about eight-thirty.'

'Is that early enough? I thought one had to check in about an hour beforehand?'

'So they say, but I never do. Flights are sometimes on time, sometimes late. I don't care for hanging about in airports, so I cut it as fine as I can. I've never missed a flight yet.'

She could imagine him strolling unhurriedly into the terminal, knowing exactly where to go and what to do.

He said, 'Although it's basically the same, this flat is much nicer than Margaret's. Are you responsible for the way it's decorated?'

'Yes, I couldn't stand the existing décor, so I re-did it. The furniture is from my mother's family home. As possibly you know, it's mostly Regency. I'm lucky to have inherited it. Jenny and Paul didn't care for antiques, so Father left it all to me.'

'Those are your parents, I presume?' He indicated a photograph of her father as a young subaltern with her mother in a white wedding dress in the style of the early 1950s.

'Yes, and that's my sister on the bookcase. We weren't much alike.'

'But no photograph of your husband, either here or in your bedroom?'

She stiffened. 'No. I—I have some snaps, but no studio portrait,' she answered, in an expressionless voice.

How like him to point out something which most people—anyone with an ounce of tact!—would not have mentioned.

'I think, if you don't mind, I'll go to bed,' she said, rising.

'By all means.' He stood up.

Christie couldn't find fault with his manners.

'Thank you for cooking that delicious dinner,' she

said, with formal politeness, 'Goodnight.'

'Goodnight, Christiana.'

She had a feeling his eyes were amused as he watched her walk out of the room.

She did not oversleep a second time, and it was she who cooked breakfast for him next morning.

'Are the things which you'll need for this trip— suitcases, summer clothes and so on—going to strain your budget?' he asked her. 'If so I'll be pleased to contribute to your expenses in bringing John out to me.'

'Thank you, but that won't be necessary. I already have several cases.'

'As far as clothes are concerned, one light dress should be enough. You can buy the rest in Antigua where cotton dresses are worn all the year round.'

When the time came to say goodbye, he swung John up in his arms and held the child perched on one forearm.

'Goodbye, John. See you soon. Take good care of Aunt Christie till I see you again, won't you?'

He kissed the boy's cheek, and John hugged him, plump arms round his uncle's strong neck. Then Ash lowered the boy to the floor and turned to take his leave of her.

'See you at the end of next week. I'll be waiting to meet you at the airport. Goodbye, Christiana.'

She forced a smile, but her silver-grey eyes were nervous. She had an uneasy feeling that, merely to tease, he might bend down and kiss her as well. But he only shook hands.

*   *   *

The days which followed his visit were busy ones. Margaret ran up one dress for Christie; she herself made another.

She completed her Christmas shopping, buying the little things to put in John's stocking, and two larger presents for him. At Margaret's suggestion she bought a gift to give to Ash. It would be merely a gesture. She could feel no liking for the man who had swept in and out of her life with the force of a hurricane, leaving desolation in her heart.

One evening before their departure she spent reading a book, borrowed from the Public Library, about her nephew's future home.

Antigua, twelve miles by sixteen, was the largest of the Leewards, she learned. The other islands in the group were Nevis, St. Kitts, Montserrat, Barbuda and Anguilla.

Although small, they have a monumental past, she read. *Around them raged many historical naval and military battles.*

Christie lifted her gaze from the page, a troubled frown between the delicately marked eyebrows which, like her long lashes, were several shades darker than her hair.

And if I don't like what I find, and don't think John will be happy, another battle will rage between Ash and me, she thought.

For although he had discouraged her from attempting to resist Ash's superior claim to the child, her solicitor had added that, if Mr Lambard's life style could be shown to be at all irregular, then she would be on stronger ground.

* * *

Christie had been apprehensive that the eight-hour-long flight across the Atlantic might prove too exacting a test of her small nephew's usually good behaviour.

She need not have worried. From the moment they boarded the huge aircraft which had ten seats in each row, separated by two gangways, he was as quiet and contented as some of the other children on board were restless.

Luckily they had been allocated side seats, and she put him in the one next to the window from which, once they were airborne, he was able to gaze in wonder at the sunlit world above the clouds.

This limitless snowscape was the view for several hours, during which time they were served first with drinks and then with lunch.

After lunch the stewardess handed out headsets to those who wanted to hear the inflight movie or listen to music. On her own, Christie would have watched the film, of which she had an excellent view because each section of the cabin had its own screen on the wall of the central blocks which housed the many well-equipped washrooms. But as John was too small to see over the seats in front of them, and too young to enjoy an adult film, she paid for one set of earphones so that he could listen to the Junior Jet Club Show, a programme specially for children.

This lasted an hour, and before it was over he had curled up and fallen asleep with his thumb in his mouth and his other arm cuddling Sammy, his toy baby seal.

Very gently, Christie removed the headset without disturbing him and was able to hear the dialogue of the last part of the film.

When it was over she leaned across John to open the shutters over the porthole which passengers had been asked to close for the film show. Now, outside, the shining white snowfields had given place to a deep blue ethereal lake on which floated hundreds of royal icing islands.

The service of afternoon tea roused John from his slumbers to find another plastic tray on the folding down table in front of him, this meal including a packet of his favourite digestive biscuits.

'I like flying, don't you, Aunt Christie?' he said, as she helped him to unwrap his scone and spread it with blackcurrant jam.

'Yes, I do,' she agreed with him, smiling.

No doubt seasoned travellers, such as his uncle, found nothing extraordinary about air travel. To her it still seemed a miracle that four hundred people, tons of luggage and the food for a three-course meal as well as this light snack could be wafted miles into the air and sped across a vast ocean which had once taken weeks to traverse.

She had already put back her wrist watch to five hours behind London time, because when they arrived it would still be mid-afternoon in Antigua's time-zone.

Thinking about landing, and of the man who would be there to meet them, she began to feel tense and keyed-up. She told herself it was merely the excitement common to all holidaymakers on nearing their destination, but deep down she knew her own feelings were more complex than the happy anticipation to be seen in the eyes of the people around her.

Half an hour before touchdown she changed John's sweater and long pants for the cotton tee-shirt and shorts she had brought in her hand luggage.

She herself had travelled in a pleated skirt with a thin blouse under a cardigan. Earlier, after the Captain had announced that the temperature in Antigua was eighty degrees, she had been to a washroom to remove her tights.

'Look . . . look . . .!' John exclaimed excitedly when, bare-legged, she returned to her seat.

Christie bent her head close to his and had her first glimpse of Antigua, a low-lying, brown-coloured island in an indigo sea paling to turquoise near the shore. As the aircraft descended towards the runway, she had the impression that most of the buildings on the island were roofed with red corrugated iron. Then the great wheels touched down and her first flight was over.

In spite of being forewarned, she was unprepared for the heat which enveloped them as they descended the steps from the cool cabin to the hot tarmac. Not everyone was leaving the aircraft which soon would fly further south to Barbados and Trinidad.

In the open there was a pleasant breeze blowing, but once inside the low buildings of Coolidge International Airport—not as large or impressive as its name suggested—the heat became really uncomfortable for anyone wholly or partially dressed for the English climate.

Queueing to have her passport examined, Christie

looked about for Ash. He had not been outside
among the people congregated behind a wire fence,
waving and calling to friends and relations. Nor was
he anywhere to be seen on the other side of the
immigration officers' desks where porters were waiting to carry baggage out to the taxis she could see
through the outer doorways.

'How long you stayin', ma'am?'

She returned her attention to the uniformed Antiguan behind the desk. 'Nearly four weeks.'

A few moments later she was being asked by a
porter to indicate her cases among the pile being
unloaded from a trailer.

By the time she had passed through the Customs
section there was still no sign of Ash. As she was
wondering what to do, someone said, 'Mrs Chapman?' and she turned to find a tall and very glamorous young woman in a scarlet sun-dress looking
down at her.

'Yes . . .'

Before she could say any more, the girl turned to
the porter and told him to carry the cases to a white
sports car.

As he moved towards it, she introduced herself.
'I'm Bettina Long. Ash asked me to meet you. He's
not here at present, but he'll be back in a day or two.'

Taking no notice of John, who was holding tightly
to Christie's hand, she added, 'If you don't mind we
won't hang about. I've had to shut up the shop, and
there's a woman staying here this week who usually
comes in to browse about this time of day. She's been
spending a lot of money, so I don't want her to find

the place closed. I run the boutique at the Turtle Creek Cottage Colony, which is where you'll be staying until Ash returns,' she explained.

As Bettina led the way to her car, Christie looked admiringly at the brown-satin smoothness of her shoulders under the shoestring straps of her bright red dress. Her dark hair, obviously long, was at present wound up in a coil held by two scarlet combs and adorned with a spray of red flowers. She would have been two or three inches taller than Christie in bare feet, and her height was accentuated by a sophisticated form of espadrille with high rope-covered wedges and long red tapes criss-crossed around her slim ankles.

She made Christie conscious that the synthetic lining of her own skirt was clinging uncomfortably to her legs, and of the pallor of her skin, and John's, compared with this girl's gorgeous tan.

'The child can sit in the back,' said Bettina, after tipping the porter who, in spite of the heat, was wearing a woolly hat pulled down over his hair.

The large number of Antiguans who wore some kind of headgear—shady straws, old-fashioned felt trilbys, or gaily coloured cotton headties knotted at the back of the head, not under the chin as in England—was among Christie's first-impressions of the island.

'I expected you to be much older . . . middle-aged in fact,' was Bettina's first remark, during the drive.

'Is that how Ash described me?'

'No, just my impression . . . from the fact that he said you were a widow, maybe.'

'You say he's not here. Where is he?' Christie was not sure whether she was relieved or disappointed at having their next confrontation postponed for a few days.

'In Montserrat. A friend of his there is in some kind of trouble—he didn't go into details when he rang up to ask me to meet you. He sent a message that you were to be particularly careful not to sunbathe except before nine and after four. You'd be amazed how many visitors don't take the warnings seriously and end up looking like lobsters and feeling like hell. Even ten minutes of midday sun here can fry anyone with a skin as white as yours,' said Bettina. 'If you haven't brought a beach cover-up and a tee-shirt for swimming and snorkelling, you'd better buy some from me. Ash won't be pleased if he comes back to find you with burns. It's something he's very strict about with his passengers.'

'What happens to them while he's away? Or has he none at the moment?'

'Oh, yes—it's the height of the season. But he doesn't sail *Sunbird* single-handed, and his crew can cope for a short time.'

They had left the airport behind and were motoring through open country which reminded Christie of films of the African bush. In places the dry grass was shaded by small, flat-topped trees which later she learned were acacias. An unfamiliar breed of cattle, some of them severely emaciated, were grazing the roadsides, trailing long chains behind them. Many of the beasts had a white egret for a companion.

'In general the roads here are terrible,' said Bettina, avoiding a rut in the much-patched macadam.

But the poor condition of the surface didn't cause her to reduce her speed. Turning to smile over her shoulder at John who was perched between the two up-ended suitcases, Christie wondered if Bettina always drove as fast, or only because she was in a hurry to re-open her boutique.

Was she Ash's girl-friend? she wondered.

Aloud, she asked, 'Do you live at the Cottage Colony?'

'Yes, it suits me. I'm not domesticated. Cooking bores me. Housework—no, thanks! Living in a hotel is ideal. Apart from fixing breakfast, which is only black coffee and fruit juice, I don't have to lift a finger. The maids clean the cottage, and I have lunch by the pool and dinner in the restaurant. That's if I don't have a date to dine in St John's or at one of the other hotels.'

They were approaching a village. Most of the houses close to the road were built of wood, gaily painted in colours such as sky blue, bright pink and turquoise which would have looked garish in England but here had a gay, fresh appearance.

The houses were all single-storey, and few were much larger than a good-sized European garage while many were tiny, like garden sheds. But on the outskirts of the village and farther away from the main road there were new, more spacious block-built bungalows with white wrought iron grilles across the windows and fenced gardens.

The gardens of the small habitations merged with

each other and were full of tropical trees and shrubs ablaze with bright flowers. The only ones Christie knew by name were the purple and red bougainvillea, and the long-stamened scarlet hibiscus.

People sitting on porches or grouped in the doorways of small shops watched the white car go past, and some waved. Christie and John returned these greetings, but Bettina ignored them and caused the elder of her passengers more than one anxious moment by not slowing where children were playing or hens were crossing the road.

Beyond the village the sound of the sports car's hooter scattered a herd of goats. They had no one with them and, when Christie expressed surprise at the absence of a herdsman, Bettina shrugged and said it was not at all unusual.

'I've no idea,' was her answer to the question as to how the goats' owner knew where to find them. She gave the impression of taking little interest in the flora and fauna of the island.

It was about half an hour's drive from the airport to the wide gateway with the name of the Colony incised on a great block of stone, and a tree-lined drive curving away out of sight.

The car jolted over the bars of a cattle-grid, then swept round the curve to where the branches of a group of tall palms shaded the forecourt of a long, low, single-roofed building. In the centre of this structure a covered walk, open at either end, gave, as the car drew to a halt, an enticing glimpse of a swimming pool.

'The staff will look after you now. I'll see you later,

probably,' said Bettina, as a strongly-built, dark-skinned young man, wearing a pale blue tee-shirt with Turtle Creek printed across the chest, stepped forward to open her door for her.

With no word of thanks for this service, she disappeared into the building.

The young man flashed white teeth at Christie and, reaching into the back seat, swung John up and over the side.

'I'll bring your bags for you, ma'am. You'll find Reception in there'—with a gesture in the direction of the walk-through.

'Thank you.' After walking round the front of the car and taking her nephew's hand in hers, Christie approached the polished counter where two attractive Antiguan girls broke off a conversation to bid her good afternoon.

'I'm Mrs Chapman. I believe a room has been reserved for me.'

'Yes, ma'am.' The taller girl took down a key and handed it over, not to Christie, but to the young baggage porter who was already at her elbow with their cases.

He put it in the pocket of his white trousers. 'This way, ma'am.' He handled the two large suitcases with an ease which, as he moved ahead, drew her attention to the splendour of his physique with very wide shoulders tapering to a narrow waist.

The fine, athletic build of all the island's young men and the loose-limbed grace of their carriage was something she was to notice repeatedly during her first days in Antigua. Each time she did, it reminded her of Ash's remark about the island being a healthier place for John to grow up than London. But whether broad shoulders and strong muscles were something island life could give to every boy, or were a genetic inheritance peculiar to the Antiguans, she could not be sure. Clearly, in the harsh days of slavery, only the most hardy people had survived the gruelling work in the canefields and the epidemics of the period.

At the inner end of the walk-through, the whole of the large, sparkling free-form pool was revealed to them, with bathers lying stretched out on sun-beds on the paved surround. Instead of skirting the pool, they turned aside and passed through an area of gardens dotted with tall palms where the grass was kept green by sprinklers. Farther on, given privacy from each other by shrubberies, were the holiday cottages, each with its name on a fingerpost where the side path diverged from the main path.

Theirs was called Frangipani Cottage, and Christie concluded that the golden-centred white flowers growing in profusion beside the front door must be those after which it was named.

The door gave into a lobby with an inner door open to show a spacious, dimly lit sitting-room. The half-light was caused by vertical louvred blinds at present arranged to shut out the afternoon sun.

After the young man had left them, Christie made a quick exploration of the rest of the cottage. It consisted of an equally dimly lit bedroom with twin beds, a small but well fitted kitchen and a shower room with a separate lavatory.

Only then did she look for the cords which controlled the blinds in the sitting-room. When the slats slowly opened to reveal the prospect on that side of the cottage, she drew in a sharp breath of pleasure.

Immediately outside the floor-to-ceiling plate glass panels was a flowery verandah with two reclining chairs and four upright chairs arranged round a white table fitted with a furled sunbrella. Beyond, seen between the tall trunks of coconut palms, was the calm and sparkling Caribbean.

'Oh, John—just look!' she exclaimed delightedly. 'I can't wait to have my first dip. I'll find our swimsuits and your armlets, and we'll unpack properly later on.'

It didn't take long to unstrap and unlock the case containing her plain green one-piece and John's stretchy tomato-red briefs with the face of a smiling sun sewn on the behind.

Mindful that the inflatable armlets would expose more of him to the still-powerful rays than was the case with an unsupported swimmer, she insisted he wear an old tee-shirt.

The part of the beach closest to their cottage had fewer people on it than the area near the thatched beach bar, and Christie was glad not to be too near the other holidaymakers. They all seemed enviably tanned, making her doubly selfconscious of the unpleasing pallor of her limbs.

She found herself wondering if, by the time Ash returned, she would have achieved a less unappetising colour; her next thought being that it should be a matter of indifference to her whether he found her skin repulsively white or not.

Although it was her nephew's first encounter with the sea, he needed no encouragement to walk into the warm, clear water and try out the bright orange armlets. Soon it was clear that, like the majority of children, he was a natural water-baby who, left to himself, would dog-paddle happily for hours.

Christie had learnt to swim at school, but had not swum a great deal since then, and never in water like this; crystal shot with pearly gleams where it rippled on the powdered coral sand, then shading from palest jade through all the blue-greens to purple above the submerged reefs. There, about fifty yards out, she could see a number of people snorkelling, occasionally blowing plumes of water out of their breathing tubes.

When she and John left the water, she felt more refreshed and relaxed than she could ever remember.

'But we won't sunbathe until later. The sun is still very hot,' she said, mindful of the message left with Bettina by his co-guardian.

A few minutes after their return to the cottage, the telephone rang and a man's voice asked, 'Mrs Chapman?' and then introduced himself as the Manager.

'We shall meet later on. For the moment I merely wish to say "Welcome", and to urge you to be sure to tell me if you have any problems, or if I can help you in any way.'

'That's very kind of you. Thank you.'

'Not at all. It's our job to ensure you have a perfect

vacation. By the way, although we routinely put flowers in all the cottages, Mr Lambard asked for a specially nice arrangement to be prepared for your arrival, Mrs Chapman. You'll also find various supplies, including milk for the little boy, provided for you in the kitchen.'

'Really? Oh, that's very helpful.'

'Some of our guests enjoy a substantial breakfast in the restaurant while they're on holiday. Others prefer to be self-sufficient first thing. There are times when guests like to socialise with each other at one of the Colony's four bars where we serve all the island specialities such as Piña Colada and Antigua Kiss. But sometimes they want some quiet refreshments on their own verandah. We start them off with a bottle of Antigua's excellent light rum. However, Mr Lambard thought that wine might be more to your taste, and we've carried out his instruction that a bottle of our best French white wine should be placed in your ice-box a short while before your arrival. Now I'll leave you to rest after your journey.'

After she had replaced the receiver, Christie looked around the sitting-room more carefully and saw, in an alcove, a lovely cascading arrangement of apricot and coral bougainvillea with frangipani flowers which had creamy petals edged with red.

She could not help being warmed by his attention to the details of her comfort, particularly when there had been other things on his mind.

She gave John a glass of milk and, seeing that the wine had already had its cork drawn and lightly replaced, succumbed to an impulse to try it, although wine at this hour of the day was far from being her usual style.

Presently she suggested a walk along the beach. Both wearing white shorts and tee-shirts, with plenty of sun cream on their exposed parts, they set out to explore the full length of the beach to the point where it came to an end in the shadow of the wooded headland behind which the sun would eventually sink out of sight.

They paddled most of the way. In places the sand was loose and coarse and clung to their feet in large flakes. Mostly it was fine and firm, a pleasant surface for walking or jogging.

As the working day came to an end, the holidaymakers were joined by islanders arriving in cars and on motorbikes for an evening dip. Their very dark skins made an effective contrast with the turquoise sea. Although the island had been governed by Britain, and was now an independent State in association with Britain, Christie found that when the Antiguans were chatting and laughing among themselves she could understand only odd words of their conversation.

It was early evening by local time, but hours past the bedtime to which John's body was accustomed, when they went to the restaurant for a light supper of fried snapper and salad.

It was dark when they returned to the cottage by way of the lanternlit paths. The child was asleep within seconds of being tucked into bed, and Christie herself felt drowsy as she returned to the sitting-room to have another glass of wine and to look through a folder of useful information provided by the management.

She had been studying a map of the island, and must have dozed off, when the telephone startled her into wakefulness. It had rung several times before she could pull herself together and recall where she was, and where it was.

'Hello?' she said, somewhat muzzily.

'If you sleep now, you'll find yourself wide awake at three in the morning.'

The speaker had no need to announce himself for her to distinguish his deep, lazy-sounding voice from the slightly Americanised briskness of the Manager's delivery.

'Ash . . . where are you?' she asked, still confused. He sounded as if he might be calling from the main block.

'Still in Montserrat. I'm sorry I wasn't at the airport to meet you. How was your flight?'

'Fine, thank you, and your friend Miss Long was there to take us under her wing.'

'It's Mrs Long, actually, although the marriage has broken up now.'

'Oh, I see. She introduced herself as Bettina Long, and I didn't notice what rings, if any, she was wearing. There was so much else to take in. This is a lovely place, Ash . . . Turtle Creek, I mean. Thank you for the special flowers and the wine. It was probably the wine which sent me to sleep just now. Oh, goodness'—after a glance at her watch—'It wasn't "just now". It was over two hours ago!'

'I'm sorry I woke you, but I couldn't get to the

phone before, and I wanted to be sure you'd arrived safely.'

'It's a good thing you did wake me,' she said, 'otherwise I might have spent all night in this chair and woken up cramped.'

'Oh, you're not in bed yet?'

'Not yet.'

'I hope you've acquired some cooler night things than the ones you were wearing when I stayed with you in London. This is no climate for thick pyjamas.'

Christie remembered the morning he had lingered in her bedroom, somehow contriving to make her as uneasy as a middle-aged spinster in Victorian times.

'Naturally I haven't brought them,' she said stiffly.

'What have you brought instead?'

She suspected him of teasing her. 'A cotton nightie made for me by Margaret Kelly. Isn't it rather expensive, telephoning from another island?' she added. 'Oughtn't we to keep this call short?'

'Perhaps you're right. I can't say yet when I'll be back, but I'll be there as soon as I can. Goodnight, Christiana. If you do wake up in the small hours, go for a stroll on the beach. It may be cooler, but I'm sure your new nightdress is very little less decorous than those pyjamas.'

On this mocking note he rang off, leaving her farewell unspoken and her hand clenched on the receiver more tightly than it had been before his derisive parting shot.

THREE

Christie did wake in the small hours, but even if she had felt inclined to go for a solitary walk on the now moonlit beach, she would not have done so in case John, too, should wake and be frightened at finding himself alone in a strange place.

However when, at half past six, it was light outside and the child was still soundly asleep, she crept out of bed and went to retrieve her swimsuit from the line in the small screened patio outside the kitchen door.

Apart from two men, one of whom was raking the sand while the other arranged the sun-beds in orderly groups, she had the beach to herself.

The sun was gilding the clouds—not the low grey unbroken clouds of a European winter, but scattered white cottonwool clouds—but had not yet risen above the low hills of the hinterland when she walked into the sea.

At waist-depth, she flung herself forward, the water momentarily cool to her sleep-warmed body, but only for a moment. She began to swim a vigorous breast-stroke, moving parallel to the shore, counting the strokes until, at a hundred, she let her feet sink to the sand and stood up, her breathing quickened by the unaccustomed exercise.

The beach was in full sunshine when she emerged

from the sea to walk to the end and then back again. Half way back to Frangipani Cottage, she said, 'Good morning' to an elderly couple who, judging by the pallor of their skin, were also new arrivals whose bodies had yet to adjust to the change of time zone.

She found her nephew awake, but untroubled by her disappearance. He was sitting on the verandah in his pyjamas, watching and being watched by a black bird smaller than an English blackbird and much less nervous of humans.

Later, when they had breakfast, they had an audience of these birds, and they also found out the purpose of a wickerwork globe which hung from a bracket on the wall. It was not, as Christie had first thought, an outdoor light fitting. Inside was a dish of sugar, and through the gaps in the wicker flew little birds with bright yellow breasts.

At lunchtime, from a waiter in the restaurant, she learned that the impudent black birds were greckels, and the smaller birds were bananaquits, known in Antigua as yellowbirds.

At lunch they were joined by Bettina, who asked if she might share their table. Christie had the distinct impression that until she entered the restaurant and saw them sitting there, Bettina had forgotten their existence and was not too pleased to be reminded of it.

But she made some effort to be affable, although from time to time, after asking Christie a question, her pale eyes would slide away to one of the other tables, making it clear she was not greatly interested in the answers to her enquiries.

Not wishing to bore her, Christie changed the subject to clothes, asking Bettina if the ones she was wearing were locally made.

'No, these are imported from Singapore,' said the other girl, glancing down at her wraparound skirt and cotton top. Both were bright sky blue, wax-printed with white flower motifs round the hem of the skirt and on the sleeves of the top.

'This shaggy bag is local—and rather fun, don't you think?' she asked, indicating the shoulder bag she had put on the empty fourth chair.

It was made from scraps of bright cotton in many colours and patterns. As Bettina ruffled them with her long, red-lacquered fingertips, Christie could see that each scrap was a narrow rectangle about four times the length of its width, stitched half way along to a backing and then folded double.

'These are a development of the rag rugs which the island seamstresses used to make from the scraps left over from dresses,' Bettina explained. 'I think they're nicer than most of the straw bags on sale. They're nearly all spoilt by having *Antigua* worked on them. Not chic!'—with a slight grimace.

'And your jewellery—that's very unusual,' remarked Christie, glad to have hit the other girl's wavelength.

'Have you never seen sand dollars before?' Bettina's fingertips went to the thin gilded discs attached to a chain round her neck, and matched by smaller disc ear-rings. 'In their natural state they're white shells, extremely brittle. These have been gold-plated. You'll find them on sale in most Caribbean resorts, and in New York too. I'm surprised you haven't seen them in London.'

'I don't live in central London so I don't very often go to the top fashion stores. Hardly ever, in fact,' Christie explained.

'Really?' Bettina looked astonished, as if she couldn't imagine anyone living in the purlieus of a city, far from the best stores and boutiques.

'You must take some back with you. They're not expensive. Would you like to come and look round the shop? It's a quiet time now, after lunch.'

They accompanied her back to her shop which was small but artistically arranged with a glass-topped counter in the centre to contain the more valuable pieces of costume jewellery, and rails and shelves round the walls for the dresses and accessories.

'No word from Ash yet, I'm afraid,' said Bettina, as she changed the sign on the door from *Closed* to *Open*, 'I thought he might call me last night, but he must have been too busy.'

Christie didn't like to say that he had rung her, in case Bettina might be piqued. With a murmured injunction to John not to touch, she had a look round, seeing many things she would have liked to add to her own very basic holiday wardrobe.

However, she knew it would be foolish to buy anything which had no place in her real life, and few of these attractive resort clothes were really suitable for England, even in a heatwave.

They were designed for people who could afford several holidays a year in places where the sun shone every day and the nights were warm and balmy. But when, once this trip was over, would she ever have the chance to wear an ankle-length emerald gauze beach wrap, or a backless black and white evening dress?

'You have marvellous taste, Bettina, but I'm afraid I'm not going to be the kind of customer for whom you were hurrying back yesterday,' she said frankly. 'Did she come in as you expected?'

'Yes, but only to bring back a skirt she had chosen the day before and then decided she didn't like. They're tiresome old bitches, a lot of the women who stay here, and whatever they wear doesn't make them look any less haggish.'

Christie glanced up from bending over the jewellery counter to see Bettina studying her own reflection in the full length mirror.

'You'd look wonderful, whatever you wore,' she said sincerely.

The other girl shrugged. 'Perhaps, but it's maddening to sell super clothes to people who look nothing in them. Oh, here she comes now. You'd better go.'

As a stout older woman entered the shop, and John and Christie left it, she heard Bettina say sweetly, 'Hello, how are you today? Did you have a good time at the Casino last night?'

Not a happy person, Bettina, Christie thought as they strolled back to the cottage. I do hope she isn't Ash's girl-friend. She wouldn't be kind to John. He would be a nuisance in her eyes.

*   *   *

On the fourth morning after their arrival, when Christie took off her nightie before going for her early dip, there was a perceptible difference between the flesh covered by her bathing suit and the rest of her. At last, if only very slightly, she was beginning to brown. Whereas one or two recent arrivals who had tried to hasten the process had only succeeded in achieving painful red patches

There had been no further calls from Ash, either to herself or to Bettina. Although she disliked having to admit it, she found herself beginning to feel some impatience for his return.

That morning she was able to swim two hundred strokes without being even mildly puffed, and she knew that already this open-air life she was leading had exercised neglected muscles and improved the tone of her skin.

Surprisingly very few holidaymakers came down to the beach before breakfast. This morning she had it to herself until, on the third and final lap of her walk, when the breezy sunshine had already dried her arms and legs, she saw a man leave the gardens and cross the beach to the sea's edge.

At first, from a distance, she took him for someone staying at the Colony. And then he turned in her direction, and his height and something about his bearing made her catch her breath slightly. But it couldn't be Ash, not at this hour. Surely it couldn't.

That it was Ash, she knew for certain when he raised an arm and waved to her. What was he doing here so early? He must have flown over last night. Even so, seven o'clock in the morning seemed a peculiar time to call on her. For all he knew, she might be enjoying sleeping late, as most of the other guests seemed to. Unless . . . unless he had spent the night at the Colony, in Bettina's cottage, and had come to the beach merely to swim, not expecting to find Christie up yet.

As these thoughts were going through her mind, the distance between them was lessening, and her heart was beginning to beat in quick, nervous thumps.

During his stay at her flat she had been aware of the strength of his tall, lithe body. Now, as he strode towards her wearing only the briefest of briefs, the pattern of muscle from his broad shoulders down to his hips made her think of a suit of bronze armour. He was as splendidly built as any of the young Antiguans who came to the beach at this hour to exercise and swim before work.

Her mind shied away from a mental picture of Ash and Bettina, both naked, in a narrow bed. For the rest of the way, until they were within speaking distance, Christie averted her gaze and pretended an interest in the goats which were grazing on the open land outside the boundary of the gardens surrounding the Colony.

'Good morning. I didn't expect you to be about for some time yet. Most people, having adjusted to Antigua time, tend to like to "lie in",' were his first words.

'But this is the best time of day. I love it down here before breakfast.'

Only after this preliminary exchange were they

close enough to shake hands, and the warm, firm clasp of his fingers sent a curious tremor down her spine.

She would have withdrawn her hand quickly, but his strong grip forced her to wait until he ended the contact, and this he did not do until he had looked her up and down, and said, 'You've been sensible, I'm glad to see. By the end of the week you'll be a very nice colour. Already you've lost that sickly look.'

'Sickly! I may have been white, but I wasn't unhealthy,' she protested.

'Wait till you go back, and see if you don't agree that people with white skins look sickly. You've been in already, I see. Will you join me in another dip?'

Christie shook her head. 'I must go back and fetch John for his bathe. He wakes up later than I do, but he has a swim before breakfast.'

'Okay. I'll see you presently.'

Ash turned to sprint into the sea for a flying header which flung up a shower of spray. He came up with his face to the sun, black hair glistening and teeth very white as he grinned at her. 'This is the life!'

Yes, for a favoured few, she thought as she turned away. But not many can live like this. Even the Antiguans themselves could not all remain in their birthplace. The maid who serviced the cottage had spoken of a cousin in London, and a sister who had gone to America.

A life in the sun, surrounded by beauty and peace, was almost everyone's pipe-dream, but one very seldom realised.

'And not by me, that's for sure,' Christie murmured aloud, as she dabbled her feet in one of the troughs of salt water in which guests were asked to rinse their feet to reduce the amount of sand going into the Colony's drains.

She found John feeding crumbs to greckels and sparrows, with an apricot-breasted Zenaida dove bobbing about outside the verandah until her arrival made it fly off.

When they returned to the beach, Ash seemed to have disappeared. Then she saw him far out in the bay, half way to the deep-water reef where a line of white breakers marked the great barrier of coral between the indigo of the ocean and the lighter colours of the protected water. Even when she had the stamina to swim as far as that and back, she doubted if she would do so. There might be no danger in it, but she had overheard snorkellers speaking of barracuda and kingfish, and she did not fancy the idea of being far from the shore with a large fish close by.

While she inflated John's armlets, she watched Ash returning with the steady, slow-motion strokes of the powerful, experienced swimmer. With him she would feel safe out there, but she wouldn't be able to keep up with him.

'Here comes Uncle Ash,' she told John, as she put on the armlets.

The little boy ran into the water and, completely fearless, began a strenuous dog-paddle in the direction of the man surging towards him.

His enthusiastic splashing did not carry him far,

but he was well out of his depth by the time his uncle stopped swimming and, in a single movement, stood up with the child in his hands.

'Hello, boy. How are you?'

He kissed him and lifted him high before swinging down with a rapid, water-chute motion which made Christie gasp with dismay until she saw that John loved it.

He was shrieking with laughter, and shouting, 'Again . . . again!'

Ash obliged him with three more upswings and rapid descents. The last time, he said, 'Close your mouth and hold your nose,' so that when he let go of the boy, although John was swamped for a moment, he didn't swallow any water and survived the experience still beaming.

'Have you got a mask and some flippers?' Ash asked him.

John shook his head.

'Later on we'll go into town and buy some for you—and for Aunt Christie too, if she likes?' Ash gave her an enquiring look as she came into the water to join them.

'Isn't he a bit small for snorkelling? Shouldn't he learn to swim first?'

'Snorkelling will teach him to swim. Like a ride, John?'

Ash crouched so that John could climb on his back, then set off with a leisurely breast-stroke.

Following a few yards behind them, Christie could not deny that the easy, demonstrative way in which Ash had greeted his nephew had been rather touching. A woman might be able to put on an affectionate manner towards a child. but she did not think men were as adept at playing a part—or not in relation to small fry. Either they were genuinely good with children, or they were not. Clearly Ash was good.

But even if, temperamentally, he might be well suited to the rôle imposed on him by his brother's death, there remained a problem. Like her, Ash had his living to earn. He couldn't give all his time to the child, and he didn't have a wife who could do so. Only a succession of girl-friends who, if Bettina was a sample, were unlikely to want a child included in their relationships with him.

'Are your friend's troubles sorted out now?' she asked, as they came out of the water.

He shrugged. 'For a while. Not permanently, I'm afraid. I doubt if anything can mend a marriage as far on the rocks as his is. It's a pity: they're both nice people, just totally unsuited to live together, particularly in the testing conditions of a small yacht. Everyone else could see it wouldn't work from the word go. But they were in love, and love overrules common sense. Or would you disagree?'

'No . . . no, I think love does blind people, not only to other people's shortcomings, but to their own.'

He gave her an intent glance which made her wish she had not enlarged on her answer. To her relief he did not pursue the subject, but said, 'Will you join me for breakfast in the restaurant? As you know, I like to start the day with something more substantial than the orange juice and coffee which is all you have here, I daresay.'

And all you would get at Bettina's cottage, she thought, as she said, 'A little more than that, but nothing substantial. Why don't you collect us when you're ready? About what time are you thinking of leaving for town?'

'The shops in St John's are open from eight until noon, and again from one until four. We'll leave here about nine, if that suits you?'

'Perfectly, but I should have thought, after being away for some days, you would have had more important things to do than taking us shopping for snorkelling kit.'

'No, I've managed to arrange my affairs so that, providing no more unforeseen emergencies crop up, I can give a good deal of my time to showing you the places of interest. See you both later.'

With a lift of the hand, he turned in another direction, towelling his head as he went, the action making the muscles ripple down his back.

His car was larger than Bettina's, with a bench seat in front so that they could both have sat beside him had he allowed it. But he made John go in the back in the interests of safety.

'There's a forty-mile limit on all roads here, but not every driver observes it,' he remarked dryly, as he slid his tall frame behind the wheel.

But he did, Christie noticed. He was a very relaxed driver, showing no sign of impatience when a large herd of goats blocked the road for several hundred yards, and stopping to pick up an elderly villager who had missed the bus into town and set out on foot.

Although she knew that it had a cathedral and a deep-water harbour for cruise ships, to Christie St John's seemed more like a country town than a capital city.

The main streets were arranged on the grid system, with broad roads sloping downhill towards the harbour, intersected by narrower cross streets.

Tucked in between the big buildings were houses no larger than village houses. Modernity, in the form of large, air-conditioned banks, mixed with tradition in the form of pavement stalls spread with trinkets made from shells and seeds.

First they went to a shop selling sports gear where Ash selected a mask and flippers for his nephew and then for Christie.

'You must let me pay for mine,' she said.

He shook his head. 'Extra gear is always useful on the boat, and they won't be much use to you in England.'

As they left the shop, he said, 'I have one or two business calls to make. John can come with me, and you can explore the shops at your leisure. We'll meet at Darcy's in St Mary's Street at eleven. It's more or less opposite the Coco Shop, which is good for clothes and presents, I'm told. Don't worry if you can't make it on the dot. If you're late, we'll have another drink.'

On her own, Christie went first to a branch of her English bank to cash a travellers' cheque. Ash had already explained that there were two currencies operating on the island, American dollars and East

Caribbean dollars, and that it was important to be sure which currency price tickets were marked in.

There were several people for whom she wanted to buy presents, notably Margaret Kelly. The shop he had recommended was a small timber house painted dark brown with a corrugated iron roof painted white like the shutters on the windows, and the guard rail of the twin flights of steps leading up to the front door. Inside it was larger than the exterior suggested, and Christie was tempted to buy Margaret one of the cotton smocks imported from a neighbouring island and hand-embroidered round the collar with lizards, hummingbirds, shells and other local motifs. In the end she decided to wait until she had looked around more. In a neighbouring building, painted royal blue and white, she found the Sea Island Cotton Shop and there, in Margaret's favourite dark red, a batik-printed overblouse which was equally attractive.

However, she had no parcels with her when she joined the others at their table in the shady courtyard which was their rendezvous.

Ash had risen to his feet when he saw her pausing in the gateway. 'Nothing tempting?' he asked, with a raised eyebrow, seeing she carried only her shoulder bag.

'Oh, yes, any number of temptations,' she said, as he pulled a chair out for her. 'But Margaret, who's travelled a lot, advised me not to do my shopping straightaway. She said it was better to wait and see.'

'What would you like to drink?'

He had a glass of lager in front of him, and John

had a pink concoction which was probably a mixture of fruit juices.

Christie was glad to be sitting down in the shade. It was extremely hot in the streets. She would have been more comfortable in a loose sun-dress, but was wearing a short-sleeved blouse to protect her shoulders. Where it was tucked inside the waistband of her skirt, making a double layer of fabric, she felt unpleasantly sticky, although Ash with a leather belt slotted through the loops on his shorts looked cool enough. But he was acclimatised and she wasn't.

'What is an Antigua Kiss?' she asked, remembering the drinks mentioned by the Manager of the Colony.

To her astonishment, he reached for one of her hands and, lifting it, pressed it to his lips before replacing it on the arm of her chair

'That's the mid-morning, public version. There are others—more exciting—which I should be happy to demonstrate at suitable moments.' As he spoke, he was looking at her mouth.

Christie felt herself turning as pink as the stuff in John's glass.

'Y-you know what I mean   .   it's a drink,' she stammered in confusion.

'Oh, really? It's a new one on me. I've heard of an Antiguan Smile. Why not have a rum punch? That's as refreshing as anything.' Without waiting for Christie's assent, he gave the order to the waitress.

At this point, much to her relief, a diversion was created by a large green lizard scuttling across the courtyard, passing under several tables and causing squeaks from some elderly female tourists sitting at them. To John's delight it ran past him before taking cover among some plants, giving Christie a moment or two to recover her self-possession.

No doubt Ash had only been teasing, and it had been stupid of her to show she was flustered. She ought to have laughed it off, not reacted like a nervous schoolgirl.

For lunch he took them to the Runaway Beach Hotel which was not very far out of town. He had told her to bring their bathing kit and, before lunch, they had a swim, but did not try out their new masks.

'Haven't you any bikinis with you?' he asked, when Christie had changed her wet green suit for a dry black one.

She shook her head. 'December is not a good time to buy inexpensive beach things. All the chain stores are selling warm clothes. It's not hard to find expensive swimsuits for people going on winter cruises, but I didn't want to spend the earth when I'm only here for a few weeks.'

'No, but you ought to have a bikini or you won't get your middle brown. Bettina's stuff tends to be pricey, I believe, but not all the boutiques are expensive.'

'Aunt Christie does brown her tummy when nobody's looking except me,' said John.

Ash's mobile left eyebrow went up. 'You surprise me. Toplessness merely, or complete nudity?'

'Neither. John means that I sometimes sit on our verandah in my underwear which, to anyone passing, would look like a bikini,' she answered. 'Is there much topless sunbathing here? I haven't seen any at the Colony.'

'No, you wouldn't. It's not encouraged. Although there are plenty of secluded coves where people can lie in the raw without offending anyone else. Personally I prefer to exert a little imagination, if not too much.'

A certain glint in his eye made her suspect that, had John not been present, he would have said something to make her blush again.

For lunch they had smoked ham with pineapple, accompanied by servings of lobster and chicken in coleslaw, these mixtures arranged on a large red-veined leaf from the sea grape bushes growing along the back of the beach.

With lunch Christie tried a Piña Colada, a mixture of pineapple juice, coconut cream and rum whipped in a blender until it was frothy. Having sipped it slowly, through a straw, she became aware that it was not as innocuous as it looked. Obviously the rum had been added with a generous hand and, not being accustomed to drinking, she would have to watch her step.

After lunch they drove a little further north to a stretch of water behind the coast road where many birds were to be seen, including the brown pelicans known on the island as boobys, and the frigate-birds often called weatherbirds. Ash had fieldglasses in the car with him, and he let John look through them to see the birds in close-up.

The sun was losing its fierceness by the time they returned to Turtle Creek.

'Now for the snorkelling lesson,' he said, as he parked the car.

John was his first pupil, and a surprisingly apt one. In no time at all the little boy had mastered the way to hold the mouthpiece between his lips and inhale and exhale through it. It happened that a shoal of small pale silvery fish were darting about near the shore, and while John was absorbed in watching them, Ash came to where Christie was waiting her turn.

He had already told her that the test of a good mask was that it should cling to the face when the wearer inhaled without the aid of a strap. Nevertheless it took him several minutes to adjust the strap to his satisfaction and, while his fingers were busy at the back of her head, she found herself intensely conscious of his closeness and the brush of his forearms against her bare shoulders.

'There: I think that should be comfortable. Now sit down here in the shallows and keep your face submerged and practise breathing until it no longer seems strange,' he instructed.

Before the lesson was over, both she and John had had the exciting experience of gliding through the water with as clear a view of the plants and creatures beneath the surface as they had of the trees and birds in the air above.

John even had no problem with his small pair of bright yellow flippers, but Christie found it more difficult to adapt her leg movements to gain maximum impetus from them. They seemed to her heavy and clumsy, but Ash assured her that many people had the same difficulty at first.

When the time came to leave the water, John flip-flopped his way up the beach with the air of a veteran snorkeller. When Christie attempted to follow suit, she tripped over her flippers and fell backwards.

Before she could struggle to her feet, Ash scooped her into his arms and, as if she were no heavier than John, carried her ashore.

'I should have warned you—it's advisable for adults to back out of the water,' he said, grinning. 'Small kids seem to manage to walk forward in flippers, but not grown-ups.'

From the water's edge to the low wall which prevented sand from encroaching on the lawns was not a great distance. But to Christie, cradled in his arms, in intimate contact with a man's almost naked body for the first time in more than four years, it seemed an eternity before he lowered her into a sitting position on the wall, and knelt to remove the flippers for her.

'I should like to stay and have dinner with you, but I have another engagement,' he said, rising to his full height and placing the flippers on the wall. 'Tomorrow morning I'm busy, so I'll come over here about two and we'll have another snorkelling session.'

Christie watched him strolling across the gardens, still wearing his wet black briefs, with a towel tossed over one shoulder, and his clothes in a canvas bag.

She wondered where he would dry and change. Presumably at Bettina's cottage.

This supposition was confirmed when, about an

hour later, leaving John playing ball with another child, she walked to the main block to mail the postcards she had bought in town that morning.

As she arrived in the entrance hall, where there was a letter box by the reception desk, she was just in time to see Ash and Bettina leaving the building. She was dressed for an evening out in a long narrow backless red dress with a side-slit skirt. Her hair was loose on her shoulders, and Christie glimpsed a cascading shell ear-ring as she turned her head to speak to her tall companion. He was probably one of the few men with whom Bettina could wear high heels and still have to look up slightly, thought Christie, watching them disappear in the direction of the car park.

When Ash arrived the next day, he tossed a paper bag on to Christie's lap.

'I hope it's the right size. If not, I can change it.'

She opened the bag and pulled out a bright pink cotton bikini. Her reaction was a mixture of the feeling that she ought to be grateful to him, and a certain resentment of his assumption that a bikini of his choosing must be acceptable to her.

Before she could say anything, he told her to go and try it on.

Slim as she was, Christie would never have chosen a bikini cut as this one was. The top was gathered into a ring between her breasts, and the thin strings which held it up were attached to the ring, thus exposing the skin normally covered by the ties of an ordinary halter top. The bottom part left the sides of her hips completely bare except where the strings tied. It also exposed a great deal more of her behind than did her other swimsuits. Even so she would not have been embarrassed to wear it in front of anyone but Ash. It was the thought of his seeing her in it which made her shrink from reappearing on the verandah.

However, when she did go back he was amusing John by making a playing card appear and disappear, and he barely glanced at her.

Even when she said, 'It fits perfectly. Thank you very much for bringing it. What do I owe you?' he continued to watch his nephew's baffled face.

'Nothing,' he said. 'It's a welcome to Antigua present.'

'But Ash, I can't possibly accept—'

'Oh, come now, Christiana, this isn't the nineteenth century and, if not related by blood, we are both *in loco parentis* to this young fellow. That allows us to dispense with most of the conventions, don't you think?'

'Some of them, I suppose. But why should you pay for this bikini as well as everything else? It must be costing you a fortune to keep us in luxury like this. I can't feel comfortable about it.'

'Ah, but you see I have a scheme to recoup my outlay.'

Having made the card materialise behind John's ear yet again, he put it in the pocket of his shirt, ruffled the child's hair, and stood up.

'Are we ready for the beach? I brought you something else; an American sun-screen with an extra high protection factor for those areas you haven't exposed yet.'

Now his dark gaze did scan her body, and she felt her colour rising, although not in the fiery blush which had suffused her face yesterday morning at Darcy's.

Striving not to lose her composure. she said, 'What sort of scheme?'

'I'll explain it some time when we're *a deux*.'

He unbuckled his belt, unzipped his shorts and stepped out of them. Taking a tube from the pocket. he handed them to her. and asked, 'Could you put these inside for me somewhere before you lock up? There's some money in the back pocket which I don't want to leave lying around.'

'Of course.' She took them into the cottage, and spent a few moments checking that the other doors were locked.

What could he mean by a scheme to recover his outlay? They hadn't discussed the future yet. but already she knew in her heart that Ash was right about this being the best place for John to grow up How could she deny him the chance to live in this wonderful climate where. already. she felt vitality bubbling up inside her like a spring.

Before going into the sea. she and John put on their tee-shirts to protect their backs from the sun. To her surprise, Ash took a bottle from his beach bag and asked her to oil his back for him

'I shouldn't have thought you were in any danger of burning,' she said.

'I'm not, but anyone who spends a lot of time in

sun and salt water needs a rub with oil occasionally. It's the equivalent of leather dressing.'

He bent forward, hands on knees, so that she could reach his shoulders more easily.

Reluctant to touch him, she dribbled a small pool of oil between his shoulder blades, and spread it with the flat of her hand.

He had spoken of leather dressing, and that was what his back felt like—as smooth and supple as her one pair of good kid gloves, with no jelly-like subcutaneous fat such as most people on the beach had. only firm springy muscle and the hardness of bone.

As fast as she could, she spread a film over his back from the nape of his neck almost to the top of his briefs.

'You can go at it harder than that,' he said. 'Try both hands. If it isn't well rubbed in, it doesn't do the job.'

Freshly irritated by his assumption that she wouldn't mind having to touch him, Christie capped the bottle and began to dig her fingers into him as hard as she could. Her nails were shaped to her fingertips, so there was no danger that she would scratch him. But she hoped that such vigorous rubbing would be rather more than he had bargained for. To complete the treatment she used the edges of her hands to perform a series of chopping movements up and down his spine

'There you are. How was that?' she asked crisply.

Ash straightened, flexing his shoulders. 'Great You've missed your vocation. You should have been a masseuse.' His eyes were amused

She felt that he knew she had been disturbed by the warmth of his deeply tanned skin under her palms. Clearly the full force of her fingers had caused him no more discomfort than if John had pummelled his fists against the flat, muscular area surrounding his uncle's navel.

She went into the water full of unease and suppressed anger, but came out with her vexation forgotten in the wonder of their first exploration of the small reef close to the shore.

There was not much of a tide round the island, but the sea did rise and fall, and that afternoon was low water. Some of the rocks were exposed, and there were places among the coral where the bottom was sandy under a shallow depth of water, so that even John could stand up.

'I'll take care that he doesn't graze himself. Don't, either of you, put your hands near any holes in the rocks. Sometimes they're the homes of moray eels, and they're anti-social creatures,' Ash had warned them, before they started.

But the hazards of the reef were more than balanced by the beauty and interest of the corals and brightly coloured fish, none of which seemed at all alarmed by the invasion of their habitat.

'Oh, that was marvellous! Thank you,' was her spontaneous reaction afterwards.

She had not been wearing her flippers, and Ash had towed her and John back to the beach. With them holding on to his hands, using only undulating movements of his big black flippers, he had surged through the water at speed, pulling them with him.

His hand had felt cool; as impersonal as the hand of a doctor or dentist. The contact had not reanimated her earlier feelings, and it was with genuine gratitude for an enriching experience that she pushed her mask up, off her face, and expressed her pleasure.

'That's only the beginning. Wait till you've snorkelled the reefs between Green Island and Fanny's Cove on the west coast. They really are something. Why not get in some practice with your flippers? I'll keep an eye on our tiddler.'

Christie did as he suggested, still finding the flippers more hindrance than help, but persevering.

By the time she came out John was perched on a stool at the beach bar, with Ash leaning beside him. She exchanged the wet pink bikini for the dry green suit before strolling over to join them.

Ash had seen her coming and ordered a banana daiquiri which the barman placed on the counter as she climbed on to the high stool on the other side of John.

The little boy finished his drink when her glass was still three-quarters full. His uncle lifted him down and sent him off to play with his bucket and spade under a palm-thatched sunshade until they joined him.

Christie concluded he was making an opportunity to speak to her alone. But when, intensely curious, she prompted him, saying, 'That scheme you mentioned . . .' his response was, 'First I'd like to know more about you.'

'But you already know everything.'

'I know the outlines, not the details.'

'What sort of details?'

Ash looked at her thoughtfully. 'I don't know much about your marriage, except that it was very brief.'

She stiffened. 'I really don't see what bearing my marriage has on anything.'

'Perhaps it hasn't. I'm not sure. There are things about you which puzzle me, Christiana.'

Why did he persist in calling her by her full name, and why did hearing him say it always send a frisson down her spine?

She tried to sound casual. 'For instance?'

'For instance, your agitated reaction to having your hand kissed, and your palpable shyness at appearing before me in a bikini by no means as scanty as some I've seen. If I hadn't known how old you were, and that you'd been married, I'd have thought you were a seventeen-year-old virgin. You're blushing again at this moment,' he added, with a quizzical glint.

'I—I can't help being sh-shy,' she stammered.

'I don't think you are shy, my girl, or not with everyone you meet. Only with men, and that's odd in a woman of twenty-four who's not so recently widowed that her interest in men is temporarily atrophied. You can't still be grieving for your husband, or you certainly shouldn't be.'

Christie glanced at the barman. But he was in conversation with a waiter. There was no one to overhear what she and Ash were talking about.

'No, I'm not,' she agreed, in a low tone. 'But if you'd known several widows, I don't think you'd find my attitude unusual. We're often on edge in male company, because most of us have discovered that the world is full of men who think we're . . . so starved of sex that they'll be doing us a favour by . . . by . . .'

Her voice tailed off and she put her lips to the straw, her eyes downcast, her cheeks burning.

'And you're nervous that, if you relax with me, I may be encouraged to make a pass at you?' he enquired.

'I don't know. I shouldn't think so, but one never knows. The fact that you—' She stopped short.

'Yes? Go on,' he prompted.

'The fact that you probably have a woman in your life wouldn't necessarily prevent you from having a shot at me. I—I'm not overrating my attractions. I don't think I'm anything special. It's just the way things are for women in my situation.'

'On the contrary, you're an extremely attractive girl, although you try to disguise the fact. Frankly, I don't think your being a widow has much to do with the number of men who've had a shot at you, to use your own phrase. After all, if you'd never been married, you wouldn't still be a virgin. The good-looking girl of twenty-four who has never had a lover must be non-existent.'

'Possibly.' She wished he would drop the subject. It was bad enough being exposed to his powerful aura of sexuality without having to discuss that aspect of life with him.

'You sound uncertain,' he remarked. 'Is it possible you disapprove of amorous relationships outside marriage?'

'No. I don't disapprove.'

'But you've never indulged in one yourself?'

'If you feel entitled to cross-examine me in this way, the answer is no,' she said coldly.

'You've presupposed that I have a girl-friend. I think I'm entitled to find out your views on sex, religion and so on. As I pointed out earlier, sharing the responsibility for John places us in a rather special relationship.'

Christie glanced over her shoulder at the small figure busy with his bucket

'I wish it were a responsibility we could share properly,' she murmured unhappily.

'Perhaps it is,' was Ash's reply. As she turned a questioning face to him, he went on, 'That's where my scheme comes in. No, I can't explain now. I have to go *Sunbird*'s due in at English Harbour early this evening, and I want to be there when she berths Tomorrow night we'll have dinner at The Admiral's Inn. The management here will lay on a baby-sitter for John. I'll pick you up at half past six. Now, if you wouldn't mind unlocking the cottage for me, I'll change and be on my way.'

FOUR

THAT night was a restless one for Christie. While John slept soundly in the other bed, she lay on her back with her hands clasped under her head, watching the black silhouette of a palm tree against the moonlit sky, its fronds fluttered by the same trade-wind which was driving a great fleet of clouds across the horizon.

Thinking over her conversation with Ash, she wondered how he would have reacted if she had answered his questions truthfully. But the truth was something she would never confess to anyone, least of all to a man who looked virile enough to bed a whole harem of women

How could someone like him ever understand someone like her? He would think her unnatural, as indeed she was; and normal people, even if they strove to hide it, were repelled by those who were not He would think she was flawed through and through, and perhaps he would be right. It was enough to warp anyone's spirit, six months of secret misery. To which, after Mike's death, had been added the even worse guilt of knowing that what everyone else had seen as a tragedy had, for her, been a merciful reprieve from a relationship which had become intolerable.

How much longer could she have borne them, those waking nightmares which had made going upstairs something to be dreaded, and their bedroom not a bower of bliss but a place of disappointment and despair?

Not that he had ever hurt her deliberately. The distress he had inflicted had been unwitting. He would have been horrified to know that what he had thought tremors of pleasure had in fact been shivers of revulsion. She had loved him until their wedding, and from that night on, gradually, hope had died that making love would ever be the rapturous experience she had once anticipated.

Now, years later, and far away from where it had happened, it still sent a shudder through her to remember what it had been like and how, on her first night alone in their white double bed, she had wept, not with grief, but with relief that never again would any man ever have the right to make so-called love to her cringing body.

Inevitably these were memories which would never be completely erased; but they troubled her less and less often, or had until Ash's probing had brought them vividly to mind.

She wondered if her explanation of her nervousness had satisfied him. He was certainly right in thinking she was not shy in the ordinary way; and not, in fact, shy of all his sex. Only of those who showed signs of being interested in her, and there were not many who noticed a woman who took pains to be as unnoticeable as possible.

Ash was the first man who had shown any inclina-

tion to flirt with her for a long time. Christie guessed
that his deliberate misunderstanding of her question
about the Antigua Kiss had been more in order to
take a rise out of her than from any strong desire to
kiss her hand or to administer the other kisses he had
referred to.

Perhaps her reserve was a challenge to him. He
might, if he knew the whole truth, find that even
more of a challenge. He struck her as the kind of man
who had enormous confidence in his prowess as a
lover, and who would feel sure that he could succeed
where others failed.

Once, wretchedly unhappy at the thought of never
having children, she had snatched at the straw that
her frigidity might not be incurable. But as the only
way to test the possibility was totally unacceptable to
her, she had put the idea out of her head.

She could never again go to bed with a man unless
she liked and respected him for his breadth of mind
and strength of character, and in that case she
couldn't endure the chance—more, the prob-
ability—of being repelled by his caresses.

Lying awake in the middle of the night, and
wondering sadly how many of the women in the
other cottages were sleeping in their husbands' or
lovers' arms, Christie knew that only if he took her by
force would she ever again be pinioned beneath a
man's body. And even the mocking-eyed, confident
philanderers like Ash did not take women against
their will; although she could imagine that he might
have been capable of doing so had he lived in an
earlier century when a man might do as he pleased

with a woman without necessarily being considered
a brute.

In the morning she could not be sure whether it had
been a fantasy before she slept, or a dream while she
slept: that vision of herself spreadeagled on a bed in
the captain's cabin of a privateer, with Ash stripping
off the clothes of two hundred years ago, the upper
part of his face in shadow but the light from a
swinging lantern showing a smile of unmistakable
meaning playing round the corners of his well-cut
but sensual mouth.

Sitting on the edge of her bed, its fine Sea-Island
cotton sheets rumpled by her restlessness, Christie
hoped it had been a dream. She didn't like the idea
that it might have been a figment of her conscious
imagination rather than one produced by her subconscious mind. The subconscious threw up all
kinds of weird images which had no relation to life,
but fantasies were another matter, a form of wishful
thinking.

Oh, it *must* have been a dream, she told herself. No
one with her history would voluntarily daydream the
sequence of events which had followed that, so to
speak, opening shot.

But when, by lunchtime, the dream remained
clear and vivid instead of fading and losing reality
as dreams usually did as the day went on, she
began to suspect that she must have invented
Ash's slow, remorseless subjugation of her struggling body.

'You're not talking to me today, Aunt Christie

'Are you cross with me?' her nephew asked plaintively.

Glad to be distracted from her thoughts, Christie forced a bright smile. 'No of course I'm not cross with you, darling. You're a good boy and I love you very much. Even when you're naughty, which isn't often, I still love you, you know. You'll be extra good tonight when a nice person comes to look after you while I'm out with Uncle Ash won't you? Her name is Mrs Jones. She sounds very much like Mrs Kelly and you know how much you liked her.'

'Yes, I'll be a good boy,' John promised. 'But why can't I come with you and Uncle Ash?'

'Because it will be long past your bedtime before we come back, and we're going to have supper at a restaurant which is only for grown-ups in the evening. I'll tell you all about it tomorrow morning.'

Mrs Jones arrived half an hour before Ash was due, and quickly made friends with her charge. Christie had already been told that she was the widow of an official of the British régime.

'I'm what's called a "belonger",' she told Christie. 'That's the name given to foreigners who have lived here for more than seven years, and I've been here for thirty. I couldn't go back to England. I should be a foreigner there now.'

'Is this dress sufficiently formal for The Admiral's Inn?' Christie asked her.

She had put on the simple dress she had run up herself, using one of Vogue's Very Easy patterns and a remnant length of white cotton gabardine.

'You could wear something dressier if you liked.'

'I haven't anything dressier with me.

'Oh, then that will do very nicely Antigua isn't a formal island. One or two hotels insist on a tie or a shirt with a collar for men after seven o'clock, and some women like to dress up with their menfolk in lightweight sports coats. But in general it's all very casual I've been to The Admiral's Inn and seen a young man wearing denim shorts with frayed hems But most of the people who dine there strike a happy medium Are you going to add a little jewellery, my dear?'

'Yes ' Christie returned to the bedroom and put on black shoes, and some black and white beads The dress made the most of her tan, still pale by comparison with those of the guests nearing the end of their holidays, but a great improvement on the pallor she had had on arrival.

'Why not wear a flower in your hair—a red flower, suggested Mrs Jones

'I'm not the right type,' said Christie.

She had no wish to displease Ash by appearing unsuitably dressed, but nor did she feel it incumbent on her to alter her usual hyper-unobtrusive style

Although she was expecting him, his rap on the door made her jump. As she went to admit him, she remembered the curl of his mouth as she had seen it during the night—whether waking or sleeping, she still wasn't perfectly certain—and she felt her throat dry up with tension

'Good evening, Christiana. Have you had a good day?' he enquired, as he crossed the threshold.

'Good evening. Yes, we have, thank you. This is Mr Lambard, Mrs Jones.'

'How do you do, Mr Lambard.'

It seemed to Christie that a flicker of perturbation showed in Mrs Jones's mild eyes, and that her acknowledgement of the introduction had a certain stiffness which had not been in her manner earlier.

Ash was wearing a suit of pale grey linen except that the top wasn't a coat but a combination of short-sleeved shirt and jacket with a vent at the back and pockets with flaps on the chest.

He said, 'We shan't keep you up late, Mrs Jones. We should be back here by eleven, and I'll run you home on my way home.'

So he wasn't spending tonight with Bettina.

'Thank you, but that won't be necessary. I didn't come by taxi, I drove myself here. I'm not nervous of driving at night. There's no one who would harm me, not even the Rastas, I'm sure,' she said. 'So there's no need to cut short your evening if you want to stay out until midnight, Mrs Chapman. I have my sewing and a book. I'll be quite happy to stay until twelve, if you wish.'

In his car, as they set out to drive to English Harbour on the south coast, Christie asked, 'Who are the Rastas?'

'The Rasterferians. They're young men who wear their hair in a style known as "dreadlocks". It looks like the head of a mop—usually a very dirty mop,' he answered, with a grimace. 'Most respectable, church-going Antiguans regard the Rastas as thieves and troublemakers, but I know one foreigner living here who has one who works in her garden. She says he's a hard, willing worker who wouldn't dream of stealing from her. Generally it's the Rastas who sometimes behave in a hostile way towards tourists, and make them feel unnecessarily nervous. The fact is that here in Antigua there are people who dislike the whites in the same way that over in England there are people who can't stand the blacks. But by far the majority of people, both here and there, have no animus towards someone of a different colour. They're happy to live and let live.'

'I must have imagined it, I suppose, but I wondered if Mrs Jones might have a slight animus towards you. Have you ever encountered her before?'

'Not as far as I recall.'

'Then obviously I did imagine it.' She fell silent, glad of the wide bench seat which left a good space between them, unlike Bettina's white sports car in which, every time Ash changed gear, his hand would almost have brushed her thigh.

It was dusk when they drove down a long hill overlooking a large stretch of water which he told her was Falmouth Harbour, a much larger but more shallow anchorage than the nearby English Harbour.

'That's Pizzas in Paradise—a good place for a cheap, filling lunch,' said Ash, as they passed a verandah restaurant, the tables packed with young people with the sun-bleached hair and tanned faces of yacht crews.

Not much farther on he stopped the car on a

parking area close to the water.

'The Dockyard is closed to most traffic. We'll dine now, before the restaurant fills up, then have our coffee aboard *Sunbird* where we can be quiet and discuss things. There'll be no one else on board her. The last lot of charterers flew back to New York this morning, and the next don't arrive till tomorrow.'

'Does that mean you'll be taking over as skipper?'

'No, not this time. Perhaps next time. It depends how things go.'

Holding her lightly by the arm, just above the elbow, he steered her along a roadway between a brick building on the left, and a high bank with trees growing on it. Ahead of them, lit by a lamp, for already the dusk had become darkness, were the gates of the Dockyard, surmounted by an old ship's bell.

Immediately inside the gates, Ash made a sharp U-turn and soon, a few steps farther on, they were in the grounds of the building which had formed one side of the roadway.

'This was the Boat House. The upper floor was a sail loft where sails were made and repaired, but it was destroyed by an earthquake in 1843, and these pillars were capped to preserve them,' he told her, indicating the immense stone pillars on their right, lit by concealed floodlamps.

Beyond the pillars was a small wet dock, and beyond this the garden terraces sloping down from The Admiral's Inn to the moonlit waters of the historic harbour.

The ground floor of the inn had a staircase ascending to the bedrooms, a bar, a comfortable sitting area with linen-covered sofas and large table lamps on the end tables, and two rows of dining tables. There were also tables outside on the floodlit terraces, and this was where they ate their meal, with a steel band playing under a tree over by the wet dock.

They began with pumpkin soup, followed by Lobster Thermidor with buttered christophene, a vegetable new to Christie. Ash said it was a squash of Mexican origin now grown throughout the tropics.

She thought the white flesh rather tasteless and wondered if, like parsnips, it might be more palatable roasted. The lobster, served in its shell, she found quite delicious, although it was not presented in the classic manner with dry sherry in it and a crisp topping of buttery breadcrumbs.

'As you probably realise, this lobster isn't the true French *homard*,' said Ash, pausing to drink some white wine. 'It lacks the delicious claw meat of the northern lobster, which is blue when it comes out of the sea This fellow is a spiny rock lobster, reddish brown with extra long antennae and most of the meat in the tail. On the French islands it's called *langouste*. Here, purists call it a crawfish. In Antigua it's almost invariably cooked like this, but I feel there must be more varied ways to serve it

'Oh, there are—many ways,' she agreed. 'I can't say I've tried them all, because lobster in England is so expensive. But if it's cheaper here one could do the whole gamut—Lobster Newburg, Lobster Américaine, parfait, Mongole, Suprême . . . the lot. With adjustments for the lack of claws.'

'I gathered you were more than a good plain cook by the spices and off-beat ingredients I saw in your cupboards. Also Mrs Kelly told me she had known you to cook superbly on occasions,' he said, leaning back in his chair.

The terrace was not brightly lit and where they were sitting, under a canopy of leaves, there were romantic shadows and patches of moonlight.

His movement put a mask of shadow across the upper part of his face from the high cheekbones up to his dark hair. Christie wrenched her gaze away from his mouth with its wide rather thin upper lip and full lower lip.

'I—I don't know about that, but I do love cooking, which is half the battle. When my father was alive we used, occasionally, to feast ourselves in the grand manner.'

'And your husband? Was he a gourmet?'

'No, he had a hearty appetite—especially on Sunday after playing rugger on Saturday—but he only liked the traditional English dishes—roast beef, Yorkshire pud, apple pie.'

'Rugger . . . hm? I was always afraid of the injuries. A broken nose wouldn't have mattered. Might even have been an improvement'—stroking his large, high-bridged nose. 'But I never fancied the idea of having my teeth knocked out. Very gutless of me, I'm afraid, but there it is.

'Not gutless   sensible. Mike had lost several teeth.'

Christie remembered the dismay she had felt on

their wedding night when, just for a joke, her husband had taken out the bridgework replacing two lost teeth. He had put it back almost at once, but it had been the first jarring note. The second had been when she had emerged from the bathroom, shy in her white chiffon nightgown, and he had said, 'You won't need that on, old girl I've been a model of good behaviour so far—not much chance to be anything else while your old man was breathing down my neck—but tonight's the night we start making up for lost time. So strip off, there's a good girl. I expect you spent a bomb on that nonsense, and I don't want to tear it.'

Had she been foolishly over-sensitive? Or had he been crude and crass? How could she ever know the answer?

'Were you really expelled from your school, or was that an exaggeration on Paul's part?' she asked, to shut out the distasteful memory.

'My father was asked to remove me. As my partner in crime was a member of the staff, it was a hushed-up expulsion.'

'What kind of crime?' she asked blankly. The only offence she could think of involving a master and a boy was unbelievable in relation to the man on the opposite side of the table.

He read her mind and his mouth quirked. 'No, I was always heterosexual. I was caught *in flagrante delicto* with one of the assistant matrons. Had a master come in and found us I should probably have got off with a beating. I was seventeen. She was twenty, and not inexperienced. Unfortunately it was the Headmaster's wife who caught us, a woman of the highest morals who was deeply shocked—and perhaps subconsciously envious, the Head being a scholarly aesthete of powerful intellect but somewhat lacking in red blood.'

'It's not brawn which makes a good lover,' Christie said shortly.

How would I know? she thought, the next instant. Maybe Mike was a wonderful lover. He wanted to do it every night, and sometimes again in the morning. So often . . . so quickly . . . oh, God, let me not think about it.

'No, it's not,' Ash agreed, his tone casual. 'But nor is it an intellectual exercise. A happy medium is desirable, wouldn't you say? Will you have pudding or cheese?'

She had the Chef's Cake, he the Stilton.

'No coffee, thank you. The bill, please,' he said to their attentive waiter.

When it came, he signed it and tipped. 'Now we'll stroll across to my mooring.'

On the way he paused by a building with tall Georgian doors and windows like those of The Admiral's Inn. But this was of timber construction, with a balustraded balcony above the wide verandah surrounding the ground floor.

'The Admiral's House. Tradition has it that Nelson lived there when he was based in Antigua between 1784 and 1787. In fact the house wasn't built until midway through the next century, and the house Nelson really occupied was on the site of the present officers' quarters. This place contains quite an interesting museum which you should come and see another day.'

He moved on towards a three-storeyed building which he said had originally been the vast copper and lumber store.

'Now it's twelve self-catering apartments, done up in excellent taste, some for four and some for two people. I would have booked you in here, except that they're full at present.'

Passing other buildings they came to the dockside itself, the moored vessels spread round the semi-circular quay like the sticks of a fan, their sterns to the quay, their cabin lights casting golden spangles on the dark still water between them.

'There she is—my *Sunbird*,' said Ash.

Christie heard the pride in his voice as he steered her towards his own vessel. So might another man have said, of a beautiful woman, 'There she is—my wife.'

'But surely this isn't the boat you told me about, is it?' she asked, as they stepped on board what seemed to her inexpert eyes an almost new yacht.

'No, that's *Sunbird One*. She's up north in the British Virgins for a month. This is a more recent acquisition. I had her built for me in Denmark. She's a staysail schooner, built to take up to six guests; seventy-four feet long, not counting her bowsprit, with a beam of sixteen feet six. She has three double cabins and six single bunks; three of the cabins have basins, and the bathroom has a proper bath. I think you'll be surprised by the size of her saloon.'

Christie was. She had had no idea that a cruising

yacht's quarters between decks could be so spacious and well-appointed. There was no question of roughing it. The saloon had a thick fitted carpet, well-upholstered banquettes and an armchair, and a library of several hundred books housed on shelves between built-in fitments of rich dark mahogany.

Ash left her to explore the passengers' cabins while he made coffee in the galley. By the time she returned to the saloon, greatly impressed by what she had seen, the coffee was ready.

'Normally we serve real coffee made from freshly ground beans, but I remembered that you prefer the decaffeinated instant stuff,' he said, setting the tray on the polished table, and turning to a cupboard containing bottles and glasses. 'What liqueur would you like? I think we have most of the best known ones.'

'Do you have Drambuie?'

'Certainly.' Having filled two small glasses, he left the bottle on the table, slid his long legs underneath it, and seated himself on the banquette at right angles to the part on which she was sitting.

'Now—to business,' he said, in a brisk tone, relieving her of the anxiety that having coffee on his schooner might be the nautical equivalent of being taken to someone's apartment to look at their etchings.

'As possibly you know,' he began, 'Antigua used to be covered with estates growing sugar cane. Nowadays, many of the mills and the Great Houses are in ruins. But some have survived in good order. Unless tourists are interested in history or architecture, they don't usually see them, except perhaps Marble Hill. It's up in the north-west corner. An artist called Dominic Hapsburg lives and works there, designing hand-printed fabrics and clothes which are sold in most of the good shops. Another fine house is Mercer's Creek. It's kept up and used by outsiders, with Antiguan caretakers. There's also a scheme whereby people can lease these old places at reasonable rents, providing they undertake to preserve them.'

He paused to swallow some coffee and, after a moment, continued, 'I've bought a Great House called Heron's Sound. Tomorrow I'll take you to see it. It's full of splendid antiques, but it's been very badly neglected and needs drastic renovations. When it's done up, I mean to run it as a very superior kind of guesthouse. But first I need someone with taste to redecorate it, and then to act as the chatelaine—supervising the servants, arranging the flowers, making the people who'll come there feel as if they were staying in the house of an exceptionally good hostess. How does it appeal to you, Christiana? Instead of going back to London, to stay here and work with me?'

For some seconds Christie was speechless.

'But I have a job,' was her first reaction.

'People change jobs. I'm sure if you wrote immediately to your Principal—perhaps a cable would be better—explaining the situation in relation to John, your Head would be prepared to release you from whatever agreement you have with the school. After all, you are John's surrogate mother even if I am his legal guardian. Had you been married, and your husband had been posted abroad unexpectedly, you would have had to go with him.'

'Yes, that's true, I suppose.'

'Wouldn't you like to stay here? Doesn't Antigua appeal to you?'

'It seems a . . . a paradise to me.'

'Nowhere on this earth is paradise,' Ash said, on a sardonic note. 'True, there are no serpents here—the mongooses have seen to that They were brought in to wipe out the snakes, and they did it a long time ago The only slithering creatures are some blindworms which live on Great Bird Island. But we do have scorpions and other unfriendly insects, and the climate isn't always quite as pleasant as it is now. It can be humid at times, and we have periods of drought, and hurricanes.'

Christie turned the stem of her liqueur glass, but she didn't raise it to her lips. She was far too preoccupied.

'But could I do it?—The job, I mean. I think you need a professional interior designer to do up a house of that order.'

'I think not,' was his crisp response. 'You have excellent taste of precisely the kind the house needs. I knew that as soon as I saw your flat '

'But my flat is a do-it-yourself job, with Laura Ashley papers and fabrics They're some of the most reasonable on the market

'So much the better. If you can achieve the same effect at Heron's Sound without spending a fortune, I shall be very pleased. I don't believe in cheeseparing, but nor do I think the most expensive articles are necessarily the best. Good design is what counts, and not everyone has an eye for it. Clearly, you have.'

'So has your friend Bettina Long,' said Christie. 'Don't you think she might like the job?'

'She is ultra-modern in her taste. She wouldn't know where to begin restoring an old house—except by getting rid of all the original contents and starting from scratch with new stuff. As for the running of the place, she'd be hopeless. Bettina has a number of talents, but they don't include the domestic arts.'

'When do you want Heron's Sound to be ready?'

'As soon as possible. If you started immediately, I should think the place could be habitable by the end of February. I can lay on a work force to help you. You can't be expected to do-it-yourself on that scale.'

'What about my flat in London?'

'I suggest you retain it for three months. I'm sure Mrs Kelly would be happy to keep the place aired and dusted in return for a holiday at Heron's Sound later on. In three months' time you should have decided whether you want to stay here permanently, in which case you can fly back to arrange for your furniture to be shipped over, or she can take care of that as well.'

'I—I don't know what to say,' said Christie uncertainly.

'Don't say anything. Sleep on it. Drink your coffee before it goes cold.'

Christie did as he bade her, but without tasting what she was drinking. 'How long have you owned Heron's Sound?' she asked.

'Not long. It's a matter of weeks since the deeds came into my hands. But I've known about it for a long time, and suffered a good deal of uncertainty as to whether it would ever be mine Eventually— although not for many years yet—I hope to be able to afford to keep it for my personal use.'

Ash refilled his glass with Drambuie. 'As it's rather a gloomy place at present, I think it might be advisable not to take John with us tomorrow. No doubt Mrs Jones would be prepared to spend an afternoon on the beach with him.'

'Probably.'

There were footsteps on deck, and a man's voice called, 'Ahoy below!'

Ash raised his voice slightly 'Ahoy there!'

The man who entered the saloon a few moments later was of medium height, very thick-set, with a neatly trimmed curly blond beard and light blue eyes in a brown face. He looked to be in his late twenties

'This is Bob Wright, *Sunbird Two*'s skipper when I'm not aboard,' Ash told Christie 'Bob, this is Mrs Christiana Chapman, whose sister was married to my half-brother.'

'How d'you do, Mrs Chapman. Nice to meet you. Sorry to intrude on you, Ash, but I thought I'd have an early night. I was pretty late getting my head down last night, and I don't want to greet the new party with bags under my eyes.'

'No intrusion, Bob We were on the point of leaving anyway. I'll be here to say hello to the new lot, and assure them that you are every bit as competent as I am.'

'In seamanship, maybe. Not at sailing downhill with the fair sex,' was Bob's quick-fire response. Then he glanced at Christie and reddened, clearly regretting his riposte.

Ash's dark face showed no reaction, nor was there any displeasure in the tone of his goodnight to the other man.

They walked back past three moonlit capstans surrounded by a low wall which was all that was left of the Capstan House.

'The capstans were restored by volunteers from two Royal Navy ships in the early Fifties,' he told her. 'I should have explained to you earlier that the whole of this dockyard was abandoned by the Royal Navy in 1899 because the winding way in was unsuitable for modern ships. Fifty years later, in 1949, an ex-Navy Commander, Vernon Nicholson, with his wife and sons set out from England to sail to Australia in their schooner *Mollihawk*. They put in here for refitting and fell in love with the place which, at that time, was completely neglected and in danger of total dereliction. A couple of years or so later the Society of the Friends of English Harbour was founded, with people like the Queen and Lady Churchill taking an interest. The wealthy Americans who had bought twelve hundred acres of land to build the Mill Reef Club were also very generous supporters. But it was the Nicholson family who were the prime movers. I envy them sailing in here and, over a period of thirty years, seeing it slowly restored to the way it is now.'

'And, on a much smaller scale, you want to do

something similar with Heron's Sound?'

'Yes, if I can. I wasn't the first person to take an interest in it, but the owner—a man in his eighties—had gone back to England, and refused to sell it. He was a distinguished old boy, so I arranged for a friend to cable me as soon as his obituary notice appeared in *The Times*. I was able to contact his heirs. Heron's Sound had been left to a nephew who arranged for a local surveyor to report on the state of the place, and estimate the cost of restoration and upkeep. On the basis of that report, the nephew accepted my offer. It wasn't a bargain, by any means, but I think it will prove to have been a sound investment.'

They had left the dockyard by now, and were almost back at the car.

Motoring up the long hill from Falmouth and then through the villages of Liberta, Sweets and All Saints, they were silent. Ash gave all his attention to the bends in the road and the ebony-skinned villagers who, unless they were wearing light clothing, tended to merge into the darkness, especially when there was oncoming traffic.

Christie had plenty to preoccupy her; not only Ash's astounding proposition, but also the several fresh insights into his nature.

With hindsight, she guessed that the cry of 'Ahoy' from on deck had been Bob's tactful precaution in case *Sunbird Two*'s owner was engaged in 'sailing downhill' with his latest quarry.

And, as Ash had told his deputy that he would be present tomorrow to welcome the next charter party, it seemed a reasonable deduction that, if not spending the night with Bettina, he was sleeping in some bed other than his own on the schooner.

She was tempted to put him on the spot by asking where he kept his belongings when the schooner was not at the dockyard. But it might be she who was embarrassed if he chose to tell her the truth. No, on second thoughts, his private life had nothing to do with her, and it was better to pretend to be blind to it.

'I'll call for you at two, and we'll be back by five,' said Ash, as the car's wheels bumped over the grid at the entrance to the Colony. He escorted her inside the main block, where he asked if she would like a nightcap at the bar.

When Christie refused, he said, 'As you wish. Goodnight, Christiana.'

'Goodnight.' She had already thanked him for dinner, so she walked away quickly.

When, before turning a corner, she glanced over her shoulder, he had already disappeared. Whether to return to the car, to go to the bar on his own, or to hurry to Bettina's cottage, she would never know.

Mrs Jones answered Christie's enquiries by saying that John had been an angel, and she had enjoyed the supper brought to her on a trolley from the restaurant.

'Yes, certainly I'll come tomorrow,' she agreed. 'Now, will you join me in a cup of tea, Mrs Chapman. I've just this minute made myself a full pot, as you kindly invited me to do so.'

'Thank you.' Christie fetched another cup.

She had already explained the reason for her

presence on the island, and John's uncle's connection with her sister.

After some minutes of small talk, the older woman said, 'So it's Mr Lambard who is the little boy's guardian. You didn't mention him by name when you were telling me about it before you went out. Had you had much to do with Mr Lambard prior to losing your sister, Mrs Chapman?'

'No, nothing at all. Neither had Jenny. The two men had kept in touch by letter, but that was all. They hadn't met each other for years.'

'I see.' Mrs Jones pursed her lips. 'That puts me in a difficult position.'

'Really? Why? I don't understand.'

'I'm not a gossip, Mrs Chapman. I have never indulged in the scandalmongering which goes on in any community where some people have little to do but to drink and discuss each other's shortcomings. However, you're very young, and I can see that the little boy is devoted to you, and you to him. So I feel it's my duty to tell you that, from all I've heard, Mr Lambard is a most unsuitable person to have charge of any child.'

FIVE

CHRISTIE felt an automatic mistrust for anyone who prefaced revelations with 'I feel it's my duty . . .'

'In what way unsuitable?' she asked, her tone stiffening.

'He makes no secret of his predilection for the opposite sex. No attractive female, married or single, is safe with him. The granddaughter of two very dear friends of mine came out on holiday last year, and became entangled with him. She came with the young man whom her family hoped she would marry. He took her to the Lord Nelson Ball at the end of Sailing Week, when the Governor presents the prizes to the winning yachtsmen. Mr Lambard won two of the trophies. No one would dispute his skill as a helmsman. But I think even his friends in the sailing fraternity were shocked by the unscrupulous manner in which he cut out Lucy's fiancé. My friends were not present themselves, but I've been told by someone who was that he flirted outrageously with her, ignored poor Roger and, quite deliberately, encouraged Lucy to drink more than was good for her. Then he took her somewhere in his car, and they weren't seen again until the following morning. Naturally her poor grandparents were quite distraught with worry, as was Roger.'

'How did her grandparents know? Were they sitting up for her?'

'Roger woke them up to ask their advice.'

'It would have been more to the point if he'd stopped Lucy going off with Mr Lambard. I don't think alarming her grandparents, and advertising her indiscretion, was very sensible of him. He sounds rather feeble to me,' was Christie's reaction.

But although she felt obliged to take a defensive stance, inwardly she thought it contemptible of Ash to filch another man's girl in the manner described. It was one thing for him to amuse himself with sophisticates such as Bettina. The seduction of less worldly girls was a different matter altogether.

'What was the outcome?' she asked.

'The outcome was that the two young people quarrelled and broke their engagement. Roger flew home immediately. When Mr Lambard had the effrontery to call on Lucy, her grandfather refused him admission. Whereupon, I regret to say, Lucy behaved even more foolishly by packing her bags and announcing that she intended to spend the rest of her holiday with him.'

'And did she?'

'No. A few days later she, too, was on her way home—sent packing by Mr Lambard who, having seduced the poor child, very quickly grew bored and turned his attentions elsewhere.'

'I see. Well, I don't know that Mr Lambard's morals in relation to women have much bearing on his role as John's guardian,' Christie said guardedly.

'I'm sorry to say it's not only his liaisons which

have made him *persona non grata* among people of integrity,' said Mrs Jones. 'Several years ago, before he was known as a libertine, some even more unpleasant rumours about him were circulating.'

Christie bit her lip and said nothing. Her instinct was to tell Mrs Jones that ancient rumours, probably with no foundation, were not of the smallest interest to her. But her common sense told her that Ash was almost a stranger. It might be wiser to listen to all the scandal attaching to him. Exaggerated it might be, but even gossip usually had a germ of truth in it.

'It was when he first came to Antigua,' Mrs Jones continued. 'He was befriended by Lady Anna Fitzwarren, the daughter of a duke and the widow of a distinguished statesman. She was old and extremely eccentric. She never mixed with the English community, and was only seen in St John's once a year when she signed the visitors' book at Government House. Young men do not cultivate old ladies, except with an eye to the main chance. When she died he inherited everything she possessed. It was thought by a number of people that he might have precipitated her death.'

'That I do *not* believe!' stated Christie. 'A rake . . yes, that he may be. A murderer—no! That's a slander I can't accept, and if you knew him personally, you wouldn't either, Mrs Jones.'

'I didn't suggest that he murdered her!' The babysitter looked put out.

'You said "precipitated her death".'

'Precisely. By which I meant he may have hastened it. It was well known that she . . . shall we say, raised her elbow. Mr Lambard encouraged that weakness which, at her age, must have been harmful. Had he not done so, she might have lived several years longer.'

'It sounds all conjecture to me,' said Christie. 'One *fact* about Mr Lambard is that he has voluntarily taken on responsibility for the child in there He could have avoided the job of bringing up John

'Perhaps if John's father was wealthy . . .'

'He wasn't—quite the reverse. Mr Lambard stands to gain nothing. John will be a charge on his income.'

'I daresay he can afford it. He charges a fortune to the people who charter his boats.' Mrs Jones looked at her watch. 'It's time I was leaving. At least I've warned you, Mrs Chapman. I will only repeat that Mr Lambard is not a man in whom I would place too much confidence, were I in your shoes.'

After she had departed, visibly ruffled by Christie's failure to accept all her gossip as gospel, Christie went to the bathroom. She had left her nightdress and slippers there in order to get ready for bed without disturbing John. Not that he was easily disturbed. Tonight when she opened the blinds—the glass louvres were already open—and the room was flooded with moonlight, he did not stir. She bent over him and brushed a feather-soft kiss on his cheek.

Ash had told her to sleep on his offer, but already—and even in the light of Mrs Jones disquieting revelations—she knew she had no choice but to accept the job. She could not part from this small boy, except if she had no alternative. She had grown to love him too dearly to reject any chance to stay with him and watch him grow up.

No one could live without someone to love and be loved by. Even the cupboard love of a cat or the silent companionship of a dog was enough to keep an old person going. But Christie was young and she needed some form of human love. And John needed her. Not for long, and not too possessively. She would never allow herself to cling to him in the stifling way of some women who, when the time came for independence, did not want to let their children go. But while he was small and defenceless—and in case some of his uncle's unsavoury reputation was well founded—she would stay and protect him.

How she would protect herself if Ash took it into his head to add her scalp to his belt, she was not sure. No doubt when she started to work for him the local busybodies would look askance at her, and perhaps she, too, would soon be *persona non grata* among the elderly members of the foreign community. If so, it couldn't be helped.

When Ash came to fetch her the following afternoon, he was wearing a pair of old jeans and a shabby tee-shirt.

'I assumed you wouldn't have any old clothes with you, so I brought you these. No point in dirtying your good clothes,' he said, handing over a similar outfit.

'The jeans are Bob's. Mine would be too long in the leg for you. His will be too big round the waist, but the belt will hold them up. The plimsolls are fives—I hope that's about right.'

'Just right.' She retreated to the bedroom to change.

The plimsolls were new. He must have bought them for her on his way to or back from English Harbour. The tee-shirt had the faded legend *I survived Antigua Sailing Week '79* printed across the chest.

Half a mile down the road from the Colony, there was something on the macadam which made Ash slow the car. Christie leaned out of the window to look at the large grey land crab which seemed to be looking at her, its eyes on the end of stalks, its huge pincer claw held still.

'Are they harmless?' she asked.

He nodded. 'Although I shouldn't care to wave my bare foot in front of it,' he said dryly, as he drove on.

'John has been trying to catch one of the small, sand-coloured crabs which live in the holes on the beach, but they're much too quick for him. Why do we need these old clothes? Is the house very dirty?'

'Pretty filthy. Nothing's been done inside yet. At present I'm having the drive cleared, and the worst of the potholes filled in on the approach road. I say "road"—it's only a dirt track. The drive was virtually impenetrable. I used to get in by a goat track between the Sound and the garden. That's how we'll get there today—hire a boat from the village and get there the back way, by water.'

'How old is the house? Do you know?'

'Not yet. Antigua's most valuable archives are

preserved in London, and the deeds I have only refer to the first time the property changed hands. The earlier history is something I shall have to have researched.' He glanced sideways at her. 'You haven't asked me how much I propose to pay you?'

'How much?'

'Not as much as you're earning at present. At least not until the place is operational.' He mentioned a figure which, converted into sterling, was rather less than half her present salary. 'Plus your keep, and the use of a car. No fixed working hours. I'd expect you to work damned hard in the early stages. You can have until New Year's Eve to make up your mind. Then I want a firm yes or no.'

It was on the tip of Christie's tongue to tell him the decision was already made. Then she decided to wait.

She said, 'Talking of New Year's Eve, I'd forgotten it's almost Christmas. Somehow, in this glorious weather, it's hard to believe it's December.'

'On Christmas Day we've been invited to join a house party at the home of some Anglo-American friends of mine. There'll be other small children for John to play with, and I think you'll find the adults congenial.'

'It sounds fun.'

Ash stopped the car for the second time, and picked up the two boys who had been hopefully thumbing a lift. It was not more than two miles further to the waterside village which was their destination.

The boys said, 'Thank you very much,' and

showed their beautiful teeth in farewell grins.

'They're not ruining their teeth with too many sweets and ice lollies,' Christie remarked.

'No, but sometimes you'll see adults with teeth worn into points from chewing cane when they were children; and there's plenty of scope here for Dr Pritikin, or whoever is the current king of the diet gurus,' answered Ash, with a discreet nod in the direction of one of the many heavyweight Antiguan matrons.

Christie had noticed that although the majority of Antiguan girls and young women were slender, with small waists and delicate wrists and ankles, many of the older women did have serious weight problems.

Ash took a small rucksack from the boot, and slung it over one shoulder. 'Cold drinks,' he explained.

A few minutes later she found herself seated in the bow of a small fishing boat with an outboard motor to propel it through the calm water.

The trip along the Sound gave her her first close-up of mangroves; strange trees growing out of the water and putting down leafless branches in the mud. The Sound was a stretch of water between the land and a number of small, barren islands. Behind the mangroves which fringed it rose a low hill covered with scrub. Presently, at a point where the mud was piled with conch shells discarded by fishermen who had used the mollusc for bait, Ash tied the painter to a mangrove and handed Christie ashore.

'I'll lead the way, shall I?'

He set off up a narrow path among the bushes,

most of which if not thorny were prickly. She was glad of the serviceable denim protecting her legs. In a dress she would have been scratched.

Long dried and more recent goats' droppings showed how the path was kept open. It wended a roundabout route to the top of the incline where Ash waited for her to catch up.

'This is the boundary of the garden. One should be able to see the house from here, but Nature has been on the rampage for over five years, and the place is a jungle. That's why the house seems so gloomy. It won't once the trees blocking out all the light have been felled.'

'Did you hack this path clear?' she asked, following him along a corridor through dense greenery.

'Yes, and darned hot work it was.'

Suddenly, unexpectedly, the house loomed out of the vegetation engulfing it—a two-storey house, built of stone blocks, with shuttered windows.

'The front door is round the other side. This way.' He mounted a flight of stone steps leading up to a covered walk level with the first floor rooms. This had only partially been cleared of the creepers which had taken over while the house was unoccupied. It extended round two corners of the building to the side where another, more imposing double flight of stairs descended from the entrance verandah.

'Brace yourself for a pretty overpowering stench of mildew and neglect,' he warned her, as he inserted a large iron key in the lock of the tall double doors.

Christie crossed the threshold, then waited while Ash strode about opening sash windows and shutters. He had not exaggerated the smell. Her nostrils flinched from the rank air.

In the limited light admitted by the open shutters, the room where she stood was revealed as an ante-room to the large drawing-room beyond it. There, mice or rats had gnawed through the upholstery materials on the chairs and sofas, and the hard furniture was filmed and mottled with dirt and damp.

To anyone without imagination it presented a depressing spectacle. But Christie had the ability to disregard the stained, dark-painted walls, the cob-webs hanging from the sconces, and the fungus growing on a skirting. She could see the room's fine proportions, and its possibilities.

Ash showed her all the principal apartments and two or three of the bedrooms, each of which had a fourposter bed, but without the canopies of such beds in old English houses. Here the posts were supports for mosquito nets.

'That's the famous Antigua Black pineapple, a recurring motif in early island-made furniture,' said Ash, tapping the part of a mahogany post carved with criss-cross grooves like the indentations on the fruit.

'What a strange chair!' Christie had noticed a low chair, its flat mahogany arms extending far forward of the seat.

'A planter's chair,' he explained. He sat down, leaned back, and spread his legs to rest them on the projecting ends of the arms. 'A chair like this was for relaxing at the end of the day. Some of the hotels have beach chairs modelled on these chairs.'

By one of the beds hung a many-tailed whip with knotted ends. At the thought of its use on human beings, Christie gave a slight shudder.

Ash saw the reaction, and took the whip down from its hook. 'Not an ornament for a bedroom, or indeed any part of the house. I'll get rid of it. Historic items of this nature we can do without, but some things I do want preserved. For example, the old water filter.'

He showed her the apparatus he meant; thick stone bowls which dripped into each other and then into a water container, all enclosed in a cage of fine mesh.

'Where's the kitchen?' asked Christie.

'In a separate building. I'll show you.'

The squalor of the scullery and the small, blackened room containing an ancient cooking range under a soot-crusted chimney made her pull down the sides of her mouth.

'Don't worry—I know it's a hell-hole. We'll preserve it as an interesting relic, and build a modern one elsewhere.'

As he spoke something made her glance down. A second later she was recoiling with horror at the sight of a scorpion rearing its sting not two inches from her left foot.

'*Ash!*' Instinctively she turned and clutched him.

His arms closed round her. He lifted her, swung her aside, and crushed the insect under the heel of his boot. Instead of putting her down, he then carried her out of the kitchen into the paved yard beyond.

'Sorry about that, but I don't think you need to worry that you're going to encounter them frequently. That's the first one I've seen here.'

Slowly he set her on her feet, still holding her close to his body, her breasts crushed against his hard chest, her arms trapped inside his arms.

'Thank you, but . . please . let me go,' she begged, in a soft shaken voice.

'Must I?' His eyes held laughter. 'Doesn't that service merit some small reward?'

Her hands were still grasping his shirt. She opened them, pushing him off, but to no effect as long as he chose to hold her to him.

'Don't flirt with me, Ash. I know it's a reflex of yours to everyone female, but—'

'What makes you think that?'

'Bob said as much, last night. Please—' She exerted more strength.

It was useless. His arms were as inescapable as iron bars. He alone could loosen his grip. Christie could only stand still and protest.

'Bob overrates my prowess because he's a shy man with women.'

'He didn't strike me as being shy.'

'Now with you perhaps. With a girl like Bettina he's tonguetied.'

All at once his arms fell away, and she stepped back, relieved but ruffled.

Attempting a self-possession she was far from feeling, she said, 'As it's possible that I may be going to work for you, I think it's much better not to . . . to fool about.'

'Is that your only reason?'

'What do you mean?'

'That I should have liked to kiss you doesn't mean it was also your reflex. But at least you prefer me to a scorpion,' was his quizzical answer. 'Come: I've something else to show you which I hope will act as a counterbalance to the off-putting aspects of the house. Why don't you wait on the front verandah while I close up the shutters?'

She did as he suggested, leaning her forearms on the balustrade, trying to visualise Heron's Sound in its heyday, and as it might be in the future, given loving attention backed by a good deal of money.

'Where exactly is the drive?' she asked him, when he had re-locked the front doors.

'You can't see it yet, but it's impressive—or will be. An avenue of forty-foot queen palms. It stops some way short of the house, so I think there must have been a large sweep where the carriages used to be parked when the house was *en fête*.'

At the end of the garden, instead of returning down the goat track, Ash went in a different direction where the slope of the hill was steeper and more rocky.

Watching where she was stepping, Christie did not notice where he was leading her until they were almost at the bottom. Then she came round a large bush and saw a small perfect cove—a half-moon of sand shelving into palest jade water.

'In the days when Heron's Sound was built, people didn't go swimming as we do. The original owners may never have come here,' said Ash, as she joined him on the beach.

'Why didn't I bring my bikini? It looks so inviting, doesn't it?' she exclaimed regretfully.

'I assumed you had it in your bag. Never mind you can swim in your skin. I won't look,' he assured her, straight-faced.

'No . . . no, I couldn't.' She blushed.

'Okay, then swim in your undies. You told me the other day they were indistinguishable from a bikini at a casual glance. I'm going in myself.' He proceeded to unzip his jeans.

'Did you bring a towel?' she asked uncertainly.

'Yes. We can share it. Come on, don't be a goose, Christiana. I had you in my arms a few minutes ago, and nothing bad happened to you, did it? I'm not likely to go berserk at the sight of you in your underwear. It's too hot for that sort of thing. I'm more interested in cooling off.'

With which he stepped out of his pants, tugged his tee-shirt over his head, and unlaced his short canvas boots. Moments later he was wading into the sea.

Stung by his sardonic tone, Christie tried to make up her mind. Her underclothes consisted of a pair of blue cotton bikini briefs and a no-bra bra of semi-transparent shimmer nylon. The briefs were no problem. The bra was. Once wet, it would be totally transparent.

On the other hand, Ash was striking out for deeper water as if he meant to swim a fair distance. If she splashed about in the shallows, she should be able to dash ashore before he came back to the beach. She

was not altogether convinced by the sarcastic tone in
which he had dismissed her reluctance as unnecessary prudery. It was not—as she had already told
him—that she considered herself irresistible. Far
from it.

It was merely that her own impression, reinforced
by what Mrs Jones had told her the night before, was
that he was a man for whom women were one of life's
pleasures, to be taken, enjoyed, and only occasionally remembered—like a rich meal, a vintage wine, or
perhaps an exhilarating yacht race.

She might be nothing special to look at, but she
wasn't susceptible to his charm; and she had an
intuitive conviction that Ashcroft Lambard was not
accustomed to being resisted, and didn't care for it.

However by the time he had disappeared into the
wider waters of the Sound, the heat of mid-afternoon
was beating down on her so fiercely that it did seem
crazy not to have a quick dip.

Swiftly she shed her clothes and removed the
plimsolls. Then she hastened into the sea, giving
vent to an ecstatic sigh as the crystal coolness refreshed her from foot to chin.

Presently, having first assured herself that there
was no sign of Ash coming back, she floated, her
arms flung wide, her head so deeply submerged that
the water lapped over her forehead.

Through half-closed eyes she gazed at the deep
azure sky. Her body was utterly relaxed. It was like
lying in an invisible hammock, alone in a blue and
gold universe, at peace, with no cares, no problems.

And then, as she lay suspended in the shining sea,

there was a disturbance beneath her which brought back a phrase from the Guide Map issued by the island's Department of Tourism.

Antigua, which is partly volcanic and partly coral, is surrounded by superb white sand beaches which are almost entirely reef-protected.

Almost entirely. Not entirely.

Her slack limbs stiffened with fear. What if this cove was not protected, and a shark or a huge barracuda had cruised in from the ocean? Only a very large creature could have caused that strong swirl below her.

Where was Ash? *Ash—help me!* her mind screamed while her body was frozen with terror. What to do? Oh, God—what to do? The few yards to the beach seemed a mile.

SIX

With a sudden convulsive movement she stood up and looked wildly round for the creature which threatened her safety.

But there was nothing there. No menacing fin. No long sleek shape under the surface.

A turmoil in the water behind her made her whirl round, her grey eyes dilating. Then a moan of relief escaped her as she saw the brown back of the man who was raking back glistening dark hair, his ribs more clearly defined by the long, deep lung-filling breath of someone who has stayed under water to the limit of their air.

'It was you!' Christie exclaimed, her voice husky.

He turned to her. 'Who else would it be? There's no one around but ourselves.'

'I thought . . . I thought . . .'

She heard her voice falter, and felt herself losing her balance as the cove seemed to tilt at an angle. Her head swam. She felt cold and sick. Then darkness blotted out the sunlight.

'Don't worry, I'm here. You're all right.'

It was Ash's voice, somewhere close by. Christie heard him speak reassuringly to her, and then she became aware of being in a sitting position, but bent forward with her head hanging down between her knees.

'W-what happened?' she murmured bewilderedly.

'You blacked out for a minute. You can sit up now . . . slowly does it.'

With an arm across her chest, gripping her shoulder, he raised her until she was upright. Then she felt his other arm behind her, stopping her from flopping backwards as she felt she might without support.

'I fainted,' she said, in surprise. 'I've never done that before.'

'Haven't you? Well, I don't think it's anything to worry about. It didn't last half a minute. Put your head on my shoulder if you still feel a bit woozy.'

She was sitting on one of his thighs, she found. He was kneeling on one leg, and making a chair for her with the other leg and his arm.

Later, she realised that, had he been a man of average build his head would have been lower than hers. Because of his height—at least ten inches taller than hers—and the fine proportions of his body with a torso to match his long legs, even in this position his eyes were still slightly above hers. Their faces were close, even closer than in the kitchen. She could see herself reflected in his pupils.

'No . . . no, I'm not woozy. I remember what happened now. You'll think it incredibly stupid, but I thought you were a shark . . or something dangerous.'

Ash lifted an eyebrow. 'There are no sharks here,

in the Sound. They live out in the deep water, beyond the reefs.'

'Don't they ever slip through the gaps? There are gaps—the guide map says so.'

'If there was any danger from sharks around here, you can take it from me that I wouldn't be swimming,' he said dryly. 'If it had crossed my mind that you might mistake me for one, I should have surfaced before I reached you. I'm sorry I gave you a fright. I take it you've read or seen the film version of *Jaws*?'

'No. I don't like that sort of book, or horror movies.'

Feeling better now, she was suddenly conscious of their closeness and her immodest state. Ash had said he preferred beachware which left a little to the imagination. The white bra, now wet, concealed nothing.

'I—I think I'd like to get dressed now.' She was uncomfortably aware of her still-pale breasts exposed by the gauzy material as clearly as if she were topless.

'Yes, a good idea,' Ash agreed.

His free arm slid under her knees and he rose, lifting her up with him as easily as if she were John.

At the moment of fainting she had been at the other end of the cove from where she had entered the water. Her clothes were about twenty yards away.

'I can walk. You don't have to carry me.'

'You're not heavy—not heavy enough. One wouldn't call you a thin girl'—with a downward glance which scanned her from neck to knee—'but you could put on several pounds without becoming over-plump.'

Christie coloured, and didn't answer. Did he think her breasts were too small? she found herself wondering. They were no smaller than Bettina's. She had a model girl's figure with almost no bosom at all. Perhaps he found that a fault, preferring more lavish curves.

Why should I care what he prefers? she asked herself sharply, and was glad when he set her down.

He put the towel round her shoulders. It was not a large one like the bath-sized beach towels provided at the Colony.

'I'll turn my back. Let me know when you're decent,' he said.

She took off the bra, dried her top and pulled on the tee-shirt. Then she did the same with her lower half.

'I'm decent.' When he turned round, she handed him the towel.

'You haven't dried your hair.'

'If I do that the towel will be soaked.'

'It doesn't matter. I have my tee-shirt to dry on. I don't need to wear it to drive back. Come here.'

He beckoned her closer. When she hesitated, he stepped forward and began to rub her hair.

She submitted in silence, aware of a sensation she hadn't felt since her father's time; of being looked after. Had Mike made her feel protected? She didn't think so, but she couldn't remember too clearly. All the time before they were married she could only see through the dark glass of subsequent experience.

Ash ceased rubbing and slung the towel round his neck. He bent to his neatly folded jeans and took a comb from the pocket.

'Hold still.'

He drew her parting—on the correct side and in the correct place: he must be extraordinarily observant—and began to comb through the tangles left by his vigorous rubbing.

'A pity I didn't bring some coffee instead of a cold drink. But there's rum in the rucksack. A little of that should warm you up.'

Having dealt with her hair to his satisfaction, his next move was to produce a plastic beaker and a small unlabelled bottle which looked as if it might once have contained cough mixture. Now it was full of golden brown liquid.

'I brought this to lace the orange juice in the vacuum flask, but I think it will do more good neat,' he said, as he handed her a tot.

Christie couldn't deny that she was shivering. It was, she supposed, delayed shock. She drank it, turning away as Ash began to dry and dress. The rum did not make her stop shivering. In spite of the heat of the sun, she felt icy and longed for a sweater.

'In the absence of a rug—'

He finished the sentence by putting his arms round her from behind. Before she knew what was happening, they were both sitting down on the sand and she was between his legs, her back to his chest, his arms folded round and in front of her.

'Don't jump to the wrong conclusion. This is not the beginning of that pass you're afraid of. It's merely the best way of warming you,' he said, close to her ear. 'Try to relax. Take some deep breaths.'

It was like leaning against a radiator, only more comfortable. For a moment or two she did relax, feeling the warmth of his body seeping into her chilled one.

She looked down at his sinewy forearms, the tanned skin lightly covered with dark hairs. His watch, on a stainless steel bracelet, was a complicated-looking Rolex.

When she asked him about it, he said, 'It's a GMT-Master, a chronometer for navigation, and pressure proof, so they claim, to a depth of one hundred and sixty-five feet. It shows precise time simultaneously in two zones.'

As he spoke, his breath fanned her cheek and made her remember an incident she had put to the back of her mind.

It had happened before she was married. Mike had come to supper at the cottage. Afterwards, when her father had gone into the hall to answer the telephone, Mike had seized the opportunity to kiss her. She had never minded his kisses, providing they remained gentle. She hadn't liked fiercer kisses, and she had resisted his attempts at other caresses. That night, when she had felt his hand sliding under her jersey, she had struggled free, protesting that her father might come back at any moment.

Not until months later—when they were married—had she understood that her father's return had been an excuse to cover the fact that she had not wanted him to touch her in that intimate way.

Yet now, as she looked at Ash's hand as it moved briskly up and down, chafing the skin between her elbow and the sleeve of the tee-shirt he had lent her, she had an unnerving moment of self-enlightenment.

If he, now, were to slip his tanned fingers under her shirt and then upwards, over her midriff, to explore and caress her bare breasts, she would not feel the same distaste she had felt long ago, with Mike.

Indeed, merely thinking about it sent a thrilling tremor through her body. A deep blush burned from her forehead down to her throat.

'I'm much warmer now. I feel fine. Don't you think we ought to be getting back?'

She moved restively in his arms, and was thankful when he let her go.

'Maybe it would be as well if you had a check-up with my doctor,' he said, on the drive back. 'I don't mean to suggest that a black-out as brief as that is anything to worry about, but it could be a warning signal that something is slightly wrong. When did you last have a check?'

'I haven't seen a doctor for years. I've always been healthy.'

'I have a check every year.'

'Do you?' she said, in astonishment. 'But you look just about as fit as it's possible to be.'

'I am, and I want to stay that way. A charter skipper is responsible for other people's lives. He can't afford to go sick. To have a yearly check seems to me like having a car serviced or boat refitted.'

'Very well, I'll have myself checked.'

'I'll fix it for you.' He took a hand off the wheel to place his palm on her forearm. 'How are you now? Your skin feels normal.'

'I'm fine, merely very embarrassed at making such a fool of myself. I'm not usually a highly-strung person—rather the reverse.'

'Perhaps you don't know what you are,' was his enigmatic comment.

Christie would have liked to ignore the remark, but her curiosity got the better of her. 'What do you mean?'

'A lot of people go through life being whatever is expected of them. It's the line of least resistance; the easy way. As children they try to please their parents and teachers. They're punished if they don't. For a while, in their teens, they may fight the system, but in most cases not for very long. Then most of them revert to conforming. It's not quite as bad as it used to be. At least now it's widely accepted that early sexual attractions are rarely a solid basis for long-term partnerships. In my observation, most people don't know themselves until they're in their late twenties, by which time it's often too late. They're trapped by their circumstances. Perhaps you're in one of those traps.'

'Not as far as I know,' she said stiffly. 'You're not, I feel sure'—with a trace of sarcasm.

She had felt there was something patronising in his reference to other people. As if he were a being apart, a natural superior to his fellows.

Ash said, 'No, but I had self-determination forced on me by my mother's death and my father's remarriage. No other woman's child could have won approval from my stepmother, and as my father was in love with her to the exclusion of all other feelings, I suppose he began to see me through her eyes, as an encumbrance.'

He took his eyes off the road to glance at her. 'I'm not complaining about it. I'd already had seven years of happy childhood with my mother. A spell of adversity didn't hurt me. It made life uncomfortable for a while, but I see now it was a good thing. Had my mother lived, undoubtedly I should now be in one of the professions in England, with a wife and children, and a small boat to sail at weekends. I should have missed my true métier; and if, at times, I felt dissatisfied I shouldn't have known it was because life had steered me away from my proper place in the world.'

'Is there only one way of life in which a person can be happy?' asked Christie. 'I should have thought there were several.'

'Maybe, but the majority of people never find even one of them. You told me the other day that Mrs Kelly had advised you to wait and see before doing your shopping here. It's the same with life. It's better to see what's available before making a commitment. What, at nineteen, did you really know about all the different kinds of men in the world, or about yourself? Not much. If your husband had lived, and your marriage had lasted, it would have been luck, not judgment.'

She could not argue with that statement. She knew she had been pressured into marriage; by Mike, by her own romanticism, by a moral code imposed on

her by her father who would have been shocked and
upset by the discovery that she was no longer the
pure, innocent girl he had wanted his daughter
to be.

Jenny had wounded him terribly by letting him
know that she and Paul had been lovers long before
their marriage. But Jenny had been a worry to both
her parents. Christie could remember several angry
scenes between Jenny and their mother in the last
year of their mother's life when her sister, then a
well-developed fifteen, had been out with boys on the
sly.

Sometimes Christie had wondered if it had been
Jenny's precocious enthusiasm for sex which had put
her off it. At twelve she had still been a child, thin
and coltish, dreamy and impressionable, more interested in books than boys.

Her sister had told her things which she hadn't
been ready to know; earthy things which bore no
relation to her ethereal idea of love.

'Your stepmother sounds a horrid person. Was
your father happy with her?' she asked.

'She wasn't horrid. She had certain faults, as we
all do. Hers were jealousy and possessiveness. I think
she made Father extremely happy. She was twenty
years his junior, very pretty and probably much less
inhibited than my mother, who had been of his own
generation. I suspect that Lorna gave him a much
better time in bed, and he couldn't believe his luck.
It's easy for a woman to enslave a man in that way,
particularly a middle-aged man who feels his virility
declining. Most women don't realise their power

over men or, if they do, they're too shy or repressed to exert it fully.'

She wondered if he had any idea that he was talking to an extreme case of shyness and repression. An incurable case.

Seizing an opportunity to change the subject, she said, 'Is that sugar-cane in that field on the right?'

'Yes, they're starting to grow it again. Before Independence, it was the island's main crop. Then it was dropped and other crops substituted. By 1975 it had virtually disappeared. But now it's being reintroduced. Actually tobacco was the very first crop, then sugar, worked originally by white indentured labourers, and then by slaves brought from Africa. Five million Africans were shipped to the West Indies in the three hundred years between 1500 and 1800.'

'Five million!' Christie echoed, aghast.

'Britain was the first country to forbid the slave trade. That was in 1808, but the slaves already here weren't freed until much later. The Antiguan planters released their slaves—thirty thousand of them—in August 1834. But the French had slaves until 1848, and the Spanish didn't emancipate theirs until 1886. Not that freedom means much where there's still great poverty and minimal education. But that's past history. It's the future which is important.'

'You spoke of hoping, eventually, to have Heron's Sound as your private house. That means, presumably, that you plan to spend the rest of your life here?'

'If Antigua remains peaceful, as I think it will, yes, I do. I'm a New World man. I feel no strong links with Europe. Had I been alive in the last century, I would have emigrated to America and gone West. The idea of pioneering new country appeals to me, but all the remaining virgin territories are too damned uncomfortable.'

They had arrived at the Colony, so Christie did not utter the comment that the American West must have been uncomfortable in the early days. But she could imagine Ash there. Not as a settler, building a cabin for his family, taming the wilderness into farmland. Ash, she thought, would have ridden scout for a waggon train, or adventured alone, free and footloose.

That evening she wrote a letter resigning her job forthwith, and explaining the reasons why she was unable to give notice in the usual way.

The envelope sealed, she went to the main block to buy a stamp from the desk. There she ran into Bettina, who said, 'I hear you've been invited to Miranda's party on Christmas Day.'

'Yes. Will you be there?'

'I was at school with Miranda's younger sister. It was she who invited me to join her on a holiday here, just after my divorce. Then the job at the Colony came up, and I stayed on. I spend a lot of my free time at Miranda's place. It's gorgeous—very luxurious. Her second husband, Joss, is an American. He commutes from Miami. I don't know why they don't have a place in Palm Beach, but they seem to prefer it here.'

Her pale sea-green eyes swept critically over the simple print sun-dress made for Christie by Mar-

garet Kelly. Christie knew that it was unfashionable.
The shoulder straps were too wide, the skirt neither
full nor straight. But Margaret had made it, in
Christie's size, with one of her own favourite patterns, and from a dress length she had had by her. It
had been a surprise and a labour of love, and Christie
appreciated it as such.

'Have you something stunning to wear?' Bettina
asked. 'It will be a very smart party. People from
Mill Reef will be there.'

Christie remembered Ash's reference to the rich
Americans who had contributed to the restoration of
Nelson's Dockyard.

'What sort of thing will you wear?' she asked.

'In the evening, a design of my own. We're invited
for midday, but they have the main meal at night,
when it's cooler and all the children are out of the
way. Then there's dancing until the small hours.'

'I imagine Ash must mean to run us back here
before that stage of the party,' said Christie. 'So the
question of something special to wear for the later
festivities won't arise for me.'

'No, maybe not,' Bettina agreed. 'Have you a
driving licence?'

'Yes, I used to drive my father's car sometimes,
but I haven't driven recently.'

'If I lent you my car, you could drive yourself back
here and save Ash missing an hour of the party,'
Bettina suggested.

Later in the evening, Ash telephoned Christie to
tell her he had arranged for her to have a medical
check in St John's early the following morning.

After which you may have some last-minute Christmas shopping you'd like to do. Bring your bathing kit. I've booked lunch at Curtain Bluff, a hotel on a stretch of the coast which you haven't seen yet.'

Having told her what time he would fetch her, he said goodnight and rang off. Whether he had made the call from Bettina's cottage, or was somewhere else on the island, she had no means of knowing.

Later, in bed, but unable to sleep, she had a few moments of panic at the thought of the letter to England now lying in the Colony's mail-box, or perhaps already removed from it. But when she rolled over and saw John's small shape in the other bed her misgivings subsided. She felt sure she had done the right thing.

Her thoughts turned to her strange reaction to being in Ash's arms that afternoon. Not so much the first time—although that had been a disturbing experience—but the second time, when she had imagined him caressing her.

What would his kisses be like? Surely there couldn't be much difference between one man's lovemaking and another's? Clearly they varied a good deal in the preliminary stages. Some were shy and diffident like Bob Wright. Some had the aplomb of much practice, like Ash.

But in the end, in bed, surely they must all be the same—possessed by a feverish urgency which made their mouths greedy, their hands rough until, their strange passion expended, they relaxed and were soon fast asleep.

Or might there be men who were not like that?

Christie gave a long, uneven sigh. It was a question she would rather leave forever unanswered than put it to the test and find out the answer was No.

Driving to town the next morning, she told Ash of Bettina's offer of the loan of her car.

'Certainly not,' was his response. 'You and I and John are expected to stay overnight, as is Bettina, I believe.'

He spoke as if he were not sure, yet he must know for certain. Perhaps he was being discreet.

His doctor was a youngish Antiguan who, after he had noted her medical history and was preparing to test her blood pressure, told her he had trained at one of the great teaching hospitals in London.

'Are you glad to be home?' she asked him.

'In most ways, yes. But after a long time away, there are some difficult adjustments. I miss the London bookshops. There isn't a first class bookshop here.'

His examination complete, he told her to dress. He was completing his notes when she came out of the curtained section of his surgery.

'As far as I can discover, you're in perfect health, Mrs Chapman,' he told her, with a smile. 'I think your faint yesterday was merely the result of having been badly scared. Ash has told me something of the recent events in your life. Having lost your sister very suddenly, it isn't surprising if you tend to be easily upset. But that will pass. Physically, you're in excellent shape.'

He accompanied her back to the waiting-room and repeated his opinion to Ash, as if he were entitled to know the state of her health.

'When you've finished your shopping, come and join us at the Golden Peanut. We'll be there from eleven,' said Ash, dropping her off in one of the main streets.

In the Scent Shop in High Street, she bought a large atomiser of Diorissimo cologne for her hostess, and one of Rive Gauche for Bettina. Many luxury items being duty-free in the island, they cost far less than in England.

It was barely ten. Having an hour to spare, she went into a shop called Bay Boutique, in St Mary's Street, and there looked through the dresses. Perhaps she owed it to Ash to wear something rather more stylish at the party than any of her existing dresses. But although there was a good choice, there was nothing she felt was right for her.

Then, looking in a glass showcase, she saw some delightful jewellery made from a coiled shell, sliced to show its convolutions and threaded into decorative bib shapes with thick, silky cord. She did not covet one herself, but she knew her sister would adore one.

Would have adored one. With a pang, she corrected herself. For an instant she had forgotten the still unbelievable fact that Jenny was dead.

She had a number of packages when she found Ash and his nephew sitting at one of the outdoor tables of a café screened from the road by a tall flowering hedge between two gateways.

'Secrets?' Ash asked, as she put her shopping on the fourth chair after he had risen to draw out the third one for her.

She shook her head. 'A small present for Mrs Hathaway, and a pair of shoes for me. The ones I brought with me are all flat-heeled, not very suitable for a party.'

'I was going to suggest that a little something for Miranda would be a pleasing gesture, but I forgot,' he said. 'I might have known you would think of it yourself. You have nice manners, Christiana— rather rare in these offhand times.'

The expression in his eyes as he praised her made her pulse give a queer little jolt. As the waitress came for her order, she had to remind herself that Ash himself had exceptional manners—those of a prac- tised charmer.

The road to where they were lunching passed through the inland villages of Ebenezers, Jennings and Bolans. Then the sea came into view again, and a beautiful, long palm-fringed beach.

As they did in England, cars drove on the left, so that Christie had to look in Ash's direction to admire the scene on the right-hand side of the roadway. She noticed him grinning, and asked, 'What's the joke?'

'I was remembering some friends of mine who were taken for a ride along this stretch—a metaphor- ical ride. They stopped to enjoy the view, and a local lad came along and sold them three coconuts. Very good coconuts. He opened them for them, and they drank the water straight away. But twenty-two E.C.

dollars was rather more than the market price, they discovered later.'

'What is the market price?'

'It varies, but certainly under a dollar each.'

She laughed. 'How galling for your friends! But I suppose anyone who can afford to holiday here is not on too tight a budget. It sounds as if that coconut vendor is going to be rich himself one day.'

Before they reached the hotel, Ash pointed out the Shekerley Mountains, with the summit of Boggy Peak, the island's highest point, rising above the others.

It was early for lunch, so they bathed, and then dried off on beach beds.

Having put some sun-cream on John, Christie protected her own skin, now toasted to light golden brown. She had done her arms, legs and chest when Ash asked, 'Want me to do your back?'

Usually, on the beach at the Colony, she would ask some friendly-looking woman if she would mind doing it for her. Here she had no choice but to hand the bottle to him.

He left his beach-bed to sit beside her on hers. Silently exhorting herself not to tense when she felt his hand on her, Christie said aloud, 'Tell me more about the Mill Reef Club. Is it strictly for millionaires?'

'Yes, people like Tom Watson, the IBM mogul, and Lord and Lady Astor. It was founded about thirty years ago, and now there are about sixty properties and five hundred members. You can see the roofs of some of the houses from the beach at Half

Moon Bay, but the grounds of the Club are strictly private. Some distinguished people have been turned back at the inner gate if they had no invitation from a member. Jackie Onassis is a regular visitor, I've heard. One can imagine the attention she would attract on a public beach such as this one.'

'Yes, I suppose if the word went round that she was staying here, the rubbernecks would come in droves,' Christie agreed.

Having trickled some cream down her spine, he was working it into her skin with firm, smoothing strokes with his fingertips. First up to the top of her left shoulder, then over the blade, then down to her waist and below it to the curve of her hip and the cleft of her bare behind.

'I'm being gentler with you than you were with me, you'll notice,' he teased her.

'You asked me to rub it in harder.'

'True, but my hide is tougher than yours. Your skin is as soft as a baby's.'

Christie was silent, her throat tight. She wanted to be as indifferent to his touch as she was when another woman applied the cream for her. But she wasn't: in fact she was so acutely sensitive that she could feel individually the pressure of the three fingers he was using on her.

'The tie of your top is in the way. If you'll stop it from coming adrift, I'll undo the strings for a minute.'

She barely had time to anchor the triangles of cotton before he had undone the bow, and was

starting methodically to cream the other half of her
back.

It seemed an eternity before he reached the base of
her spine; and then, when she thought it was over,
she felt his thumb running up the line of her verte-
brae and sending a violent frisson of intense and
unfamiliar sensation rippling upwards from the pit
of her stomach.

'There you are: all done.'

But the ordeal wasn't quite over. As her hands
sped behind her to re-fasten the strings, they collided
with his hands about to perform the same function.

As their fingers tangled, the loosened bra became
displaced. With a murmur of dismay, Christie
snatched it back into position.

'Sorry. Lose your spinnakers?' said Ash. 'Never
mind. If that chap caught a glimpse of your breasts,
I expect he thought, as I did yesterday, that
they're one of the nicest exposures he's seen for
some time.'

He was referring to a man who was strolling along
the water's edge, looking up the beach in their
direction. But it wasn't what he might have seen
which was causing her to blush, but the reminder of
being virtually topless while Ash was carrying her in
his arms.

In an effort to sound unflurried, she asked, 'Why
do you call them spinnakers?'

He stood up and went back to the other sun
bed.

'A spinnaker is a special racing jib set on the
opposite side to the mainsail when a boat is running.

Most spinnakers are coloured and patterned, and when the wind fills them they're much the same shape as a well-filled bra.'

'I see.'

'The time to see spinnakers out in force is in April, in Sailing Week. Maybe by then I'll have taught you enough about sailing for you to help crew one of the *Sunbirds*. But, if not, Miranda Hathaway always takes a brunch party up to Shirley Heights above English Harbour. It's a great place to see the start of the first yacht race from Falmouth to Dickenson Bay.'

'Is that one of the races which you've won?'

'It's a race which includes seven classes, each one starting at ten-minute intervals over a period of an hour. So there's more than one winner. The top trophy, the Lord Nelson Cup, goes to the boat with the best overall results at the end of the week. *Sunbird Two* has won it a couple of times, and some of the other trophies as well. But who told you that? Bettina?'

'No, John's baby-sitter . . . Mrs Jones.'

Recalling what else she had said Christie must unconsciously have frowned, because the next thing Ash said was, 'You look displeased, Christiana. Not put out by my likening your bra to a pair of spinnakers, are you?'

Her expression lightened. She smiled. 'I'm not quite as straitlaced as that!'

'You haven't got a straitlaced mouth.' His dark eyes were focussed on her lips. 'Rather voluptuous, in fact.'

Her frown returned. 'Please, Ash . . . don't.'

'Don't what?'

'Don't flirt with me. I thought we'd already agreed on that.'

Before he could answer, John came running back from the hole he had been digging. Soon afterwards it was time to go to the hotel for lunch.

Built on a tongue of land jutting out between two glittering bays which gave guests there a choice of beaches, the hotel was very attractive, its public rooms grouped round a spacious, tree-shaded court-yard. The décor was sky-blue and white, and Christie was interested to see that, in one of the lounges visible from their table, there were built-in cupboards with fronts of white-painted wickerwork. They reminded her of her own pretty Regency cup-board with its brass grilles backed by pleated silk. She made mental notes of various other pleasing decorative touches which might have applications at Heron's Sound.

The hotel's boutique, near the entrance, was an unusual shape—octagonal. She would have passed by, but Ash said, 'You haven't bought a Christmas present for Aunt Christie yet, have you, John? Let's see what we can find her in here.'

And before they had been inside for more than two minutes, he said, 'Ah, I see the very thing.'

'What?' asked John and Christie, simultaneously.

Her impression, from two or three price tickets, was that nothing here was likely to be within John's minuscule budget.

'These.' From a perspex container Ash picked up

a pendant and ear-rings made from gilded sand dollars.

'Much too expensive,' said Christie firmly.

'Not expensive at all,' countered Ash. 'What do you say, John?'

'It's pretty,' said the little boy, as his uncle swung the pendant by its chain. 'Mummy has one like that. Where is Mummy?'

Their glances met over his head: Christie's grey eyes distressed, appealing to Ash to help her in a dilemma which, although she had been prepared for it, she still didn't know how to handle.

SEVEN

Ash went down on his haunches, still gently swinging the sand dollar.

'Mummy and Daddy have had to go away, John But they know that however long they're gone, you'l be quite all right with Aunt Christie and me, so they don't have to worry about you. And even though the houses here don't have chimneypots, Father Christmas will come just as usual. He'll come in the middle of the night. When you wake up tomorrow morning it will be Christmas Day and your presents will be or your bed.'

He straightened. 'We'll have these please. Could you gift-wrap them for us?'

Intent on the child's reaction to the answer giver by his uncle, Christie was only vaguely aware of the words he addressed to the woman in charge of the shop.

She knew she could never have matched the level matter-of-fact tone in which he had spoken to John Her own voice would have been unsteady, so that whatever she had said, an awareness of some terrible happening would have been communicated to him disturbing his sense of security which somehow almost miraculously, had so far remained intact.

While the jewellery was being boxed and wrapped, the boy's attention wandered to the things or display. Suddenly, in the way of very young children, he edged closer to his uncle and put his hand on his leg. Ash glanced down and took the small, still-plump hand in his own.

Behind them, Christie looked from the tiny figure to the tall one, and found herself deeply moved by the contrast between child and man; the vulnerability of the one, and the strength and confiden e of the other. Was there any situation in life which Ash would not be able to cope with? She found it impossible to imagine one.

'We're going back a different way, up Fig Tree Hill which is the only part of Antigua with the sort of rain forest vegetation you find on the islands farther south,' he said, as they climbed in the car. 'But don't expect fig trees. Fig is the island name for a banana. In the French-speaking islands, dessert bananas are known as *figues* as distinct from the plantain called *banane*.'

'Have you been to all the other islands?' asked Christie.

'Not all. Most of them.'

Not far beyond the village of Old Road, they passed two small boys riding donkeys accompanied by a baby donkey. Ash braked to let John have a good look, then in a low gear drove slowly up the steep hill, pointing out to Christie the massive silk cotton and breadfruit trees, the thickets of bamboo fern, and the trees of the mango, lime and soursop.

'I hope you won't mind spending Christmas Eve on your own,' he said, on the last lap of the drive. 'I have an engagement I can't break, and in which I

can't include you. But I think you'll find a friendl-
atmosphere in the bar at the Colony tonight if yo
want to keep John up a little later than usual.'

'What time do you want us to be ready tomorrow?

'About eleven will be early enough.'

It wasn't until John was soundly asleep tha
Christie investigated the contents of the large carrie
bag which Ash had locked in his boot. He ha
handed it over with the flicker of a wink and n
comment, from which she had guessed it containe
some parcels for John to open with his stocking in th
morning.

Each parcel was Christmas-tagged, with the boy'
name written on the tag in clear black capital letters
But the soft-feeling parcel at the bottom was not fo
John. It had her name in a neat script in the space o
the label.

What had he chosen for her? she wondered. It wa
obviously something made of fabric. Perhaps
might be a beach sarong, or maybe one of thos
colourful cover-ups she had seen in the Sea Islan
Cotton Shop.

After several minutes of striving to contain he
curiosity, she gave up the struggle and opened th
present. What it was was not instantly apparen
except that it was black and white, and interleave
with much tissue.

Christie shook it out and held it up. As the piece
of tissue floated free, so did a folded sheet of paper o
which, as it reached the floor, she could see lines o
writing.

Tossing the mysterious mass of material on to

chair, she snatched up the paper, and read—*It appears unlikely that you will have packed a dress for the dancing tomorrow night. This seems your style, and is guaranteed to fit. It also doubles as a skirt. Happy Christmas. A.*

She picked up the fabric a second time. Before she had been holding it by the hem, she discovered. Knowing now that it was a dress, it didn't take long to find the right way of it.

And such a dress! She had never possessed anything like it, not even among the trousseau of pretty clothes she had taken with her to Guernsey on her honeymoon.

A voluminous swirl of pure silk, the dress which Ash had selected for her was cut in three tiers, the top one gathered by a double row of elastic, and the bottom one narrowly hemmed. The white flowers and leaves of the pattern were wax-printed on the thin silk. The effect was of moonflowers reflected at midnight in a pool lightly stirred by a breeze.

Quickly shedding all but her briefs, she lifted it over her head and wriggled it into position with the gathered top under her arms. Only then did she find that it had narrow strings of self-fabric to be tied in bows on her shoulders.

What luck that the shoes she had bought were slender-heeled black kid sandals, intended to go with the white dress she would have to have worn but for this one.

It also doubles as a skirt. She undid the bows and transferred the top to her waist. Yes, with a black or white silk shirt, and perhaps a black velvet belt, it would make an equally attractive long skirt.

Looking down at herself, now naked from the waist up, she wondered if there might be somewhere at Heron's Sound where she would be able to brown herself from top to toe instead of still having pale patches.

She was glad Ash had referred to her breasts instead of using Mike's slang terms. She had never told her husband how much she disliked the words he used, with their subtly derogatory undertones. Perhaps it would have been better if she had. She seemed to remember reading somewhere that it was the small trivial pinpricks, the unspoken minor irritations which were the cause of most break-ups.

It was only when she took the dress off that she noticed the swing-tag, a slip of pasteboard decorated with a drawing of two palms with a building and four boats in the background. Beneath the drawing was *The Galley Boutique, Nelson's Dockyard, Antigua W.I.* The style of the dress was Stephany, but the price had been carefully crossed out.

How much had it cost him? she wondered. It was unquestionably silk; the fragile, diaphanous, floating silk of some Indian saris.

Now, whatever anyone else wore, even the rich Mill Reefers, she couldn't feel out of place, a sparrow among the hummingbirds.

The next morning, for the first time in years, Christie woke in a mood she had almost forgotten. This was how she had felt at eighteen—carefree, confident, eager to jump out of bed and begin an exciting day.

John, far from waking at first light, as Ash had precast, was still asleep. Longing to see him open his presents, she kissed him awake.

'Happy Christmas, darling.'

For a few moments he remained sleepy. Then he saw his stocking hanging from the chair she had placed at the end of the divan. Instantly, he shot up like a jack-in-the-box, his eyes large with anticipation.

When Ash arrived shortly before eleven, they were ready to go. Earlier Christie had told John to be sure to thank his uncle for his present as soon as he saw him. The child needed no second prompting. He had already tried out the inflatable green and yellow crocodile, and had loved perching on its back with Christie pushing it from behind. It wouldn't be long before he could paddle it unaided.

'And thank you for the lovely dress, Ash. It's stunning . . . terribly generous of you,' she said, when her turn came. 'This is a very small present from John and me.'

He unwrapped the Liberty silk scarf which had been the only thing she could think of to buy for a man she scarcely knew, whose way of life was unknown territory to her in every sense. Because he had seemed to like blue—a navy silk dressing gown, a sky blue cotton shirt—she had chosen a scarf with a paisley design outlined in navy on a silver-grey ground.

Whether he really liked it was impossible to tell. He gave every appearance of being pleased.

The drive to the Hathaways' house took about half

an hour. Christie was wearing separates she had bought in a sale at one of the Jaeger shops two years before. But like most of their clothes, the button-through cotton skirt and the voile shirt printed to match had not dated. The colours were black and cream which had looked rather dull on her in England but now, with her tan, had a new chic. Also she had left the two bottom buttons unfastened. She told herself this was because, when it was known she was going to do up Heron's Sound, she didn't want the word to go round that she had no sense of style.

While in the scent shop the day before, she had indulged herself with bottles of Madame Rochas talc and body cream. The cream gave her brown skin a silky sheen, and she looked with satisfaction at her legs and feet in the new black sandals. Probably she would be the only woman there with unpainted toenails, but at least her toes were straight and unblemished.

The Hathaways' front door was hung with a Caribbean adaptation of a Christmas wreath, made with glossy green leaves and scarlet hibiscus. Ash pressed the bell, and a few moments later the door was opened by a man almost as tall as himself, but about thirty years older, with steel grey hair and piercing blue eyes behind horn-rimmed spectacles.

'Ash, my dear fellow—welcome!'

Their host gave him a hearty handshake, then turned to Christie, his shrewd eyes making a swift ten-second assessment as he put out both hands to enfold hers between his large palms.

'Mrs Chapman—a very merry Christmas to you.

May I be permitted to use your unusual and charming given name? Your parents were admirers of Bunyan's great work, *Pilgrim's Progess*, I presume?'

'Merry Christmas. With pleasure. My father was,' she agreed, smiling. 'But it's not read a great deal nowadays, so very few people recognise the source.'

'I would probably not have myself, except that I'm currently engaged on a ten-year reading programme which will cover all the greatest works of literature. I spend a great part of my life in airports and aeroplanes, and I use that time for what I call mental jogging. More people should do it. No sense in keeping the body in trim and letting the mind go to seed.'

His accent, so Ash told her later, was that of a Bostonian. But his wife being English, he had incorporated many British turns of phrase into his speech.

He offered his hand to the child. 'Hi, John. Father Christmas made a double delivery for you last night. There's a big package with your name on it beneath the tree in our living-room.'

He ushered them into a wide hall opening into a very large room on several levels. The whole of one side was made of sliding sheets of glass, most of them doubled to leave large open spaces. Through this enormous window, perhaps sixty or seventy feet long, could be seen a beautiful garden descending in terraces to the beach.

A small blonde woman, perhaps in her early fifties, wearing a fuchsia pink housecoat, appeared.

'Ash, darling! Happy Christmas.' She lifted her

arms invitingly, and he bent to give her a hug and
kiss her on both cheeks.

Like her husband, Miranda Hathaway greeted
Christie and John with great warmth. Indeed, all
that happy day, and in spite of about thirty other
guests to attend to, she felt they were keeping a
special watch over her, so that not even for a few
minutes should she feel a stranger at a party where
everyone else knew each other.

At first John was shy of the other children, whose
ages ranged from two to fourteen. Then a little girl of
seven took him under her wing. Christie continued to
keep an eye on him, but she was amused to notice
that Susie's manner towards him was as protective
as that of a fussy elderly nanny.

Until a light lunch was served about two o'clock,
the festivities centred round the pool. A number of
people had only just arrived from England and had
to cover-up between swims. Christie was glad she
had passed that stage and, still liberally sun-
creamed, could stay in the sun without danger.
Although in fact most of the chairs and loungers
round the pool were semi-shaded by the gently
rustling fronds of the palms surrounding the paved
area.

Ash came to exchange a few words with her from
time to time, but mostly he chatted to the other men.
The only women he paid much attention to were his
hostess and Bettina Long, a greyhound-slender
figure in a white bikini.

That night John was put to bed in a room which
had been specially designed to accommodate the

Hathaways' grandchildren. It had twelve built-in pinewood bunks. Tired out with activity and excitement, John was already half asleep when Christie kissed him goodnight. Above him Susie was also in bed, but with a book to read.

'I'll come and tell you if he wakes up and cries, Mrs Chapman.'

'That's kind of you, Susie. Thank you. But I don't think he will—he's exhausted. Goodnight.' Christie blew her a kiss, and departed to change for the evening.

She had been given a single room with its own shower room, but Miranda had asked her if, for changing purposes, she would mind sharing it with two other girls who were not house guests.

Christie had had her shower, and dried her hair with the dryer which belonged to the pretty cool blue and white bedroom before the other two joined her.

While Mara, from New York, was having her shower, Christie chatted to Kate who worked on a glossy magazine in London. Both were young married women, holidaying with their husbands who were connections of the Hathaways and who were using Ash's room to change in.

'I can guess where that came from,' said Kate, as Christie took her evening dress out of the wardrobe. 'The Galley Boutique, yes?'

'Yes.'

'I thought so. I remember when the woman who runs it was starting with a few bikinis. Now it's crammed with all kinds of super things. It's one of the two best places for clothes on the island.'

'Which is the other?'

'The shop at the Long Bay Hotel which is over on the east coast by Devil's Bridge. The proprietor's wife is an American artist. You'll see her appliqué hangings, signed Laf, in several hotels. I bought a couple of her pen and wash drawings of buildings in St John's for our flat. She also designs very good clothes. I'm wearing one of her dresses tonight.'

From another section of the wardrobe she produced a short scarlet dress of cotton voile splashed with white flowers. It was cut in three tiers of fullness, but not in the same way as Christie's, on which the tiers joined each other. Kate's were separate and flared, not gathered, each one trimmed with a narrow white edging.

'What are you wearing, Mara?' Kate asked as, wrapped in a bath sheet, the American girl joined them.

Mara showed them her green chiffon dress, and then Christie lay on her bed in her bra and briefs—fortunately one of her bras had detachable straps—and watched the other two sharing the wide dressing stool to put on their faces.

'No make-up for you, Christie?' asked Mara.

She hesitated. 'I left it behind. It doesn't matter—I don't wear much.'

'My dear girl, why didn't you say? Use mine. There must be something here which will do in an emergency,' said Kate, indicating her well-stocked make-up case.

'Yes, have a look through mine as well. All my

cosmetics are non-allergic, if you have that problem,' said Mara.

Wondering what had possessed her to distort the truth—it had not been a lie: she had left some unused cosmetics in London—Christie accepted their invitation to select from their joint resources.

It felt strange to be painting her face again; using an eye-shadow and mascara from Kate's box, and one of Mara's lipsticks. Her skin needed no embellishment. Always fine and clear, it now had the best of all cosmetics, a light but glowing tan.

But when she put on the black dress her mounting excitement ebbed suddenly.

'Oh . . . I hadn't realised how transparent it is. It needs a slip, and I haven't got one,' she wailed. Last night she had not seen the dress in a full-length mirror with the light behind her.

'Don't be silly: it's *supposed* to be see-through. And what have you got to hide? Not a bulge anywhere, lucky creature,' said Kate. 'It doesn't show anything that all the men haven't seen already when you were in your bikini.'

'Except that somehow veiled glimpses always look a hell of a lot sexier than a clear view,' said Mara with a twinkle. 'It's a pretty dress on the hanger. With you inside it, it's a knock-out,' she added generously.

Christie gazed uncertainly at her reflection. Had Ash realised how revealing the dress was when he had bought it for her? Perhaps not, but if he had she was damned if she'd let him know thàt she was selfconscious. With a resolute lift of her chin, she

fastened the golden sand dollars in her ears, and the
necklace round her throat.

'Hey! What about scent? You must have some
scent on,' exclaimed Katy. 'Try some of this. It's a
classic which suits everybody.' She offered a bottle of
Blue Grass.

When all three were ready, they left the bedroom
together, but whereas the other two went directly to
the living-room, Christie went to look in on the
children.

Several more had joined John and Susie, and a
good deal of noise was going on, but her nephew was
soundly asleep.

'You do look pretty tonight, Mrs Chapman,' said
Susie admiringly.

Half way back to the living-room, Christie caught
sight of herself in a mirror, and she knew that she did
look quite different from her everyday self.

A soft blend of olive green and silver eye-shadows,
and brown mascara, made her eyes look larger and
more sparkling. The curves of her mouth were accentuated by the apricot-rose lipstick, and altogether
she had a lit-up-inside look about her.

A record of West Indian steel band music was
playing when she reached the living-room where
most of the men and a few women had already
foregathered.

A few men were wearing white dinner jackets, but
most were informally dressed. Ash, instantly noticeable as the tallest among them, had on his grey linen
suit with the Liberty scarf knotted casually inside the
collar.

As Christie approached the two or three steps leading down to the lowest level, her host came to meet her.

'Perhaps you haven't noticed, but we now have a bunch of mistletoe—not plastic, please note. The real stuff, flown in from England—strategically placed right above you. And I propose to kiss every one of the pretty women here tonight,' he added, bending to brush a light kiss on her smiling cheek.

'And here's Ash to enjoy the same privilege,' he added, stepping to one side as the younger man joined them.

'Good evening, Christiana.' Ash gave a slight bow, his dark eyes gleaming appreciatively as he looked her up and down.

Stepping closer, he bent and, instead of kissing her cheek as Joss Hathaway had, put his lips to her startled mouth.

It was such a brief kiss that, to anyone looking on, it must have seemed merely a playful Christmas Night salute of no special significance.

But to Christie, unkissed for four years, the warm, soft pressure of a man's lips—particularly his—was a profoundly sensuous experience. As before, in his arms on the beach below Heron's Sound, she felt a vibration of her nerve ends, a deep inner trembling.

He smiled down into her dazed eyes, a flicker of devilment in his own.

'Come and have something to drink—a restorative after that shock,' he added in an undertone which, Joss having already moved away, no one else heard.

She allowed him to take her by the elbow and lead her to a garlanded table where, from a large silver bowl, one of the Hathaways' staff was dispensing the traditional rum punch, except that here it was chilled instead of mulled.

'You look as beautiful as I knew you could if you made the most of yourself,' Ash murmured, as she took the glass offered to her.

Christie smiled at the butler, and said, 'Thank you. Merry Christmas,' before returning what she hoped was a composed 'Thank you' for the compliment.

'No problems bedding John down?'

'No, he's out like a light, but I'll peep in from time to time.'

They were joined by Mara and her husband, and all four walked out on to the terrace to look at the lanternlit gardens and the silver sea.

At half past eight dinner was served at tables for groups of six. Like the large artificial silver Christmas tree hung with pale pink and crimson baubles, the tables were laid with pink cloths and crimson napkins, with arrangements of crimson flowers amid silver-grey foliage, handsome sterling silver and crystal wine glasses.

To her surprise Christie found herself seated opposite Ash, with Bettina at another table. The tables being round and the groups small, conversation was sometimes general, sometimes with neighbours. A good deal of her attention was occupied by the man on her right, a surgeon whose relaxation was sailing.

He was both personable and amusing, and separated from his wife. When he learned that she was a widow, he became even more attentive. He was staying at The Admiral's Inn, sailing all day and hoping, she guessed, to find a feminine companion to share his evenings.

From time to time she was aware of being watched by Ash. His expression gave nothing away, but she wondered if he might be displeased at seeing someone else trying to charm her. Without analysing her motive, she was more forthcoming with Ian, the surgeon, than she would have been had Ash been seated elsewhere.

After dinner, the dancing began. She danced with Ian twice, then with Joss, then with Kate's husband, then with Ian again. She wondered when Ash would dance with her. He would surely do so at least once.

After three successive dances, Ian suggested a stroll round the garden. Their last dance had been a slow number, and he had held her too close for her liking.

She smiled, and said, 'I'm afraid you'll have to excuse me for a few minutes, Ian. I have to go and check on my nephew.'

'Don't be long. I'll be waiting for you.'

As she hurried away, Christie regretted her foolishness in giving him the impression that her attitude to him was the same as his to her.

All was silence in the darkened children's room. Not wanting to return to the party immediately, she sought a few minutes' sanctuary in her own room.

Had she switched on the light, what followed

might never have happened. But the moonlight was flooding in, and she sank down into the armchair next to the window to enjoy five minutes of solitude. And also to consider how, without being ungracious, she could make it clear that she was not in the market for a holiday affair.

'A delicious meal, but hideously fattening, I'm afraid,' said a woman's voice, somewhere close by. 'What a bore it is, never being able to feast without having to fast the next day.'

Leaning forward to peer round the open curtain, Christie saw a man and a woman having a quiet cigarette on the low wall surrounding the neam tree in the centre of the small lawn outside her window.

'Yes, it is,' agreed the man. 'But I'm playing golf with George tomorrow, so that should work off some blubber.'

As their conversation was not of a private nature, Christie relaxed. Preoccupied with her own problem, she only half-heard their next remarks.

Then a question, put by the man, regained her attention.

'What do you think of young Lambard's gorgeous new chick?'

'You mean the girl in black, with the huge grey eyes? Oh, she's not one of his chicks, Bill. I was told about her at dinner. Her brother was married to his sister, or maybe the other way round. Anyway, they were killed in a car smash. This girl has brought out the son, the little fair-haired boy. Ash is going to look after him, apparently, but she's going back to England early in the New Year.'

Christie heard a fruity male chuckle. 'That gives him plenty of time to become more than friends with her.'

'I don't think he has that in mind. He's still involved with Bettina as far as I know . . . unless that affair's over now. I did wonder why Miranda had put them at separate tables.'

'You weren't sitting where I was, Joanie. I had a good view of both Lambard and the girl in black. Believe me, she's in his sights, even if she doesn't know it yet. Can't say I blame him. She's a stunner— a much cosier armful that that skinny giraffe, Bettina. I wonder if she knows she's become redundant. Don't think she can, judging by the sultry looks she was giving him earlier today. Still, any woman who tangles with Lambard is bound to be jettisoned sooner or later.'

'Bettina won't be heartbroken if he has ditched her. What she really wants is a rich, indulgent older man. It was just sex between her and Ash—if you're right, and he really has dropped her. Oh, listen . . . isn't that *My Way*? Let's go and dance . . . work off some Christmas pudding.'

The couple strolled back to the party, their voices fading.

For a few minutes more Christie stayed sitting still in the moonlight. Then she switched on the dressing table lights, and began to repaint her mouth. She found that her hand was trembling slightly. She had to rest her elbow on the table to draw a clean line.

When she returned to the party, she did so

cautiously, on the look-out for Ian whom she wanted to avoid if possible.

'My dance, I think, Christiana,' a voice said, making her jump.

She turned and looked up at Ash. For a man at a Christmas party, his expression was curiously grim. Without waiting for her assent, he swept her into his arms and propelled her on to the dance floor.

EIGHT

THEY danced in silence.

Ash held her close, his hand warm on the small of her back through the delicate silk. She could feel the hardness of his thighs, the solidity of his broad shoulder under her palm.

He made her conscious that, young and fit as she was, her strength was puny compared with his. He was a big, powerful man, and at the moment, for a reason she couldn't quite fathom, he seemed to be extremely annoyed with her.

Pressed against him, she could no longer see his expression. But she felt anger pulsing inside him, and her own trembling started again. Only the tight clasp of his left hand stopped her right one from shaking.

The slow music ended. There was a short pause before a livelier number began. But by that time Ash, with a vice-like grip on her upper arm, was steering her away from the lights and voices and music, into the moon-dappled shadows of the garden.

It was more extensive than she had realised, and they were far away from the party before he let go of her.

He said curtly, 'I thought you didn't care for men who took it for granted that every young widow must be sex-starved.'

Christie didn't pretend to misunderstand him. 'I don't think Ian is one of those. He was merely doing his duty as a guest, and making an effort to be entertaining.'

'He's on holiday by himself. The Hathaways fell into conversation with him the other night at The Admiral's Inn, found he was alone, and invited him here today out of kindness. Of course he's looking for a woman. No man without one of his own is averse to some no-strings sex to complete his holiday.'

'Perhaps you shouldn't assume that everyone is like you, Ash,' she answered coolly.

'You know the saying—It takes one to know one. Anyway, even if his interest in you were not of that nature, he's years too old for you. Forty-five if he's a day.'

'You surely don't imagine that, on the strength of sitting next to a man at dinner, I'm in danger of losing my head over him. How ridiculous!' she expostulated.

'The moment when a butterfly breaks out of the chrysalis and spreads its wings for the first time is precisely the moment when it's most in danger of being snapped up by a predator,' he told her dryly.

'In that case, it's highly imprudent to be out here with you,' she retorted. 'Of all the bare-faced predators, you must be the—' She broke off, regretting the quick flare of indignation.

'You've been listening to gossip, Christiana.' His response was as cool as hers had been heated. 'I've never done anything to you to justify that statement.

One light Christmas kiss under the mistletoe hardly constitutes a pass, would you say? Unless its effect was more potent than I had intended.'

He knew, she thought furiously. He knew what that brief kiss had done to her.

'Come, let's not quarrel, tonight of all nights. It's supposed to be the season of goodwill. If I'm prepared to accept that your intention was not to lead the man on but merely to make him feel liked, perhaps you can accept that my motive was, for once, a desire to protect.'

'Very well, I accept that,' she answered him, in a low tone.

'Good. Then I suggest that we rejoin the others and dance again.'

His gesture invited her to precede him along the path by which they had come.

She hesitated. 'In a moment. First there's something I think I should tell you. I—I've decided to accept your offer, Ash. I know you gave me until New Year's Eve to make up my mind. But as it's made up already, there seems no point in delaying. I should like to stay in Antigua and help you to run Heron's Sound.'

He was silent for such a long time that, remembering her letter of resignation airmailed to England and by now received by the Principal, she felt a quiver of panic.

'You . . . you haven't changed your mind, have you?' she asked anxiously.

'No, no—certainly not. But I've been thinking it over, and there is one proviso I must make.'

She gave a small sigh of relief. 'A proviso? What kind of proviso?'

Again he was silent for some moments and, with his back to the moonlight, she could not read his expression.

At length he said quietly, 'I think, for a number of reasons, that if we're going to work together and, at times, live in the same house, it's advisable for us to marry.'

Christie stepped back a pace, as if from a physical blow. For some minutes shock struck her dumb. She couldn't believe she had heard him correctly. That Ash, the island's arch-philanderer, should now be proposing marriage to her—to her, of all people!— was as paralysing as being told that a tidal wave was on its way and would strike Antigua in fifteen minutes.

'You can't be serious,' she said, at last.

'Perfectly serious, I assure you. It's not a spur-of-the-moment suggestion, but something I've thought over carefully. Would you like me to enumerate my reasons?'

'Yes . . . yes, I should. Frankly I think it's the maddest, most outrageous suggestion I've ever had put to me!'

Ash folded his arms across his chest. 'It's clear from your earlier remark about my predatory tendencies that you've heard various things which don't redound to my credit. Probably grossly exaggerated, but not without an element of truth. At any rate my reputation is such that no young and attractive woman can associate with me without some people concluding that our relationship is far from platonic. Were we both to sleep at Heron's Sound, with only the staff to chaperone us, not many people would believe we'd occupied separate bedrooms. I don't wish that kind of gossip to attach to you.'

He paused, his dark eyes unfathomable in the deeper shadow cast by his frowning brows.

'Not only for your sake,' he went on, 'but also for John's. He's going to grow up here. I don't want him to overhear slighting remarks about us such as I heard about my father when he married a much younger woman. The knowledge that one's parents are held in contempt by other people can be very wounding to a child. We stand *in loco parentis* to John, you and I. You've decided to stay here and run the house which I regard as my home. It's the logical course of action to regularise the situation.'

'But we're almost strangers!' Christie expostulated. 'Do you realise it's less than a month since we first laid eyes on each other?'

'A valid objection in the case of a youthful infatuation. But I'm not a boy, nor are you a green girl,' Ash reminded her. 'We are both mature, experienced people, capable of making sensible judgments based on practical considerations rather than overheated emotions. I feel the most important factor is that John is going to depend on us for at least the next fourteen years. So from that point of view our lives will be linked anyway.'

'Linked—yes. But what you're suggesting is a legal bond, a life contract. And surely that, without love, could become more like a life sentence?'

Ash shrugged. 'In other periods of history, love was something which developed after marriage—or found expression in discreet extra-marital relationships. Marriage was an essentially practical institution. It's only comparatively recently that people have been brainwashed into believing it must begin with both parties up in the clouds—even if they crash-land in the divorce courts a few years afterwards.'

The warm night wind blew a silky strand of Christie's hair across her cheek. She put up her fingers to stroke it back into place.

She said, 'But although those marriages by arrangement sometimes worked out well, we know from memoirs and biographies that some were intolerably wretched. Not everyone can come to terms with being married to someone they find . . . intensely incompatible.'

'Not everyone, no,' he agreed. 'But when you speak of incompatibility, are you thinking chiefly of the physical side of marriage?'

'Yes . . . yes, I was,' she admitted.

'And does that apply in our case? Do you find me repulsive, Christiana?'

'No, not repulsive—of course not! It's just . . . oh, you don't understand.'

'Then explain to me,' was his suggestion.

She glanced uneasily round them. There seemed to be no one about, but who knew where their voices might carry.

'I—I would rather not discuss it here. Just a short

while ago I couldn't help overhearing a conversation which wasn't meant for my ears. Can't we talk about it some other time?'

'I would rather we thrashed it out now. We'll walk on the beach, on the hard sand. We can leave our shoes on the steps. This way.'

He took her hand and led her further along the path until they came to a staircase which led down to the beach.

'What was this conversation you shouldn't have heard?' he enquired at the foot of the flight.

'Nothing sensational. But the people were discussing some others in a way which they wouldn't have done had they realised there was an unwilling eavesdropper near.'

Ash did not press her for details, but took a clean handkerchief from his pocket and spread it on the third step up. 'Sit on that and I'll take off your sandals.'

Christie obeyed, and with surprising dexterity he released the straps from the little gilt buckles. He must have done it before for some other woman. Probably he was adept at undoing all the fastenings on women's clothing from zippers to snap-clips on bras.

She found herself wondering how many women he had made love to since being caught with the assistant matron while still a schoolboy. Dozens, probably. He knew so much about her sex, and she, in spite of being married, so little of his.

Having placed her sandals side by side, he removed his own lightweight black slip-ons of well-polished leather, and his socks of pale-coloured silk.

'I feel overdressed for a beach walk. You don't mind if I peel off a bit?'

'Not at all. It's a very warm night.' She averted her gaze, but was aware of him loosening the scarf she had given him, and then unbuttoning his jacket. Having folded and placed them by her sandals, he said, 'Okay, let's go.'

They crossed the stretch of yielding sand between the back of the beach and the firmer part by the water.

Reluctant to return to the subject they had been discussing, Christie said, 'It must be nice, swimming by moonlight.'

'But not always advisable. Such accidents as have occurred have generally happened at night. But I daresay some people here will have a dip in the pool before the night's out. The only hazards there are insects.'

They were walking into the breeze. It moulded her dress to her body and lifted her hair off her neck.

'How warm the wind always is here,' she remarked. 'I expect it's perishing in England.'

'Enough of this weather talk, Christiana,' he said dryly. 'We're well out of earshot down here. What was it you were going to explain to me? That I wasn't repulsive to you, but . . . Go on from there.'

She swallowed and took a deep breath, bracing herself for the effort of saying what must be said in the face of his extraordinary proposal.

'But I can never marry anyone because . . . because, however attractive a man is, I don't want that close relationship with him. I . . . I suppose you would call me a born celibate.'

He was strolling along with his hands in the pockets of his trousers. Her admission didn't make him alter his pace. Nor did he glance at her.

'I see,' he said calmly. 'I wondered if that might be the explanation. You didn't discover this until after you were married, presumably?'

'No, or I should never have married. It lasted such a short time that Mike never found out. It would have been terrible if he had.'

'It must have been bad as things were—for you,' he said shrewdly.

'It wasn't . . . easy,' she admitted.

'Either you must be an excellent actress, or your husband must have been remarkably unobservant. I should know if a women in my bed was gritting her teeth.'

His sardonic tone made her say, 'Mike hadn't your vast experience. I suppose he had had other girls, but not very many. He wasn't much older than I, and he went in for sport, not womanising.'

'Has it ever occurred to you that you might have had a more satisfactory relationship with someone of your own sex?'

'Oh, no—no, never!' she exclaimed vehemently. 'There was a woman at school once who confided that she . . . who thought I . . . but no, I know I should find that equally unacceptable.'

'So now you've got off your chest what I'd suspected all along,' he remarked, in an equable tone. 'But I don't see it as an insuperable obstacle to a marriage between us. I told you I should like a son, and I find John an adequate substitute. As for my other needs, I've had no problems up to now, and expect to have none in future. I should have to be a good deal more circumspect, but that's not impossible.'

'You're suggesting that we should marry and you should go on . . . having mistresses?'

'Why should you mind? If you don't want to sleep with me? Jealousy springs from possessiveness, and you and I would not possess each other. Ours would be a marriage of companionship and shared endeavours. I think it could work out splendidly. If, after a time, you decided you wanted more children, it might be possible to achieve that by scientific means rather than the usual ones.'

He stopped walking and turned to face her, his bare chest and shoulders like sculpted bronze in the moonlight.

'People aren't all of a piece. We don't have to conform to a pattern laid down by others. Nowadays anything goes. Men live together. Women live together. Men and women live together and few people think less of them because they don't have official permission to do so. Live and let live is the new watchword. If what I'm suggesting suits us, we shouldn't be influenced by what anyone else might think of our arrangement. If they knew, which of course they wouldn't.'

'I don't know, Ash . . I don't know,' Christie murmured, in helpless confusion. 'It seems so cold-blooded . . . unnatural.'

'There's nothing cold-blooded about friendship. That's what it would be—a close friendship.'

He took her slim hands and held them firmly in his. 'If you have some doubts about throwing in your lot with a charter skipper, you needn't worry about my solvency. I've worked hard and made a lot of money, and Antigua is a place where a man can keep most of what he earns. Also, some years ago I took the advice of a knowledgeable passenger—the only advice worth having is from people who are rich themselves—and invested my funds in Mexico, at a very favourable rate of interest. If you marry me, we shall have a joint bank account, and joint title to all my assets.'

'I'm not concerned about those things. I have my own career to fall back on. It's the personal side which disturbs me. May I . . . may I ask you something very personal?'

'Go ahead. People who are contemplating marriage should be able to discuss anything and everything with each other.'

'Are you and Bettina Long lovers?'

'We were at one time,' he answered. 'Not since I came back from London.'

'You haven't stayed at her cottage since John and I came to the Colony?'

'No, I haven't. What made you think so?'

'That first morning we met on the beach. I assumed you'd spent the night with her.'

'Did you indeed? Did that supposition account for the coolness I detected in your manner?'

'Not entirely. You made me nervous—you still do

at times. I suspect that you do it deliberately.'

'Such as kissing you tonight under the misletoe? But I didn't know then that you disliked physical contacts. Do you find even this unpleasant?'—swinging her hands to and fro.

'No, I don't mind being touched in a friendly way. I don't even dislike being kissed. If I had I should never have reached the point of getting married.'

'It's when the kissing leads on to other caresses that you take fright and freeze—is that it?'

There was no derision in his voice. His tone reminded her of the detached kindliness with which doctors questioned patients about symptoms.

'Yes, that's it,' she said, very low, avoiding his eyes and fixing her gaze on his chest.

He was not as hairy as her husband. Mike had had a thick mat of coarse curls all over his chest and stomach. In spite of playing rugger every Saturday, he had also had the beginning of a beer-drinker's belly.

There was little or no hair on Ash's chest, and none on his flat hard midriff. His only visible body hair was on his sinewy forearms and long muscular legs.

He said, 'I take it there's nothing in your background which could account for your aversion? You were never frightened as a child? You didn't find out about sex in an offputting way?'

'No, never . . . there was nothing like that. My mother gave me a book which made it sound rather peculiar, but not in any way unpleasant.'

'She didn't tell you herself? But that's not so

unusual, I suppose. Do you think your parents were happy together?'

'Yes, very happy. I know that. My father adored her, and missed her for the rest of his life.'

'She died some time before he did?'

'Yes. She'd been a semi-invalid as far back as I can remember, and she died when I was thirteen. He lived without her for seven years, and never considered remarrying although he was very good-looking, and several women we knew would have liked to marry him.'

Ash had let go of her hands. As they turned back to walk in the direction of the Hathaways' garden, Christie went on, 'I'm sure there's no psychological reason for the way I am. I was born asexual, that's all.'

'It would seem so—yes. It doesn't change anything as far as I'm concerned. You'll make me a very capable and decorative wife, and I'll do my best to be a considerate husband and generous provider.'

'But Ash, supposing that one day you fall in love—really in love. Then you won't want to be tied down to a loveless marriage.'

'In nine cases out of ten, falling in love is a matter of physical desire which quickly wears off once it's satisfied. If I wanted a woman, and she was willing, I should take her. I shouldn't break up my home for her. Haven't you noticed? Men don't.'

'Not very many,' she agreed, thinking of the women she had known who had fallen for men whose wives didn't understand them, but who nevertheless seemed to have an unbreakable hold on them.

'I gave you time to think over my last proposition, and you've made up your mind well in advance of my deadline,' he said, as they reached the stone steps.

'This time I want a quick decision. I'd like to know by tomorrow.'

'Tomorrow!' she gasped. 'But this is a *much* harder decision. I can't make my mind up overnight.'

'Certainly you can. You may not get a lot of sleep, but if I allow you to mull it over for several days, you'll become more uncertain, not less so.'

Ash bent to pick up his coat. Shrugging into it, fastening the buttons, he met her worried grey gaze with a calm, steady look.

'The big decision, Christiana, was to throw up your safe job and stay here. Having made up your mind to that, I'm sure you'll have the courage to take this plunge,' he said casually.

She stepped into her sandals and fastened them while he was replacing his scarf.

'You didn't explain why it ended—your affair with Bettina,' she said.

'For the reason that all such things end. We grew bored with each other.'

You mean you grew bored, was her thought. Aloud, she asked, 'Does she know? That it's over, I mean?'

'Naturally. It ended by mutual consent. We aren't an embarrassment to our friends, like people who break up fighting. Bettina is on the look-out for a rich husband. She makes no bones about it. I was merely a brief diversion,' he added, with a shrug.

But although he made it sound as if the affair had

ended on Bettina's initiative, Christie wasn't convinced of the truth of this. If it were the case, why had the man called Bill remarked on the sultry looks he had seen her throw in Ash's direction?

They walked back through the night-scented garden and, although he was half a pace behind her, his tall shadow stretched ahead of hers on the path.

Several people observed their return—Bettina, Ian Scott, Miranda.

Bettina was sitting between two men who were talking to each other across her. She was smoking and looking bored, until she saw Ash coming back and began to watch her companions, as if whatever they were saying was amusing and included her. Christie felt very sorry for her if, not meaning to, she had lost her heart to Ash and didn't wish to be jettisoned.

Miranda came up to them. She put her arm round Christie's waist. 'You've monopolised her long enough, Ash. Now I want to stroll round the garden with her. We haven't talked properly all day. You can go and peek at your nephew.'

Like her husband with his English idioms, she had adopted some Americanisms.

Ash took his dismissal with a smile, and Miranda said to Christie, 'Let me show you my favourite place in the garden. Or have you already discovered the gazebo Joss had built for my last birthday?'

Christie shook her head, and was taken, with Miranda chatting all the way, to a corner of the grounds where there was a small stone-built tower with a cedar-shingled roof.

The upper part was open on all sides. When they had climbed the staircase to it, Christie found that a cushioned bench ran round three sides of the square, with a table in the centre.

'There are blinds to let down if it's too hot, but the roof is enough shade for me. I come here to write my letters, or to do my needlepoint, or sometimes just to sit and think,' explained Mrs Hathaway.

'Ash and I are very old friends,' she went on, hardly pausing for breath. 'He's one of my favourite people. He's told me a lot about you, including the fact that he wants you to be in charge at Heron's Sound. He must have great confidence in your taste. Are you going to take on the task, or haven't you made up your mind yet?'

'Yes, I am. That's partly what he and I were discussing while we were walking just now.'

'That's wonderful. I'm very glad. It will solve a lot of problems for him to have you remain here.'

'And for me. I was dreading leaving John.' Christie hesitated before asking, 'Why is Ash one of your favourite people, Mrs Hathaway?'

'Call me Miranda, please. Well now, why do I like him? Let's see. I suppose the main reason is that he has the rare combination of a cultivated mind in the body of a man of action. Sailing men can be horribly boring, you know, if they have no interests *but* boats. With Ash one can talk about anything, even women's subjects. He's an excellent cook. Did you know that?'

'Yes, he cooked a meal for me and a friend of mine in London.'

'He was forced to acquire that expertise. You could say that the success of a charter boat depends on the standard of the cuisine. When he started out Ash had to be skipper and crew, chef, bottle-washer, the lot.'

She paused for a moment before continuing, 'I'm attracted to people who love life in all its aspects. Joss is one, and Ash is another.'

'And a lover of women, so I gather?' As soon as she had said it, Christie wished the comment unspoken.

But Miranda smiled, and replied, 'Yes, I can't defend him on that charge. He is rather ruthless with women. But nobody's perfect, I guess, and there is a side to his nature which *I* think more important. Do you know where he spent all last evening?'

Christie shook her head. She had assumed he had spent it with Bettina.

'I do,' said Miranda. 'Not because he himself told me. I learned it from a mutual friend, the doctor who looks after us if ever we have any health problems during our stays here. He told me how, for some time now, Ash has been going to the hospital to see an old seaman from St Lucia who had no relations to visit him. Last night the poor old fellow died. If he'd been alive today, I feel sure Ash would have slipped away for an hour or two. He's like that. He cares about people—provided they're old or young, or middle-aged like myself. It's only bedworthy girls who have to watch out, and nowadays most of them are well able to take care of themselves.'

There was a pause before she added, 'I hope I haven't made you nervous about his intentions towards you. You're a very lovely young woman. I could see that our lonely surgeon, whom I put beside you at dinner, was completely neglecting poor Lucy Grant on his other side. But I don't think you need to worry that Ash will step out of line where you're concerned. Because of the child, you and he have a special relationship, and I feel sure he'll respect that—unless you indicate otherwise. You must find him attractive, don't you?'

Christie said guardedly, 'His height alone makes him striking. I wonder how he came by it. The Greeks aren't noted for their tallness, and he certainly takes after his mother as far as his colouring goes. Perhaps his father was a tall man, although my brother-in-law wasn't.'

'You poor child: that was such a tragedy.' Miranda reached over and squeezed Christie's hand for a moment. Then she said, in her usual bright tone, 'I think we'd better go back now. I shan't be popular if I keep you out of circulation too long.'

Ian waylaid them at the edge of the terrace.

'Will you dance with me, Christie?'

This time she had no excuse. She went with him on to the floor. The music was slow, as it had been the last time they danced, but he did not attempt to hold her close again.

Almost immediately he said, 'I believe I've made rather a fool of myself. I didn't realise during dinner that I was poaching on another man's preserves—and one whom I shouldn't care to get on the wrong side of. He's so much bigger than I am,' he added with a rueful smile.

'What makes you think you were poaching?'

'I saw you dancing together, and disappearing together. I realised it had been too much to expect that such a very attractive young woman would be unattached. You should have put me in my place, but I suppose you're accustomed to every Tom, Dick and Harry making a set at you, and you bear with them kindly—too kindly.'

'I think you exaggerate, Ian. I'm not as attractive as that,' she returned, suspecting him of flattery.

But he sounded in earnest as he said, 'No, I'm serious. If your yachtsman hadn't seen you first, I should have pursued you most vigorously. In spite of the difference in our ages. It's a long time—years— since I last felt so strong an attraction. It's a shame I can't follow it up. I should have enjoyed taking you sailing, and having your charming face on the other side of the table at The Admiral's Inn tomorrow night. However, it isn't to be.'

Christie was taken aback by this seemingly sincere declaration. Ian lacked Ash's physical distinction, being a man of only medium height with thinning brown hair and grey eyes. But he was a leading London surgeon—he had not said so, but she had gathered as much—and sophisticated and witty. She would have been less than human not to be pleased by his admiration.

Later, when he was leaving, he gave her his card and expressed the hope that, when she returned to London, she would ring him up. She had not told him she did not intend to go back.

He left the party at midnight, but it went on much

later and was still in progress at one-fifteen when she slipped away to her room.

Surprisingly she slept almost at once, and awoke at her usual early hour.

Today was the day she had to give Ash her decision—and what an impossible decision. How could she commit her whole future to a man who was still, in many ways, an enigma; and on the extraordinary basis which he had put to her last night?

After a while she threw back the sheet, and sat up and pulled off her nightdress. After brushing her teeth and her hair, she put on her bikini and walked through the gardens to the beach. To her relief, it was deserted. With any luck she would have it to herself for at least an hour. If most of the others had stayed up until two or three, they would not be rising very early. Surprised that she didn't feel more jaded after losing three of her usual eight hours' sleep, she plunged into the clear water, and struck out for a white raft moored about a hundred yards out.

From the raft she had a full view of the whole of the Hathaways' property; the rambling one-storey house with its silver-grey shingled roofs half hidden by palms and other trees, with Miranda's gazebo marking the boundary at one end, and the flight of stone steps at the other. Two Sunfish and a Hobie Cat were beached close to the stone retaining wall, and there was a rack for four windsurfers.

When Christie had asked Miranda why they didn't live at Mill Reef where many of their friends had properties, she had answered that she and Joss had no need to avoid the public eye, and she liked to live on a beach which was shared by the islanders and anyone else who discovered it.

'All my family are mad keen snorkellers. Me, I'm a people-watcher,' she had said, with a laugh. 'I find them far more interesting than fish.'

Her host and hostess certainly had an enviable life style, thought Christie, as she dangled her legs over the edge of the raft and admired the luxuriant cascades of crimson and magenta bougainvillaea along the retaining wall.

A life style which would, in some measure, be hers from now on, whether or not she accepted Ash's offer of marriage.

She was conscious of a sense of relief at having told someone the truth. And how calmly he had received it, as if it were nothing very unusual, and certainly not a disability which made her unacceptable to human beings with normal reactions.

Yet she had kept it a secret even from her own sister; seeing it as something to keep dark, in the same way that, years ago, people who had petit mal had hidden it from public knowledge, and often suffered more from the secrecy than from the affliction itself.

For perhaps as long as half an hour—she did not have her watch on—Christie sat on the raft, thinking over all the reasons Ash had put forward in favour of their marriage.

But balancing the pros and cons brought her no nearer to a decision. Not that she could marshal many reasons for refusing his proposal. Her dubiety was all instinctive. As Ash said, all her life she had been brainwashed into thinking of marriage as the culmination of romantic love. The idea of accepting a husband selected by her parents, or of being one of a man's several wives, was totally anathematic to her. Yet such things had been, and in some parts of the world still were, a normal way of life.

A movement among the trees caught her eye, and a moment later she recognised the tall figure strolling down to the beach. When he reached the sand he must have seen her perched on the raft, but he didn't wave. Nor did she.

She watched him walk into the sea, panic rising inside her. What was she to say? Yes or no?

At waist-depth, Ash flung himself forward and began a fast crawl towards her. At the same time the sun rose higher and the sea took on its daytime brilliance, like jewels with a spotlight turned on them.

'Good morning.'

He grasped the edge of the raft and heaved himself upwards, muscles bunching in his upper arms. The next moment he was seated beside her, the raft swaying beneath them.

'Good morning,' Christie answered, her mouth dry.

He raked back his crisp dark hair. It was typical of him to say, at once, without any preliminaries, 'What's it to be, Christiana?'

'I—' She swallowed, and licked her dry lips. 'It' . . . yes, I will marry you.'

'Good. In that case we'd better go to the cable office first thing tomorrow and get a wire off to the school. Better still, if you know the Head's private address, you can telephone him this morning.'

'Actually I wrote to him several days ago, as soon as I'd made up my mind.'

Now that she had committed herself, she was suddenly amazingly calm.

'Did you indeed? But you thought you'd keep me in suspense?'

'I don't think suspense is something which you often suffer from. I'm sure last night you slept like a log.'

'As I didn't turn in until three a.m. it didn't take me long to drop off.' He studied her face for a moment. 'I don't see any shadows under your eyes. Don't tell me you haven't slept a wink?'

'No, I slept quite well, in the circumstances. Ash, there is just one thing . . .' She hesitated, before adding, 'I do have your word that you won't ever . . . that this will be a marriage of companionship only?'

'I thought that was made clear last night.'

'I'd still like your solemn promise.'

Without hesitation, looking straight into her eyes, he said, 'You have my word, Christiana. I will never do the things you don't like.'

Secure in the feeling that his word was his bond, she began to relax slightly. As she had already discovered with the revelation of her secret last night, it was better to act than to vacillate.

Life was not unlike sea-bathing in England. It was best to dive or run in. To hover uncertainly on the brink was only to prolong the agony.

Here, in the lukewarm seas surrounding Antigua,

it was never necessary to muster one's will power to swim. Perhaps, from now on, in a close but platonic partnership with Ash, her life would proceed more smoothly and pleasurably than it had during her first marriage and widowhood.

'There seems no point in a long engagement,' said Ash. 'I suggest we arrange the wedding as soon as possible. Then, for appearances' sake, we'll go to London for a week or two, ostensibly on honeymoon, but really for you to pack up your flat and to choose the furnishing fabrics you'll want for Heron's Sound. You could buy them in New York, but as the majority of our clientele will be Americans, I think the house should be totally English in atmosphere.'

He stood up, and held out his hand to assist her to her feet. For a moment they stood side by side, adjusting their balance to the rocking motion caused by their movements.

'You'll enjoy that, won't you? Most women seem to enjoy shopping.'

'Yes, I shall love it. But what will you do with yourself? London in January doesn't seem exactly your scene.'

'I shall spend some time trying to unearth the early history of the house, and I'll go round the galleries and buy some more paintings. I've been collecting paintings of schooners for a number of years, but have never had a place to display them. We could do with one very large painting for the drawing-room.'

Ash glanced towards the Hathaways' garden. 'That looks like Miranda and Joss coming down for their pre-breakfast bathe. We may as well break our news to them.'

'Yes, why not?' Christie agreed.

But inwardly she felt a fresh stirring of trepidation. It was going to be difficult, facing the congratulations of people who had no idea of the true nature of their arrangement.

Ash said, 'I see no reason to advertise that our marriage will be different from other people's. The Hathaways are probably watching us. So I'm going to kiss you. But don't worry—it will be the first and last kiss of our engagement.'

He stepped closer, took her face between his hands, and she saw his eyes close as he bent to press his mouth on hers.

At first it seemed like the kiss he had given her under the misletoe. But this one became more prolonged, his mouth moving softly on hers, like someone savouring the taste and texture of a fruit.

There was no contact between their bodies. Only the feel of his palms holding her face still, and that soft, searching movement of his mouth which seemed to go on and on until, not realising it was her own fault for holding her breath, Christie began to feel weak and dizzy, as if she might faint again.

All at once it was over. She could breathe out and gulp fresh air in. As she stood there, dazed and unsteady, Ash turned away and dived into the sea. There was a small splash as his legs disappeared underwater, a moment of turbulence on the surface, and then he was gone and she was alone.

It took only a very few moments for the bobbing

raft to stabilise; much longer for Christie's disturbed emotions to quiesce.

She was conscious of curious sensations; of a strange pain deep inside her, of trembling thighs and tingling breasts, of the skin on all parts of her body feeling suddenly intensely sensitive. As for her face, she could still feel the pressure of his hands, and the toothpaste freshness of his lips trying to coax her to open her closed ones.

But perhaps that was not actually so; it could have been merely that he had kissed her in the manner of an experienced man, not deliberately trying to be invasive, but seeming to be because of her own inexperience.

Four years was a long time to live untouched and inviolate. She was almost like a virgin again, and an old-fashioned virgin at that; one who dreaded and shrank from the pain of being made a woman.

NINE

'Christie! Christie . . . come here!'

The halloo from the beach was Miranda, beckoning excitedly. Ash was talking to Joss.

With an effort, Christie pulled herself together. She dived off the raft and swam, but less vigorously than he had, towards the group on the sand.

'Christie, you sly puss! I bet you knew this last night, and you never breathed a word. Well, I can understand that. You want to hug it to yourself for a while before the world knows. Oh, I'm so . . . so . . . so *deeply* delighted. Let me give you a big hug, you sweet thing!'

Rushing into the shallows to meet her, Miranda embraced her most warmly.

'And a kiss from me, my dear girl. This is great news. Couldn't be better.' Joss, wearing a thick towelling bathrobe, gave her an even more vigorous hug.

'As a matter of fact Miranda and I thought that Ash might have met his match yesterday. "If he doesn't snap her up," I said, "he's a bigger fool than I take him for".'

'You're very kind,' Christie said, blushing. 'I—I think I'm the lucky one.'

'You're both lucky. Everyone's lucky when they're young and in love, with a wonderful future ahead of them,' said Miranda, beaming. 'In fact, if you want to know the truth, it's marvellous, even at fifty, when you meet the right man at long last, and know that you haven't missed out on the best thing in life after all.'

She gave Joss a loving look, then clapped her hands, and exclaimed, 'This calls for champagne! Come on, darlings.'

But as she would have led them up to the house, Ash stopped her by saying, 'There'll be plenty of time for a champagne breakfast when you and Joss have had your swim, Miranda. Right now I have something I want to give Christiana. We'll join you on the terrace in half an hour.'

'Yes—all right. That'll be lovely,' their hostess agreed.

Christie went with him up to the garden where she said, 'Have you really something to give me, or was that a pretext to cut short Miranda's somewhat embarrassing enthusiasm?'

'I don't think you need feel embarrassed. We *have* a good future ahead of us, if not the romantic idyll which Miranda envisages. Certainly I have something for you. An engagement ring.'

'Oh, but that isn't necessary. I mean, if we're going to be married almost immediately, a wedding ring is perfectly adequate.'

'Not for my wife.'

'But, Ash, you need all your money to spend on the house. If you have a ring in your room you must have been totally confident that I would fall in with your plans.'

'I'm always confident that my plans will work out successfully, and they always have,' he said smoothly. 'Go and get ready for breakfast. I'll come to your room in fifteen minutes.'

'Do you know where it is?'

'Yes, I made a point of finding out yesterday.'

'Really? Why?' she asked, puzzled.

She could think of only one reason for a man to find out where a woman was sleeping. Was it possible that his intention, before she told him the truth about herself, had been to finish the Christmas party in her bed?

'Antigua has earthquakes,' he told her. 'Not very often, and not usually in the tourist season. But even a minor tremor can be terrifying. Just in case of emergencies, I wanted to be able to get to you and John quickly.'

'I see. You're very considerate.' She felt ashamed of her unworthy supposition.

'Being responsible is part of my business,' was his answer, before he walked off.

Christie had rinsed the salt water out of her hair and was dressed when he tapped on her door.

'Come in,' she called from the dressing-table

She was combing her hair and did not turn around. She could see his reflection in the mirror as he entered and closed the door behind him. He had on a pair of white shorts, and a short-sleeved white cotton shirt, unbuttoned.

'St John's is not the place to buy jewellery,' he said, sitting down on the bed immediately behind

her. 'For the moment I'm going to give you a ring of
my mother's. You can choose a permanent ring
while we're in London.'

She swivelled to face him, her heart beating oddly
fast considering he was only going through the mo-
tions of what, for most couples, was a moment of
deeply romantic symbolism.

'Give me your hand.' He had taken the ring from
its case but was keeping it hidden in his right hand.

Christie put out her left hand on which she still
wore her wedding ring, but not her first engagement
ring. She had never liked it. It had been a tiny
diamond on a white gold hoop. It had not been the
smallness of the diamond she had minded. She
would have been happy with a cheaper ring. But
those she preferred—antique rings set with am-
ethysts, or garnets, or turquoise—Mike considered
unsuitable. So she had deferred to his taste. After
his death, she had put the ring away and never looked
at it again.

'I think it would be appropriate for you to take
that ring off now, and wear only this for the short
time until we're married,' Ash suggested.

'Yes, of course.' She twisted the wedding ring over
her knuckle. Although her fingers were slim, it left a
slight indentation and a circle of pale skin.

As he replaced it with his ring, she saw a glint of
rich red and the lustre of gold.

'It's beautiful!' she exclaimed, when he took his
hand away. 'Why must I choose something else? Or
would you prefer that I didn't wear this ring permanently?'

'It's up to you. If you like it, by all means wear it. I thought you might think it too heavy.'

It was indeed a large ring; a ruby cut in an oval and held between eight points of gold. The top of the jewel was hollowed and embellished by a minute spray of flowers and leaves in gold embedded with diamond chips. The bezel was beautifully chased. Christie turned her hand this way and that, admiring the blood-red gleam, so different from the icy glitter of her first ring.

'I like it very much. Thank you. I promise to take the greatest care of it.'

'You have beautiful hands,' he remarked. 'They're more like the hands of a dancer than of a domestic science teacher. I'm glad you don't paint your nails, or grow them too long. Now about the wedding. Are you content to let me arrange it at the earliest possible moment, so that we can get to grips with our project with a minimum of delay?'

'Yes . . . yes, by all means,' she answered. 'I wonder if John is awake yet?'

'Let's go and see. If he is, he can join us for breakfast.'

John was not only awake. He was dressed and, with Susie, was playing ball outside the children's room.

'I helped him to wash his face and hands, and brush his teeth, Mrs Chapman,' she announced importantly.

Ash scooped up John by his armpits and swung him high in the air. There he twirled him around so the child could sit on his shoulders.

'Aunt Christie isn't going to be Mrs Chapman for much longer,' he told him. 'She's going to marry me and become Mrs Lambard.'

'Mummy's name is Mrs Lambard.'

Christie tensed, but Ash replied evenly, 'That's right, and Daddy's name was Mr Lambard, like mine, because Daddy and I were brothers. Our daddy was your grandfather, and his name was Robert Lambard. When Aunt Christie marries me, we shall all be called Lambard.'

Susie, who had been listening to this with interest, said, 'Could I be your bridesmaid, Mrs Chapman? My cousin Emma has been a bridesmaid three times, but I've never been one, not once.'

'It's nice of you to volunteer, Susie. But it's going to be a very quiet wedding, not the kind where the bride has a bridesmaid.'

'Oh, what a pity. But you'll have a lovely white dress and a veil, won't you?'

'Not this time. I've been married before, you see, and when people have a second wedding they dress rather differently.'

The subject of Christie's wedding dress came up again half an hour later when Miranda asked her if she had given the matter any thought yet.

'No, none.'

'You could get Heike Peterson at the Studio in Church Street to design a dress for you. Or I have an excellent dressmaker—seamstress, they're called here—who would run up something very quickly. For fabrics I think the best shop is Lolita's in Market Street.'

'It depends when the wedding is to be. If it's very soon, I should think I might find something off the peg where my black dress came from. the Galley Shop.'

Later, the Hathaways were taking most of their house guests to a regular Boxing Day event, racing at Cassada Gardens. But Ash opted out of this expedition, saying that he was going to give Christie her first sailing lesson in a Sunfish

Nobody thought it unusual that the newly-engaged couple should prefer to be alone together, with John and some other young children in the care of Miranda's housekeeper

Christie enjoyed her lesson. The Sunfish was a simple craft which John would be able to handle within a few years, and Ash was a relaxed teacher.

'Well done. A most promising beginning,' he said, as they carried the boat up the beach. 'Do you want to have a go on a windsurfer?'

She shook her head. 'Not just now. I'm going to laze for a while.'

'You don't mind if I desert you for an hour?'

'Not a bit.'

Presently, with a newly-published bestseller borrowed from the Hathaways' well-stocked bookshelves, she settled herself in a hammock slung between two palm trees and began to read.

But no book, however gripping, could hold her attention that afternoon. There was too much else on her mind. Her decision, so rashly taken, to share her life with a man she had known less than a month. The bewildering impact of his kiss. The basilisk flash of dislike with which Bettina had glanced at her when she heard the news. The awkward pause after someone, meaning no harm, had said jocularly, 'You know what they say—reformed rakes make the best husbands.'

Now, the book lying unread on her lap, Christie looked out to sea and watched the man who would soon be her husband, if only in part, speeding over the surface of the water on the red-sailed windsurfer which he controlled with such ease.

Being responsible is part of my business, he had said that morning; and Christie felt confident that even if a disastrous world-wide recession affected the yacht charter business and caused a reverse of his present fortunes, Ash would always find some way to ensure that she and John never went without basic comforts.

She knew that from time to time the island was swept by hurricanes. But she had no fears for her safety at Heron's Sound. If danger threatened, he would be there, and if he was there they would be safe, or as safe as it was possible to be when natural forces were on the rampage.

Thinking of Nature out of control turned her thoughts to the violent emotions which beset human beings—the jealous dislike she had seen in Bettina's pale eyes, and the hot desire which Ash must have felt for the other girl at the beginning of their liaison.

He had given Christie his word that he would never attempt to assert the normal rights of a husband. Whatever his other shortcomings, she would stake a great deal on the creditability of his promises. He was, she felt sure, a man of rock-like integrity in matters of business. He would disdain to lie. His handshake on a deal would be as binding as another man's signature on a legal document.

At the same time his reputation did not suggest that he was equally scrupulous in his relationships with women. Even Miranda, whose affection for him was plain to see, had admitted that he could be ruthless with bedworthy members of the opposite sex. According to island gossip he had filched and seduced another man's fiancée. And, whatever he might say about it, it was clear that the break-up with Bettina had not been by mutual consent.

Supposing, at some time in the future, he needed a woman but had no affair in progress. Would he then turn to her, his wife, his promise driven from his mind by the overpowering strength of his lust?

Her mind shied away from the possibility. No, no—he wasn't a savage to force himself on a woman who didn't want him. He would always have someone to turn to . . . an old flame such as Bettina . . . or else some 'gorgeous new chick'.

She was still reclining in the hammock when Ash came up through the garden, and strolled across to her.

'What are you reading?'

She showed him the cover. 'But I haven't been reading . . . just lotos-eating.'

To her surprise, he quoted the opening lines of Tennyson's *The Lotos-Eaters*.

There is sweet music here that softer falls
Than petals from blown roses on the grass,
Or night-dews on still waters between walls
Of shadowy granite, in a gleaming pass:
Music that gentlier on the spirit lies,
Than tired eyelids upon tired eyes . . .

She remembered Miranda's remark that Ash was
a lover of life in all its aspects, but Christie would not
have imagined that poetry would be among them.

It had long been one of her own pleasures, a taste
inherited from her mother, but not shared by her
sister or Mike. The only verses her husband had
known had been the bawdy lyrics of rugger songs.

'You look slightly shocked,' he said dryly. 'Do you
feel there's something effeminate about a liking of
poetry?'

'Oh, no—not at all,' she replied. 'I was merely
surprised . . . and impressed. I've always loved poetry myself, but I've never met a man who did.'

'The greatest poets were and are men. Women
may read it more, but they don't seem inclined to
write it much.'

'No, I wonder why not?'

His inscrutable half-smile lifted the corner of his
mouth. But he explained it a moment later by saying,
'One of the things I like about you, Christiana, is
that you don't feel obliged to refute every statement
of that sort. There are so many women around who
take every unqualified generalisation as an outrageous slur on their sex which they must indignantly repudiate.'

'I wasn't upset by that statement, but I do become outraged occasionally. I think we should stick to poetry. It's a safer subject than Women's Lib. Do you like modern poems as well as the classics?'

'There's one modern American poet whose work I like—James Kavanaugh. You probably wouldn't have come across him. He was a priest, but gave it up. I have two books of his stuff—I'll lend them to you. I've never had much of a library because there's been nowhere to keep it. But there's a room at Heron's Sound which I thought we might make into a book room.'

They began to talk about the house, a subject on which their minds were so much in accord that Christie forgot the doubts which had troubled her earlier.

In the week between Christmas and New Year, they went several times to Heron's Sound. Between them they measured the rooms and Ash made a plan of the layout to which Christie attached various sketch-notes and several pages of written reminders of her ideas about décor.

Miranda had insisted that she and John should vacate the cottage at the Turtle Creek Colony, and move to the Hathaways' house. To the older woman's vexation, she could not be present at the wedding as she and her husband had an unbreakable engagement in Florida on the same day, and were flying there the day before.

Secretly, Christie was glad of this circumstance. She felt sure Miranda would have insisted on organising a wedding party, and her own preference was for a minimum of fuss and ceremony.

She had thought they would leave for London immediately, but Ash said no normal couple would choose to spend their wedding night crossing the Atlantic. He had booked to fly out the next night.

Some of his efforts to conceal the true nature of their relationship were rather disturbing.

One evening, before dinner—he was also staying with the Hathaways—he picked a spray of crimson bougainvillaea and divided it into two pieces. One he tucked behind Christie's ear. The other he slipped behind the clip of her front-fastening bra, having first unfastened the modestly high top button of her dress and opened it up to show the soft mounds of her breasts.

Miranda and Joss were both present, and there was nothing about the gesture which could have offended any but the most prudish of onlookers.

It was the act of a man in love adorning his beloved with the flowers which bloomed in such profusion that the house could be filled with their brilliance without denuding the garden.

But as Ash was not a professional actor, it made Christie oddly uneasy that he brought such conviction to his rôle. And even the brush of his knuckles against the tops of her breasts sent a strange little tremor down her spine.

He never kissed her goodnight or good morning, even when their first and last encounters were in public, and it would have been normal to do so. But, invariably, the first and last words he addressed to her were accompanied by an ardent look which gave the impression that, during the day or the night, he would kiss her—and very thoroughly.

Their bedrooms were not far apart. Christie guessed that Miranda, a broad-minded woman, would take it for granted that they were already sleeping together. No doubt she would feel that, as they were both mature adults, there was no reason why they should defer the pleasures which she and Joss enjoyed.

She showed Christie the large, air-conditioned master bedroom with its seven-foot-wide double bed.

'You must have this room on your wedding night,' she said. 'Apart from anything else'—with a lurking twinkle—'it will be more comfortable for Ash. I'm sure his feet overhang the end of the guest bed he's sleeping in at the moment. In our bed he can lie diagonally, and really stretch out. When Joss and I stay with other people, we always feel so cramped. I don't like twin beds. I like to sleep cuddled up close, but before I sleep I always read, or maybe do a little needlepoint, and for that one needs elbow-room.'

Christie gazed intently at a painting, hoping to hide her heightened colour.

'I have some black crêpe-de-chine sheets,' Miranda went on. 'Joss dislikes them. He says they feel slithery. He prefers percale. But they look very naughty and sexy. I'm sure Ash will approve, especially with you lying on them.'

She noticed Christie's embarrassment, and said, on a slightly puzzled note, 'I'm not shocking you, am I? Sometimes—' She stopped short.

'Sometimes what?' Christie tried to sound casual.

Miranda hesitated. 'Sometimes you have a very ingénue air, Christie. It's part of your charm in a world full of hard-boiled young women. Frankly, if I didn't know it, I should never have guessed you'd been married. I should say you'd come straight from a convent. You don't smoke, you don't swear, your conversation is never risqué, and—'

'You make me sound a sanctimonious horror!' exclaimed Christie.

'Why, no. I didn't mean that, dear. If you were that, Ash wouldn't love you. No, I find you very refreshing. Worldliness can become boring. There's only one place a man likes a woman not to be modest, and that's in bed with him.'

She caught sight of herself in a mirror, and paused, her expression critical. 'I wonder if I need a neck-lift. Am I starting to look like a turtle?'

To Christie's relief she began to discuss cosmetic surgery.

The day before their wedding coincided with *Sunbird Two*'s return from a charter.

In the evening, when the outgoing charter party were on their way home by air, and part of the turn-around procedure had been accomplished, Ash gave a party on board for those of his sailing friends who were in harbour at the time.

Christie had expected it to be a stag party. She would have been happy to spend the evening alone, with John in bed and only the staff in residence now that the Hathaways were away.

But Ash dismissed this idea. 'Stag parties are for young men without too much sense. I have no intention of spending my wedding night nursing an almighty hangover. You don't want a pale green, cross-eyed bridegroom, do you?'

She laughed. 'Are you ever pale green and cross-eyed?'

He shrugged. 'I've committed all the usual follies, but not for some years.'

It was a good party. She enjoyed it.

By now she had become used to the curiosity in the eyes of people meeting her for the first time—the young widow from London who had succeeded where so many others had failed.

The men probably came to the conclusion that, behind the demure façade, she must be hot stuff indeed for old Ash to give up his freedom for her. The women were more likely to think that the child had a great deal to do with it, and that it wouldn't be long before Ash was off on another of his escapades.

Whatever their theories about the marriage, none of them would guess, or perhaps even believe it if they were told it, that Ash had promised his bride a separate bedroom in his house and, if not a separate cabin, a separate bunk whenever they spent nights on board either of the two *Sunbirds*.

Although, when she came to think of it, he had not actually made this plain in so many words. But when they were studying the plan he had drawn, he had not contested her suggestion as to which should be his room and which her room. The rest was a tacit agreement based on his sworn word on the raft.

At midnight the party broke up and, followed by a chorus of good wishes, some of them ribald, they walked to the car park and Ash drove her home.

'You seemed very relaxed this evening. No eleventh-hour jitters?' he enquired, when they were nearly there.

'Not so far. What about you?'

'Why should I be nervous?'

'It's a big step . . . a confirmed bachelor giving up his freedom,' she pointed out.

'What makes you think I was ever a confirmed bachelor?'

'Weren't you?'

'No. Merely a man who'd never met a woman he wanted to marry.'

'And you haven't now—not really,' she said, in a low voice.

She knew that he glanced towards her, but he didn't say anything. What was there he could say?

Miranda's housekeeper was waiting up for them. She and George, the butler, were married and lived in a cottage in the grounds. They had three grown-up children who were all overseas, doing well for themselves.

'Can I get you anything, Mr Lambard? Some coffee maybe?'

'No, thanks, Rose. We'll just have some brandy. Thank you for baby-sitting.'

'You're welcome, sir. Mrs Hathaway left orders for you to have breakfast in bed tomorrow, Mrs Chapman. What time would you like me to bring it, ma'am?'

'About eight o'clock, please, Rose. I'll have it in bed if it will please Mrs Hathaway, but I'm sure to wake up early as usual, and I'll probably have my usual swim.'

'The bride shouldn't see the bridegroom before the ceremony, ma'am,' Rose said seriously.

Miranda had mentioned that, like many Antiguans, her housekeeper seldom missed church on a Sunday. Clearly Rose did not assume that Ash and Christie were already sleeping together.

'As I'm driving the bride to the ceremony, we shall have to disregard that tradition,' said Ash.

After Rose had bidden them goodnight, he poured out one large and one smaller measure of French brandy.

'Drink it. It will help you to sleep,' he said, as she looked doubtfully at the glass he was offering to her.

As she took it, he raised his own glass. 'To us.'

They both drank to the toast. Then Ash said, 'I suppose, inevitably, you're remembering your first wedding, and all the eagerness and excitement you must have felt the night before. That may be lacking this time, but where there are no expectations there can't be any disappointments. You may find, this time next year, that what we have together is as satisfying, in its way, as a marriage based on romantic love.'

'I—I hope so . . for your sake as well as my own. I'm the one who has most to gain. You're the one who's . . losing out,' she said uncomfortably.

'In one respect only, and very few people have everything they want from life. Finish your brandy in your room. I'll look in on John.'

He took her hand, gave a curiously formal bow, and brushed a light kiss on her knuckles. 'Goodnight, Christiana.'

'Goodnight.'

She left him and went to her room, carrying in her mind's eye the image of the tall man, informally dressed for the schooner party, saying that formal goodnight to his bride-to-be.

She felt her heart aching for him; that he would never know the bliss of holding in his arms a girl whom he truly loved and who loved him. with all her heart.

She would never experience that either, but somehow her sorrow for him was sharper than the resigned acceptance she felt on her own account.

But perhaps Ash had never dreamed of the world well lost, of a love that would last for ever, she thought, as she prepared for bed.

Although it was now one o'clock in the morning, she had never felt less like sleeping. She decided to read for a while. For her, it was not important to look clear-eyed and radiant tomorrow.

Today, she corrected herself. In less than twelve hours from now she would be Mrs Ashcroft Lambard.

The bestseller, begun in the hammock, was on her night table. But as she stretched out her hand, she remembered that in her bag was the book of poems by James Kavanaugh which, earlier that night, Ash had found for her on the schooner's bookshelves.

She slipped out of bed to fetch it; a book with a

dark brown wrapper and paler brown pages, decorated with drawings of trees. At the back was a section with a drawing of a man and a woman embracing in a field of flowers. The first of the poems in this group was called *Where Are You Hiding, My Love?*

It was a long poem. She read it through once, then again. Could it be that Ash *had* shared the feelings expressed in this poem? For the third time her eyes skimmed the verses, lingering on certain lines.

Where are you hiding, my love?
   I have sought you for so long
That surely you must feel the pulsing
   Of my endless longing!

And farther down,

I care not whose you were—or even whose you are—
   Your eyes will tell me that you are mine
And that you are waiting.

Where are you hiding, my love?
   Each day without you will never come again.
Even today you missed a sunset on the ocean,
   A silver shadow on yellow rocks I saved for you . . .

Deeply troubled by what she felt might be an insight into an unsuspected region of Ash's being, Christie put the book aside, switched out the lamp and lay down

But for a long time she remained awake, wondering if, behind his self-sufficient, sometimes arrogant manner, he concealed the *wounds and weariness and hopes grown dead* of the poem.

She did not, after all, wake up early.

Rose woke her, bringing her breakfast tray, and accompanied by John. Already firm friends with the housekeeper and her husband, he was going to stay with them in their cottage after Ash and Christie had left on their so-called honeymoon, and until the Hathaways returned.

'Uncle Ash and me have had breakfast. This afternoon we're going shelling,' John announced, climbing onto her bed.

'Are we? What fun!' Christie hadn't thought about the rest of the day after the wedding. 'You should say "Uncle Ash and I", darling,' she added.

'Uncle Ash *and I* went out in the little boat,' John continued. 'He says when I can swim a long way I can have a little boat of my very own. He's going to teach you to sail, Aunt Christie, and then we can go on adventures in his big boat sometimes, just the three of us.'

'That sounds terrific,' she said, spreading butter on toast.

Whatever else was wrong about this marriage, it was going to be good for John. That was the important thing.

He stayed with her until she had finished eating. Then he ran off to play, and Christie slid out of bed and went to have a shower.

She had not, after all, bought a new dress in which

to be married. Her clothes included a very plain ivory silk shirt-dress, made in Hong Kong, and advertised as a special value mail order offer by Selfridges, the great department store in Oxford Street. It was the kind of undating classic which had been worn in the Thirties and would be worn in the Nineties. With it she wore the small real pearl earrings which had been her mother's, and a fine fourteen-inch gold chain which circled the base of her throat, the last birthday present given to her by her sister.

Ash, when they met, was wearing a pale grey tropic-weight suit with a dark terracotta shirt, and a cotton tie patterned in pale terracotta and blue. He looked, as always, exactly right for the occasion, and he looked approvingly at her.

Accompanied by John, and with George and Rose to be their witnesses—looking far more bridal than the bridal couple—they drove to St John's. Little more than an hour later it was all over and they were driving back to change into beach clothes for the shelling expedition.

Mr and Mrs Ashcroft Lambard. Christie looked at the gold wedding band now encircling her finger next to the ruby engagement ring, and couldn't believe the deed was done. There could be no turning back now.

By noon they had shared a bottle of Dom Ruinart with the two Antiguans, reverted to shorts and beach shirts, packed two cool bags and a picnic basket into the car, and were beach-bound.

He took them to one called Seaforth, well shaded,

deserted except for themselves, with a group of
fishing boats some way off, and an offshore island
with a cottage on it.

They swam, played with John on his crocodile,
then dried off and sat down to eat.

'It's so *beautiful* here. I just can't believe this is
home now,' said Christie, gazing around her, an
ackee patty in one hand, a glass of iced water in the
other.

Ash was lying on his side, Roman-fashion, propped on one elbow. 'You haven't begun to know the
island yet. A lot of the best places are away from the
main roads, like this is, or only accessible by sea. It
will take a long time to show you everything. You'll
want to do some exploring on your own. When we
get back from London we'll have to find you a car.
Maybe one of the Hillman Hustlers which the tourists hire to buzz around in would suit you, although
they haven't much lockable storage space.'

'I shall have quite a lot of money when the flat is
sold. I shan't be too great an expense to you.'

'I didn't marry you for your dowry, Christiana,'
he said dryly.

No, for my housekeeping skills, she thought, with
an odd little pang.

After lunch they went searching for shells; finding
fragile tellins, the home of sand-dwelling clams, and
lucines, a stronger clam shell, as well as little striped
cowries, and many of the Atlantic Bulla shells known
as bubbles.

Later, they bathed again. Then it was time to go
home.

That night, Ash and Christie had dinner after
John was in bed. Rose had prepared a special meal,
and George had set up a table for two on the terrace
and laid it with napery and china which Christie had
not seen before; a pale green circular cloth, with a
border of exquisite pulled work with matching motifs
on the napkins, and a service of white French porcelain patterned with tiny wild strawberries and rim-
med with gold. The cutlery had vermeil handles of a
beautiful lustre in the light from the storm-shaded
candles on either side of the centrepiece. This was an
arrangement of white flowers and dark green leaves
in a frosted crystal bowl, too shallow to obstruct their
view of each other.

Ash had been listening to a record on Joss's stereo
when Christie returned from Miranda's bedroom.
When she joined him, he lowered the volume, but the
music—Chopin—continued to play while they ate.

The Hathaways' cook, who lived in the nearby
village, had excelled herself. They began with jellied
orange consommé, served in chilled bouillon cups,
garnished with slices of orange and having a faint
hint of cloves.

'No, this is a Grenadian speciality, Mrs Lambard,' George told her, when she asked if it was a
local dish.

The main course was striped bass baked on a bed
of potatoes, served with a green sauce and accompanied by a French white wine selected for them by Joss
from his specially-built wine store, air-conditioned
to stay at fifty-eight degrees all year round.

The meal had been light enough for Christie not to

feel satiated before the pudding appeared, a lime meringue pie with whipped cream. Finally, they both had a little Brie on Miranda's favourite Bath Oliver biscuits, before George reappeared to enquire whether they wished to have coffee at the table or in the living-room.

'Inside, please, George.'

Ash laid aside his napkin and pushed back his chair. He came round the table to assist her to rise. 'If we have it inside, George can clear the table and go off duty,' he said, to explain his choice.

They moved to one of the several groups of comfortable chairs and sofas in the huge room. Very soon the butler came back with coffee in a tall silver pot. He set the tray on a low table between Christie's chair and Ash's end of the sofa next to it.

'Cream, Mrs Lambard?' he asked, before he had finished filling a black and gold demi-tasse.

'No, thank you.'

He placed the cup and saucer within her reach, and performed the same service for Ash. It took him less than five minutes to clear the dining table, loading everything on to a rubber-wheeled trolley. Then he came back to where they were sitting.

'If you should require anything else, you have only to ring, sir.'

'Thank you, George, but we shan't need anything more. Goodnight.'

'Goodnight, sir. Goodnight, ma'am.'

A few moments later they were alone. It was not quite fifteen minutes past nine—much too early to go to bed for people only pretending to be on their

honeymoon. When, shortly afterwards, the music
came to an end, the ensuing silence seemed to
emphasise their seclusion.

'Would you like some more music?' Ash asked.

'Yes, please.'

'What would you like? If it's classical, Joss probably has it.'

'Some Tchaikovsky, perhaps?' Christie suggested.

The music centre was in another part of the room.
She watched him stroll away from her, moving from
the hips with the straight-backed, indolent grace
which was as pleasing to watch as the paces of a
thoroughbred horse or the fluid movements of a
leopard patrolling its cage.

She poured herself another cup of coffee, and
wondered how soon she could excuse herself. Not
before ten o'clock. It wasn't that she was tired; it was
just that tonight was an awkward time. Surely he
must be equally conscious that a normal couple, if
not already in bed together, would at least be exchanging passionate kisses.

Mike had hustled her up to their room as soon as
they had finished dinner at their Guernsey boarding
house. But she didn't want to remember that now. It
was part of the past; not part of her new life with Ash.
He would make no repugnant demands on her. With
her second husband she could relax, knowing the
night held no shattering disillusionment, only undis-
turbed rest, alone in the Hathaways' bed.

'Have you seen this American *Vogue*?' He came
back to where she was sitting with a magazine and a
heavy coffee-table book with *Mexico* in large letters

on the dust jacket. While she turned the pages of the fashion magazine, he seemed immersed in the colour plates of the book.

'George forgot to offer us a liqueur. Would you care for one?' he asked presently.

'What? Oh, no . . . I don't think so, thank you.' Her absorption in an article on a raw food health and beauty régime was no pretence. With a start she realised that the time had passed much more swiftly than she expected. It was already five minutes to ten. 'In fact I think, if you don't mind, I'll turn in.'

'Why not? We shall be lucky to have more than two or three hours' sleep on the plane tomorrow. For reasons best known to themselves, since everybody has already eaten, they serve dinner forty minutes after take-off.'

Christie put the magazine down, then decided to take it with her. 'Goodnight, Ash.'

He rose to his feet. 'I hope you don't find yourself suffering from agoraphobia in the Hathaways' bed. I've seen it. Six people could sleep there,' he said, with a gleam of amusement.

'Yes, it would have been better for you to occupy it, and for me to stay where I was. Well . . . goodnight,' she repeated.

In Miranda's luxurious bedroom she took off her dress. Rose had cleared one section of the wall-long bank of hanging cupboards, and left the door wide to indicate that Christie could use it. Having hung up her dress, and taken off her light make-up, she went to the bathroom to shower, borrowing a bath cap she found there to protect her hair which, in spite of her afternoon swim, would not need another shampoo until tomorrow.

The bed had been turned down, and her night-dress laid across it. A cool, pretty Tana lawn night-dress, but not the seventh-veil garment most brides chose for their honeymoon.

Shedding the bath sheet, she slipped the nightie over her head, then returned to the bathroom to hang up the towel and brush her teeth.

She was in the bedroom again, brushing her hair, when there was a light tap on the door. It sounded as if it might be Rose. Perhaps John had had a bad dream and woken up frightened and calling for her.

'Come in.'

It wasn't Rose. It was Ash. He was wearing the navy silk dressing-gown she had seen at her flat, but not the apple green pyjamas. His long brown legs were bare between the hem of the robe and his leather slippers.

'Is something wrong?' she asked concernedly.

He came in, closing the door. 'No, nothing is wrong, Christiana.'

'Then . . . what do you want?' she asked, puzzled.

He strolled into the centre of the room, his hands thrust into the square patch pockets of the robe.

'I want you,' he said, very softly. 'I'm going to make you want me.'

Christie froze. Her knuckles whitened on the handle of the hairbrush as she realised what he meant.

'B-but you promised . . . you gave me your word!'

'I gave you my word not to do anything you

wouldn't like. You will like our *nuit de noces*. It won'
be like your first wedding night.'

'Y-you can't . . . you wouldn't . . . you don't mea
it.' Her voice was ragged.

Ash didn't move, but a dark flame burned in hi
eyes.

'It's useless to argue with a woman who believe
she is frigid. Words will never persuade her she
wrong. There is only one way to convince you, m
nervous bride.'

TEN

STILL he didn't make a move towards her, and for perhaps fifteen seconds Christie remained on the dressing stool, paralysed. Terror turned her to stone; a sick, mindless, abject terror such as people must feel when they knew they were going to be tortured.

It was the most horrible moment she had ever experienced; the knowledge that she had been betrayed; the feeling of being utterly helpless, with no possibility of escape.

Escape.

The ancient human instinct for self-preservation flickered to life again. She knew there was only one chance, one place where Ash could not touch her.

She leapt to her feet and flung herself towards the bathroom.

He caught her before she reached it, spun her into his arms, and held her fast. She struggled and squirmed, but in a very few moments he had both her wrists pinioned behind her, manacled by his steely fingers, while his other arm bound her against him, only the silk of his robe and the thin flowered lawn of her nightgown insulating her body from the warmth and strength of his tall frame.

'Let me go . . . *let me go*,' she implored. 'You promised . . . oh, God, you promised.'

'And I'll keep that promise,' he assured her. 'Calm
down, Christie. I'm not going to hurt you.'

It was the first time he had used the familiar form
of her name.

'You will,' she burst out, in anguish. 'Oh, how I
hate you—you bastard!'

The way she ground out the epithet—itself so
uncharacteristic of someone who rarely uttered an
expletive stronger than "damn"—expressed all her
bitter sense of betrayal. She had believed him; had
trusted him; even, last night reading that poem, had
felt compassion and sadness for him.

And now he was about to rape her.

The thought iced her veins with dread, but she
forced herself to pull back from the brink of hysteria.

'If you don't let me go, I shall scream the place
down!'

'No, you won't.'

Suddenly his free hand was holding her head still
and his mouth was pressed fiercely on hers, effective-
ly stifling any sound but a muffled groan of despair.

Christie closed her eyes, strove to keep her lips
tightly compressed, her body rigid with resistance.
Let him see how much pleasure he gained from
taking her by force. None, unless he was so sated
with normal lovemaking that the idea of taking a
woman against her will stimulated his jaded appetite.

His grip was hurting her captive wrists and yet, as
he went on kissing her, less fiercely now but more
sensuously, she was appalled to realise that, already
it was having an effect on her. She could feel the

strange trembling of her thighs, the ache low down in
her body, the desire to open her lips to the lips
moving softly on hers.

Then all at once terror revived as Ash let go her
wrists and, using that hand to pull her closer, made
her suddenly, fearfully aware of the hard, aroused
state of his body.

This was how it had been before. She could not
endure it again. With clenched fists she beat on his
chest, wrenching her mouth from under his, fighting
him with a desperation which gave her twice her
usual strength.

But it was no defence against Ash. Her violence
merely amused him. She saw his teeth flash in a grin
as he let her go for an instant, then grabbed her and
tossed her bodily on to the bed.

She landed flat on her back, was rebounded by the
excellent springing and, for a few moments, lay still,
breathing hard and glaring up at him, her grey eyes
glittering with tears of impotent fury.

As she started to struggle up, he flung himself
beside her, pinning her down with one arm stretched
across her to clamp her right arm at the elbow. Her
other arm was trapped underneath him. When she
raised her legs, intending to strike at him with her
heels, he foiled her by throwing his right leg across
her slim thighs.

'Who would have thought you could be such a
termagant?' he teased her.

But the mockery in his voice was not matched by
the look in his eyes. They were brilliant with undisguised desire. Christie could see that her struggles

had excited him, and he would not play with her for much longer.

When he tried to kiss her again, she whipped her face aside, twisting her neck as far as she could to keep her mouth out of his reach.

His lips were hot on her throat, travelling slowly up to the delicate hollow behind her ear. His teeth softly nibbled the lobe. She felt the tip of his tongue exploring the spirals of her ear, and the heavy beating of her heart, and resistance dying down inside her.

'Give me your mouth, Christiana.'

The low-voiced command made her shiver.

'No . . . never . . . never,' she whispered, keeping her face averted.

He gave an almost soundless laugh at her futile refusal to submit to a conquest she could not avoid.

'You will,' he said softly. 'You will. And there are other places to kiss.'

With a sudden change of position he shifted himself lower down, the weight of his chest on her hips, and his face on a level with her breasts, still heaving after her struggle with him.

The pressure of his hands on her outflung arms was lighter now, but she guessed it would rapidly harden if she attempted to move them. So she lay inert and despairing while his breath scorched like fire through the flimsiness of her nightie, and instead of nibbling her ear-lobe he found a more sensitive spot to concentrate, for the moment, his siege of her body.

But it wasn't the expected disgust she felt as his

mouth kissed its way from one soft quivering breast to the other. And when he said, 'Too many lights on,' and suddenly rose and left her, she lay still for at least twenty seconds, not quite grasping that she was free, if not for many moments.

When she realised, she leapt to her feet and fled for the bathroom yet again, only to be caught at the threshold and hauled backwards into his arms.

'If you think that door would protect you, you don't know me,' his voice mocked.

Before she knew what was happening, her night-dress had been whipped upwards to hamper her flailing arms and cover her head. Then, naked from the chest down, she was thrown on the bed a second time and kissed as before, but now with not even thin lawn between Ash's lascivious lips and the tremulous, satin-smooth flesh which the sun had not touched.

Knowing it was useless to attempt to pull down her nightie, she struggled to extricate herself from it in the other direction. Sprawled as she was, this was not easy, and it took her many agitated seconds to rid herself of its folds. For all the time she was struggling, Ash's hand was exploring the rest of her until, when at last she had freed herself, and given a gasp of relief, he reached the top of her thighs and drew another sharp gasp from her.

'No!' She tensed every muscle against the insidious caresses.

'Yes,' was his hoarse-voiced response.

She could feel the pounding of his heart, his heavy breathing. Yet there was no impatience in his touch.

She had not known a man could throb with so fierce an ardour, but keep his passion in check. He seemed to have total control.

All at once she herself had none.

She began to tremble from head to foot, as if she were shivering with cold instead of burning all over. Then, as her braced muscles slackened, Ash slipped his hand between her legs and her shivering became violent shudders.

Only dimly aware of frantically clutching his shoulders, she heard her own laboured breaths, and no longer felt any shame as her body writhed in abandon to the waves of delicious sensation induced by his expert caresses.

Again and again he drove her to the point of frenzy. Not until she was almost exhausted with pleasure did he let go his iron self-discipline. For an instant, eyes wide in the moonlight, she saw him looming above her, and felt his hard, muscular flanks between her soft, spreadeagled thighs. As their bodies fused, she cried out; not a cry of pain, but rather of astonished joy at being unafraid and ready for his final possession.

And when he had taken his pleasure, and kissed her softly on the mouth, she burst into tears of relief at not being condemned to relive the misery she had known before.

He seemed to know why she was crying and, instead of moving away, he continued to hold her in his arms, and was still there when she was calm and almost asleep.

*   *   *

When Christie woke in the morning, she was alone. Ash was not in the bedroom, nor was there the sound of water running or the buzz of an electric razor from Joss Hathaway's dark blue bathroom next to Miranda's pink one.

Perhaps Ash did not use an electric razor. He might be in there, shaving quietly with an ordinary one. For a dark-haired man with a strong beard, he had been very smooth-cheeked last night. There was not a mark on her body, she discovered, peering at herself.

None of the bite marks and bruises, none of the red stubble-grazes which had marked her pale and tender skin on the morning after her first night in bed with Mike. When she stretched it did not make her wince. In fact, although she didn't want to admit it, she had never felt better in her life.

Rested, refreshed, invigorated; all her hormones the right way up.

Where had that phrase come from? she wondered. She had read it somewhere, but where?

When she sat up, she saw that the door of Ash's bathroom was open. He must have gone down to the beach for an early swim. How long before he came back?

At the thought of having to face him, after all he had done to her last night, her face grew hot and she had a revulsion of feeling.

It wasn't only what he had done which was mortifying, but that she had allowed it—and responded. He had virtually raped her—not brutally, not like a beast. But that didn't alter the fact that his slow

invasion of her body had been against her will, or by
a coercion of her will.

That he was her husband made no difference
However carefully he had phrased his assurance that
he would not expect her to sleep with him, it was still
a despicable ruse for which she could never forgive
him.

Yet even while she wanted to hate him, a part of
her mind held the thought, Why did Mike never
make love like that? Why did I have to go through all
that disillusioned unhappiness, thinking it was my
fault, thinking there was something terribly wrong
with me?

It was a distasteful idea: that enjoyment in bed
had nothing to do with the emotions, but was merely
a matter of technique. She did not want to accept
that any man with Ash's experience could have
inflicted the same rapturous sensations on her. But
the only other explanation—

'Good morning. How did you sleep?'

He had caught her lying on her side, with her head
cradled on her arm and her other hand absently
smoothing the lustrous black silk crêpe-de-chine of
the undersheet.

At the sound of his voice, she rolled over, clutching
the oversheet to her. Ash was standing in the space
left by one of the sliding glass doors which gave on to
the Hathaways' private breakfast patio.

'Good morning.' Without answering his question
she sat up, returning his quizzical half-smile with a
look of smouldering hostility.

Her glare made his smile more pronounced. He

strolled to the bed and sat down on the edge of it. 'It's usual for husbands and wives to exchange a good morning kiss—especially after a night as pleasurable as last night.'

He held out both arms, inviting her to come to him from her place in the centre of the bed. He must have removed his wet trunks down on the beach as now he was wrapped in a small towel which covered him from waist to mid-thigh.

Christie's bosom heaved with indignation. 'Have you *no* compunction?' she burst out.

'No, none. Should I have?' he asked equably. 'Perhaps there was a slight risk that your claim to be frigid was justified. But you know what they say— There's no such thing as a frigid woman, only an inept lover. And if my judgment of a situation is ever in doubt, I favour the S.A.S. motto—Who dares wins. Last night was a mutual victory. Can you deny it?'

She wanted to burrow under the sheet to hide her scarlet confusion.

'No, you can't,' said Ash, with a low laugh. 'Because you remember as well as I do that when you gasped and cried out it wasn't because I was hurting you.'

'How can you! Oh, God!' She buried her face in her hands, unable to bear the reminder of those moments of total abandonment.

She felt a movement on the mattress. The next moment he was beside her, pulling her into his arms, making her uncover her face.

'Twenty-four, and so shy,' he teased her. Then the

mockery died out of his eyes, replaced by a curious expression which she could not fathom.

'It was like taking a virgin,' he told her, his voice low and vibrant. 'Not that I speak from experience, having always avoided them before—endangered species that they are. But perhaps, just once in a lifetime, there's something to be said for being the first man to hear those whimpers of pleasure which you gave last night.'

'I hate you . . . I hate you,' she ground out. 'You're disgusting . . . a disgusting satyr!'

'If you think that, my dear, on the basis of last night's experience, you have a great deal to learn. So much that I think I'd better continue your tuition immediately.'

It must have been at least an hour later, while Christie was staring at a hairline crack in the ceiling plaster, with nothing else in her mind, like someone in a deep trance, that Ash raised his head to look at her.

Big and broad as he was, she was not in any way cramped. His weight was all on his own arms.

Her gaze fixed on the crack, she wondered if her face was still dewed with the moisture which, earlier, she had felt breaking out on her forehead, under her eyes, everywhere.

The same thing had happened to Ash. She had felt the sudden dampness of his back, like the moment of crisis in a fever when the high, burning temperature falls, and the restless delirium is eased. But that had been some time ago, since when she had lain in a daze of emotional exhaustion.

After studying her face for some moments, he kissed the tip of her nose before rolling aside to sit up.

'Time for breakfast, I think, don't you? Then perhaps another tutorial. A sailing lesson,' he added blandly. 'I'm going for a shower, and then I'll organise breakfast. Don't be too long having your bath.'

She watched him walk to his bathroom, his buttocks only a little less tanned than the rest of him. They had concave planes at the sides, and tighter curves than her own still partially white behind on which, when she went to her bathroom with its mirrored walls, she discovered one small dark love bite in a place which only Ash would see.

Like a brand, she thought, anger reviving. His property now, his woman. For although his caresses were gentle as long as she submitted, he had left her in no doubt that if ever she attempted further resistance, he would use his superior strength to enforce his mastery.

Without any love between them, she was in the position of a new addition to a harem. And although she had his undivided attention for the time being, how long would it be before he tired of her?

During breakfast she discovered that Miranda and Ash had arranged for John to spend that day and night at the home of some of the children he had met at the Christmas Day party.

'Fond as I am of him, I don't want a child at my heels during my honeymoon,' said Ash.

Reluctantly, Christie was forced to say goodbye to

her nephew many hours before she had expected to part from him. John himself seemed unconcerned. He promised to be a good boy all the time they were away, hugged her, hugged Ash, and went off happily with his hostess when she came to fetch him.

They spent the rest of the morning sailing, first in the Sunfish and then in the Hobie Cat. After lunch, Ash suggested a drive to Devil's Bridge on the eastern side of the island. He told her it was an area which had been bought by the Mill Reefers and presented to the Government of Antigua to remain an unspoiled beauty spot.

Although it was a lovely day, the heave and surge of the deep green water under the bridge of rock, carved by centuries of pounding by the sea, made her unaccountably nervous.

She did not step on the bridge, but Ash did. When he was half way across she felt a sharp thrust of fear in case it should suddenly give way, plunging him into the turbulent water beneath.

Even he, powerful swimmer that he was, might not be able to save himself from that cauldron of conflicting currents. The thought of his splendid body being lacerated by the rocks, and herself standing helplessly by, made her turn away, hating the place.

From there they went to Long Bay which had a reef close to the shore of a crescent moon beach with unobtrusive hotel buildings at either end. When, after an hour of snorkelling, they were having a drink at the beach bar of the Long Bay Hotel, Christie remembered Kate's praise of the hotel's boutique.

She asked Ash if he would mind waiting while she
went to have a look for an extra present for Margaret.

'I'll come with you. There might be something I
should like to buy you,' he answered.

The shop was full of temptations. She bought a
dress length for Margaret, and several small presents
for former colleagues whom she hoped to see and say
goodbye to.

Ash insisted on buying her a pair of black coral
ear-rings, and a white evening skirt from Mexico,
covered with vivid embroidery. Attractive as it was,
she would have preferred not to accept it, but was
prevented from demurring by his obvious determination and the presence of another customer.

It was late afternoon when they returned to the
Hathaways' house. They had supper earlier than
usual, to allow an interval before the meal which
would be served to them on the aeroplane.

'I'll go and finish my packing,' said Christie, after
supper.

She felt badly in need of some time alone. In the
same room with Ash she was continually conscious
of the things he had already done to her. At least she
would be spared any further lovemaking tonight.

But her respite from his disturbing presence lasted
less than ten minutes. She had turned the Mexican
skirt inside out and was folding it to be as little
creased as possible when she heard the door open
and close behind her.

Surely he hadn't followed her to—?

As she bent to lay the skirt in her case, lean brown
hands slipped under her arms and closed firmly over

her breasts, drawing her upright. She closed her eyes
as a kiss burned the nape of her neck, and his fingers
fondled her softness.

'You can finish your packing later. There's plenty
of time.'

She wanted to hate it: the feel of his hard male
body already pulsing with desire for her, the prac-
tised assurance with which he unbuttoned her shirt,
pushing the strap of her bra off the curve of her
shoulder to make it easier to slip the warm palm of
his hand between the cup and her bare flesh.

But the truth was she didn't hate it. Already,
though her mind rebelled, her body had signalled
its surrender. The peaks of her breasts had swollen.
Her thighs were quaking. She was panting.

'Shall we have our first shower together? Hot
water makes the skin more sensitive.'

Christie stifled a groan at the thought of becoming
even more responsive than she was at this moment.
She had almost no control left. It horrified her that,
in less than twenty-four hours, Ash had changed her
from the woman she thought she was into the eager,
pliant wanton he held in his arms now.

It was this self-disgust which made her say, 'What
a fool I was ever to trust you! And it's not as if I
wasn't warned.'

'Were you? By whom?' As usual, he sounded
amused. His fingers didn't stop their soft effleur-
age. With his other hand he began to loosen her
skirt.

'By someone I didn't listen to at the time. I should
have. I should have known that anyone capable of

seducing another man's girl would make mincemeat
of someone like me.'

Ash withdrew his hand and turned her round.
'Whose girl am I supposed to have seduced?'

'Their names were Lucy and Roger. I expect
you've forgotten her by now. A quick bash, or
whatever you'd call it, in the back of a car, after a
dance.'

His hands fell from her shoulders. He tilted a
sardonic eyebrow. 'Was your informant an eye-
witness, or is that an assumption on your part? A
rather curious assumption in view of your own recent
experience of my approach to women. Last night and
this morning didn't come in the category which
you've just described in those rather unbecoming
terms, did it?'

Christie coloured. 'I'm sure you've heard worse.'

'Much worse,' he agreed, on a dry note. 'But I'd
rather not hear them on your lips.'

'That's a red herring,' Christie said shortly.

'All right: you answer my question, and then I'll
tell you the facts about Lucy and Roger.'

She bit her lip. 'No, it didn't, but presumably, as
your wife, I rate preferential treatment.'

'Another remark like that and you'll rate an old-
fashioned spanking!' He moved a few paces past her
to a table where Rose had left a try with glasses and a
flask of iced water. He filled the glasses before he
said, 'Lucy was engaged to Roger for two reasons—
because her family were in favour, and because she'd
panicked.'

'Panicked?' she echoed, as he came back to where

she was standing and put one of the glasses into her hand.

'She was pregnant by an older man. He already had a wife and a child, and he didn't want to know about hers. She couldn't face telling her family, and she couldn't face an abortion. The only alternative was Roger, poor chump.'

He paused to drink some of his water. 'On the night you were told about, I could see that she wasn't used to drinking and was well on the way to being tight. I could also see Roger wasn't the type to handle the situation with any finesse. So I danced her off and took her across to *Sunbird One* where I gave her black coffee and some fatherly advice. Someone must have seen us leaving the festivities, and warned Roger that my intentions were usually dishonourable. He came to her rescue, by then rather tipsy himself, and was too aggressive for his own good. He took a swing at me, and I dodged it. He fell over, hitting his nose, and bled like a pig.'

He grinned at the memory of it. 'He couldn't go back to the dance with his shirt all bloodied, and he wasn't fit to drive her home. To avert a quarrel between them, I left him on board with another chap who was there, and took her for a stroll round the Dockyard. Then she wanted to see it by moonlight from Shirley Heights, and I like it up there on a fine night, so up we went. On the way she unburdened herself, and asked my advice.'

'What did you tell her?' Christie asked curiously, wondering how a man would see the girl's problem.

'That it would be asking for trouble to palm the

child off on Roger. Either she had to be honest with him, and hope that he cared for her as much as he claimed. Or she had to face up to bringing up the baby single-handed, with aid from her people and the State. She wasn't a girl with much spirit, but one couldn't help feeling sorry for her. She'd been pretty badly conned, poor little wretch.'

'By the wretched man who made her pregnant. Yes, what a rat he must be.'

'By him, but not only him. By all the people who promote claptrap ideas about free relationships and open marriages, and so on. There are quite a few girls like Lucy who do things they don't really want to because they think "everyone" does it, and they'll either miss out or be laughed at if they don't go along with the herd. She's not the only person to have her fingers burned in the permissive Seventies, but it looks as if the Eighties might see a revival of commonsense.'

Such views, coming from him, astonished her.

Ash guessed her reaction, and said, 'A life style which works for a man in his thirties can be disastrous for a girl in her twenties. Anyway, Lucy and I had a long talk up there on the Heights, and by the time we returned Roger had gone home in a huff. So she stayed the night on *Sunbird*, chaperoned by a retired Naval chaplain and his wife who were spending Christmas here. The next day she told Roger the truth. At the time he couldn't take it and shot back to England on the first available plane. However, I heard from her later that he'd come back to her and they were going to be married.'

'Could it ever work out?' said Christie doubtfully. 'Two not very sensible people, and another man's child?'

'I believe so. If they both want it to work, and concentrate on each other's happiness rather than their own.'

He was watching her very intently as he made this statement.

'Is that an oblique way of saying that I should concentrate on your   well-being, even if it conflicts with mine?'

'Is there a conflict?'

'You know there is. We agreed to a certain kind of marriage, and you've changed that. You . .   you've forced all this on me.'

'I've never yet known a woman who wanted a man to ask her permission to make love to her. Any man who says "May I?" is going to be refused on principle,' was his dry response.

'A convenient theory, but not well founded,' she said coldly. 'The dozens, perhaps scores, of women who have welcomed you into their beds don't represent their entire sex. Just as not all men—very few, I should think—would have acted as ... high-handedly as you have.'

She had not yet drunk any of the water he had given her, but he took the glass away from her and replaced it, with his own, on the table. Then he came back towards her, and something in his expression made her shrink back a pace before standing her ground.

About two feet from her, he halted, arms folded.

'Let me make something clear to you, Christiana. I don't want to hear any more of these cutting allusions to my past. No normal man of my age has not had some—not scores and not dozens!—relationships with women. In my case they've always been women like myself, adults and free agents. Contrary to gossip, I've never seduced a young girl or been the first person to cuckold another man. For practical reasons as much as moral ones. Inexperienced women are unsatisfactory partners, and the number of divorcees floating about makes it unnecessary to break up any more marriages.'

He paused, his lips momentarily compressed in a grimmer line than Christie had ever seen before. She discovered that when he was displeased he could be daunting indeed.

'However, all that's in the past. I now have a wife to warm my bed and'—and the grimness lightening—'although you're inexperienced now, I detect signs of natural aptitude. So no more shrewish cracks, please. One more and you'll find that pretty backside of yours smarting!'

The dark eyes were smiling now. 'This time I'm going to be lenient, although perhaps you won't think so.'

'W—what do you mean?'

He reached out and drew her to him.

'I'm going to give myself the pleasure of undressing you, and then we'll take that shower I suggested, and then—'

He left his intentions unfinished, and his mouth came down firmly on hers.

Their take-off that night was delayed. Owing to
some mix-up in the bookings, there were more passengers boarding at Antigua than had been expected. In consequence some of the aircraft's fuel
had to be discharged to compensate for the extra
weight of people and baggage.

Christie heard, without really listening, the grum-
bles of the homegoing holidaymakers. Some had
small fretful children to cope with, and all were sorry
to have come to the end of their holiday in the sun,
and to be returning to everyday life with three
months of the English winter still to come.

She knew how she would have felt had she been in
their shoes, with the added anguish of leaving her
nephew behind. But what were her feelings as things
stood?

As the aircraft soared into the night, and they
waited for the illuminated safety-belt sign to be
extinguished and the cabin crew to pass along the
aisles with the drinks trolleys, she wondered if all she
had gained by becoming Mrs Ashcroft Lambard
could outweigh being forced to submit to the passion of the man beside her.

In a way it would have been easier to bear if he had
been like her first husband, intent on his own satisfaction and achieving it without delay.

But Ash was at pains to ensure that she shared his
enjoyment, and it was that which, somehow, made it
unbearable. At least Mike had loved her, and said so.
Ash abstained from using any endearments. A few
hours earlier he had forced her to a high pitch of
ecstasy, and never once called her darling.

She was beginning to think that an act of love, however clumsy and frustrating, was preferable to an act of lust performed with great virtuosity but no real affection.

It was one o'clock in the morning before, at last, dinner was served. The menu that night was seafood cocktail, roast sirloin of beef, and Black Forest Gâteau. It sounded better than it tasted, and Christie was not hungry anyway. Nor, apparently, was Ash.

He had bought her a headset in case she wanted to follow the film, but immediately after the meal he settled down to sleep. They were in the Economy Class section because, in his view, the extra comfort of First Class was not worth the extra fare. But their part of the plane was extremely cramped for a tall man, and some of the passengers were not considerate of their fellows and went on wandering about and chatting to people they had met on holiday. Ash had the aisle seat, Christie the one in the middle, and the window seat was occupied by an unsmiling dark-skinned woman who had got on at Barbados or Trinidad.

Christie watched the film because she knew it would be impossible for her to sleep. But Ash, having closed his eyes, did not stir. It gave her, when the film was over, her first opportunity to study his face in minute detail.

A fine face to match a fine body, she thought. With his eyes closed so that one wasn't distracted by the sardonic gleam which often lurked in them, it was possible to appraise his features as critically as those of a sculpture. A strong face, bold and decisive.

She remembered him referring to the motto of the Special Air Service, the élite British regiment of commandos whose exacting training was only survived by men of exceptional fitness, initiative and guts. He would have survived it, she was certain.

Who dares wins. Last night was a mutual victory. Can you deny it?

Suddenly she remembered the source of the phrase which, on and off, had been plaguing her memory all day.

It had been in an article by Katherine Whitehorn, the well-known journalist and columnist. She had read it ages ago, probably before her first marriage, and one sentence had been filed way in her mind, like an obscure fact in a computer, and had never since been retrieved, until she woke up this morning.

She still couldn't recall the theme of the article, only that single sentence about waking with all one's hormones the right way up after a smashing night with one's true love.

But Ash was not her true love.

She stared at his sleeping face which was half turned towards her, emphasising the high slant of his cheekbone and the strong, uncompromising jawline.

Then it hit her with a force of a blow; the sudden shattering discovery that Ash Lambard *was* her love.

In almost every respect he personified all she admired in men. He was courteous, capable, responsible; he had a ready sense of humour and, to quote Miranda, 'a cultivated mind in the body of a man of action'. He was kind to old ladies and

children. Physically he was the most attractive man
she had ever met. As a lover she knew him to be both
painstaking and imaginative. What more could a
woman want in a man?

Only that he should love her was well as desire
her.

But that doesn't make any difference to my having
fallen in love with him, she thought.

For the next hour or more, as they flew east, into
the early sunrise, she sat motionless, trying to come
to terms with this new and amazing complication of
an already complex situation.

She could see now why she had been nervous when
Ash had crossed Devil's Bridge. It had been one of
several signals which she had not understood at the
time.

She did not remember becoming drowsy, but she
must have dozed. Because the next thing she knew
was that breakfast was about to be served, and she
was no longer sitting upright but leaning against her
husband.

He had put the arm-rest out of the way, and had
his arm round her, with her head cushioned on his
broad shoulder.

'How long have you been awake?' she asked,
drawing away.

'About an hour. I went to have a quick shave
before the main rush to the washrooms, and when I
came back you didn't look too comfortable, so I got
rid of this'—putting the arm-rest back in position.

'Thank you. I hope I haven't given you pins and
needles.'

She avoided his eyes, afraid that he might see in hers some clue to the revelation which had come to her during the night.

It was late morning when the aircraft touched down. Immediately the ebony face of the woman on her right was split by a beaming smile. She began to chat, making Christie realise that she wasn't as sullen as she had seemed. She had been afraid, but now, safely back on the ground, was cheerful and friendly.

How easy it is to form a wrong impression of people, Christie thought, as Ash handed down the woman's belongings from the the locker.

As they left the aircraft, she noticed how the smiles of the two stewardesses standing by the exit became more animated as they saw the tall man behind her. She wondered if he was looking appreciatively at them. Even if he were in love with her, she would not expect him never to take note of a pretty face.

All that's in the past, he had said, of his close relations with other women.

But could a wife hold a husband who did not love her once making love to her had lost its novelty?

ELEVEN

NEVER having landed at Heathrow before, Christie had no idea of the procedure at a very large airport. But Ash had and when, after landing, some of the people around them began to stand up and open the lockers for their belongings, he said, 'There's no hurry. The last off the plane will get clear just as fast as the first.'

There was some way to walk from the aircraft to the barrier where their passports were briefly inspected. Then they entered a large baggage hall where passengers from several flights were waiting to see their cases appear on the various baggage carousels.

'Wait here.' He strolled off and, some minutes later, returned with a trolley.

When their cases appeared, he hoisted them easily off the conveyor belt and pushed the trolley towards the Green section of the Customs hall. Only a couple of officers were on duty there, and they showed no interest in Ash and Christie.

On the other side of Customs, a large crowd of friends and relations were waiting to meet arrivals. Christie assumed that now Ash would make for the Underground, or perhaps take the airport bus to the Victoria Air Terminal in Central London.

Instead, she was amazed to find, he had laid on a

chauffeur-driven car. The address he gave to the driver was not that of her flat where she had expected to be staying, but somewhere in the West End.

'Where are we going?' she asked him, as the car set off.

The driver had put a plaid wool rug over her knees, but the morning, although cold, was bright and sunny—a pale, soft sunshine compared with the golden light of Antigua.

'I've booked one of the apartments where I always stay when I'm in London. I prefer them to a hotel, and they're more conveniently situated than your place. A lot of the stores are within walking distance. If you want to go over to the Sloane Street–Knightsbridge area, you'll have this car to call on. Taxis can be hard to come by at lunchtime and towards closing time. You're going to have a full enough schedule without hanging about in the cold, or the wet, waiting for a taxi to bring you and your parcels home.'

'You're very considerate,' Christie said stiffly.

'My consideration is not entirely disinterested. I don't want my wife to be too exhausted at the end of a wearing day's shopping to have any energy left for me.'

He reached for her hand, raised it to his lips and, when she glanced at him, gave her a smile of unequivocal sensuality.

Flushing, she snatched her hand free, and looked quickly at the driver. But the glass panel between the front and back seats was closed. If the man could see them in his rear-view mirror, he had not been looking in it just then.

The entrance to the flats was in one of Mayfair's quieter squares. They stayed in the car until the driver had announced their arrival on an entryphone and the electrically-operated door had been unlocked by whoever was in charge of the flats.

When the lift brought them to the sixth floor, they were met by a woman in an overall whom Ash introduced as the housekeeper. She showed them to their apartment, followed by the driver with their cases. Ash asked him to call for them at four.

When they were on their own, he said to Christie, 'I expect you'd like to have a bath after that uncomfortable night. I'm going out to buy something to eat and drink. I'll be back in about forty minutes.'

This was an unforeseen respite. As soon as the outer door had closed behind him she expelled a long sigh and relaxed slightly.

The sitting-room seemed small by comparison with the Hathaways' exceptionally spacious rooms, but it was well furnished with a fitted carpet, a sofa and two armchairs, a glass-topped coffee table to match the round dining-table, and good quality lamps and pictures. There was a television set, and a coin-operated telephone. The green and white glazed chintz curtains were lined and interlined, and when Christie drew aside the white net glass curtains she looked out on the topmost branches of the plane trees growing in the square gardens. Double-glazing reduced any noise from the traffic circling the gardens, and the flat was centrally heated.

The rest of it consisted of a small fitted kitchen, a pink bathroom, and a bedroom with a double bed and plenty of storage in drawers and cupboards.

In much less than forty minutes, or so it seemed to her, she heard Ash's key in the lock. She was in the bedroom, wrapped in a bath towel, unpacking and hanging up her clothes. Had she realised how much time had passed , she would have dressed sooner. However, having seen that he had two large paper carriers with him, she thought he would unload and put away his purchases, giving her a chance to dress.

But she barely had time to unwrap the towel and scramble into briefs and a bra before he strolled into the bedroom.

Moving to the head of the bed, he took hold of the cover and pulled it away from the crisp white pillowcases and neatly folded down top sheet. At the same time, his other hand was starting to loosen his tie.

'Are you g-going to bed?' she asked uncertainly. She had picked up the towel and was holding it in front of herself.

'I am. How about you? I should think you could do with a nap after having so little sleep last night.'

'No, I—I'm not tired at the moment.'

'Good, because I'm not tired either. I wasn't intending to sleep.'

He threw aside his tie and came to her, reaching out to take away the towel with which she was concealing her scanty underclothes.

Christie backed away 'No   please . not now.'

'Why not now? We have half an hour to fill before the wine will be chilled. What better way is there?'

She shrank back until the wall behind her made

further retreat impossible. 'I—I don't want to . . .
you have no right to force me.'

'I'm not going to force you. Only coax you.' There
was a smile in his eyes.

Her grip on the bath towel tightened. The stub-
born line of her chin became more pronounced as she
braced herself to resist him.

'Are you going to fight me again? I don't know
why, since it's now established beyond doubt that,
far from being frigid, you're a normal, warm-
blooded girl with all the right reflexes. You also
have a beautiful body, so there's nothing to be shy
about.'

As he spoke, he moved close and reached out, not
to take hold of the towel she was clutching, but to put
his arms round and behind her, and open the clasp of
her bra.

'Don't . . . *don't*—'

But her angry protest was smothered by the
hungry pressure of his mouth.

He kissed her for a long time and then, with his lips
to her cheek, he said, in a husky murmur, 'You want
this as much as I do. Why not admit it?'

'I don't . . . I do *not*! It's degrading.'

At that he lifted his head, looking down at her
tormented face with eyes which had narrowed and
hardened.

'Degrading? Why, for God's sake?'

Forgetting the clasp he had undone, she let go the
towel and, placing both palms on his chest, gave him
a vigorous shove. She succeeded, because he let her,
in pushing him off a couple of paces. But the sharp

movement also made the cups fall away from her breasts.

As she snatched them back, she said furiously, 'Because we don't love each other. To me, sex without any love is a . . . a disgusting travesty.'

'It didn't seem to disgust you the night before last, once I'd overcome your initial reluctance.'

A deep blush suffused her face and spread down her neck. She said in a low, goaded voice, 'If you torture someone you can make them admit to anything. If you use your sexual skills on me, of course my body will respond. But not my mind . . . not my heart. You can never impose force on them.'

Ash had been unbuttoning his shirt. He pulled it free of his pants, unbuttoned the cuffs and shrugged it off, his dark gaze intent on her face.

'At least my despised sexual skills have relieved you of the depression of believing yourself to be abnormal. I thought you might have been glad to be freed of that burden.'

'But now I have a new and worse burden imposed on me,' she retorted bitterly.

She saw anger flare in his eyes. He jerked down his zip and stepped out of his trousers.

'Yes,' he said curtly. 'If that's how you choose to regard it, I'm afraid you have. Because for me, the delights of your body are better than all the other pleasures of the flesh. And one day you're going to agree that what we are about to do together is not degrading. It's a gift from the gods which I don't intend to deny myself because of your scruples, my girl.'

He was fully undressed now, as naked as the statues of ancient Greek athletes. Except that they had not been sculpted at the moment described so graphically in the poem she had read on the eve of their wedding.

She was afraid that, because she had annoyed him, this time he might take her swiftly, before she was as ready for him as obviously he was for her

The still unforgotten misery of past ordeals made her cringe as he came towards her. But it was an inward cringing which she was too proud to let him see.

She might have known he would have a far more subtle way of punishing her than by hurting her. The first thing he did was to refuse her uneasy appeal. 'Can't we draw the curtains?'

Now that she knew she loved him, she was terrified of revealing it; of having him watch her face as he drove her mad with his devilishly skilful hands and his knowledge of all the most sensitive parts of her body.

'No, I like to look as well as touch.'

He smiled as he said it, but there was a vengeful glint in his eyes which made her quail. She could tell that her angry outburst—and particularly that last lie, that he would never reach her heart—had only served to fuel his determination to conquer her completely. She felt sure that, without loving her, he meant to make her love him.

As usual, she tried to resist and, as usual, he soon overcame her. It was not long before his kisses had deprived her of all rational thought.

Aroused as she knew him to be, he still held himself in check until, though she strove not to show it, her pulses were racing with a fever of desperate excitement. But this time Ash did not allow her to reach the lovely sensation she had experienced on the island.

Suddenly he stopped kissing her and touching her. She kept her eyes closed, but felt a movement on the bed which made her feel sick with disappointment. She thought that now, for the first time, he was going to indulge his own hunger without the delectable prelude she had already learned to expect.

Ash parted her legs, and his mouth seared the tender flesh inside one quivering brown thigh. She waited for him to enter her, and then gave a gasp of shock and a smothered scream.

Her body coiled like a spring as she reached down to grab with both hands his thick, springy hair. Her tug on his head must have hurt him, but it didn't stop what he was doing to her. His strong hands snapped over her wrists, biting painfully into her flesh until she released her hold on him.

Christie's shoulders sank back on the bed. She surrendered to waves of ecstasy.

When, presently, he moved upwards, covering her body with his, the exquisite ripples of pleasure were still coursing out to her nerve ends. She arched her hips to receive him, and her slender arms twined round his neck.

It was not until later, when Ash had gone to have a shower, and she was alone with her hot face buried in the pillow, that she realised how refined a punish ment he had inflicted upon her. Inhibited as she still was, the act which had given her such pleasure now caused her agonies of shame.

How could she have lain back and let him? How could she face him when he returned from the bathroom? And what other shameful delights did he mean to impose on her?

At four they set out for the suburb where she had lived.

Christie had telephoned Margaret before they left the apartment, and they went to Mrs Kelly's flat first. She was delighted with her presents, delighted to see Christie again, and doubly delighted at what she obviously took to be a whirlwind love match.

After spending some time in Christie's flat, they took Margaret out to dine at a good Italian restaurant before returning to the West End.

The next day Ash arranged for two international removal firms to come and give estimates of their charges. She spent the whole day sorting through her possessions, deciding what to have shipped and what could be given to Oxfam or some other charitable organisation.

That night, Ash took her to hear Kiri te Kanawa sing at the Royal Opera House. It had long been one of her ambitions to attend a performance by the singer whose face and figure were as beautiful as her voice. As they took their seats, Christie was aware of interested glances from people nearby. Unaccustomed to being stared at in that way, she wondered what was attracting their attention. Then she realised that she was unusual in having bare shoulders—she was wearing the dress Ash had given her—and being golden brown in January. Perhaps she was thought to be a member of the jet set. Little did they know, she thought amusedly.

Afterwards they dined at the Arlington, a quiet, spacious rose-coloured restaurant where people who had been to the theatre could order a meal until midnight. They began dinner with deep-fried mushrooms, followed by roast duck with fresh vegetables and a bottle of red Burgundy which Christie found rather dry. But obviously it suited her husband's palate, and he drank most of it.

It was the kind of luxurious evening which Christie had never experienced before, and the fact that she was dining with by far the most personable man in the restaurant, with whom she was in love, made it an almost perfect occasion.

The next day it was necessary to spend several hours at the flat. In the afternoon she called on former colleagues who were still on holiday. They could not conceal their amazement at seeing her so greatly altered, accompanied by an attractive husband, and being driven about by a chauffeur.

Her final call was on the Principal, to apologise in person for deserting his staff so precipitately. To her relief, for her action had weighed on her conscience, his attitude was sympathetic rather than aggrieved.

'It's always inconvenient when a valued member of the staff has to be replaced, but I'm delighted that, after many misfortunes, your future promises to be much happier,' he told her kindly.

To Ash, he said, 'Unlike many bridegrooms, you won't have to suffer a period of burnt offerings and inexpert household management, Mr Lambard. I've long known that Christie has a disposition which greatly endeared her to her pupils, but I must confess—and I don't think she'll mind my admitting it—that I hadn't realised what a very good-looking young woman she is. Your enviable climate and the well-known glow imparted by falling in love have worked a remarkable transformation. I congratulate you, and wish you both every happiness.'

'Thank you, sir. I'm well aware of my good fortune,' was her husband's smooth reply.

It wrung her heart to hear him sound so sincere, as if theirs was a marriage made in Heaven, not a practical partnership leavened, but perhaps not for long, by his physical desire for her.

That night he took her to Boulestin's where the walls lined with apricot silk, the chandeliers and the eighteenth-century oil paintings turned her thoughts to the drawing-room at Heron's Sound. She wondered if the same colour might be a good choice there.

They began their dinner with quail mousse served in hens' eggs, and followed by turbot cooked in a leaf of spinach with watercress sauce. Throughout the meal, which ended with fruit brulée, they drank vintage Krug.

'I don't think you liked the wine I ordered last night. You should have said so,' Ash remarked, watching her take her first sip of the champagne.

'I know which wines are correct with which dishes, but that isn't to say I have an educated palate,' she answered.

'The "correct" wine is the one you like. Don't be fooled by people who pretend to be connoisseurs. Few of them are; they're practising winesmanship, and it can be very amusing. But nowadays not many people, unless they're professionally involved or have large expense accounts, can afford to educate their palates. The expense account has ruined many restaurants. They don't have to bother any more because the majority of their clientele don't know good food from mediocre food, or fine wines from moderately good ones.'

'This tastes delicious to me,' said Christie.

'Good. I want to give you pleasure.'

Ash raised his own glass and drank, watching her over the rim with a look which made her face flame.

The night before last, tired out by her wakeful night on the aircraft, she had been asleep before he had come out of the bathroom. Last night, seeing that she was weary after the long day sorting out the flat, Ash had not attempted to make love to her. But she guessed he would not allow a third night to pass without touching her, and perhaps he intended to repeat the thrilling caresses about which her feelings were still torn between shocked shyness and unwilling excitement.

On the way back to the flat, Ash announced that they were going to spend the weekend with friends in the country, and would leave London by road at eleven o'clock the following morning.

'We're going to stay with Hugo and Emily Ffar-

ington. I hope you'll like them. He's my oldest
friend. We were at school together and it was his
father, dead now, who taught me to sail when I spent
several holidays with them,' he told her. 'There's to
be a dinner party tomorrow night, so pack something
suitable. It's an old house, but not a cold one.'

At the flat he switched on the television, explaining that earlier, while glancing through the evening's
programmes, he had noticed a thirty-minute documentary which should be interesting.

'I think I'll go and do my nails,' said Christie.

It was not that the programme didn't appeal to
her, but that she was glad of an opportunity to attend
to aspects of her grooming which she didn't want to
deal with in his presence. Since the wedding she
hadn't had a chance to shave her legs or renew the
pale pearl lacquer on her toenails.

If Ash was going to watch television for half an
hour, it would give her time to catch up with various
feminine rituals and embark on the visit to his friends
with the confidence that, whatever else they might
find lacking in her, at least his friend's wife wouldn't
be able to fault her grooming.

While she was shaving and doing her eyebrows,
which luckily needed very little attention to keep
them in shape, she kept the bathroom door locked.
Afterwards she decided to have a shower and to use
an after-bath lotion she had bought during the day
and which was still in her tote bag.

When she went to fetch it, she could hear the voice
of the television narrator coming from the other
room. She wondered if Ash would watch whatever

followed the documentary, or if he would switch off and join her.

If he did the latter, she would have to postpone painting her nails until the morning. Perhaps she wouldn't paint them at all. If the Ffaringtons lived in the country, and were sailing people, Emily might be the open-air type who didn't go in for cosmetics and varnished nails.

Christie herself, after four years of going without make-up or French scent, was thoroughly enjoying their use again. But she was very willing to modify her eye make-up and leave off coloured varnish if it would help her to establish a rapport with the wife of her husband's closest friend.

Returning to the bathroom, she didn't bother to lock the door a second time. A few moments later she was under the shower, slowly revolving to get herself thoroughly wet before turning the tap off while she soaped herself.

Working up from her feet, she was busily lathering her thighs when the shower curtain was swept aside, making her give a smothered exclamation of surprise.

'You sound happy tonight,' said her husband, appraising her wet brown form.

Until he spoke, she had not realised that she had been singing to herself.

He took the tablet of soap from her and turned her round to stand with her back to him. Then he rubbed the tablet over her upper back and spread the lather with his other hand.

'Are you happy?' he asked.

'I ... I'm not unhappy,' she conceded, sharply
ware of the pressure of his long fingers sliding
aressingly over her moist skin.

He had already undressed and was as naked as
he. Did he mean to take another shower with her?

The last time he had had to keep her under the
hower with him by force. She had not realised that
he had fallen in love with him, and had still been
onsumed with rage at his breaking his promise not
o make love to her.

Now, in spite of her protests and her continued
esistance, she knew in her heart that he had been
ight to take her. If he hadn't, she would have spent
he rest of her life convinced that she was frigid,
ever knowing the delicious sensations which were
eginning to course through her as his hand glided
ver her back.

Ash stepped over the side of the bath and pulled
er backwards into his arms, holding her there with
strong arm clamped round her waist while he
arted to lather her front.

This time she did not squirm and struggle, but
ood in motionless submission while he stroked her
lky wet flesh.

'Is that the best you can say—that you're not
nhappy?' he murmured, some moments later.

'What do you want me to say?' Her voice was
reathless and uneven, betraying the disturbance
ithin her.

He didn't answer, but his hands began to do
ings which made passive resistance impossible.
gainst her will, her head sank back on his shoulder

and her body relaxed and responded to his skilfu
mastery of her senses.

He began to nibble her ear, softly biting the lob
with his teeth, and kissing the side of her neck. Wit
one hand spread below her navel, he pressed he
against him, making her feel his desire for her.

'I'm going to turn the shower on.' His voice wa
husky but steady.

The warm water, already mixed to a comfortabl
temperature, began like a light summer rain whic
became a tropical deluge as he turned the pressure t
full. As it poured down on Christie's body, he re
sumed his slow, patient caresses. She was beginnin
to know that, with him, love was never a rush
However fiercely he wanted her, he would not un
leash his own passion until she was trembling with
pleasure, her inhibitions swept away.

'No, Ash . . . no . . . please,' she said faintly
feeling the tremors beginning.

But she didn't really want him to stop and, know
ing that she didn't, he ignored her stammered pro
test and went on making love to her under th
cascading water. Not until she was on the edge o
ecstasy did he stop: but only to turn off the showe
and wrap her in warmed white towels, and carry he
through to the bedroom

There, on the thick pile carpet, not once but agai
and again, he reduced her to rapturous shudder
which swept away all her control. When, scarcel
knowing what she was doing, she mutely beseeche
an embrace which included them both, he told he
thickly, 'Not yet.'

Finally, when she felt exhausted with pleasure, he gave her a brief, bemused respite by drying her wet hair and gently towelling the rest of her until, incredibly, she found herself quivering and trembling.

All at once his self-control snapped. As delight zinged along her nerves, more piercing this time than before, he took her with a fierce, silent urgency.

Some time later she was dimly aware of being lifted, but although it woke her she did not open her eyes. As soon as she was placed on the bed she felt sleep enclosing her again, like a fog which had thinned for a moment, only to become even more dense.

The next time she woke, the room was no longer quite dark. It was very early in the morning, and the faint grey light before sunrise was beginning to filter round the edges of the curtains.

Ash was lying close behind her, his arm heavy on her ribcage, his hand enclosing her left breast. At first she was only aware of being warm and snug, and at peace in a special kind of way. It was allied to a feeling she had occasionally experienced after vigorous exercise; a long, brisk winter's day walk, or a bracing spring swim in the sea off the south coast of England. All her muscles felt toned and relaxed, not a single tension left anywhere.

But as she remembered the reason for this agreeable sense of well-being, and how not one word of love had been exchanged, the peacefulness left her. She began to fret against the possessive intimacy of his hold on her, and to be ashamed of her abandonment the night before.

She remembered, years ago, coming across a copy of the Victorian bestseller *Trilby* in which a Hungarian musician and hypnotist called Svengali had mesmerised an artist's model into becoming a famous singer. After his death the spell was broken. The girl lost her wonderful voice and died of a broken heart.

Christie was beginning to feel that, when Ash made love to her, he exercised the same kind of power which Svengali had had over Trilby.

Suddenly he stirred in his sleep, withdrawing the slack weight of his arm as he rolled over on to his back. Secure in his love for her, she would have turned and snuggled against him, her head on his shoulder, her arm on his smooth, sun-tanned chest. Instead she remained where she was; physically fulfilled, but emotionally as starved as she had ever been.

Having expected to arrive at an ordinary small country house, Christie was taken aback when next day, about an hour's drive from London, the hired car turned in at a very large, impressive gateway with lichened stone peacocks on top of the tall brick gateposts, and the crest from a coat of arms incorporated into the design of the wrought iron gates which were standing open to admit them.

The long, well-kept drive was fenced off from the surrounding parkland, sheep grazing on one side of the drive, cattle on the other.

'This used to be a fine avenue of elms, but they all fell victim to Dutch elm disease, and Hugo has had to

replant with these limes,' said Ash, indicating the
new trees. 'In the spring these wide grass verges are
thick with daffodils.'

'You didn't warn me your friends lived in a stately
home,' Christie said, a little apprehensively.

'Does it make any difference?' he said. Then,
before she could reply, 'It's not the most salient fact
about them. *That* is that they have achieved what I
hope you and I will, some day.'

'What do you mean?'

He gave her an enigmatic glance. 'You'll see for
yourself very shortly.'

The house which now came into view was a
battlemented Elizabethan manor, built in the 1560s
of Kentish ragstone, although Christie did not learn
these details about it till later.

Her first impression was of a very large yet somehow cosy-looking house, mellowed by more than
four centuries of English summers and winters until
it looked as natural to the landscape as the several
splendid cedars of Lebanon growing on the lawns in
front of the principal entrance.

When the car drew up Ash sprang out, and turned
to help Christie step on to the gravel. Their arrival
had been seen. An elderly man in black trousers and
a grey alpaca coat had come out to greet them.

Ash grinned at him. 'Hello, Johnson. How are
you?'

'Very well, thank you, Mr Lambard. You're in
your usual good health, I hope?'

'Yes, thanks.' Ash turned to Christie. 'Darling,'—
unaware of the pang the endearment caused her, he

put an arm round her shoulders and drew her nearer to him—'this is Johnson who's been in charge of the household since Hugo and I were at prep school, and long before that, as a matter of fact. Forty years, isn't it, Johnson?'

'Forty-two years, to be precise, sir. Good morning, madam.' The butler inclined his head to her. 'Sir Hugo and Lady Emily asked me to express their apologies to you and Mrs Lambard, sir. They both had to go out this morning, but should be back very shortly. Lady Ffarington is in the family room and looking forward to your arrival.'

'Then we'll go up to her immediately.'

Taking Christie by the hand, Ash led her into the house and across the large hall where dark rose red walls gave a warm and welcoming atmosphere, and were a good background for the many gilt-framed family portraits slanting up the wall behind the wide stone staircase.

At the top of the stairs he led her along a corridor to a doorway where he paused to knock. Then, opening one of the tall double doors, he gave Christie an encouraging push into the room within.

The interior was not what she was expecting. In size and proportion it was a room of immense grandeur, with columns of marmalade-coloured marble dividing it into three sections, and some very elaborate classical plasterwork ornamenting the ceiling.

But the floor was covered with wall-to-wall natural jute matting, and the chairs and sofas—some modern, some eighteenth-century—were upholstered and cushioned in every shade of yellow from honey to banana, with one or two light blue accents.

A television set, a child's first tricycle, an easel with a half-finished painting, the pieces of a jigsaw puzzle all spread face up on a table—these were some of the things Christie noticed in her first glance around her.

Then, although it seemed no one was there, a woman's clear voice—a voice with a smile in it—said, 'My dear Ash, how lovely to see you! Always so beautifully brown and now, at long last, with your bride. Come and give me a hug, dearest boy.'

Then Christie saw, rolling towards them, a light metal invalid chair, its occupant a woman with curly white hair and a mesh of crow's-feet no doubt caused by and now accentuating the charm of their owner's smile.

'Aunt Diana—how are you?' He bent to kiss her on both cheeks.

'I'm well. We all are. And this is your lovely Christiana. Welcome to Peacocks, my dear. I've hoped for a long time that Ash would eventually find someone to make him as happy as my sweet daughter-in-law has made my son. You'll meet them both very soon.'

She extended a thin, mottled hand, but in spite of its fragile appearance her handshake was a firm one.

'How do you do, Lady Ffarington.'

Christie, not usually shy with strangers, knew that her response sounded stiff. It was caused by renewed embarrassment at being taken for a radiantly happy bride. She thought the adjective Lady Ffarington had applied to her must have been a compliment on her part, rather than a reference to anything Ash had said in his telephone talk with her son.

It was true that, when making love, he would tell her how beautiful she was, but she thought this was part of his technique, something he said to all the women he bedded.

'I think you should call me Aunt Diana as Ash does,' said Lady Ffarington.

As she spoke, a black pug trotted towards them. followed by a tall man and woman, both wearing navy blue fishermen's slops over sweaters and corduroy trousers. The man was fair, the woman redhaired. They were followed at a leisurely plod by an elderly golden retriever.

'So sorry we weren't here when you arrived, Ash.' The woman was the first to greet him, offering her cheek for a kiss

Then the two men exchange hearty handshakes, and Sir Hugo clapped Ash on the shoulder. 'You look disgustingly fit as usual.'

His own face was far from pale, having the ruddy colour of someone outdoors in all weathers.

Christie stood by, waiting her turn, liking the look of these people. wanting them to like her.

Emily Ffarington didn't wait for Ash to present his bride to her. She said, 'Christiana— hello. As you realise, I'm Emily We've been so looking forward to meeting you. We could hardly believe our ears when Ash rang up to ask if he could pitch up for the weekend, bringing a brand new wife.'

'As I should have been your best man, Ash, if you hadn't already done the deed, I'm going to insist on the right to give the bride a kiss,' said her husband. Having done so, he bent a very kind smile on Christie, saying, 'Ash didn't exaggerate when he told us to expect a stunner. As he's long past the age of being dazzled by a lovely face, I'm sure you're as nice to know as you are to look at, Christiana.'

'Thank you.' She returned his smile.

She noticed he had hazel eyes with green flecks while Emily's eyes were amber with golden flecks in them.

'Ah, Johnson, well done,' was his next remark, as his butler came in with a bottle of champagne in an ice bucket.

It was not long before they all had a glass in their hand, and their host was completing his welcome with a toast to the hope that Christie and Ash might find marriage as agreeable an institution as he and Emily had done in their eight years' experience of it.

Presently, Emily said, 'I expect Christiana would like to wash before lunch. I've put you in the room at the end of the east corridor, Ash. Will you show her where it is, or shall I?'

'I'll take her. I need a wash too.'

'We'll still be in here when you're ready. With a party tonight, we thought a light lunch would be enough.'

As he took her to the room prepared for them, Christie asked, '*Did* you tell Hugo I was a stunner, or was he merely being flattering?'

'I think knock-out was the word I used—as indeed you are. The first time I met you I saw your potential. By the time you'd been in Antigua a week you

were starting to look a different person. Now the
transformation is complete. There are not many
flowers out in England, but it's certainly your blos-
som time. There's nothing like sexual fulfilment for
putting a bloom on a woman.'

'Oh, hush . . . someone might overhear!' She
looked nervously over her shoulder.

'There's no one to hear, or to see.'

Ash stopped, caught her to him, and kissed her. It
began playfully, but before long she knew that he
wanted to do more than kiss her.

She wrenched her mouth free. 'Please, Ash . . . not
now . . . please!'

'No, there isn't time,' he agreed reluctantly. 'And
after lunch they'll suggest a tramp in the woods. We
shall have to wait until we come up to change for
dinner.'

His embrace had slackened, and she was able to
free herself.

She was provoked into saying, 'You may be impatient—I'm not.'

The moment the words were out, she wished she
hadn't said them. Ash recaptured her, pressing her
close, making her feel the impatient surge of his
desire for her.

'I could make you retract that jibe,' he said, with a
punitive gleam. 'And you know it, don't you, little
spitfire?' His lips to her ear, he added in a husky tone,
'I could bring you to the very brink, and leave you
there—all afternoon. Don't try me too far, Christiana.'

She knew it was no idle threat. In some moods, he

was capable of anything. To make them both late for lunch because he had taken the time to force her beyond the point when she could resist him, to reduce her to the helpless victim of his infinite skill and her own unsuspected wantonness, would not cause him any discomfiture.

It would be she, and only she, who would sit through the meal hardly able to swallow for embarrassment; afraid that one of the others would sense the pitch of voluptuous excitement to which he had driven her.

'I didn't mean it,' she said hurriedly.

Ash gave a short, humourless laugh. 'You meant it—but it wasn't true.'

He let her go and walked on.

Their bedroom was decorated in shades of terracotta, and dominated by a tester bed with curtains of printed cotton at its four corners, and the same cotton, quilted, as a cover.

The air was deliciously scented by a fragrance emanating from the small golden flowers on the otherwise naked branches in a vase on one of the windowsills. Later Emily told her this was witch hazel, although she, being a gardener, used its botanical name, *Hamamelis mollis*, and the popular one for Christie's benefit

Their cases had been unpacked for them, and her hairbrush and some of her make-up arranged on the dressing-table which stood in the angle of the two window walls. The bedroom, being on a corner, overlooked two sides of the house, one pair of windows looking out on a large lake amid parkland, and the other pair giving a view of the gardens.

'I learned to sail on that lake,' said Ash, in his normal voice, not the impassioned tone he had used to her in the corridor.

Relieved that his ardour had subsided, she said, 'Do I take it Hugo is a baronet?'

'Yes, it's a hereditary title. Emily's father is a duke, so she's always been Lady Emily, which saves the confusion of there being two Lady Ffaringtons. She was twenty when Hugo married her, so she's four years older than you are.'

'Have they children?'

'Three—twin sons of seven, and a younger boy of just three whose trike you may have noticed in the family room. They'll have been out of doors all morning, as the weather's good. We'll meet them at lunch.'

Christie used the bathroom first and when she came out, replacing her rings on her left hand, Ash said, 'Don't wait for me. You can find your own way back, can't you?'

'Yes. All right, I'll go on ahead.'

She was nearly back to the family room, as he had called it, when she paused to admire a fine painting of a battle scene. While she was standing there, not three yards from the door which Ash must have left partially open, she heard Lady Ffarington say, 'How very unfortunate that Celia is coming tonight. I can quite see you couldn't put her off, but it's not an ideal situation—a man's bride and an old flame at the same dinner party.'

'Particularly when the old flame is Celia, who will

flirt outrageously with him just to be tiresome.' This was Emily's voice.

'She won't get any encouragement. He'll soon make it clear that that party is long since over.' Now it was Hugo speaking.

'That will only egg her on,' was Emily's answer. 'She's like Ash himself used to be. Celia adores a challenge. If a man appears to be indifferent, she can't rest till she's made a conquest. I should think that's what attracted him about Christiana. She's rather reserved, isn't she?'

'Yes, but that may pass off when she gets to know us. Do you think she'll hold him, Hugo? Do you think Ash really has changed?' The question came from his mother.

'I don't know, Mama. Perhaps. It's a side of his life I've never really understood, not being the type women fling themselves at.'

'Nonsense! You're just as attractive as he is.'

'You're prejudiced, Emmy. Ash always had a hell of a lot more opportunities than I ever did, but whether he made the most of them because womanising is his nature, or because he hadn't then encountered the one absolutely right girl for him, I honestly wouldn't know. He's never discussed women with me.'

'I have a sinking feeling the leopard doesn't change its spots. I hope I'm wrong. I like what I've seen of his wife so far,' was the comment made by his mother.

At this point the sound of children's voices coming from another direction roused Christie to an aware-

ness that the conversation she had heard had not
been meant for the ears of any but the three people
inside the family room.

There was no time to wonder when, and for how
long, the unknown Celia had been Ash's bright new
flame before the Ffaringtons' three sons and a
pleasant-faced woman in her forties appeared round
a corner and approached her.

'You must be Mrs Lambard. I'm Nanny Maitland. How do you do?'

They shook hands, and then the twins, Harry and
Ranulf, and the little boy, Duff, were introduced.

Lunch was eaten round a large table at one end of
the huge family room. Although simple, it was delicious, beginning with puréed chicken livers baked in
a buttery *brioche* dough. This was followed by gar-
licky hamburgers with a tomato sauce and spinach.
The pudding was poached pears.

Christie noticed approvingly that the children ate
everything which was put in front of them. John was
inclined to look askance at anything but the conveni-
ence foods which her undomesticated sister had fed
her family on, but Christie hoped to cure him of his
faddiness eventually.

The twins joined in the conversation, but without
any showing off. Duff concentrated on his food, with
some discreet assistance from Nanny Maitland.

As Ash had predicted, after lunch his friend pro-
posed a walk. But Emily said, 'You two chaps go off
for a tramp. I'm going to show Christiana the house
and the garden.'

Later, alone with Christie, she explained, 'I'm

being careful not to overdo things at the moment. I had two miscarriages between the twins and Duff, and I don't want to lose this baby which I'm just starting, so a gentle ramble round the garden is better for me than a strenuous hike with the men. Anyway, they'll enjoy an hour or two on their own. They're almost like brothers, you know. It's a shame they can't see more of each other. But Hugo is rooted here, and Ash belongs in the sun.'

In a gesture of impulsive warmth, she linked arms with Christie for a moment or two. 'It's going to be even nicer coming out to Antigua, as we do every year, now that Ash is married to someone of my own sort. Some of his girl-friends have been a bit chicken-witted. I'm dying to see this lovely old place he's bought. What fun for you, doing it up. Marrying Hugo, I could have been deprived of all that. But his mother is such a darling, she insisted I should re-do everything just the way I wanted it.'

They had come to a small lobby, leading into the garden. It was hung with old macs, tweed coats with leather-patched elbows, oilskins and a variety of headgear and footwear.

From this selection Christie borrowed a wind-cheater and a pair of green gumboots.

As they left the house, Emily went on, 'Diana's mother-in-law was the most appalling old battleaxe who went on ruling the roost until she died at ninety-three. She would never hear of any changes. By the time Diana had a free hand, she'd been struck by this wretched illness which keeps her in a wheel-chair. Also my father-in-law hated spending money inside the house, although he lavished it on the estate. The gardens have always been heaven. One must give Hugo's grandmother her due. She was a brilliant gardener, and a working one, too, unlike most of that generation.'

Even in January it was possible to see that, when spring came, the gardens at Peacocks would be heavenly indeed. Christie had had no idea there were so many winter-flowering shrubs and heathers. She saw that old flagstones, old bricks used for paths, and old statuary contributed a great deal to the beauty of the place, and gleaned many ideas that she felt could be adapted to good effect in a Caribbean garden.

But it was the interior of the house, even more than the grounds, which she enjoyed being shown.

'Have you had some training in interior design?' she asked Emily, impressed by her colour sense.

'No, but while Hugo's immersed in *Country Life*, I pore over *House & Garden*, and I've filched a lot of ideas from professional designers like David Hicks and David Mlinaric who specialise in dealing with this kind of house.'

Talking to Emily, feeling pleased by the rapport which had sprung up between them, Christie forgot the disturbing conversation she had overheard before lunch.

She remembered it while she was dressing for dinner. Ash had not come upstairs with her, as he had said he would. He and Hugo had walked several miles, coming back to the house at dusk to find the women and children enjoying hot buttered crumpets, home-made strawberry jam, shortbread and' Dundee cake.

Later, when Emily had suggested it was time to change, Hugo's comment had been, 'You girls go ahead. It'll take you an hour at least. Ash and I can be ready in ten minutes. Time for a drink, I think, Ash. What'll it be? Whisky and soda?'

For some seconds, not very long, Ash had turned his dark gaze on his wife, his expression inscrutable.

Had he been remembering their conversation before lunch and deliberating whether to find some reason for accompanying her?

Whatever had been in his mind, after a brief hesitation he had accepted the offer of a whisky and soda.

Before leaving London that morning, Christie had been into Liberty's and bought herself a red silk shirt to wear with the white Mexican skirt which had red flowers among its embroideries. She had also bought a kid tie belt of the same colour to link skirt and shirt together.

Her eyes and lips were made up with the cosmetics given her by her sister, and she was dressed and ready when Ash entered their bedroom.

'Will I do?' she asked, a little uncertainly, as he closed the door and she turned from her own final inspection of herself in the cheval-glass.

'Admirably,' was his answer. 'But I should take off those sand dollars.'

'Oh . . . yes, if you feel they don't look right.'

Although the skirt was embroidered in brilliant

colours, she had felt that the plain silk shirt needed a necklace of some sort

While she was removing the sand dollars, Ash crossed the room and she saw him take his shoulder-strapped travel bag from his part of the wardrobe. From the bag he extracted a package. Having stripped off the wrappings, he crumpled them and tossed them in the dressing-table waste box. He then placed two leather cases in front of her.

'I think these will look better,' he said.

The larger of the two cases was an unusual shape, more or less round with a projection at the back and front. She touched the catch and lifted the lid.

'*Ash!*' she gasped.

Lying in a serpentine groove in the dark velvet bed was an early Victorian snake necklet of overlapping gold scales. The snake's eyes were rubies, and its head was ornamented with rubies and diamonds, as was the heart suspended from its jaws.

'You like it?' He leaned over her shoulder to lift it from the case and put it round her neck.

The tip of the snake's tail fitted into a tiny slot at one side of the head. His hands rested on her chest as he dealt with the fastening.

'It's magnificent, and perfect with my lovely engagement ring.'

'That's what I thought when I noticed it in Asprey's window on my stroll this morning.'

'Asprey's! Oh, Ash, how extravagant of you. Thank you . . . thank you *very* much.' She controlled an impulse to take one of his hands, which now were on her shoulders, and kiss it.

After a pause, he asked, 'Aren't you going to open the other box?'

'Yes, of course.' She had been transfixed by the beauty of the jewel now lying at the base of her throat.

The second case contained a pair of small ruby ear-rings. He kept his hands on her shoulders while she fixed them in place and reiterated her thanks.

'Were you relieved or disappointed that I didn't come upstairs with you earlier?'

The question caught her unprepared. She opened her mouth to reply, but could find nothing to say.

He flicked the necklet with a forefinger. 'I suppose, now, you don't like to tell me that you were relieved,' he said, in his most sardonic tone.

'That's not fair! I wasn't—' she began.

'You weren't relieved?' He lifted a sceptical eyebrow. 'Then you must have been disappointed. In that case, let's hope the guests don't linger too late.'

His hand slid down from her shoulder to cover a breast. Within seconds his gentle fondling had exacted an involuntary response which brought a thin smile to his mouth.

'Shall I teach you something new tonight?—After you've stopped resisting and your alter ego has taken over?'

'I . . . hadn't you better start changing?' Already her voice was uneven. In a moment, if he didn't stop, she would start to tremble.

He gave a harsh laugh. 'Very well. I'll let you off for the moment. But later, when the party is over, we'll perform that degrading exercise which your mind rejects but your body seems to enjoy.'

With which he strode to the bathroom, leaving Christie upset and bewildered, all her pleasure in the jewels he had given her doused by the hostility in his manner.

TWELVE

As Christie made her way to the main staircase, intending to go down to the drawing-room on the ground floor which Emily had shown her earlier and where household and guests would meet, she encountered Nanny.

'How nice you look, Mrs Lambard. What an unusual skirt!'

'Thank you. It's from Mexico. My husband chose it.'

They chatted for a few minutes. To postpone the moment when she would have to put on a party smile and meet fifteen strangers, Christie asked, 'Might I say goodnight to the twins? I expect Duff is already asleep.'

'Yes, he is. But the twins are not. Do come.'

Christie lingered in the children's wing as long as possible. Eventually, Nanny said, 'I think they may be wondering what's become of you, Mrs Lambard.'

'Yes, I'd better go down. Goodnight, Nanny.'

Suddenly wishing she could spend the evening in the cosy day nursery, browsing through some of the Victorian and Edwardian children's books she had noticed on the crowded shelves, Christie left Nanny knitting, with a television set to switch on later if she wished.

A party of six people had recently arrived when

she reached the gallery which led from the top of the staircase round three sides of the upper hall, with corridors leading off it.

As she paused to look down, these three couples moved out of sight and Ash came into view below her, talking to an elderly woman. At the same time the butler opened the door to some new arrivals, two men and a much younger and extremely glamorous blonde woman in a black velvet cloak with a glittering clasp. At the sight of Ash she gave a loud exclamation.

'*Darling!* What a *super* surprise. I wasn't told *you* would be here. You're *exactly* the person I need to restore my morale. I've been having *the* most *ghastly* time—too unutterably vile. How *are* you? How *divine* to see you!'

After which enthusiastic outburst, delivered in a deep plummy drawl, she flung her arms round him and kissed him, full on the mouth.

Celia, I presume, thought Christie.

As she walked down the stairs she saw Celia let go of Ash and, smiling radiantly at him, reach up to unfasten her cloak.

'May I take that for you, Miss Dane?' the butler enquired, at her elbow.

'Thank you, Johnson.

Ash was wiping her lipstick off his mouth with a linen handkerchief. He caught sight of his wife, and said, 'Ah, here comes Christiana.'

'Christiana?' Celia swung round to see at whom he was looking.

As Christie descended the last few stairs, he introduced the other woman to her. Then, to Celia, he added, 'Christiana and I are in England for our honeymoon. We were married just under a week ago, in Antigua.'

'Married! *You* . . . married, Ash?' she exclaimed incredulously. 'Oh, darling, I can't *believe* it!'

'Looking at Christiana, I should think you would find it very easy to believe it.'

'How do you do, Miss Dane.' Christie offered her hand.

'How do you do. Well, yes, I do see what Ash means. You are rather a bobby-dazzler, as my father used to say.' Her large topaz-coloured eyes, fringed by long thick lashes, some her own and some not, appraised Christie's figure and clothes.

She herself was wearing clinging black silk, high-necked and long-sleeved but slit to mid-thigh on one side, revealing one black-stockinged leg and the four-inch-high heel which had enabled her to kiss Ash on the mouth.

By this time the two men who had arrived with her were in conversation with the elderly woman. Celia remembered their presence and summoned them.

'Peter . . . Leo . . . come and meet the honeymoon-ers.'

She made the introductions, Ash introduced Christie to the older woman, who was Mrs Leigh, and a few minutes later they all moved towards the drawing-room; Leo with Christie, Peter with Mrs Leigh, and Celia with her hand tucked in the crook of Ash's elbow and her blonde hair gleaming close to his shoulder.

It should have been a delightful evening and, in many ways, it was. All the men were in dinner jackets and white voile or soft piqué shirts, except one, a theatrical designer, who was wearing a navy silk polo under an emerald velvet jacket, and Ash. His dinner jacket was white, worn with a dark red silk waistcoat which Christie thought gave him the air of an unusually young commanding officer in tropical mess dress.

The drawing-room at Peacocks had been refurbished during the Regency. It was all white and gold and pale yellow satin. Emily had introduced several comfortable modern sofas in addition to the original ones, and everywhere there were porcelain cachepots filled with white hyacinths or with charming arrangements of dried and handmade silk flowers.

It was an elegant setting for a gathering of urbane, distinguished-looking men, and stylish women with well-kept figures and good clothes.

Emily, like Christie, was wearing a shirt and skirt, hers being of pale grey crêpe-de-chine and cashmere, with a rope of large amber beads, and her red hair caught up in a knot at the back of her head, in a way reminiscent of the fashion when the drawing-room had been redecorated.

Diana Ffarington was in black chiffon, a shirtdress, with which, having a long neck, she was wearing a Queen Alexandra collar of pearls with the emerald and diamond clasp at the front. Several magnificent rings flashed on her emaciated fingers.

Ash was known to most of the other guests. Before dinner, while everyone sipped dry Madeira and

moved about greeting each other and making civilised chit-chat, Christie was asked more than once
now he and she had met each other. She deduced
that a number of people took her to be the daughter
of one of his wealthy charterers.

Two of the women to whom she chatted admired
the snake necklet She noticed that they, and indeed
all the women present. wore antique jewels rather
than new ones.

'Yes, isn't it lovely? My husband gave it to me
tonight,' she replied. with a somewhat forced smile,
recalling the bitter mockery of his parting shot.

Admittedly Ash had paid her a graceful compliment when she came downstairs, but she still felt the
wound of his scathing words in their bedroom

They dined in the Chinese Parlour where, earlier
Emily had shown her the pipe enabling the beer once
made on the Peacocks estate to be drawn in the
dining-room. The room took its name from the
wallpaper with its duck egg blue background and
bright birds and insects flying about in a tracery of
white foliage An early English Axminster carpet,
with a ground of the same soft blue, reflected the
design of the ceiling

Christie was surprised to find that she had been
placed on Hugo's right Seeing that Ash was on
Emily's right at the other end of the long polished
table. she supposed this to be in honour of their
recent marriage

On her right was a retired Brigadier, now a dedi-
cated gardener, and on Hugo's left was a woman
potter with. beside her, the theatrical designer. Celia

Dane was near the centre of the table, on the sam
side as Ash, and thus unable to see or to be seen b
him.

A deliberate strategy by Emily, Christie guessec
She had not failed to notice that Celia had monopol
ised Ash throughout the pre-dinner period. It migh
have been difficult for him to get away from her, bu
not impossible for a man of his aplomb.

Remembering Emily's remark about her reserve
Christie made a great effort to be more vivaciou
during dinner, and was rewarded by twice makin
her companions laugh at episodes during he
teaching career.

She had expected the food to be even more delic
ous than at lunch, and it was.

'I think I should tell you that my beautiful, cleve
wife cooked everything we are eating tonight,' sai
Hugo, when they had begun the meal with Frenc
rarebit, the cheese flavoured with wine and garli
with Cognac as well as Worcester sauce in it.

'I don't know how she does it. I can cope with si
or eight, but twenty people would be beyond me
said the potter, whose name was Angela.

Emily had confided to Christie that her culinar
achievements were dependent on a French foo
processor, and a deep freezer which allowed her
stagger the cooking for a special occasion.

'She's a disciple of some Frenchwoman who ran
cookery school in Paris about thirty years ago,' sai
Hugo.

'I wonder who that was?' Angela remarked, look
ing surprised.

Christie said, 'I think it must have been Simone Beck. As far as I know she is still alive. The school was called L'École des Trois Gourmandes and one of her partners in the enterprise was an American, Julia Child, who is famous now as a television cookery demonstrator.'

Her guess was confirmed when the main course was served by Johnson and a team of women from the nearby village who were also the daily cleaners. It was turkey breasts baked with potatoes and cream, which Christie knew to be a Simone Beck adaptation of a classic presentation of veal.

Several times during dinner she noticed Hugo and his wife exchanging glances. Once he raised his glass of white wine in a wordless toast to the excellence of the meal they were enjoying.

The gesture made Christie remember Ash's remark in the car before their arrival: *They have achieved what I hope you and I will, some day.*

She would have liked to believe that he had meant the warmth of their love for each other. But a more realistic interpretation was that what he admired was the skilful way they had enhanced this beautiful old family house, and the gracious life style they enjoyed here.

Although Heron's Sound had fallen into a disrepair much more serious than the lack of any innovations imposed by Hugo's grandmother and father, it was not impossible to visualise Ash's Great House recovering its original splendours

The turkey was followed by a caramelised apple tart accompanied by a custard cream delicately

flavoured with almonds. No cheese was served. Emily
had told Christie that, at an informal meal, she
would serve cheese in place of a pudding. But in an
era when most people disliked over-eating, she
thought it unfair to tempt them to indulgences which
they would regret the next day.

Nor, out of consideration for her helpers, did she
let her guests linger at the table as was usually the
case when they ate upstairs in the family room.
Tonight coffee and liqueurs were served by Johnson
in the drawing-room, in order that the table could be
cleared and the very valuable Georgian silver returned to the strong-room for the night.

While people were forming new conversational
groups, Christie was approached by a woman who
said, 'I'm Beatrix Browning, Mrs Lambard. I'm
intrigued by your skirt. I feel it must be Mexican.'

'It is,' Christie agreed, with a smile.

'I thought so; only the Mexicans seem to be able to
combine all those vivid colours without any garish-
ness. Are you by any chance a fellow needlepointer
to use your American term for what we call canvas
work?'

'I'm afraid not. Nor am I American.'

'You're not? Oh, I'm sorry. I suppose I formed
that impression because the Caribbean is a mainly
American playground now, I believe, and also because you have the famous American bandbox look.'

'Do I?' said Christie, startled. 'Tell me about your
needlework, Mrs Browning. I've been admiring the
beautiful antique needlework in this house, and
know Lady Ffarington and Emily both do it.'

'*All* the most civilised women do it,' answered Mrs Browning, with a laugh. 'You should try it. I'm sure you'd enjoy it. My daughter-in-law, who has to travel a great deal, says flying about the world would be unbearable were it not for her needlepoint. She always has a piece with her in case the plane is delayed, or she can't get to sleep on night flights.'

'Where could I buy the materials to try my hand at it?'

'In London, either at the Royal School of Needle-work in Princes Gate, or there's an excellent shop in the Pimlico Road. Start with something small like a case for your sunglasses, or a coin purse. Canvas work is extremely hard-wearing. I'm still using a spectacle case which I made over twenty years ago.'

'Did you recognise my skirt as Mexican because you've visited Mexico?' Christie asked her.

'No, I only wish I had. That's a treat which my husband and I are reserving for when he retires. At present we don't really have the time to go farther afield than Europe. Every five years we go back to Paris, which is where we spent our honeymoon. It was there, last spring, celebrating our thirtieth anniversary, that I came under the influence of Manuel Canovas, the French interior designer.'

'Manuel Canovas sounds a Spanish name.'

'It is. His father was Spanish, but his mother was a Frenchwoman and Manuel was born in France. If you're ever in Paris, you must go to his showroom. It's in the Rue de l'Abbaye, opposite the palace of Cardinal de Furstenberg. He designs the most enchanting fabrics and wallpapers and carpets; and now his wife, Sophie, who designs bed-linen and accessories, has opened a boutique in the Place Furstenberg. If I could refurnish my house, regardless of expense, I should use nothing but their designs. As a young man he spent two years in Rome and two in Mexico, and he was one of the first designers to bring Mexican colours to Europe. Before that nobody had thought of using vibrant combinations like pink, orange and red together.'

'My husband and I are just about to do up a house. Not regardless of expense,' Christie added 'but perhaps we could splurge in the drawing-room. Is there anywhere in England where one can see Monsieur Canovas' designs, or are they only obtainable in Paris?'

'I feel sure they are available here, although I can't tell you where. But a firm I can recommend for beautiful fabrics in the English taste is Colefax and Fowler in Brook Street. All their chintzes are based on old designs. But of course, being English, you'll know them.'

'I've heard of them,' Christie agreed. 'But I imagine they're rather expensive. I've always subscribed to the maxim that it's better to have curtains made from yards of cheap fabric than to skimp on expensive fabric.'

'Oh, absolutely,' the other woman agreed. 'Did you know that one pair of silk curtains with a swagged pelmet can cost three thousand pounds? Or that mohair velvet is now eighty pounds a metre? But even very expensive material looks nothing if it's not properly lined and interlined.'

'I agree about the lining. I don't think interlining would be necessary where we live,' said Christie.

'Perhaps not in the bedrooms, but I should have it in your drawing-room curtains,' advised Mrs Browning. 'Interlining isn't only for warmth, you know. It absorbs noise, and protects the curtain from dust blown in when the windows are open. I'm rather an expert on the subject because we spent Christmas with some people whose daughter has made a profession of curtain-making in London. She does those elaborate festoon curtains which look so delightful in old houses, and Roman blinds, and swags and tails. She was telling me the ideal lining for bedroom curtains is something called Black Italian, and there's a finer than usual interlining called Domette. According to her, good curtains are such an investment that in about fifteen years' time one should be able to sell them for twice as much as they cost despite their being used in the meantime.'

Their conversation lasted for some time, and would have absorbed all Christie's attention had she not been conscious that Celia was again beside Ash. A wife who knew herself to be loved would not mind how many attractive women cast seductive glances at her husband, she thought, half listening to Mrs Browning. And a wife who did have some qualms, and more savoir-faire than she possessed, would probably wander over and nip the attempted flirtation in the bud.

Having always despised jealousy, Christie was unwilling to admit to the nature of her feelings when she saw Celia rest her hand on Ash's forearm.

Jealousy springs from possessiveness, and you and I would not possess each other. Ours would be a marriage of companionship and shared endeavours.

Since Ash had said that to her, the terms of their marriage had undergone a drastic change, and now he did possess her—entirely. It was too much to expect that she should remain indifferent when another woman threw out lures to him. Surely everyone must think it was very strange for a bridegroom to spend so much time with a woman with whom he was known to have had an affair?

To her relief, the next time she allowed her glance to stray in that direction, it was Hugo to whom Celia was talking in her affectedly emphatic style. Ash was now in another part of the room with two other men.

But Christie had a dispiriting feeling that he had not cut short the tête-à-tête with Celia. More than likely Emily or Lady Ffarington had discreetly suggested to Hugo that he should break it up.

About midnight, after several of the older guests had taken their leave, Lady Ffarington retired to bed. Late nights taxed her limited strength. But the younger Ffaringtons' contemporaries showed no inclination to break up a party which might, Christie gathered, continue well into the small hours, with more coffee or drinks being offered to the latestayers.

At one o'clock she murmured to Emily, 'Would you think it rude if I went to bed? I believe I'm still suffering from jet-lag'—although this was merely an excuse. The flight east had not been as disruptive to her sleep pattern as the flight to Antigua before Christmas.

'Of course I don't mind,' said Emily. 'you should have gone earlier, Christie. Perhaps Ash is tired, too, although he does seem to be one of those people with almost inexhaustible energy. I think you'll find him in the library with Nicholas. They were going to refer to the encyclopaedia to settle an argument they were having.'

Without saying goodnight to anyone else, Christie slipped away. In the deserted hall, she paused, debating whether to seek out her husband. If she did, would he take it to mean that she wanted him to come with her for other purposes than sleep?

But if she did not, he would think it cowardice on her part; a deliberate avoidance of the act to which, as he well knew, she had ambivalent feelings of desire and dread.

Eventually, knowing that tired as she was it would be impossible to sleep until he came up, she made her way to the library. She wouldn't mention going to bed. She would merely sit in on their conversation, and leave the initiative to Ash.

Looking round the library earlier, she had breathed in the ineffable odour of hundreds of old leather bindings and thousands, perhaps even millions, of leaves of the handmade paper of earlier centuries.

She smelt it again as she quietly opened the heavy door. The library was almost in darkness. Only at the far end of the room was one reading lamp casting a pool of light on a table piled with old volumes.

Behind the table was the man who had been
introduced to her as Nicholas Fitz-Something. On
the nearer side, seated face to face in a pair of
high-backed leather chairs, were her husband and
Celia Dane.

The shaded glow from the lamp flattered Celia's
broad-cheeked Slavic facial structure, and the hair
which, dyed though it might be, was a very subtle
silver-gilt blonde, in excellent condition. The slit in
her dress had ridden up, revealing shapely legs
which were crossed and slanted to one side to display
them to their greatest advantage.

'. . . couldn't *bear* to be tied down. I'm for living life
free; untrammelled by husbands and children, and
the thousand and one *dreary* chores which the female
flesh *still* seems to be heir to,' she was saying, as
Christie paused on the threshold.

'Speaking of chores, I've promised to spend
tomorrow chopping a tree down for my mother. I'd
better be off,' said Nicholas. 'Goodnight, Lambard.
Goodnight, Celia.'

Christie waited for Ash to stand up and say that
he, too, had been thinking it was time to turn in. But
he said only, 'Goodnight. I hope we'll meet again
next time I'm over here.'

And the younger man walked towards the door
the other two stayed where they were, causing
Christie swiftly to withdraw before Nicholas spotted
her.

There was no time to fly up the stairs before he
emerged into the hall. She whisked herself inside the
room next door to the library which she knew to be

the seldom-used morning room.

Through a narrow aperture she watched Nicholas cross the hall to say goodnight to his host and hostess. As soon as he had disappeared, she emerged from her hiding-place and ran up the staircase. She was breathless when she reached the bedroom and flung herself into an armchair.

She had assumed that Celia had left the party with the two men who had entered the house with her. But now it was clear that the three of them had merely arrived on the doorstep at the same moment, having travelled to the party in different cars. Now she came to think of it, Celia was not the type of woman to rely on lifts from friends. She would have her own car, probably something rather dashing like a Mercedes sports or a two-seater Porsche.

It was almost two o'clock by the time Christie had undressed, taken off her make-up, paced about the room for a while, and finally climbed into the curtained tester bed.

The perfect hostess, Emily had placed or caused to be placed on the night table an airtight tin of biscuits and a vacuum flask of iced water.

After a while, Christie switched off the light and lay down. She had left three of the windows curtained, and drawn back the pair at the window with the witch hazel on the sill. Its sweet scent permeated the room.

The shaft of winter moonlight coming in through the window did not reach the bed. But the travelling clock she had brought with her had hands which could be read in the dark. She lay on her side, and watched them creep round the dial until they reached three. A few seconds later, from somewhere far along the corridor, she heard the muffled chimes of a longcase clock.

Was the party still in progress? Surely not. A more likely explanation of her husband's continued absence was that Celia lived not far away, and had prevailed on him to drive her home and walk back across the park. For all her talk of freedom, she would not disdain the gambit of playing the nervous female, glad of a strong man to see her home safely. And once she had him on her own ground . . .

Tormented by visions of Ash making love to Celia while his wife lay alone and sleepless, Christie's temper began to boil with rage, and with what she was forced to admit was jealousy.

For a while she dozed, to be woken by a slight sound which, instantly alert, she recognised as the door closing. She lay rigid, holding her breath until she heard the bathroom door being opened and closed. It was now half past four in the morning.

He was in the bathroom for a little more than five minutes. Then she heard him emerge and soundlessly cross to the bed. She forced herself to breathe with the shallow, even rhythm of the sleeper.

Whoever had turned down the bed had placed his pyjamas on the pillow. But Ash would not put them on. In Antigua, and in warm houses, he slept naked. The pyjamas were for night-time emergencies.

She felt the mattress move as he climbed in beside her, but he settled down quickly, leaving a space between them. She heard him yawn. Soon after wards he was sleeping as deeply and peacefully as she had pretended to be.

Less than one week married, and already he had been unfaithful to her. Hot tears coursed down her cheeks, but she made no sound as she wept.

THIRTEEN

CHRISTIE woke up in the morning feeling heavy-eyed and jaded. Ash was still asleep, lying on his stomach with his forearms under the pillow and his dark head turned away from her. He appeared to be sleeping heavily, and no doubt would continue to do so for several hours.

Fortunately Emily had suggested that they should get up when they felt like it. Hugo, normally an early riser, on Sundays liked to lie in bed reading the newspapers until it was time to drive his mother to morning service at the parish church.

Not from any religious conviction, but out of his strong sense of noblesse oblige, he sat through the service and drove her home. Sometimes Emily went with them, but not every week.

Sliding stealthily out of bed, Christie went to the bathroom where, slowly, to make as little noise as possible, she ran a hot bath. Meanwhile she brushed her teeth, combed her hair, and splashed her eyelids with cold water.

She felt immeasurably depressed that the not unexpected disillusionment had come so much sooner than even she had expected. Clearly, although Ash had transformed her attitude to making love, he had found her an unexciting partner. What did Celia do which made her so much more satisfactory? she wondered.

She had scarcely sat down in the water when, to her astonishment, the bathroom door opened and Ash strolled in. He was wearing his navy dressing-gown.

'You don't mind if I shave while you bath, I hope?'

She had been about to lie back, but now she stayed as she was with her knees drawn up to her chest.

'I—I thought you were asleep.'

'No, I've been awake for half an hour.'

There was no hint of guilt in his expression before he turned to the handbasin and opened the mirror-glass doors of the hanging cupboard to take out his tooth and shaving brushes. A moment later he shed the dressing-gown and stood there as naked as she was, the muscles rippling on his back as he started to brush his teeth.

Christie, who had intended her bath to be a relaxing one, now began briskly to lather herself. In the circumstances, she resented the casual intimacy of his invasion of the bathroom while she was using it, and regretted not locking the door.

Her resentment fermented as she used her soapy bath mitt, loofah on one side and friction terry on the other, on her legs and arms. By the time she used the hand shower to rinse off, her temper was again at boiling point.

Suddenly she saw a way to put him out of countenance for a change; to indict him for his despicable behaviour far more subtly than by a direct accusation.

All men, but particularly men like Ash, were vain

about their virility. She remembered her sister telling her about a local *crime passionnel* in which a
woman had narrowly escaped being killed by her
normally inoffensive husband, not because of her
infidelity but because of her cruel taunts about his
inadequacy as a lover.

After a debauch with Celia, and less than four
hours' sleep, it seemed unlikely that Ash's potency
would be equal to any further demands on it.
Obviously he had made love to Celia relying on the
certainty that his still-timid wife would never dream
of inviting a repeat performance before he had recovered his powers. But there were situations which
could goad the shyest people to take bold initiatives,
and this was one of them.

'Shall I leave the bath water for you?' she asked.
'It's not dirty, and I didn't put any scented essence in
it.'

'Yes, there's no point in running a fresh bath.
While there's no shortage here in England—
although heating the stuff is expensive—there's often
a shortage on the island. To use water more econo-
mically is something most people have to learn. I'm
glad you're already economy-minded.'

She stood up and reached for a towel. Meeting his
glance through the mirror with an affable smile, she
said, 'As you say, hot water is expensive. I've never
wasted it.'

Although she deliberately paused before wrapping
the towel round herself, she noticed that his gaze
didn't stray to her wet body but returned to his jaw,
now covered with creamy lather. That in itself was

unlike him, and an indication that he was not in a
lecherous mood.

Christie made a performance of drying herself so
that Ash had almost finished shaving before she
stepped on to the bathmat, leaving the bath free for
him.

As he lowered himself into the water, she let down
her hair which had been pinned up out of the way.
Then she discarded the towel and sat down on the
cork-topped stool to rub lotion into her legs. The
stool was near the foot of the bath where she was in
full view of her husband.

She did not look at him, and was sure he did not
look at her. But if he hadn't already got the message,
she would make sure he had before she had finished
with him.

Her legs and elbows satisfactorily moisturised, she
capped the bottle and stood up, one hand on her hip.
'Shall I scrub your back for you?'

'If you wish.'

His tone held a guarded note. For the first time
since they were married it was his turn to show
reluctance, she thought vengefully. Not that it gave
her any satisfaction to have her suspicions confirmed. It made her feel sick with misery.

She re-lathered the loofah side of the mitt and,
perched on the rim of the bath, a little behind him,
she began to apply it vigorously to his broad shoulders and down his spine. At the same time her other
hand stroked the nape of his neck, and several times
she leaned closer and allowed her breasts to brush
against him.

By now, in his usual frame of mind, Ash would have looked over his shoulder and given her the predatory grin which indicated that the signal had been received loud and clear, and very shortly she would be the one being tantalised.

But he didn't look round. He just sat with his long legs drawn up and his forearms resting on his knees.

Carefully concealing the evidence that her ministrations were having no effect whatever, Christie thought furiously.

Suddenly her wish to humiliate him by forcing a situation in which, if not admitted in words, his temporary impotence was clear to them both, changed to a profound despair. Even if she was not frigid, she lacked the power to hold her husband even for the short duration of their honeymoon.

'There you are,' she said listlessly, tossing the mitt into the water in front of him.

'Thank you.' His tone was that of a man thanking a middle-aged waitress for bringing him a cup of tea.

Christie dried her hands, and her breasts where they had been moistened by contact with his back. Looking down at herself she saw that, ironically, it was she who had begun to react to the slippery smoothness of his tanned skin.

She went through to the bedroom, closing the door behind her. She saw the room through a shimmer of tears, and longed to crawl back into bed and weep as she had in the night.

Oh, God! What sort of life could they have together if Ash was going to be continually unfaithful to her?

With drooping shoulders she crossed the room towards the drawers containing her clean underwear. Before she reached them, strong arms swung her off her feet, and she found herself cradled against Ash's chest. As she opened her mouth to protest, he kissed her—the demanding kiss of a man confident of an equally passionate response.

Before the kiss ended, and he straightened to smile down at her, she was on her back on the bed, and it was instantly clear that, far from being impotent, he desired her with the utmost urgency.

'I enjoyed that seduction,' he said. 'I suspected you had it in you, but I thought it would be much longer before you could bring yourself to make love to me.' His voice was husky, his dark eyes alight with hunger. 'Move over a little.' He made to lie down beside her.

Christie moved, but not to make room for him. She flung herself across the bed and sprang to her feet on the other side.

'Hey, where are you off to? Come back here.'

'I don't want to come back.' She snatched up her robe from the ottoman at the foot of the bed and hastened to cover herself. 'Do you think you can ignore me all evening, come to bed when it's practically morning, and then do as you please with me? I wasn't trying to seduce you. I was simply scrubbing your back, and trying very hard not to show how furious I was.'

Ash sat up and put his feet to the floor. 'Come now, Christiana, I wasn't born yesterday. You were inviting me to make love to you, and you know it. What's all this nonsense about my ignoring you last night?'

'You didn't speak to me all evening.'

'It wasn't necessary. You were never left alone. A husband and wife aren't supposed to stick together at parties. When a couple do talk to each other, they're either bored out of their minds by uncongenial company, or they're not pulling their weight as guests.'

'Miss Dane certainly wasn't pulling *her* weight. She was concentrating exclusively on you, except at dinner when she was forced to speak to other people.'

At first she couldn't read his reaction. His eyes narrowed slightly. She thought he was starting to scowl at her. Then she realised he was amused; not only amused, but also pleased.

'So that's it,' he said, his voice silky. 'You were jealous of Celia.'

'Not jealous. Annoyed,' she said shortly. 'And I think with good reason. We had an agreement not to advertise the peculiarities of our marriage.'

'Which is now a great deal less peculiar than you had intended it to be,' was Ash's dry comment. 'In fact it's becoming more normal all the time. You must have grown fond of me, Christie, if Celia's antics made you jealous.'

'I was not . . . *not* . . . NOT jealous!' she blazed. 'I just thought it extremely bad manners for you to devote almost the entire evening to a woman who used to be your mistress when you're honeymooning with someone else.'

'Who told you that about Celia? Not Emily, I'm certain.'

'Nobody told me. It was obvious from the way she kissed you, and from your own reputation. Yes, I know you warned me never to drag up your past. But you also assured me it *was* past. It didn't seem to be last night.'

'That's rubbish,' he told her roundly. 'As a matter of fact, a wife with a little more nous would have come to my rescue. It's none too easy for a man to avoid the clutches of a really determined man-eater without being churlish. Eventually Hugo detached her.'

'Are you saying she was never your mistress? I don't believe it.'

'I think the term mistress suggests a different type of relationship from a very brief fling with Celia five years ago.'

'And your even briefer fling with her last night.'

Recklessly, Christie went on, 'I was awake when you crept into this room at half past four in the morning. When I came to tell you I was going to bed, you and she were alone in the library. I'm not a *complete* fool, Ash.'

'You think I let Celia seduce me . . . here, in this house, after the party?'

'If not here, at her house perhaps.'

For some moments he didn't speak. Finally, his voice very soft, he said, 'You don't trust me even half an inch, do you?'

'In certain respects. Not that one.'

'Would you believe me if I denied it?'

'You haven't denied it.'

'No, I'm damned if I will.' He stood up and moved

round the bed. As Christie edged backwards, alarmed by the glint in his eyes, he said, 'Words prove nothing. But there's one certain way to convince you I'm not having it off with anyone else.'

'W-what do you mean?'

'We shall have to make love more often—as often as it takes to assure you. Starting now.'

'No!' she backed away.

'Yes.' He was closing in on her, forcing her into a corner from which her only escape was across the bed.

Usually careful with other people's property, but just now oblivious to everything but the punitive light in Ash's eyes, Christie made a wild leap on the bed, only to measure her length as he Rugby-tackled her legs and made her sprawl helplessly forward.

Then he flung himself bodily on top of her, and she felt his warm lips pressed against the top of her spine, and his hands sliding underneath her in search of her breasts, and his hard, desirous male body pinning her, breathless, beneath him.

Christie writhed and squirmed, to no avail. As her futile efforts subsided, Ash rolled off and turned her over, the front of her robe falling open above and below the loose sash.

As she tried to clutch it and cover herself, he sprang on her again, face to face, for a moment kneeling between her thighs, his arms braced, preparing to swoop.

For the first time, he did not delay but took her with fierce immediacy.

Afterwards, calmed and relaxed, he made gentle,

patient love to her until her slim body arched in the final voluptuous paroxysm. With a long shuddering sigh she lay still and, exhausted, let sleep overcome her.

Her idea that a few hours' rest would have not been enough to restore his depleted virility after making love to Celia was conclusively proved to be an error when Ash awoke her with kisses.

After making love to her again, he said, 'Perhaps that will relieve your mind for the rest of today.'

She flinched from his sardonic tone.

'I think it's time we got up,' was his next remark.

As he rose from the bed, she saw that it was nearly noon.

He was dressed before her, but he waited until she was ready. In silence they left the bedroom. Christie could not help feeling embarrassed by their belated appearance. She hoped very much that Emily had gone to church with the others, and that none of them would have returned yet. If so, they need never know how late she and Ash had stayed in bed.

Neither Hugo's wife nor his mother was in the family room, but he was there, drinking black coffee.

Having said good morning, he went on, 'I hope you're feeling as fragile as I am, Ash. You should be. You drank a hell of a lot more of that ruinous gutrot than I did. Why didn't I stick to whisky?'

'Gutrot! It was a particularly fine old rum which has been maturing in the cask for the better part of twenty years,' Ash returned equably.

'I have to admit it slid down very smoothly last night, but this morning—oh, God! What a headache. I suppose lack of sleep doesn't help. Did Christiana give you hell when you finally tottered to bed, reeking of rum and raw onions?'

'I didn't have onions—you did. I had only cheese in my sandwich.'

'And I suppose your wife's still too new to raise Cain when you misbehave,' said Hugo, with a rueful grin. 'Mine's not. To say that Emmy was cross is an understatement. I think it was mainly the onions. Being pregnant, she's temporarily rather intolerant for my weakness for them.'

'I heard that, you drunken beast,' said Emily, wheeling her mother-in-law's chair into the room. 'Good morning, Christiana. Was your beloved as revoltingly smelly as mine was when these two reprobates finally staggered to bed? Rum and raw onions! Ugh, what a nauseating combination! And what sacrilege, too, after feasting like kings earlier on.'

'Yes, but darling, that was seven hours earlier. One gets a bit peckish at half past three in the morning,' Hugo pointed out.

'I've forgiven you, actually. You can even kiss me—on the cheek, please, to be on the safe side,' she added, with an affectionate twinkle.

He gave her a light kiss, and left his arm on her shoulders. Catching sight of Christie's expression, he said, 'Christiana looks shocked. Maybe Ash managed to slip into bed without waking her, and she thinks we really were tight. I can assure you we weren't'—smiling at her, 'merely genial. Isn't that so, Ash?'

'Quite right. If I did wake her up, she didn't let me know. But as you pointed out, Hugo, a bride is inclined to overlook her husband's shortcomings, and to think—for a few months at least—that he can do no wrong.'

Ash looked at his friends, not at her, as he made this remark, but she knew it was directed at her, for being so ready to mistrust him.

Even so, she could not quite dismiss the possibility that the two men were in collusion. It was not unusual for friends to tolerate each other's peccadilloes even though, in a general sense, they did not approve of such behaviour. To betray Emily's trust might be unthinkable to Hugo. He might deplore Ash's conduct. But simply to spare her feelings, he might be prepared to cover for him.

'I went to bed early,' she said. 'What time did the party break up?'

'About half past one,' said Emily. 'The last to leave was our local *femme fatale*, Celia. She's always a stayer, especially now that she's on her own for a while. I suppose it's catty to say so, but I think she's going to have problems finding eligible lovers from now on. At twenty-five she was spectacularly good-looking, but now she's nearer to thirty-five the gloss is beginning to wear off. Anyway, having listened to her problems, I pushed her off home, made tea, and left these two chaps to gossip. Goodness knows what they found to talk about all that time.'

'The future, mainly,' said Hugo. 'Now that Ash

has a house and a family, he's equally concerned about the future. Although you've always been interested in making money, haven't you, old chap? I suppose it's the blood of your Greek shipping forebears coming out. My lot, all basically farmers, have been mainly concerned to conserve what they already had. But that isn't enough in the modern world.'

The talk turned to world inflation, and remained on that topic until lunchtime.

When the car came to fetch Ash and Christie the following morning, Emily left Peacocks with them. She owned, as a *pied-à-terre*, a tiny mews cottage in Chelsea. It had been a wedding present from her father whose ancestors had once owned half Belgravia, the area which had succeeded Mayfair as London's most fashionable residential area.

When Christie asked Ash the origin of the word mews, he said that originally it had meant the place where the king's falcons were kept. Later it had come to refer to the stables behind the great mansions. As cars had succeeded carriages, the stables had become garages for the Rolls-Royces, Bentleys and Lagondas of the Twenties and Thirties. After the Second World War, in which many great houses had been reduced to rubble by bombing, people had begun to realise that the garages could be converted into attractive little houses, perfect as a first home for a young married couple. Since then the demand for them had steadily increased until now cottages in the most desirable mews were fetching prices far beyond the pockets of all but the most affluent newlyweds.

'Hugo tells me that the place next to yours was sold for a hundred and fifteen thousand pounds—for a thirty-year lease,' Ash remarked to Emily, who was seated between them.

'Yes, and it isn't as nice as ours. But the price I find most incredible is two million one hundred thousand, which is what is being asked for a penthouse in St James's Place. I suppose two million is a fleabite to an oil millionaire. But they say that most of the sheiks have left London now, and moved on to America. I suppose they can't stand our climate.' Emily turned to look at Christie. 'It was amazing what an influence they exerted on the things in the shops, wasn't it? Not so much in my favourite places, but certainly on stores like Harrods. The change in their window displays was quite dramatic.'

'Was it? I hardly ever shopped in central London. Partly for lack of time, but largely for lack of money,' Christie said candidly.

She knew Emily would think no less of her for admitting to having been hard up. People like the Ffaringtons were not impressed by wealth *per se*. Even if rich themselves, which was not always the case, they had an outlook quite different from that of the newly rich.

Emily and Hugo used the cottage about once a month for shopping and going to the theatre, and more often during the season for events such as the Chelsea Flower Show and London weddings. Emily took Ash to task for not borrowing the cottage for his honeymoon.

For the rest of that day and all the next one, she and Christie went shopping together. As she had said, Christie had never had the time or the money to shop in the West End, but Emily knew all the best hunting grounds around Sloane Street, Walton Street and Ebury Street.

She was an invaluable guide to the shops frequented by the owners of England's "listed" country houses, large and small; and Christie knew it was these people's style she must emulate to achieve the right atmosphere at Heron's Sound. Fortunately her own taste already inclined in that direction. She doubted if Ash would have married her had it not. He was far too much of a realist to marry someone whose taste differed drastically from his.

Because she and her husband did not stay there long enough to get tired of it, Emily had chosen the strawberry as her theme for the decorations at the cottage. Her bedroom was papered with tiny wild strawberries, and the sitting-room had berry red linen on the walls, a soft leaf green carpet overlaid with a red and white Portuguese rug, and white glazed chintz curtains. The effect was very fresh and pretty, and it gave Christie a brainwave for a similar if less concentrated theme at Heron's Sound.

'Do you think it would be a good plan to use the Antigua Black pineapple as a recurring motif in our house?' she asked the other girl. 'We've a lovely bed with pineapples carved on the posts.'

'I think it's a splendid idea, and a practical one, too, because it's no use settling on a motif which is almost impossibly hard to find,' was Emily's reaction. 'But the pineapple is something one sees on fabrics and braids, and the ends of curtain poles and those big stone finials for gateposts. Which reminds me, a place I must take you to is Beardmore's. They're the best architectural ironmongers in London, with a tremendous range of reproduction antique drawer handles, period door furniture and all that sort of thing. I shouldn't mind betting they'll be able to produce some pineapples for you, perhaps in the form of curtain hold-backs.'

While the girls were busy shopping, Ash had his own things to do. These included having a look at the facilities offered by London's newest club, the St James', which had film stars Roger Moore, Michael Caine and Liza Minnelli on its committee under the chairmanship of actor Sir John Mills.

Ash thought the club, conveniently situated in Park Place, a quiet cul-de-sac off St James's Street, would be even more suitable for them than the block of flats they were staying in.

On Emily's second day in London, he arranged for them to lunch with him there, and afterwards they were shown one of the air-conditioned suites, and one of the fifteen studios which had fabric-tented ceilings and stylish Italian furnishings.

When Emily had returned to the country, and Christie was shopping alone, there were intervals during the day when a coffee break or light lunch at the General Trading Company—one of her friend's favourite haunts both for its merchandise and restaurant—gave her time to think about her husband and her marriage.

She had not forgotten the satisfaction in his eyes when he said, *You must have grown fond of me if Celia's antics made you jealous.* Nor had she forgotten Emily's remarks: *She's like Ash himself used to be. Celia adores a challenge. If a man appears indifferent, she can't rest till she's made a conquest. I should think that's what attracted him about Christie. She's rather reserved, isn't she?*

The more she thought about it, the stronger became her conviction that the only way to hold her husband was to respond with enthusiasm to his lovemaking, but always be a little cool, a little withdrawn at all other times.

One day, together, they went out of London to a place near Syon House, a great mansion with a magnificent Adam interior which they both would have liked to see, had it not been closed in the winter. However, the object of the expedition was the eight-acre showgrounds of a firm specialising in antique garden furniture. Ash wanted to choose two or three choice ornaments to have shipped to Antigua in time for the opening of his house the following December.

After some seasonably cold weather, the forecast the night before had been for a fine, milder day, and he had ordered a hamper from Fortnum & Mason which Ellis, their driver, had collected before coming to pick them up. He would have his own lunch in a pub.

Christie had never dreamed that there was a place where one could choose from hundreds of pillars and arches, fountains, lead cisterns, statues, sundials and ancient stone benches. There were urns, balustrading and porticos, the piers and finials of gates, pedes-

tals, obelisks and temples, all set out in a haphazard
way among shrubberies and groups of trees. Everything came from the grounds of an old house and
had, like old family furniture, the lovely, inimitable
patina of genuine age.

With few other people about, and the forecast
proving to be correct for once, it was an enchanted
place in which to ramble for an hour or two.

'Are you sure you aren't cold? Let me feel your
hands,' Ash said, at one point.

'Warm as toast.' She slipped off a glove and gave
him her hand to prove it.

He would have kept it in his and walked on with
interlaced fingers. But, although it cost her an effort,
deliberately she disengaged herself and replaced the
glove. She could not afford to indulge in romantic
moments in romantic places. To let him see that she
adored him was the surest way to lose him.

Her experience of unnecessary jealousy had been
bad enough. Justified jealousy would be hell.

Another day they went to Hamleys, the famous
Regent Street toy shop, to buy a homecoming present for John, and one to put by for his birthday
several months hence. Some of their purchases Ash
had decided to take back as excess baggage, but most
would be air-freighted later, and some things shipped.

On alternate nights they dined out, and went to a
show. Between times they ate at the flat, sharing the
cooking or eating delicious cold delicacies from Harrods' and Selfridge's food halls—smoked salmon
from Scotland, imported French pâtés seasoned with

truffles, stuffed prunes from Agen, game pie with pickled walnuts, caviar, fine English ham carved from the bone, and all kinds of cheese from one of Ash's favourite shops, Paxton & Whitfield in Jermyn Street.

Then they would relax and watch television until, often an hour after supper, he would say something such as, 'Are you interested in the next programme, or shall we make our own entertainment?'

Always she would be reluctant, and always he would ignore that, knowing that if he persisted there would come a point at which she ceased to resist him.

Then, and only then, was she able to indulge her longing to touch him, to feel the texture of his hair and skin, the warmth and strength of him, to breathe in his clean male scent.

As soon as their transports were over, instead of staying in his arms as she longed to, Christie would find an excuse to move apart.

If, as often happened, during the night he moved on to her half of the bed, she would slip out and climb in on his side. When, the first time, he remarked on it, she explained, 'I can't sleep if I'm cramped and hot. Don't you think, when we get back to Antigua, twin beds would be more comfortable?'

'No, I'm damned if I do,' he had answered curtly. 'As far as I know I don't snore, and neither of us has insomnia. A man and his wife should sleep together in both senses. Twin beds are for people whose marriage is lacking in some way.'

She had looked at him coolly and steadily before replying, 'As you wish.'

She knew that he had been put out. Like Celia and
~~nen~~, he would not be content until he had total
~~s~~urrender.

On the final night of their honeymoon, the Ffar-
~~i~~ngtons came to London for a farewell dinner *à quatre*
~~a~~t Mark's Club in Charles Street. The club took its
~~n~~ame from Mark Birley who also ran London's most
~~f~~ashionable night-club, Annabel's, where Hugo and
~~E~~mily had met each other. Annabel's was too noisy
~~f~~or them now. They preferred to dine quietly at
~~M~~ark's in a setting not dissimilar from their own
~~h~~ome. Hugo was the member, but Ash was going to
~~b~~e the host.

'When is the baby due?' he asked Emily, during
~~th~~e evening.

'August.'

'Why don't you come and stay with us in late
~~N~~ovember or early December? We'll have done all
~~th~~e hard work by then, and be ready for a breather
~~b~~efore our first season opens on December the
~~f~~ifteenth. We're going to be high season only. You
~~c~~an be our test-guests, and perhaps suggest some
~~im~~provements. Although I hope that won't be poss-
~~ib~~le. I want Heron's Sound to be something special,
~~li~~ke this place'— with a gesture encompassing the
~~m~~useum-quality of most of the Club's paintings and
~~d~~ecorative pieces.

'We should be delighted, wouldn't we, Emmy?
~~W~~hy high season only?' asked Hugo.

'For one reason because mid-December to mid-
~~A~~pril is when the people who will appreciate Heron's
~~S~~ound want to spend time in the sun. I'm hoping to

build up a largely repeat-booking clientele of the kind of guests who will find each other congenial as well as the setting. There aren't many places with atmosphere, good food and good water sports. People don't want to pay top dollar, as the Americans put it, for a level of comfort and cuisine below their own standard at home.'

'That's one reason. What's the other?' asked Emily.

He smiled at her; a smile he never gave Christie. It was warm and friendly, even loving. Emily had a share of his affection for Hugo; a young and beautiful woman but set apart from all others because he felt no desire for her, only brotherly fondness.

'Because I want part of the year for other activities. Although one or two of my forebears did well in shipping, farther back they were simple seamen. I need the sea in the same way that Hugo needs his forefathers' acres. And I want my half-brother's son and my own sons and daughters, to enjoy the sea as much as I do.'

'Oh, you're planning a large family, are you?' Emily included them both in this remark.

'I hope so.' Ash changed the subject by starting to tell them about the paintings he had bought for his house.

The discovery that, having acquired a house, a wife and an adopted child, he was now bent on founding a dynasty gave Christie something new to trouble her.

During her first marriage, she had never avoided becoming pregnant. After Mike's sudden death, she had been in dread for a while that she might bear a posthumous child. That fear dispelled, she had never given any thought to her failure, in six months of marriage, to start a baby.

Now she wondered if there might be something wrong with her. The possibility made her realise how much she wanted his children. Tall, brown, long-limbed sons and dark-eyed daughters, all taking after their father, on whom she could lavish love freely, and be loved in return.

But if that could never be, he would be bound to regret marrying her. To a couple who truly loved each other, the inability to have children was a disappointment, not a disaster. When a man and a woman were all in all to each other, there was no misfortune which could not be shared and overcome.

She parted from the Ffaringtons with sincere regret, having taken to Emily more than anyone she had met for years.

'Do write, if you have a spare minute. And keep your fingers crossed for me in August. It would be nice to have a daughter,' said Emily, before she gave Christie a farewell hug.

Later, seated at the dressing-table, preparing to take off her make-up while Ash had a shower, she remembered the night before her first flight to Antigua. What a different reflection she had seen looking back at her then!

A pale face. Worried grey eyes. A look of tension round the unpainted mouth. A figure five pounds too thin, clad in serviceable winceyette pyjamas.

Now, in a peach silk and lace slip which Ash had

seen in one of the windows in Old Bond Street and
bought for her, she still had her narrow waist, but the
curves above and below it were fuller and more
feminine. If a hint of some inner disquiet still lurked
at the back of her eyes, it was less noticeable than the
glow of her skin, the sheen of her hair.

*There's nothing like sexual fulfilment for putting a bloom
on a woman,* Ash had said, on their visit to Peacocks.
And, looking round the shops in London, she had
been aware of men eyeing her in a way they had
never done before.

But what was the use of that if only one man
mattered to her, and her hold on him was tenuous?

FOURTEEN

January . . . February . . . early March.

The golden weeks of Antigua's winter passed swiftly for the basking holidaymakers, and equally swiftly for Christie, whose days were not idle but busy.

She still found it hard to believe that this was her permanent home now; the island said to have a different beach for each day of the year, and the house beginning to recapture its original elegance.

In her task of putting it to rights, she was aided and advised by an Antiguan woman called Lillian. Without Lillian's local knowledge of where to find what, and how to enlist a team of reliable maids, Christie knew she could never have managed.

The bedroom which she and Ash shared now had screens of fine mesh at the windows to keep out all insects, and an overhead fan to stir and refresh the night air. A mosquito net over the bed was no longer necessary.

The first room to be redecorated, their bedroom had an inexpensive Laura Ashley paper, very eighteenth-century in feeling, with a pattern of birds and butterflies among twining sprays of leaves and flowers. The design was in terracotta on a cream ground, with floor-length curtains to match, made and lined by Christie herself.

The pineapple posts of the bed were now bees-
waxed and gleaming again, as was all the rest of the
furniture. She kept her clothes in the bedroom, and
he in the adjoining dressing-room. The bathroom
they shared was part of their private balcony. It had
slatted walls, liked fixed jalousies, through which she
could lie in the bath and gaze at the garden without
being seen from outside.

By day she was far too preoccupied with the house
and garden, with John, and with learning to cook the
Caribbean way, to have any time for introspection.

Each day began with a swim in the cove at the end
of the garden. They would swim again before lunch
and in the cool time before sunset. Then she would
shampoo her hair which, to please Ash, she was
growing longer, and lie in the bath while he dealt
with his mail in the bedroom. The water would have
cooled when he took her place, but he wouldn'
bother to top it up from the hot tap. He only wanted
to rinse the salt from his skin.

By the time he was dry she would have an iced
drink ready for him.

Later, when John was asleep, they would eat in the
candlelit dining-room, which now had apricot walls
and curtains to match. Christie had already finished
the first of a set of needlepoint seats for the ten dining
chairs, and was busy on the second. On the first seat
already in use, the design was a stylised pineapple
which she had found in a London embroidery shop.

The second she had designed herself, and was
working with canvas and wools posted to her by
Emily. For this she had chosen a cross-section of a

watermelon with its dark green rind and vivid coral-red flesh. The scarlet-shelled, black-seeded ackee fruit was next on her list, to be followed by bananas, mangoes, pomegranates, a coconut, limes, a pumpkin and peppers. Having mastered tent stitch she was adding other stitches to her repertoire and considering the possibility of introducing texture as well as colour into some of the seat covers. It would take her the best part of a year to complete the whole set. In the meantime the drop-in seats had covers of the same linen as the curtains.

For the time being she was doing all the cooking in the newly-built modern kitchen, and this was no burden to her. Her training, and Emily's two aids, made catering a painless exercise after Lilian had introduced her to sources of freshly caught fish, and good fruit and vegetable produce.

Later in the year Ash was importing a French-trained West Indian chef from Guadaloupe. Christie knew all the French culinary terms, but was otherwise not at all fluent. Fortunately Ash was, so the chef's arrival should pose no problems and would relieve her of all but the general supervision of the household.

In some ways she would be sorry not to be in charge of the kitchen. She was enjoying cooking for Ash. He never looked askance at anything she chose to serve him, unlike her first husband who, whenever she had attempted to infiltrate a foreign dish into the traditional English fare he preferred, had reacted with a dubious 'What's this?'

Ash had a much more sophisticated palate. There

was no ingredient or dish she had to avoid because he refused to eat it; nor had he the irritating habit of automatically reaching for the pepper and salt before he had even tasted the food on his plate. The knowledge that everything she prepared would be appreciated was a spur she had missed in the past.

But she tried not to let him see the glow evoked by his praise for something particularly successful.

'I'm glad you enjoyed it,' she would say coolly.

He must not guess that whatever it was she had set before him had been literally a labour of love.

Having eaten their evening meal, they would have coffee in the drawing-room. She would work at her needlepoint, and he would read or listen to music.

Sometimes, when he was reading, she would allow herself the pleasure of watching him for a few moments; but always poised to resume her stitchery should he raise his eyes from the page and detect the softness in her eyes as they rested on his strong, dark face.

After more than two months of marriage, with her days filled with interesting activities and her nights spent in deep, dreamless sleep preceded, still very frequently, by her husband's passionate lovemaking she should have been filled with contentment.

But she sensed that the reason his ardour remained at a honeymoon level was because she was still elusive. Sometimes, at dinner, she would glance up from her plate to find his dark gaze bent upon her with a searching look which she pretended not to recognise. She knew he could not understand why she wasn't his adoring slave.

One night, when she showed her usual preliminary reluctance, he had asked her angrily, 'For God's sake, are you never going to let me forget that I overruled your ridiculous plan for our marriage?'

And then, before she could answer, he had begun fiercely to kiss her.

Sometimes she felt that her life was like that of Scheherazade, the bride of a Shah who had sworn, because of his first wife's infidelity, to take a new one each day and strangle her the next morning. Only by keeping him interested in her tales, the Arabian Nights, had she managed to avert her fate for a thousand and one nights, after which he had revoked his vow.

Christie was not optimistic that her power to keep Ash enthralled was equal to Scheherazade's. She remembered him once remarking, apropos his father's second marriage, that it was easy for a woman to enslave a man. But in the case of his own marriage, she was the one in danger of being enslaved.

Although he spent part of his time in the dockyard at English Harbour, particularly when either *Sunbird One* or *Two* was in harbour, she was nearly always at Heron's Sound.

For this reason, every weekend he took her to lunch at the Blue Waters Hotel which was famous for its Sunday buffet of seafoods, half a dozen hot dishes including a spectacular joint of tender roast beef carved in generous slices by the chef, and a good selection of rich puddings.

At least one night a week they dined out; leaving

John in the care of the wife or eldest daughter of the caretaker who, with his family, now lived in a cottage in the grounds.

One night they went to a housewarming party given by a couple who had been chartering *Sunbird One* for several years, and who had now bought themselves a holiday house on the island.

During the later stages of the party, Christie was taken away from the main room by a man who professed to be an artist. Whether he was she never found out. It could have been a ploy he had invented for persuading unsuspecting women to go into bedrooms with him.

'I know Jim and Betty won't mind if I show you the very interesting painting they have in one of their guest rooms,' was his gambit.

He was fifty, and not overtly a lecher, so Christie went with him. She was struggling in his embrace, when a freezing voice from the doorway said, 'I should let my wife go, if you don't want a bloody nose, Morris.'

While the older man scuttled from the room, she wiped his wet kisses from her lips. Her husband looked thunderously angry. Surely he didn't think she had invited the incident?

He said, 'Betty warned me that chap liked to paw if he had half a chance. What on earth made you come in here with him?'

She was about to explain when she remembered his comment on her suspicions about Celia.

'Jealous, Ash?' she asked lightly.

His furious scowl lightened. 'I believe I can hold

you against ruttish little runts of his sort. Come here.'

He was standing with his hands behind his back, perhaps to restrain himself from the temptation to seize hold of Morris and shake him like a large dog worrying a rat.

When she came within reach, he took her firmly in his arms and kissed her until she was dizzy.

'More to your taste?' he asked mockingly, when he raised his head to look down at her.

'Anyone's kisses would be preferable to that man's slobbery lips,' she said guardedly.

Ash was not deceived. 'I think you'd like to go to bed. And why not indeed? Come on: we'll say our farewells, and be on our way.'

'No, not yet,' she objected. 'It's too early. And besides, I don't want to lea—'

He kissed her again, his hands sliding down her back to pull her hips hard against his.

'I want to,' he told her huskily. 'So do you, but you won't admit it.'

That night marked a lovely but poignant develop-ment in their relationship. Ash had always given her great pleasure but, long after midnight, when she thought herself drained of all feeling, he took posses-sion of her body and she found herself panting and shaking in the throes of a new kind of delight.

For one pulsating, mind-bending instant, she had an implosion of feeling more sublime than any be-fore. Afterwards, it was terrible to have to make herself move away from him. Tears squeezed be-neath her closed eyelids. If sex without love could be like that, what would it be like if ever they made love *with* love?

But that was something she would never find out.

There came a day, not long after that special high summit of bliss, when Christie knew she had to go away and be by herself for a while, out of reach of the disturbing magnetism of her husband's dynamic personality.

In the nautical terms which she was beginning to learn, she felt that her mind was like a compass without its corrector box. She could never take an accurate reading of her attitude to the future while living in the same house with Ash.

He had only to glance at her or touch her for her to suffer a "compass error". Sometimes even hearing his voice, as he spoke to a member of the staff, was enough to deflect her capacity to think straight.

The flat in London having been sold now, and the money partly invested and partly—at his insistence—put into a special account apart from their joint bank account, she was not without independent means.

She decided to go to Barbados, an island further to the south which, so she had heard, had more and better housekeeping cottages than anywhere else in the West Indies. It sounded a good place to lose herself for a week or two.

She left the freezer filled with dishes to last two weeks, and she wrote out a suggested meal plan for Ash and for John. Anyway, he could manage perfectly well on his own. He was the least helpless of men.

In the letter she left for him, she wrote—

I'm not going to say where I'm going, because I don't want to be hauled back before I'm ready. Please try to understand how I feel. Coming to Antigua, marrying you, all happened so fast—like a hurricane. Since then we've both been involved in making Heron's Sound liveable as fast as possible. Now I need a lull . . .'

To her nephew, she said, 'I have to go away for a little while, darling, so be a good boy while I'm gone, won't you? Do just as Uncle Ash tells you, and don't leave Sammy out in the rain again. Even though he's a seal, I don't think he likes to be caught in a downpour like last week. It could given him mildew, and that would make him smell horrid.'

John seemed to accept her departure without any worries. She had been afraid that it would remind him that his parents had gone and never come back. Had that been the case, she could not have gone. As much as she needed a period of calm reflection, her love for the boy was stronger than any personal needs.

It was only because she was sure that he now loved Ash and her equally, and felt safe and secure with either of them, that she could contemplate going away.

In her note to Ash she had not stated categorically that she meant to return. She felt a little uncertainty might be good for him. He wouldn't suffer it for long. John had her promise that she would be back, and would not need a great deal of prompting to report that assurance to his uncle. Surely Ash knew her well enough to know that her word to her nephew was as binding as a promise could be.

When John asked her where she was going, she said, 'Not very far. I may not be able to send you a picture postcard, but I'll bring some back with me, and perhaps a present as well. What would you like? Or shall it be a surprise?'

'A surprise,' he decided.

Christie hugged him, thinking, as she held him close, how nice it would be if she could be as demonstrative with Ash.

Often she longed to touch him; but theirs was not a relationship which admitted affectionate contacts. Even when they made love it was always he who caressed her. She had never dared to make love to him, even though she guessed that, in a perfect marriage, the wife's rôle was not merely passive.

She had been in Barbados two days when, shopping for food in a supermarket, she was astonished to run into Ian, the surgeon she had met at the Hathaways' Christmas party.

She wouldn't have noticed him, having eyes only for the goods on the shelves, but he recognised her.

'Christiana! What are you doing here?'

'Oh . . . Ian. Hello. How are you?' It was only with an effort that she could recall his name.

He was wheeling a grocery cart for a woman who he introduced as his sister. Her husband, also a medical man, had retired to Barbados two years ago. Ian stayed with them every year, and was gradually exploring the other islands before deciding where to buy a property for his own eventual retirement.

'Who are you staying with?' he asked. 'Laurel may know them.'

'I'm here on my own, in a housekeeping cottage.'

'What happened to that tall, dark young yachtsman you were involved with at Christmas?'

'He's in Antigua.'

'Then you're free to have dinner with me.'

'Thank you, but I'd rather not.'

But he wouldn't take no for an answer, and in the end she gave way. But she didn't want to be seen in public with him. She suggested he come to her cottage for a simple supper.

'As long as you don't misunderstand that I'm not free for anything but supper,' she added pointedly, his sister having left them to chat while she continued her shopping.

Her uncertainty as to whether she should tell him what had happened since their previous meeting was resolved when, soon after arriving at the cottage that evening, he said, 'It seems to me that last time we met you were wearing a platinum wedding ring, and now you have a gold one. I also detect other changes. I can't quite define them, but they're there. I think there must be some special reason why you're here alone, Christiana.'

'Yes, there is,' she admitted.

Suddenly the need to seek someone's advice was overwhelming. She found herself telling him everything.

'What makes you believe he doesn't love you?' was his first question, having heard her out.

'If he did, he would say so. Ash isn't bashful.
Anything but!'

By now they had finished the light meal. They
moved to the small private patio with a view of the
beach and the moonlight ocean.

Ian thought about this for a while. At length, he
said, 'One of the differences between my sex and
yours is that women need verbal and other assur-
ances of love . . . flowers, presents, romantic gestures.
That's what caused the collapse of my marriage. I
was too preoccupied with my career. I didn't take
enough time to make my ex-wife feel loved, and
another man stepped in and made up for my de-
ficiencies. I did love her. I thought it was enough to
make love to her often, and with enthusiasm. Men
tend to express love with their bodies, and to find it
difficult to put their feelings into words.'

They sat talking until very late. It was the first of
many conversations with him. Ian never said or did
anything to overstep the bounds of friendship between a wordly-wise man and a troubled young
woman twenty years his junior.

Then, one day, he said, 'Christie,'—as he had
taken to calling her—'I told you at Christmas that I
was strongly attracted to you. Getting to know you
during these past days has reinforced my opinion
that you could make me very happy. I believe I could
make you much happier than you are at present.
Marriage is not as unbreakable as it used to be, and
your present marriage was entered on very ill-
advisedly. Perhaps, after your being sexually incompatible with your first husband, and emotionally

incompatible with your second, it might be a case of third time lucky.'

'Oh, no, Ian—no. It's very kind of you, but I couldn't ever marry *again*,' was her instant reaction.

'My motive was not to be kind,' he told her, with a rueful smile. 'I'm in love with you, my dear.'

Having declared himself, he moved along the sofa on which they were sitting, and took her in his arms to kiss her.

Not counting one or two long since forgotten teenage kisses at parties and after dates, Christie had been kissed with passion by Mike and Ash, and by that revolting man Morris. She did not push Ian away because she was curious to know what effect his kisses would have on her.

At first they had none. They were not unpleasant, but neither did they excite her. And when he became more excited, and began to kiss her the so-called French way, and to touch her breasts, she was seized with revulsion and hurriedly extricated herself.

'I'm sorry . . . I'm so sorry, Ian.'

'My fault—rushing my fences again! Let's pretend it never happened, and revert to our very pleasant friendship, shall we?'

Christie felt this would be very difficult, but he had another week's holiday—or so he claimed—and refused to leave her on her own. He arranged to meet her the next day, to drive her across the island for a walk on the rugged, surf-pounded Bathsheba coast in the north-east.

Before she went to sleep that night, she thought over what he had once said to her about the differences between the sexes, and how men tended to express their feelings bodily rather than verbally.

If Ian was right—and she credited him with a good deal of wisdom, even though his own marriage had not lasted—perhaps it was foolish to hanker for more than she already had.

There was no denying that Ash made love to her 'often and with enthusiasm', and she knew that only with him could she ever experience the delights she had once thought denied to her. Ian's embrace had proved that. He was an attractive man, and probably an adroit lover; but the moment he had become passionate he had turned her off, even sickened her.

Yet she had only to think of her husband's firm, cynical mouth to be pierced by a sharp stab of longing to feel his kisses on her lips, and his lean brown hands on her body.

For the first time she saw that perhaps her concealment of her true feelings might not always have the effect intended. After a while, if she never made love to him, perhaps instead of feeling challenged, he might become bored and look for a more response partner.

Suddenly she was possessed by a feverish desire to find out how he would react if, for a change, she invited his caresses, or even took the initiative from him. Why not? That would test his sang-froid, she thought, with a gurgle of amusement, if his normally reserved wife took to demanding her conjugal rights at all hours of the day and night.

The idea made her laugh aloud; and, as she did so, she had the strange feeling that, all at once, she had found her true self again.

It was as if, for years, from a time even before her first marriage, she had lost the ability to take life lightly, with a sense of humour. Now, suddenly, she had it back. She was a whole person once more, and eager to take a more positive approach to making her marriage a success.

The idea of prolonging Ash's desire for her by keeping him guessing about her feelings towards him seemed now a negative attitude. Worse than negative: ungenerous. How many men, if the truth were known, cheated wives who were always warm and loving towards them? Probably a tiny minority.

It wasn't only that the sexual side which had made her first marriage a disaster, she realised belatedly. There had been other incompatibilities, equally serious. But that was all over and done with, and now she had a husband with whom making loving was a delight, even if she never admitted it to him.

From now on she would admit it; would demonstrate in every way possible how much his lovemaking pleased her, and how grateful she was for having her way of life changed and greatly enriched, not merely in that one respect but in many. Instead of constantly longing to feel that her love was returned, she would concentrate on being loving and warm towards him.

She was so excited by the thought of trying this new approach on him that she hardly slept a wink all night. Consequently she felt a bit jaded the next morning, and not in the mood to cook breakfast,

although the importance of a high-protein breakfast
was something which had been drummed into her by
her domestic science teachers and which she in turn
had always impressed on her pupils.

This morning even yogurt and fruit didn't appeal
to her. She had a piece of dry toast, knowing that it
was a poor foundation for an energetic tramp with
Ian; an excursion she meant to cry off if she could get
a flight home that day.

It wasn't the first time she had felt slightly queasy
in the morning, and she thought it was probably
caused by a change of drinking water. She remembered Lilian remarking that whenever she visited
other islands the water often upset her for a few days.

Upon calling the airport, Christie was disappointed to learn that the flights to Antigua were
heavily booked. Unless there was a cancellation, she
would have to wait several days.

Ian took her to lunch at a seafood restaurant
where, after enjoying the meal, she had suddenly to
bolt for the rest-room.

Without any blusher in her bag, there was no way
of disguising her pallor when she rejoined him, some
ten minutes later. He took one look at her face, and
said, 'You've been married three months. You may
be expecting a baby.'

He asked her some questions, and the answers
supported his suggestion. Being engrossed in doing
up the house, she had overlooked an important
non-event.

'I have medical contacts here. If you like, I can
probably organise a quick test for you,' he offered.

'Could you? Yes, I wish you would.'

The possibility that she might be carrying Ash's child was so wonderful that a few bad minutes in the rest-room seemed unimportant.

Forty-eight hours later, he told her the result of the test: positive. Christie was overcome with joy and excitement.

'You may not continue to feel sick, but I'll give you a prescription which should help,' he said.

'I don't want to take anything which might harm the baby.'

'Pyridoxine is one of the B vitamins. Check with your own doctor when you get home. He will probably encourage you to take several vitamin supplements.'

Ian had already flown back to London when Christie departed from Barbados. This was just as well because her take-off was delayed and, in the departure lounge, she fell into conversation with a grey-haired woman.

Her acquaintance explained that she and her husband had been spending a week in Barbados with one of their married children. They were now on their way to Antigua for a week's quiet holiday before Sailing Week. For eight or nine years her husband had crewed on one of the yachts which always took part.

'Oh, really? Which one?' asked Christie.

'*Sunbird One.* It used to belong to an old relation of my husband's.'

'Lady Anna Fitzwarren?'

'Yes, or Tugboat Annie as she was usually called. Do you remember her?'

'No, I've only lived in Antigua a short time, but I've heard of her.'

'Good heavens, is all that tittle-tattle *still* going the rounds? Those stories make me cross, especially the malicious nonsense put about by spiteful old harpies who have got their knife into Ash—Ashcroft Lambard, the skipper of *Sunbird*,' she added explanatorily. 'Have you met him yet? He's a sweetie. We both love him like a son, and he was like a son, or grandson, to poor old Anna. But for him she would have died in lonely misery. You've probably heard that she drank. In her last years she did, poor old soul. She had a terminal illness, and it was only brandy which kept her going.'

She paused to draw breath, then went on, 'We knew nothing of this at the time. We couldn't come out here in those years, and she wrote her usual cheery letters to us every month. She was one of those indomitable old dears who had gone out to India as a bride—her generation always pronounced gone as gorn and off as orf—and still felt it her duty to uphold British traditions. At the end, Ash had to nurse her, as well as buy stamps for her letters and the brandy and medicines she needed. I was told the truth by her doctor. Without Ash, she would have died in debt, and—'

She broke off as a burly, grizzled man joined them, saying, with a smile, 'I see you're talking ten to the dozen as usual, darling.'

She laughed. 'This is my husband. We're Patrick

and Rosamund Alleyn.'

'I'm Christie Lambard,' said Christie. 'Ash and I were married soon after Christmas. But perhaps he hasn't written to you since then.'

Mrs Alleyn threw up her hands. 'Yes, he has, as a matter of fact. He wanted us to stay at Heron's Sound, but we thought, with a bride of three months and a house still at sixes and sevens, he might find us a nuisance. So we're having our usual apartment in the Old Copper and Lumber Store. How lovely to meet you so much sooner than we expected! Ash didn't describe you at all, which was very maddening of him. Where is he now?'—looking about for him.

'He's not with me. He—he was too busy to come to Barbados.' Christie searched for some convincing reason for her own visit.

But Mrs Alleyn said only, 'Yes, up to his ears in preparations for the most important week of the year, as far as yachtsmen are concerned. Now, Christie—may I call you that?—do tell us how you and he met?'

They were able to sit together on the aircraft, and for most of the flight the loquacious Mrs Alleyn talked about Ash, and of his compassion for and kindness to the eccentric old woman whom nobody else had cared to be bothered with. Christie learned that the schooner, in those days, had been in danger of becoming a hulk. Only Ash's energy had restored it to seaworthiness.

It was pleasant to hear his praises sung. She wondered if he would receive her with relief or anger.

When her taxi arrived at Heron's Sound, she was dismayed to see at least ten people on the verandah. It looked as if they might be late-stayers after a luncheon party.

As she climbed out, holding some notes with which to pay the fare, she saw Ash coming down the steps. The sight of him sent a tremor of nervousness through her and, with it, a flutter of anticipatory excitement.

'Hello. How are you? Had a good trip?'

Nothing in his manner indicated that her absence had been anything other than a normal journey away from home; except that he did not kiss her, as a husband of less than six months would normally have done on his wife's return from an absence.

'Not bad. I — I missed you,' she answered.

He showed no reaction to this. Taking her case from the driver, he waited while she paid and tipped. Then, his hand resting lightly on her shoulder, they walked up the steps and he introduced her to his guests.

Like the Alleyns, they were all early arrivals for Sailing Week. Christie smiled and said Hello, How do you do? and Thank you, I'm glad you think so—this last in response to a complimentary remark about the house.

After several minutes of polite chit-chat, Ash remarked, 'Would you all excuse us for a few minutes while I take my wife's case to our room. By the way, would you like tea or a drink, Christie?'

'Tea would be nice.'

'Hear, hear. I think we could all do with some tea,

old boy. It will sober us up after all this boozing,' said one of the men, in a jocular tone.

'Right. Tea for everyone.' A hand under Christie's elbow, Ash steered her inside the house.

Not until they were well out of earshot did he say, 'Are you back for good, or merely to pick up more clothes?'

She swallowed to correct a certain tightness in her throat. 'For good. Where's John?'

'He's down at the beach with Elijah's kids. You realise, I suppose, the harm it would have done him had your disappearance been permanent?'

'But it wasn't. Don't be angry with me, Ash. I *had* to have that time alone. I had to think everything out.'

They had reached their bedroom by this time. He followed her in, set the case down, closed the door and remained near the threshold.

'May one ask by what process of reasoning you reached the decision to come back.'

'I — I never meant to stay away . . . just to stand back and sort my mind out.'

'I see. Can I rely on your not repeating the vanishing act?' His tone was coldly sarcastic. 'It causes a certain embarrassment, not to know where one's wife has gone, or for how long, if not for ever.'

'Yes . . . I'm sorry. I do realise that. But if I had told you where I was, I'm sure you'd have come and fetched me back.'

'Where did you go?'

'To Barbados. I met some friends of yours on the flight back. The Alleyns, Patrick and Rosamund.

They asked me to give you their love. We're invited
to dinner with them tomorrow, if you have no other
engagement.'

He shook his head, gazing forbiddingly down at
her upturned face, the set of his mouth more severe
than she could remember.

'I wanted to come home sooner, but the flights
were all booked,' she went on. 'It seems ages since
. . . you kissed me. Oh, Ash, won't you give me a
hug? I — I can't tell you how much I've missed you.'

This was as far, in the face of his present displeasure with her, as she felt she could go in confessing
the depths of her feelings. But although it was not the
unqualified declaration of love which she longed to
make, her heart was in her eyes as she said it.

For a second or two she thought he was going to
rebuff her. Then, with a smothered exclamation, he
shot out a long arm and hauled her into an embrace
which made her realise how carefully he must have
regulated his natural strength whenever he had held
her before.

Now it was not under control and, for the first few
seconds, as he crushed her against him and pressed a
fierce kiss on her mouth, she thought her ribs were
going to crack.

Not that she cared. To be back in his arms was all
that mattered.

Almost at once he seemed to realise that her body
was not made to withstand the full muscular power
of his own much taller and harder frame. His vice-
like grip eased a little and, finding her mouth soft and
yielding, his kiss changed, becoming less punitive.

Christie slid her arms up round his neck, responding as passionately and totally as she knew how. It was the first time she had ever surrendered at the outset, and she hoped he could feel the difference between her present response and her previous reactions.

That, whether or not he had found consolation during her absence, he was strongly aroused by her return was a fact which he could not disguise; and her own body throbbed and pulsed with the longing to be in bed with him.

'Damn those people . . . but I can't desert them,' he murmured huskily, a little later.

She opened her eyes. She had forgotten his visitors, John, everyone . . . everyone in the world but the two of them, locked together, kissing.

'Don't go back for a minute,' she murmured.

'I must. They're waiting for tea. In an hour they'll be gone, and then—' He left the sentence unfinished, but his hands slid down to her hips and pressed her more closely against him.

Before her time in Barbados, Christie would have avoided his eyes and tried to withdraw.

Now her smile held a sparkle of coquetry. 'And then?'

His eyes glittered with desire, and he gave her a wolfish grin from which, once, she would have shrunk.

'Then I'll bring you back here and punish you for running away.'

'You may have cooled down by that time, and be less . . . annoyed with me.'

Deliberately, she gave a slight sinuous wriggle; an incitant movement which would have been inconceivable before.

She heard his sharp intake of breath, and felt the electric surge of his vital force.

'Do that again and I'll deal with you now,' he warned hoarsely.

She was tempted to accept the challenge. It was exciting to feel that she had the power to drive him beyond his control; to make him take her swiftly and fiercely.

As she hesitated, Ash gave her a quick, hard kiss and put her away from him. An instant later he had gone, leaving her breathless and aglow.

With a sudden excess of exuberance which she had not felt since her teens, Christie flung herself on the bed and sprawled in luxurious abandon, longing for the moment when he would be there beside her, the door locked, the world shut out.

For some time she lay in a daydream of happy anticipation; wondering why it had taken her so long to see that holding back would never win any man's affection. Loving and giving was the answer, and from now on she would give love to Ash as unstintingly as she gave it to John.

Thinking of the little boy made her rise from the bed and tidy herself. She was running a comb through her hair when she heard his voice in the garden, and ran to the window to call to him.

He was overjoyed to see her, and they had an ecstatic reunion after which he stayed close to her side for the rest of the afternoon so that, even when the guests had departed, it was impossible for his adopted parents to seek seclusion before his bedtime.

Later, when Ash was opening a bottle of champagne before dinner, he said, 'While you were away, John asked me about his father and mother. He seemed to think you might be bringing them back with you.'

'What did you say to him?'

'I told him they'd gone to heaven. I feel it's the only explanation one can give to a child of his age.'

'Did he seem disturbed at the thought of not seeing them again?'

'No, not at all. It appears that Elijah's children had already suggested to him that his parents might be with God. They're a religious family. John went to church with them last Sunday. I see no harm in it occasionally, unless you object?'

She shook her head.

'We don't want him brainwashed,' he continued, 'but he needs to grow up with some understanding of the things which are important to other people, including all the major religions. As Joshua Liebman put it: "Tolerance is the positive and cordial effort to understand another's beliefs, practices, and habits without necessarily sharing or accepting them." I think we might make that our guideline with John . . . and with our other children.'

'I agree. It's a very good guideline.'

It was on the tip of her tongue to tell him her news, but some instinct made her refrain; a feeling that it might be better to hug her secret to herself for a little longer.

So when Ash came towards her with two glasses, and put one of them into her hand with the question, 'What shall we drink to?' she did not say, 'To the baby I'm expecting,' but, 'To John's future. You were right when you said there was a better life for him here. For him and me—thanks to you, Ash.'

His shrewd dark eyes searched her face for a moment before he touched his glass to hers, and said, 'For all three of us.'

Before they sat down to dine they had finished the bottle of champagne. With the meal they drank another, and because she was in her own home, alone with her husband, Christie didn't prevent him from refilling her glass as she would have done after one or two glassfuls at a dinner party. Indeed she was scarcely aware of what she was eating and drinking. It could have been flat beer and cold porridge and she would have enjoyed it just as much.

His presence, the sound of his voice, the movements of his hands as he peeled a pear to eat with the cheese; these things filled her consciousness to the exclusion of everything else.

She felt like a bride on her wedding night. On their real wedding night, she had not expected him to make love to her. Tonight she felt sure that, as soon as they had drunk their coffee, he would take her to bed immediately. This time she could hardly wait to be there; to have those long fingers undressing her, stroking her skin.

It was the combination of excitement and rather more wine than she was used to which made her change her earlier decision not to mention the baby yet. Suddenly she couldn't keep it to herself any longer.

'I — I have a surprise for you, Ash.'

'A present? Where is it?' he asked, looking at her as if she were a present which, very soon, he was going to enjoy unwrapping.

'No, not a present. Some news. Do you remember telling Emily you wanted to emulate Hugo in having a large family? I . . . I shall be emulating her before the end of the year.'

With his glass half way to his lips, Ash set it down on the table. There was a long pause before he said, 'Are you telling me that you're pregnant?'

She nodded. 'I felt a bit queasy once or twice in Barbados, so I had a test. It was positive.'

His mouth thinned. His whole face hardened.

'I see,' he said, in a cold tone. 'So that's what brought you back, is it?'

'No, it wasn't . . . it wasn't,' she protested. 'I had made the decision before I knew about the baby. Truly I had. You must believe that.'

He pushed back his chair and stood up. 'Only a fool would believe it. You came back because you had to.'

'I didn't . . . I swear it . . . where are you going?'— this as he strode towards the door.

'To the harbour. I'll sleep on the boat tonight.'

A moment later he had gone.

FIFTEEN

It was a miserable night. In the morning Christie overslept. She emerged from the bedroom to find John and Ash at breakfast on a sunny part of the main verandah.

Her husband rose when she joined them, and drew out a chair for her. She saw that he appeared to have eaten his usual substantial morning meal. But there was no warmth in his eyes as they returned her anxious upward gaze. She could tell he was still fiercely angry with her, an anger probably exacerbated by the frustration of the surge of desire he had felt for her the day before.

Presently he left the table, saying as he did so, 'When you've finished breakfast, I'd like to have a word with you in my study.'

'Is Uncle Ash cross?' asked John, when they were alone.

'I shouldn't think so,' Christie said, with forced lightness. 'Who could be cross on such a beautiful morning?'

'He was cross while you were away. He was like a bear with a sore head,' her nephew informed her.

'I don't know who you heard say that, but it's not at all polite, and probably not true either,' she told him reprovingly. 'If Uncle Ash did speak sternly to someone, I'm sure they deserved it. Perhaps they

adn't done something he'd asked them to do. 'If
ou've finished you may get down, pet. I'll be busy
or a while, but not for long.'

'Then will you read to me?'

She nodded, inwardly bracing herself for the con-
rontation in the study. Ash's manner, which even
he child had noticed, made her very nervous.

Since she had been bidden to go there, she did not
ap on the door of his study but turned the handle
nd walked in to find him sitting behind his desk,
nore grim-faced than ever.

As she entered, he rose.

'Sit down, Christie.'

But he remained on his feet, his hands thrust into
he pockets of his white shorts. He was wearing a
rick-red cotton shirt, the long sleeves neatly rolled
p to the swell of his well-developed biceps. He
ooked very clean and fit, and overwhelmingly
ttractive.

He said briskly, 'I've decided that from now on
ur marriage will be on the terms you wanted in the
rst place. You can stay in the room you've been
ccupying. I'll have my things moved to one of the
ther bedrooms.'

For a moment or two she felt stunned.

'Y-you can't mean it, Ash. It's not fair. I don't
vant those terms any more. I—I want to be fully
our wife.'

'I'm afraid that's no longer possible,' was his
rctic rejoinder. 'Although, as you've frequently de-
nonstrated, a woman can submit to a man's
mbraces as a duty rather than a pleasure, a man

can't simulate passion for a woman he no longer
desires. Even if I could accommodate you as dutiful
ly as you used to fulfil your obligations, I doubt i
you'd find it enjoyable. Perfunctory sex is a poor
sport, and a pretence of enthusiasm for reasons of
expediency isn't much better.'

'But it wasn't expediency which brought me back
I missed you . . . I missed you very much. I think you
missed me. You kissed me as though you had. I
those people hadn't been here, you would have made
love to me at once.'

If the desk hadn't been between them she would
have jumped up and flung herself into his arms
testing the truth of his claim to have lost his desire for
her with the eager pressure of her body.

But the desk was a barricade which made such a
gesture impossible. Ash would have time to fend her
off before her bare arms round his neck and the feel of
her breasts against his chest revived the hot, impatient passion which had flared between them the day
before.

'Perhaps. And regretted it later, no doubt—as I've
usually regretted forcing some sort of response from
you. But not any more.'

'You mean we . . . we're never going to share a
room again?' she asked incredulously.

Ash took his time answering that; and the fact that
he paused gave her a modicum of comfort before
someone knocked at the door and, with his immedi-
ate, 'Come in', he avoided replying to her question.

As the day passed Christie tried to convince her
self that he would be sure to change his mind; and

he blamed herself much more than him for this emporary impasse. It had been the height of stupidty to blurt out the news of the baby so soon after her eturn. She should have kept it to herself until she ad been back some time, and their marriage had e-established itself on a better footing than before.

However, as the rest of that slow week dragged ast, Ash seemed to grow more and more distant. he begun to wonder uneasily if he *had* meant that icy ltimatum. Or perhaps it was only that he was nusually busy with preparations for Sailing Week. he hoped so. The prospect of reverting to the oveless existence she had led before she met him did ot bear thinking about.

Sailing Week began with the inter-island race om Des Hayes, Gaudeloupe, to English Harbour. hat night there were dinner parties at The Admirl's Inn, several other hostelries and the Catamaran nd Antigua Yacht Clubs.

The main events of the next day were a Fishing nd Workboat Race, a welcome party at the Yacht lub, and a special Sailing Week Dinner held in four laces at once to fit in all the people who wished to ttend it.

On the third day came the First Yacht Race, with sh, Patrick and Joss all taking part, and the women atching the start from high up on Shirley Heights.

The Heights took their name from Major-General ir Thomas Shirley, a Governor of the Leeward slands in the late eighteenth century. At that time ntigua had been an important sugar island with, ecause of its flatness, more arable land than many islands. While Britain was at war with France, it had to be well defended from French invasion, and Shirley Heights had once been covered with extensive fortifications.

Most of these were in ruins now. Earthquakes, erosion, and the ruthless vegetation of the tropics had demolished all but a few empty buildings and arches.

But for the large crowd of tourists who watched the race start from The Lookout, nearly five hundred feet above sea level, it was easy to see why this had been an important bastion.

Even with Ros to explain it to her, and sharing Miranda's field glasses, Christie found it hard to make sense of the seeming confusion of yachts moving counter to each other on the blue sea far below. It wasn't really a muddle, merely different classes beginning the races at different times, the others told her.

Yet even as the wife of a leading contender she could not help dividing her attention between the movements of the yachts, the people around them, and the distant view of Guadeloupe, forty miles to the south, Montserrat twelve miles closer in the south-west, and Redonda Rock to the west. Perhaps the race would be more riveting when she was a qualified yachtswoman—if Ash still intended to teach her some of his skills. Perhaps he didn't, not now. She felt suddenly hot, weary of the buzz of many languages going on around them, and uncomfortable sitting on the ground. She longed for a cool, quiet room filled with dim green light, and Ash lying still in her arms after making love to her.

That night, with him and the others, she attended a dinner dance at Halcyon Cove. Two more lively race days followed, and when it came to the day when the Yacht Club held windsurfer and rubber boat races, and a tug-of-war and a riotous beer-drinking contest, she began to appreciate the full meaning of those *I Survived Sailing Week* tee-shirts.

On the night of the fourth big race, she went to a shipwreck party on Curtain Bluff beach, and the next day the Antigua Distillery gave a party with free rum punches at the dockyard.

Christie went, but she drank only fruit juice. Ash and his crew were doing brilliantly, she was told. It seemed certain that *Sunbird Two* would again win the Lord Nelson Cup.

Apart from an incisive warning, expressed at the outset of the week, that she should take care not to tire herself, her husband had had very little direct conversation with her.

Neither Ros nor Miranda, with a woman's swift response to undercurrents, seemed aware of anything amiss. Christie knew this from several remarks they made which would have been incredibly tactless had they sensed a rift between the Lambards.

She had not mentioned the baby to them. She wished it were still her secret, known only to Ian and whoever had done the test for her.

On the last day of Sailing Week—which had now been in progress for nine days—Christie saw and enjoyed the hilarious Non-Mariners Race in which all the "vessels" competing had to have cost not more than one hundred EC dollars, and must never have been in the water before.

The race, with a Le Mans start, was from the South Quay to a line off The Admiral's Inn. According to the rules, piracy and sabotage were forbidden, and as well as a prize for the first vessel to reach the finishing line, there were prizes for the most original craft and the one with the largest crew.

It was an event which caused most of the onlookers to become helpless with laughter and, for a short time, she forgot her unhappiness and was convulsed with amusement like everyone else.

About four in the afternoon, Beat the Retreat was performed by the band of the Royal Antigua Police Force. Afterwards, leaving Ash at the dockyard, Christie drove home to rest until it was time to dress for the Ball. It did not begin until ten o'clock, but they were going to have drinks with the Alleyns in their apartment beforehand.

Tired by the strenuous pace of the week, as soon as she reached Heron's Sound, she went to bed, setting her alarm clock to wake her after ninety minutes.

As on the rare occasions when she had had a nap during the day, she had always woken feeling groggy, it did not surprise her to do so on this occasion. She felt sure it would wear off presently.

She had bathed and made up, but was still in her blue cotton dressing-gown, when she heard Ash come home. Knowing it would not take him more than half an hour to shower, shave and change, she put on her dress and went to the drawing-room to wait for him.

Still feeling oddly below par, she decided to have a drink to perk her up. The doctor had said that spirits, which she almost never drank anyway, were inadvisable, but a moderate consumption of wine could do no harm.

Having poured herself a glass of sherry, she sat down to drink it. The beautiful aquamarine room never ceased to give her intense visual pleasure, and she concentrated on that and ignored her continuing malaise.

By the time Ash entered the room she had finished the sherry and seemed to be feeling more herself. She saw him looking at her dress and stood up to show it off better.

It was made of the same airy silk as the one he had bought her for Christmas, but she had chosen a print in the colours of the sea; jade shading into turquoise into amethyst into violet. It was cut in layers of handkerchief points, and the edges of the points were serrated. They floated around her when she moved.

'I hope you approve?' she said.

'Very much. Will you have some more sherry?'

The clipped response to her question, the total absence of the flame which once would have lit his dark eyes at the sight of her looking her best—and she knew that she did look nice, even if she felt rotten—did nothing to raise her morale.

'No, thank you.'

'In that case we may as well be off.'

Even Ash's well-sprung car could not absorb all

the jolts from the patched and unpatched places on the road. On the drive to the dockyard, it seemed to Christie that the bumps jarred much more than usual. She wondered if she could possibly be coming down with 'flu, and longed to be back in bed instead of on her way to a ball which, from what she had heard, would become more and more boisterous as the evening wore on. Not all, but many sailing types were as obstreperous as rugger types. She could only pray that Ash would not want to dance the night away. Not that he was likely to dance with her much.

The tables on the verandah of Pizzas in Paradise were already crowded with young people, having an impromptu party, when they passed the place. In the next day or two, many of them would be sailing away from Antigua, some to return the following year, and some never to come back because crewing was a phase of their youth and soon they would be caught up in the less free-and-easy pattern of careers with a pension at the end of them, and raising children and becoming settled and responsible. Some yachts would remain at their moorings until the day of the Antigua-Bermuda Race which was sponsored jointly by the Antigua Yacht Club and the Royal Hamilton Dinghy Club.

Patrick and Rosamund were in high spirits when they arrived. Christie heard them laughing before Patrick opened the door, and put on a bright smile to greet them.

'You look very splendid tonight, Ros,' was Ash's greeting to the older woman.

She was wearing a shocking pink dress which did

look well with her grey hair and brunette's tan. Like most rather overweight women, she had good shoulders, tonight shown off by narrow straps.

As he kissed her hand, she replied, 'It's sweet of you to say so, my dear, but I must confess that when I look at your truly beautiful wife, I can't help feeling my years. Oh, to be young and slim again! Christie, you look *so* lovely. What a heavenly dress. Isn't she a beauty, Patrick?'

'She is indeed, and Ash is a lucky chap to have snaffled her. But wasn't it Donne who wrote, "No spring nor summer beauty hath such grace as I have seen in one autumnal face"?' he answered, smiling at his wife.

'Oh, darling, how nice you are!'

She tried to take the compliment lightly, but her voice had a quiver in it and tears came into her eyes. Christie had to pretend to be looking for something in her evening bag because her own vision was blurred.

She knew that Patrick and Rosamund had been married for more than thirty years, and that Patrick's tribute was not a suave piece of lip-service. Time had not diminished their love. It would last all their lives, and whoever outlived the other would pay a terrible price in loneliness and irreparable loss for their long years of happiness together. But oh, how willingly she herself would pay such a price for thirty years of their touching accord with her husband.

'What may I give you to drink, Christie?' Patrick asked her.

She pulled herself together. 'Sherry, please.'

Ash and Rosamund began to talk, and she listened, waiting for the sherry.

'Oh, good lord! I'm most frightfully sorry,' Patrick exclaimed, a few moments later.

Rosamund, seeing what had happened, gave an exclamation of dismay. 'All down your lovely dress! Take it off quickly, and we'll sponge it.'

Only Ash understood at a glance what had caused the sherry to be spilt.

'Never mind the dress. She's not well.'

He took the glass from her hand, gave it back to Patrick and, scooping Christie up in his arms, carried her to one of the divans, where he laid her down.

Christie sank back, grey-faced, her forehead beaded with sweat, recovering from the stab of violent pain which had ripped through her just at the moment when her fingers had closed on the glass.

It had been low down in her abdomen. She put her hands to the place and wondered what could have caused it. She could not remember eating anything to bring on the kind of colic which presaged food poisoning. Nor did she feel any nausea.

'Are you bleeding?' Ash asked her quietly.

She realised then that she was, and gave a groan of despair. Oh, God! Let it not be that—*please*!

She heard him say to the others, 'She's pregnant and may be miscarrying. I'm going to telephone for an ambulance.'

And then he had gone, and Rosamund was sitting beside her, saying reassuringly, 'Don't be frightened, Christie. I've been through this, years ago, and I didn't lose the baby. But you must have absolute rest, my dear. Just lie still and it won't be long before we get a doctor to look at you.'

To her husband, she added, 'Get some towels and my roll of cottonwool, and then wait outside for a bit, would you?'

By the time Ash returned, she had done what she could to help Christie, and surrendered her place to him.

He said, 'They're coming immediately. It won't take them long to get here, and then you'll be in expert hands. Were you feeling unwell earlier on?'

'A little . . . but I never thought . . . Ros says I may not . . . not lose it.' She closed her eyes, but the tears seeped between her lashes.

'Hush! Don't cry. Of course you won't lose it.'

He took both her hands and held them, and she clung to his fingers as if the contact could transfuse some of his strength into her. The pain had left her so weak, and the bleeding seemed to be increasing.

It seemed hours before the ambulance arrived. They transferred her on to a stretcher and carried her out of the building, passing people in evening dress who stood aside, looking concerned at the sight of someone being rushed to hospital on a night of gaiety and celebration.

When she realised that Ash was getting into the ambulance, Christie mustered the strength to protest.

'There's no need for you to come too. You can't miss the Ball and the prizegiving. Please . . . I don't need you to come with me.'

'I want to be there,' he said tersely.

'But the Alleyns . . . the Ball . . . your trophy . . .'

'To hell with the Ball! Do you think I give a damn for any trophy when my . . . child needs hospital treatment? Don't argue, Christie. Just rest,' was his low but adamant answer.

Then the pain struck again, like a sword, and she gasped at the agony of it.

They must have given her something to make her sleep. When she woke, it was daylight. For a few seconds she couldn't think why she wasn't in her own bed in the room at Heron's Sound where she now slept alone but had once slept with Ash.

Then she rolled her head on the pillow and saw that, for the first time since she had left him, he was in the room with her, but not in the high narrow bed in which she was lying.

He was slumped in a chair by the window, asleep and looking as if it were the first sleep he had had for days. She had never seen him so haggard, with dark rings under his eyes and the fine lines round his eyes and the laughter-grooves down his cheeks far more noticeable than they usually were. He looked worn out, gaunt with exhaustion.

As she gazed at him, he opened his eyes. She remembered then what had happened; the pain and distress of the hours before they had put her to sleep.

She had lost his child.

They hadn't said so, but she knew it. There was no other life in her body; no embryo being who would have been their son or daughter; nothing left of the seed implanted in one of those moments of ecstasy which were now only bitter memories.

Her lips trembled. Her eyes brimmed, the tears trickling slowly down her cheeks.

The death of her parents, of Mike, of her sister and brother-in-law were as nothing to this greater grief. To have known someone and to lose them was a shock and pain hard to bear. But to lose, unborn, her first child, the treasured creation of the man she loved . . . A long shuddering sob burst from her.

Ash rose from the chair and strode swiftly to the bedside. But at the same moment the door opened, and a nurse entered.

'Ah, you're awake, Mrs Lambard. How are you feeling?'

She took Christie's wrist in her dark hand, her eyes kind and sympathetic as she pressed lightly on her patient's pulse point.

'All right, thank you,' Christie said croakily.

Ash had turned away to the window and was standing with his back to them.

The nurse said, 'I think you should go home and rest now, Mr Lambard. You've been up all night, and it won't help your wife to worry about you. We're going to give her some medication which will make her drowsy again. Why not come back this afternoon?'

'Yes, I'll do that. Take good care of her. Goodbye for the moment, Christie.'

His voice was level, his face showed nothing but fatigue. She knew she must have imagined that, when the nurse entered the room, there had been tears in his eyes.

*　　*　　*

She wasn't kept in hospital long, but she had to convalesce slowly at home, and she went through a period of deep melancholy. She was warned that she would feel depressed, and assured it would pass off in time, and that nothing had happened to prevent her having a normal pregnancy whenever she felt like it.

'What caused the miscarriage?' she had asked.

Her doctor had said, 'Nothing specific. These things happen sometimes, Mrs Lambard, and usually for the best. Maybe Nature knew something was wrong which we wouldn't have detected until later. But I see no reason why, next time, you shouldn't have a fine healthy baby who'll probably get me out of bed at three o'clock in the morning to deliver him or her.'

The day came for her final check-up, at the end of which he said, 'You're fine, Mrs Lambard. Maybe you still feel a bit low, but physically you're back to normal. And you and your husband can resume your normal relations whenever you want to,' he added.

Except that my husband doesn't want to, she thought dully, leaving the surgery.

She had forgotten to pick up the mail from their box at the post office, but Ash had also been to town and collected it. He came home while she was playing with John in the garden, and handed her an airmail letter with an English stamp and Emily's handwriting on the envelope.

With only two months to go to the birth of her baby, Emily described herself as 'looking like Mrs Buddha, but feeling terrific. No problems this time, thank goodness and, it being my fourth, I hope to

pop him or her out with the ease of a pea from a pod.
Talking of which, we're gorging on delicious man-
getouts. The asparagus is almost over—'

At this point, although John was present, Christie
could not repress a burst of tears.

'Why are you crying, Aunt Christie?' he exclaimed, in alarm.

She struggled for control. 'I don't know. It's silly
of me, John.'

Ash put a large clean handkerchief into her hand,
and took the letter from her. While she mopped her
cheeks, his eyes skimmed the lines in search of what
had upset her.

'I should have written to her,' he said, frowning.
'It hadn't struck me that she would write in this vein.
I'm sorry.'

'It's I who should apologise for being so stupid,'
she said, forcing a cheerful tone and a smile for her
puzzled nephew.

It was not until the end of dinner that night that
Ash asked, 'What was the result of your check?'

'I'm completely recovered, physically if not quite
mentally.' She began to stir her coffee, although it
was black, with no sugar in it. 'He . . . he said that if
. . . if we wanted to, it was all right to . . . to start
another baby.'

'Did he?' was her husband's only comment. He
rose from the table, picking up his cup as he did so.
'Would you excuse me, Christie? I have some letters
to answer.'

He left her and went to the book-room which, for
the time being, served as his study. Presently she

heard the muted metallic chatter of the typewriter. He was still typing when she went to bed.

For a long time she lay awake, wondering if she ought to have followed him to the book-room and insisted on having it out with him—the undiscussed question of their future, if they had a future together.

Most of the time she had the feeling he was now completely indifferent to her. Only two things sometimes made her wonder if the courteous detachment of his treatment of her could be a veneer.

She remembered how, in the ambulance, she had seemed to hear a slight hesitation when he said, *Do you think I give a damn for any trophy when my child needs hospital treatment?*

Had he meant to say *my wife?*

Also she had not forgotten her impression of seeing tears in his eyes the next morning at the hospital.

A hundred times since that day she had argued with herself about this. Ash wasn't the emotional type. He had lost his mother very young, and been packed off to be a boarder first at his preparatory school and than at his next school.

The English public school ethic might no longer include the ferocious bullying and caning of the period from *Tom Brown's Schooldays* to the time of Ash's and Hugo's fathers, but she felt sure it hadn't yet eased to the point where boys were encouraged to shed tears.

Englishmen—and although Ash had Greek-dark eyes and Greek-black hair he was predominantly English—did not weep, or only very rarely.

There were a few special circumstances in which

they could allow themselves to be visibly moved.
Prince Charles had shown grief in public at the
funeral of the widely admired old man who had been
like a grandfather to him, the murdered Lord
Mountbatten. Men wept at the loss of a child, but a
child they had known and loved, not one still unborn. And they shed tears when women they loved
had died, or been close to death.

But her life had not been in danger, and nor did
Ash love her. It must have been the tears in her own
eyes which had seemed to cause a shimmer in his.
Only . . . why had he turned away then, if not to
conceal some emotion he preferred not to show?

The days passed and all at once, as she had been
promised, her lethargy wore off and left her responsive to the beauty of the garden as, watered by some
heavy showers in May, the flowering trees of the
summer began to put out brilliant blossoms.

The temperature rose a few degrees. The humidity
increased slightly. But not as much as in the autumn
when, said Lilian, it could become a little uncomfortable. Meanwhile the extra heat was not unwelcome
at Heron's Sound with its breezy verandahs and
shady parts of the garden, and the cove so near and
inviting.

But her change of mood was not matched by a
change in Ash's manner. He continued to be courteous but aloof.

At last she could bear it no longer. She had to do
something positive. The impulse crystallised one
morning when she was in Lolita's looking for material for a kanga. This was the huge diaphanous scarf

which the most fashion-conscious tourists were wearing as beach cover-ups. It was tied in a knot near one armpit, and covered them from chest to ankle, except where the sides came apart to reveal a hip, thigh and calf as they walked.

Browsing among the bolts of materials piled in the centre of the shop, and studying those stacked on the shelves behind the counters, she saw at last what she wanted—a thin cotton voile in the colours of a ripe melon, the very dark green near the selvedges merging with a band of paler green which in turn merged with the deep golden peach of the greater part of the fabric.

As she asked for the yardage she needed, and watched it being cut off the bolt, she knew she was going to have it hemmed before nightfall, not to wear on the beach but when she went to Ash's bedroom.

He seemed keyed up and restless that evening. She would have liked to believe it was sexual frustration which made him on edge, but she didn't delude herself that, because he had not made love to her for so long, he had remained celibate all the time. He was always at home for dinner, and never went out again later. But during the day he had plenty of opportunities to keep assignations with one or more accommodating women.

Tonight he did not make one of his most frequent excuses to avoid spending the rest of the evening with her—that he had correspondence to handle. Half an hour after supper, while he was pacing restlessly about the drawing-room and she was pretending to read, he said abruptly, 'I'm tired. I'm going to turn in early. Goodnight, Christie.'

'Goodnight,' she echoed, pleased that she wasn't going to have to endure another two hours of her own mounting tension.

Of course if he really *was* tired, it could ruin her plan of action. But somehow she didn't think he was.

After giving him time to reach his bedroom, she switched out the lights and tiptoed to her room. As usual, she had bathed before dinner. Now she only had to undress and apply the Vent Vert she had bought specially for the occasion, and perhaps lightly retouch her lips.

Having draped herself in the new kanga, she had a couple of afterthoughts and took it off again. First she fastened a fine gold neck chain, given to her by Miranda Hathaway as a cheer-up present, to one inherited from her sister, converting them into a waist chain. Then she painted her rose-red nipples with a deeper red lipstick to make them more noticeable through the voile.

That done, she had an even better idea and added a design of petals and dots to make them even more eye-catching. This time when she fastened the kanga, the golden gleam of the waist chain and the patterned points of her breasts gave a much more erotic effect to her thinly veiled body.

Light showed under her husband's door as she paused outside before tapping. She was trembling with nervousness, but a couple of deep breaths steadied her.

Who dares wins, she reminded herself.

'Come in,' his voice called, in answer to her light triple knock.

Christie opened the door, walked in, and closed it behind her.

Ash was stretched out on the bed, his shoulders propped against pillows. He was naked, the upper sheet thrown aside for maximum coolness. One long leg was extended towards the footboard, the other drawn up to form a rest for the book he had been reading when she disturbed him. He looked no more tired than he had earlier.

He did not say *Is something wrong?* or *What do you want?* She felt he had only to look at her to see why she had come to his room.

As he took in the filmy kanga, and all that showed through it, she saw, before he used the book to conceal the fact, the spontaneous reaction which proved that, although he might profess indifference, he was not indifferent to her. If nothing else, she could still make him want her physically.

She walked slowly towards the bed, and seated herself on the end of it, not far from his outstretched foot.

'I—I think John needs brothers and sisters. If we delay too long, there'll be too great a gap between him and them,' she began.

Ash said nothing. His expression had never been more enigmatic. Not the slightest flicker of reaction showed in his dark, steady gaze.

'Besides which, I'm already in my middle twenties,' she went on, 'and one can't have children in too rapid succession. If, as you told Hugo and Emily, you want to have a large family, to have three would take nearly five years . . . unless we had twins,' she added awkwardly.

This wasn't at all what she had meant to say; but somehow the things she had planned were impossible to utter while he fixed with that penetrating stare which seemed to read her mind while revealing nothing of his own thoughts.

She forced herself to persist.

'You . . . you once spoke of a skipper's responsibility to his passengers. Is your sense of responsibility towards John strong enough to overcome your aversion to me?'

At last he responded. 'My aversion to you, Christiana? Surely it's the other way about?' he said coolly.

'I've never found you repulsive, Ash.'

'No? One could frequently have been forgiven for thinking so. You were never eager for my embraces until, as you once pointed out, I'd managed to force a response from you.'

He sat up and reached for the sheet, drawing it upwards to cover himself to the waist.

The movement made the muscles of his arm and shoulder ripple under the tanned skin. The oblique beam of light from his reading lamp emphasised the powerful structure of his torso. It was a long time since she had felt those strong arms enfolding her, the broad shoulders bowing under her hands.

A tremor shot through her; a surge of intense, urgent longing to relive the embraces they had once shared, to feel their flesh joined and made one.

For the first time, before Ash had even touched

her, she was ready and eager for his possession.

Ash heard her quick intake of breath, and his smile was not pleasant as he leaned towards her, grasped her wrist and drew her towards him.

'Why not be honest? You haven't come here to do your duty by John. I taught you to enjoy your body, and now you find you can't do without the pleasures you used to be so reluctant to indulge in. You've become addicted, my girl. Look at you—eyes half closed, lips half open, breasts quivering! He touched the sensitive centre of one of her lipsticked adornments. 'The personification of a woman panting to be taken. Shall I rip this thing off, or can you wait while I undo it?'

As his hand moved towards the knot of her kanga, she struck it away and tried to jerk free of his grasp.

'No . . . *no*! That's not true,' she blazed. 'You don't understand. I—'

She stopped, choking back the admission of how much she loved him.

'On the contrary, I understand perfectly. I share your impatience,' he told her.

The next moment she was crushed against him, his fingers forcing her face up to meet the fierce, famished kiss with which he stifled her protest.

Once she would have resisted and struggled. Now, the instant he pulled her into his arms, her whole body melted with ecstasy. A hurricane tide of sensation coursed through every nerve of her being.

The convulsive delight which, before, she had only experienced after many kisses and caresses now engulfed her as soon as she felt herself roughly caught and imprisoned in that first hard, demanding embrace.

His fingers at work on the knot, Ash felt the climactic shudders which racked her soft, slender body. At once she was flung on her back, and he was upon her, taking her with an unrestrained passion which, although it might once have frightened her, now prolonged and intensified her pleasure.

As a purely physical experience it was, without question, the most exalted of her life. When, all too soon, it was over, she burst into tears of reaction; uncontrollable tears which there was no way of concealing from the man lying relaxed in her arms, his dark head close to her own.

At first he seemed not to notice the soundless weeping, as if she were struggling to breathe. His tall frame weighed heavily on her, compressing her lungs. He lay still, his violence spent, his broad back as damp as her cheeks where the tears seeped between her closed eyelids.

'Oh, God! Have I hurt you?' He raised himself on his elbows. 'My love . . . my darling . . . don't cry.'

As he spoke, his voice hoarse with concern, she felt his hands on her face, the touch of his fingertips gentle as they stroked aside tendrils of hair.

'Don't cry . . . I can't bear you to cry. I went mad for a minute. I've been going crazy for weeks. It seems like ten years since I held you like this, my sweet Christie.'

Light kisses rained on her forehead, and on her wet cheeks and temples.

'I wouldn't hurt you for the world. I'd give my life

for you, darling.' His deep voice rasped with re-
morse.

'You didn't . . . you didn't hurt me. Oh, Ash . . . I
love you . . . *I love you.*'

Choked by sobs, she was hardly coherent, but her
heart was swelling with joy because of his anguished
contrition, and the tacit admission that he loved her.

Ash rolled aside, breaking their fusion, but immediately drawing her beside him to cuddle and
soothe her until, gradually, her weeping diminished.
At last, as her ragged breaths steadied, he reached
across her for a tissue, then tenderly turned up her
face and blotted the tear-stains.

'I thought I'd made you loathe me . . . that you
couldn't stand it any longer, all those things I'd
forced you to let me do to you, and that that was why
you ran away. God, the hell I went through till you
came back!' he admitted, scowling at the memory.
His hold on her tightened. 'Then you announced you
were pregnant, and I thought that had brought you
back to me. I felt I was going to have to live the rest of
my life like a monk. I knew I could never force myself
on you again, and you'd killed my interest in other
women.'

'You mean there's been no one else . . . all
this time . . . since I left you?' she whispered un-
steadily.

'How could there be? I love you, Christie.'

'You love me . . . you really love me . . . I can't
believe it!' she murmured, with a shaky sigh. 'I've
been insanely in love with you since the night we flew
to London.'

'I can't believe it either; that you're here, in my arms—and willingly.'

'Oh, much more than willingly,' she told him, beginning to smile. 'That's the understatement of the year.' Very softly, she added, *'Please stay, my love, and share the life I saved for you, each drop it guarded against all invasion till now.'*

He drew back to look in her eyes.

'You know that by heart?'

'I've read it so many times, wishing you were that kind of man . . . wanting only one woman . . . me.'

'I am. I do.' His dark, virile face was transformed by the tender expression with which he was watching her.

'But when did you start to love me? And why did you never tell me?' she asked.

'I realise now that I recognised you as the woman I'd been looking for the morning I came into your bedroom at the flat in London. You blushed like an old-fashioned virgin—and look at you now. Where did you get this idea?'—tracing the patterns she had painted.

'I'm not sure. I think it was a fashion in ancient Crete.' Already his touch was having an effect. 'But, to get back to London, we'd only just met, and I was so dull and defensive.'

'I care not whose you were—or even whose you are—your eyes will tell me that you are mine and that you are waiting,' he quoted. 'Naturally my rational side rejected that, but all the same it was the principal reason I went out and booked you on a flight here. The boy could have come on his own. In special circumstances, airlines will take unaccompanied children under six.

But apart from the fact that he needed you here, I needed you here to see if my instinct was correct.'

His whole hand was stroking her now, not only the tip of one finger. She slid an arm over his shoulder and began to caress the strong brown column of his neck.

'When did you find out that it was?'

'Within a few days. But even when I asked you to marry me, I hadn't admitted to myself that I was as crazy about you as my father had been about my stepmother. For a long time I overlooked the fact that you're nothing like she was, and therefore being yours to command wouldn't make a weakling of me as it had of him.'

'Because I am *yours* to command. Anything you want, I will give you.'

She gave a soft, sensuous sigh and moved her hips closer to his. Her lips were parted, her grey eyes openly inviting. It was wonderful not to conceal her increasing excitement, her eagerness.

Ash's dark eyes held the same light of mounting desire, but he kept it in check as he said, 'If you'd ever looked at me with love, I should have told you at once. But you never did, Christie. There was always reserve in your eyes. You never once asked me to love you—not even tacitly. It was always an act of aggression on my part, and reluctant compulsion on yours.'

'Because I was terrified that as soon as you guessed I love you, you would lose interest in me,' she explained. 'I could never forget that you'd said, at the very beginning, that you found your life ran more smoothly without the continual presence of a woman in it.'

'I must have meant it at the time, I got my come-uppance when you left me. Every day seemed as long as a year. As for the nights . . .'

'For me, too. I couldn't—'

She broke off with a gasp as he bent his head to her breast and, between his hot lips, she felt the caress of his tongue. Her fingers delved in his hair, not to tug his head away but to signal her unresisting pleasure. A low moan escaped her as thrilling waves coursed through her body.

When he lifted his head, smiling at her look of undisguised rapturous abandonment, she thought it was time she displayed a little aggression. With both hands on his chest, she pushed him to make him lie back. Then she leaned over him and, her parted lips light on his mouth, licked his lips with the tip of her tongue.

His reaction was very satisfactory. A shudder convulsed his tall frame, and he clamped her against him and kissed her with a frenzied urgency which she thought could only conclude with another swift, fierce possession.

But she ought to have known that Ash's command of himself was too strong and sure not to make this ecstatic reunion a very special memory. At one stage of their wild love game he pulled her astride his lean flanks while he took the gold chain from her waist with hands which he managed to steady while they dealt with the intricate fastening.

Then he placed his palms on her hips, and she felt his long lean brown fingers pressing her satiny flesh while his narrowed eyes scanned the rest of her from this new perspective.

How she would have hated it once, kneeling over him in the lamplight while he slowed the pace of their game, his hands taking gentle pleasure in the softness of her buttocks and thighs compared with his own. His skin had a smooth pleasant feel, but it covered muscle and bone, with none of her yielding contours.

She stretched her arms high and tossed back her long, sun-streaked hair, looking down at him through her lashes. Only faint smudged traces remained of the russet patterns. The Kanga was a crumpled swathe of colour against the whiteness of the sheet, its purpose served.

She had dared and won, and she wished she had dared much sooner. For here, in this lamplit room, on the tumbled bed, was at last the ultimate joy which would bring to perfection a future more rich in fulfilment than any of her girlhood dreams.

A husband. A home. One child, and probably others. A project to share in a setting of idyllic beauty. At last she had it all together.

'Oh, Ash . . . how I love you,' she breathed, as she bent her breasts to his chest and her lips to his mouth.

In the end it was he who looked down on her, as he had many times in the past, and with no less total a mastery of her enraptured senses. But this time she stayed in his arms for the rest of the night; and woke with her head on his pillow, and the sun streaming through the screens, and her love still asleep.

Legacy of
PASSION

BY CATHERINE KAY

A love story begun long ago comes full circle...

Venice, 1819: Contessa Allegra di Rienzi, young, innocent, unhappily married. She gave her love to Lord Byron—scandalous, irresistible English poet. Their brief, tempestuous affair left her with a shattered heart, a few poignant mementos—and a daughter he never knew about.

Boston, today: Allegra Brent, modern, independent, restless. She learned the secret of her great-great-great-grandmother and journeyed to Venice to find the di Rienzi heirs. There she met the handsome, cynical, blood-stirring Conte Renaldo di Rienzi, and like her ancestor before her, recklessly, hopelessly lost her heart.